I0651645

Anonymus

The Commerce of Montreal and its manufactures, 1888

Anonymus

The Commerce of Montreal and its manufactures, 1888

ISBN/EAN: 9783742842466

Manufactured in Europe, USA, Canada, Australia, Japa

Cover: Foto ©Andreas Hilbeck / pixelio.de

Manufactured and distributed by brebook publishing software
(www.brebook.com)

Anonymus

The Commerce of Montreal and its manufactures, 1888

THE

Commerce * *

OF

Montreal *

AND ITS

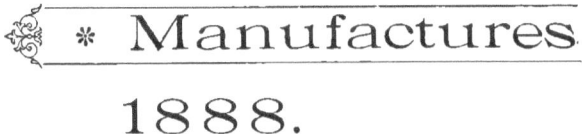

* Manufactures

1888.

PUBLISHED BY

HB George Bishop Engraving and Printing Co'y., Ltd.

CONTENTS.

MONTREAL FROM THE MOUNTAIN.

PART I.

From the Discovery of Montreal to the Conquest.

MONTREAL'S title to the commercial metropolis of British North America comes to her by inheritance. Her right to that title is older—much older—than Queen Victoria's title to the succession of the British Crown. History tells us that Jacques Cartier, who discovered Montreal, found in 1535, when he landed at Quebec, that Montreal, then called Hochelaga, was at that early age the metropolis of the savage state, the capital city of the Indian tribes. His own narrative of the discovery has the charm of romance that surrounds all North American stories. He found Quebec on the 15th of August, 1535, and met Donacona, the Lord or King of Quebec, then called Stadacona. He could not be dissuaded from a visit to Montreal, and from the 19th of September to the 28th he was engaged in sailing as far as Lake St. Peter where he was compelled by shoal water to leave his ships and take to the boats. He reached his destination on the second of October, having landed at the foot of the island. Having arrayed himself in the most gorgeous finery, he left his boats, and, accompanied by twenty mariners and four gentlemen, set out for Hochelaga. He was guided by three Indians, and says, in his description of the journey, that "all along he found the way as well beaten and frequented as can be, the fairest and best country that could possibly be seen, full of goodly great oaks, as any in the woods in France, under which the ground was all covered with acorns." After he had gone about four miles, he was met by one of the principal chiefs, who paid him some honor, made a speech to him, and insisted upon him taking a rest before he presented him to their great King, Agouhanna by name. This King had no throne but the brawny arms of his braves; and, supported on the shoulders of several of these, he received the man whom the simple natives looked upon as a god,—a man who taught them Christianity as he understood it, but who tarnished his name by unchristian and traitorous conduct afterwards. He recited the Gospel of St. John to these natives—it were crime to call them savages then—and prayed that God would open their hearts. He doubtless hoped that they would fill his pockets. They did, and did the same for thousands of his fellow-countrymen, long afterwards when not a vestige of their houses was left.

Cartier had taken thirteen days from Quebec to Montreal, which nowadays can be encompassed in five hours by train. He thus describes the town:—

"It is placed near, and, as it were, joined to a great mountain, very fertile on the top, from which you may see very far. The town is round, encompassed about with timber, with three rampires, one within another, framed like a sharp spire, but laid across above. The middle-moat of these is made and built in a direct line, but perpendicular. The rampires are framed and fashioned with pieces of timber, laid along the ground, very well and cunningly joined after their fashion. This enclosure is in height about two rods. It hath but one gate or entry thereat, which is shut with piles, stakes and bars. Over it and also in many parts of the wall, there be places to run along, and ladders to get up, all full of stones for the defence of it."

"There are in the town about fifty houses, each fifty paces long, and fifteen or twenty broad, built all of wood, covered over with the bark of the wood, as broad as any board, and cunningly joined together. Within are many rooms, lodgings, and chambers. In the midst of everyone there is a great court, in the middle whereof they make their fires. They live in common together, then do the husbands, wives and children, each one retire to their chambers. They have also in the tops of their houses, certain garrets, wherein they keep their corn to make their bread. The people are given to no other exercise, but only to husbandry and fishing for their existence."

Here was a paradise. A nation of peaceful people were making a god of Cartier. He in turn was introducing to them a civilization that was to ruin them body and soul, and ultimately wipe them from the face of the earth. He ascended the mountain near by, which he called "Mont Royal." It was no wonder the sight of the surrounding country "filled him with feelings of joy and gratification." To-day, the fashionable tourist who views the same scene, altered by civilization, will say that its grand in beauty, even after four centuries have stamped it with the iron hand of commerce and garnished it with the golden sheen of agriculture. Then Cartier saw the broad St. Lawrence and the sombre Ottawa, encircling the Island of Montreal. Looking southward, he beheld the foam of the Lachine Rapids, dashing over the leaps in the rocks, and beyond, the mountain ranges known as the Adirondacks. Westward, up the Ottawa Valley a vista of forest glade and the waters of the Lake of Two Mountains shining in the distance. Northward, a succession of forest ranges, denoting a well watered country and a range of hills beyond. Eastward, the Town and Bay of Hochelaga, the St. Lawrence hurrying past St. Helen's Island, Boucherville and Belœil Mountains beyond all. The forest luxuriance was upon every hand, and these lovely tints of Autumn had overspread the whole country. Cartier had never seen its like before. He never came back to see it again. The scene has changed. Now the gazer looks from Mount Royal as Cartier did; but takes his view from a high tower that overlooks the homes of over three hundred thousand people, the spires of a hundred churches, most of them in Montreal, but spires that gleam in the sun wherever the eye turns. Bridges span the St. Lawrence and the Ottawa Rivers. Steamers ply the rushing waters, and the shriek of the locomotive resounds where Cartier heard only the rushing waters. Huge ocean steamers in dozens, tall masts of heavy ocean sailing vessels fringe the river, where Cartier saw the rushes and the waving shrubbery. Tall grain elevators, smoking chimneys, dense blocks of limestone warehouses, miles of streets, with houses and public buildings to the value of over one hundred and fifty millions of dollars, exclusive of their contents, public schools and universities, convents and hospitals, princely emporiums and palatial hotels. Cartier would to-day have seen all this. He would not have been compelled to hurry away on the same day he came. He would have seen, too, how an artificial river—the Lachine Canal—enabled ships that could carry his entire fleet on the deck of any one of them, to pass around the Lachine Rapids, and the water turning the machinery of scores of mills upon its banks. Instead of the barter for beads and gew-gaws in the Mount Royal he saw then, he would find to-day banks in Montreal, with a capital of forty-six millions of dollars, merchants worth millions of dollars to their credit, factories by the score employing twelve to fifteen thousand workmen and valued at more than fifty million dollars, hotels, some of which could house the then whole population of Hochelaga. Cartier's visit to Montreal was succeeded by one which Samuel Champlain paid to it in 1603, when he found Montreal almost deserted, and was himself stopped by the Lachine Rapids, which tourists to-day find so very interesting as a natural curiosity. He again visited the spot in 1609, where he found the Huron Indians friendly, and he formed an alliance with them against the Iroquois. De Monts, whose lieutenant Champlain was, now lost his monopoly of the trade of the St. Lawrence, by the King's decree. Champlain returned to France, and was authorized by Count de Soissons, the new Viceroy of New France, to return and act as the latter's lieutenant. In 1611 Champlain put up the first dwelling made by Christian men in Montreal. He also in the following year induced four Recollet Fathers to go to Montreal and attend to the spiritual wants of the people. He now spent eight busy years of exploration and war against the Iroquois, who were fierce foes.

Mr. Alfred Sandam's work on *Montreal, Past and Present*, says:—"In 1620 Duke de Montmorenci, Lord High Admiral, purchased the Vice-royalty from Prince de Condé, for the sum of eleven thousand crowns.*** In 1621 Montmorenci deprived the Merchants' Association of their charter and transferred all the colonial trade to the Sieurs de Caen. These gentlemen actively engaged in the fur trade, and seem to have behaved in a very arbitrary manner, which finally led to a disagreement between Champlain and themselves. Added to this dissatisfaction was the fact that the De Caens, being Huguenots, were not likely to further the interests of the Catholic Church in Canada. In 1623 the De Caens and the old Merchants' Company had formed a union; but being continually engaged in disputes as to their rights, the Duke de Montmorenci to relieve himself of trouble, disposed of his Vice-royalty to his nephew, the Duke de Tentadone, who had entered holy orders, and whose sole object, in thus purchasing it, was to use his influence towards the conversion of the Indians. In 1625 he sent out three Jesuits, and added three Brothers to the Recollets already in Canada. These Jesuit Fathers, L'Allemand, Masse and Brebeuf, were men of exemplary character and piety, and cheerfully undertook the mission.

The disputes between the De Caens and the colonists were settled by the formation of a company under the direct auspices of Cardinal Richelieu, and this company was called the "*CENTS ASSOCIES*," or Company of One Hundred Associates.

They agreed to send out colonists and tradesmen and were bound to have six thousand Roman Catholic Frenchmen in Canada before 1643, to provide three priests to each settlement and give them all necessary comforts for fifteen years; and afterwards to give the clergy cleared lands in order to maintain the Catholic Church in New France.

But before this, came the British upon the scene, and the result of war between France and Britain was the first conquest of Canada by Sir David Kirk in 1629, when Champlain surrendered the whole of Canada. Five years afterwards Champlain returned as Governor, the British having given up Canada to the French by the treaty of St. Germain. Champlain's death followed in 1635, and he was succeeded by M. de Montmagny. Thus far Quebec was receiving all the attention of the colonists; but in 1640, the whole Island of Montreal was ceded to the Missionaries for the purpose of converting the Indians. The manner in which this was brought about is most romantic and reads more like a leaf from St. Paul's life than anything in Montreal's history.

Jérôme le Royer de la Dauversière, who lived in France, an enthusiastic devotee, heard a voice telling him to go to Montreal, in Canada and establish the Hôtel-Dieu Hospital of Nuns. As he was then a tax-collector in Anjou, France, the father of six children, and with but a moderate salary, he hesitated. Jean Jacques Olier, a young priest, was at about the same time praying in the old church of St. Germain de Paris, France, when he thought he heard a voice from Heaven telling him to go and form a Society of Priests in Montreal, Canada. Though both these men were ignorant of the precise shape of Montreal, yet they mysteriously found themselves in possession of exact details of the Island.

Dauversière was further conformed in his resolve to go after he had gone to Paris, for here he had a vision in which he heard Christ ask the Virgin Mary three times " Where can I find a faithful servant?"

Upon this the Virgin took Dauversière by the hand, saying, " See, Lord, here is that faithful servant."

Christ received him with a smile, and promised him wisdom and strength to do his work.

The most curious part of it all was his meeting with Olier. D'auversière went to the Chateau of Menden, not far from St. Cloud. On entering the gallery of an old castle he met a priest, and though he had never seen him before, he called him Olier, while Olier, who never had met or heard of him before, called him Dauversière; and, each as if by inspiration, knew the other to the depths of his heart.

They discussed their plans, and whether the reader may smile or not at the story, these men believed most firmly in the work that they set out upon, for they soon found supporters, and soon afterwards, joined by Baron de Fancamp and three others, formed the Société de Notre-Dame de Montréal, and had a capital of seventy-five thousand livres. With such incentive, nothing could stop the enthusiasts, and after some negotiations with the One Hundred Associates they secured the whole Island of Montreal, except part of the west, which was reserved by the Associates for a fort and stores. The king confirmed the bargain, and these six became Lords of the Island of Montreal.

Their plan was to locate forty men upon the Island, raise crops, and build houses for the priests and convents for the nuns. Paul de Chomedy, Sieur de Maisonneuve were chosen commander of the expedition, and Mademoiselle Mance was prevailed on to take charge of the new hospital. She, with the wives of two men and a female volunteer, were the only women in the party, which in February, 1841, assembled at the Church of Notre Dame in Paris and consecrated Montreal to the Holy Family, to be called "Ville-Marie de Montréal." The party arrived in Quebec in the same year, but were compelled to winter at the Island of Orleans, and were there received with suspicion and distrust by their fellow-countrymen. Madame de la Peltrie joined the party here, and on the 8th of May, 1642, Maisonneuve embarked and was in Montreal on the 17th. They lost no time, and before the Indians were aware of what they were doing, had several houses built, pallisades erected, and were ready either to pray, work or fight. That same year the first flood that ever troubled Christians in Montreal arose until it filled the ditch of Maisonneuve's Fort, and threatened the fort itself. But worse than this were the attacks of the Indians. Being accused once by his men of cowardice, Maisonneuve sallied forth to attack the Indians, leaving D'Aillebout within the fort to act as a reserve.****They were themselves attacked by the Indians, who killed three of them and wounded several others. Finally they broke ranks and retreated in great desorder towards the fort. Maisonneuve, with a pistol in each hand, held the Indians in check for some time. They might have killed him, but they wished to take him prisoner. Their Chief desiring this honor, rushed forward, but just as he was about to grasp him, Maisonneuve fired, and the Chief fell dead. The Indians fearing that the body of their Chief would fall into the hands of the French, rushed forward to secure it, and Maisonneuve passed safely within the fort. From that day his men never dared to impute cowardice to him. In 1644 the Island of Montreal passed into the hands of the Sulpicians of Paris, and was destined for the support of that religious order.

In 1661 there was a tremendous earthquake or series of shocks lasting from February to August. This terror is described with most vivid power. In one day 180,000 square miles of land were convulsed, many rivers were totally lost, the St. Lawrence River appeared totally white. At Tadousac such a heavy shower of volcanic ashes fell that the water became much agitated as during a tempest.   An entire forest was loosened at Point Alonettes and slid into the St. Lawrence.   Yet there was not a single life lost, nor a single person harmed in any way, a most curious affair truly.

It is surprising that even as early as 1664 New York commenced to compete with Montreal.   The Province of New York sought and obtained a large portion of the fur trade theretofore exclusively centred in Montreal.   Then commenced the trouble that afterwards led to wars and reprisals.   The Iroquois were on the side of the English, and the fighting was severe, treachery despicable, and losses heavy on both sides.   In 1687 a peace was declared at Montreal ; but by the treachery of an old Seneca Chief, the whole of this effort on the part of the French was made to appear only a treacherous plot, and in 1689 fourteen hundred Iroquois swarmed down upon the doomed settlers, wasted and burned Lachine, burned two hundred persons alive, and made their track one carnival of pillage, outrage and torture, such as only the savage knows how to inflict.   A war with the British followed, and for several years the country was ravaged now by one party and again by another.   Montreal was constantly the point of attack.   In 1713, however, the cession of Acadia, Newfoundland and Hudson's Bay Territory to Britain left Canada at peace until 1749, when the British again threatened Canada.   Montreal at this time had become a city of consequence.   French troops, with their Indian allies, were quartered in the city in large members, and the Baron de Longueuil had been appointed Governor.   It had prospered greatly.

But a day of British glory was dawning upon North America.   Wolfe's army and Saunders' fleet were to attack Quebec ; General Amherst was to attack by way of Crown Point and Ticonderoga ; while Sir William Johnson was to capture Niagara and descend the St. Lawrence.   On the 8th of September, 1760, Montreal passed into the hands of Great Britain.   The French troops were permitted to march out with the honors of war.   Wolfe had already captured Quebec, and the British flag waved over the whole of North America.

PART II.

From the Conquest down to the Present Day.

THE people of Montreal now looked forward to an era of peace and prosperity. General Amherst, the British Commandant was elated over the success of his soldiers, and the French-Canadian people were glad the war was at an end. One paragraph in the General's orders thanked Sir William Johnston, who commanded the Indians, for keeping them within bounds so that Amherst could write: "I have the pleasure to assure you that not a peasant, woman or child has been hurt by them, or a house burnt since I entered the enemy's country." A Military Government was established in Montreal, under General Thomas Gage, who treated the conquered people in the most humane manner. In 1763 the Treaty of Paris ceded the whole of Canada to Great Britain. General Murray was appointed Governor, and chose a Council comprising a Lieutenant-Governor at Three Rivers and one in Montreal, with the Chief Justice and eight citizens. The next event of importance to Montreal was its capture by General Montgomery of the United States army in 1775. The invading army had sent to Longue Point their advance guard, under Ethan Allen, to attack Montreal. They landed on the 24th of October and on the 25th, General Carlton assembled thirty regulars and 200 militia under Major Carden. The troops of Allen had entrenched themselves in some barns but were routed, and the whole of the enemy captured and sent to England. It was after this that General Montgomery took the city. After he had been killed, and his army routed at Quebec, the United States troops evacuated Montreal at the end of May, 1776. The treaty of Versailles, unfortunately for Canadians, was very favorable to the United States. Canada's territory was much curtailed, the country having been left without a winter sea-port; but, to-day, Halifax supplies the want, Portland, however of right belongs to Canada.

In 1792 the first Protestent Church was built in Montreal, St. Gabriel Street Church, the congregation of which still exist under the pastorate of the Rev. Robert Campbell. In 1791 the French-Canadian people were separated, to some extent from the British-Canadians by the division of the country into Upper and Lower Canada, each with its own Legislative Council and Assembly.

In 1792 Montreal City was defined and devided into two Wards, the East and the West. The first Parliament of Canada assembled at Quebec, and the East Ward was represented by Joseph Frobisher and John Richardson, and the West by James McGill and J. B. Durocher. Montreal borrowed money even in these early days to erect a Jail and Court House. In 1799 they appointed a city surveyor, in 1801 authorized Water Works. The rights of the conquered French people were respected to a fault, take one instance:—When the French army took property on which to build the city walls they did not pay for it; but agreed that if ever the walls were thrown down or in disuse they would return the property to the owners. French law had been replaced by English law but the property was returned to the original owners or their heirs by the conquerers.

The first Newspaper libel on record was one by the *Gazette*, which reflected upon the Governor. It was because of the publication of toasts at a dinner, April 1st, 1806, and a Parliamentary warrent was issued for the arrest of Isaac Todd, the chairman of the dinner, and Edward Edwards, the printer. Neither could be found when wanted and the matter dropped. The toasts were considered a sarcasm on the Government.

In 1805 an Act was passed providing for improved navigation between Quebec and Montreal, and the Trinity House Board was established, which was afterwards converted to the Harbor Trust or Harbor Commissioners of Montreal, a quasi-government body. There were in that day two streets in Montreal—the Upper Notre Dame, and the Lower St. Paul. Some of the quaint discriptions of the city in these days are interesting. For example, in *Acrioi Travels* we find " Montreal is divided into the Upper and Lower Towns, although the level between them exceeds not twelve or fifteen feet. A natural wharf very near to the town is formed by the depth of the stream and the sudden declivity of the bank. * * * * The environs and town contain 12,000 inhabitants." One event of note was the advent of the first steamer, fitted out by Mr. John Molson, and she made the voyage to Quebec in 1809 in thirty-six hours of sailing. She was a wonder in her day. A description of her says : " No wind or tide can stop her, she has seventy-five feet keel and eighty-five feet on deck." She was the second steamer built on the American Continent, Fulton's steamer having first cleaved the waters of the Hudson. Monopolists were as keen then as they are to-day, for Mr. Molson was granted the monopoly for fifteen years.

The war of 1812 followed, and Montreal witnessed the entry of General Hull as a prisoner, with his army. The *Herald* of that day thus facetiously alludes to Hull's arrival :—" That General Hull should have entered our city so soon, at the head of his troops, rather exceeded our expectations. We were, however, happy to see him, and receive him with all the honors due to his rank and importance as a public character.

* * * * The General appears to be about sixty years of age, and bears his misfortunes with a degree of resignation that but few men in similar circumstances are gifted with." Montreal played no active part in the war of 1812, and from that time until the rebellion of 1838–39 suffered no serious check from disturbances. Enterprise was commencing to appear in every part of Montreal. Street lighting by lamps, paid for by private subscription, was commenced in 1815. In 1819 the Bank of Montreal was organized, and in 1821 the Lachine Canal was commenced. In that year the British and Canadian School was founded " for the education of the children of the laboring classes." In 1831 Montreal became a port of entry ; in 1832 there was a riot in which troops fired upon the mob and killed three and wounded two, and in the same year 1904 persons died of cholera. There was cholera in 1834 and three years of constant confusion were followed by the rebelion of 1837–38. Subsequently there were riotous political demonstrations and 1849 the Parliament Buildings were destroyed by fire to mark the displeasure of people, who believed that the Government had had no right to pass the Rebellion losses bill. Lord Elgin was rotten-egged for daring, as Governor-General, to sign the bill. Riots in 1850 ; a great fire in the same year, and general depression, were followed by the opening of the St. Lawrence & Atlantic Railway in 1851, another great fire in 1852, and the Gavazzi riot in 1853. The opening of the Grand Trunk Railway to Portland, and the commencement of the Victoria Bridge in the same year were events in Montreal's history, each of which marked forward movements in Canadian trade.

It is curious that while New York has held her place as the commercial metropolis of the United States for three centuries, Montreal has done likewise, so far as Canada is concerned. The Montreal of to-day, as a commercial city, is to Canada what London is to Great Britain and New York to the United States. Montreal occupies a specially advantageous position at the head of oceanic navigation and at the commencement of lake and river navigation, having direct railway communication with the chief cities of Canada and the United States. In order to accommodate the magnificent fleet of ships that come to her port from all lands, the ship channel of the river St. Lawrence has been deepened to twenty-five feet at the lowest condition of the river and a further deepening is now in progress ; in order to achieve this, she had to borrow some three million dollars, and the removal of this debt will lift from her shoulders the last and greatest burden she has had to bear. In consequence of this debt the scale of harbor dues imposed was necessarily heavy, giving smaller and in other respects less convenient ports an unfair advantage over Montreal. In compliance, however, with many urgent representations the Federal Government has assumed the responsibility of this debt. The city is the terminus of one of the completest railway systems in the world. Two divisions of the Grand Trunk Railway, and various lines run in connection with its magnificent system, afford easy access to the United States and the principal cities of Canada, while the marvellous monument of national enterprise and engineering skill, the Canadian Pacific Railway traverses the continent from sea to sea, opening up magnificent tracts of fertile country and developing stores of wealth hitherto unknown, while it is becoming the great highway for commercial intercourse between the eastern and western limits of the old world. In addition to its great importance as the chief port and forwarding station of Canada, Montreal is also the largest manufacturing cenare in the Dominion. Among its industries are foundries, sugar refineries, tanneries, silk mills, manufactories of hardware, carriage and sleighs, corn brooms, woodenware, glass, paints and drugs, edge tools, locomotives, steam engines, boilers, india rubber goods, printing presses, agricultural implements, musical instruments, paper, rope, sewing machines, types, pins, tobacco, woolen and cotton goods, boots and shoes, and other smaller industries. There are besides saw and flour mills, rolling mills, lead works, brass foundries, and many other industrial establishments. The educational means of the city comprise the University of McGill with faculties of law, science, art and medicine, a branch of the Laval University with faculties of divinity, law, medicine and arts. Theological colleges belonging to Roman Catholic, Anglican, Presbyterian and Methodist bodies, a Jesuit College, a high school, two Normal Schools, several classical and scientific academies. The elementary schools are under the control respectively of the Catholic and Protestant School Commissioners, and there are also two affiliated medical colleges one to Bishops College, Lennoxville, the other to Victoria College, Cobourg. As a sign of the business transactions carried on by the community, it may be noted that there are no fewer than sixteen banking establishments, twenty-six Fire and sixteen Life Insurance offices located in the city. There are thirteen public markets, whose total sales of farm produce amount yearly to some $650,000. In order to facilitate the vast intercourse with foreign countries, the following nations are represented in the city by Consuls and Vice-Consuls, viz: the Argentine Confederation, Austro-Hungary, Belgium, Chili and Peru, Denmark, France, the German Empire, the kingdom of Hawaii, the Netherlands, Sweeden and Norway, the Republic of Uruguay, Spain, Switzerland and the United States. Montreal is the centre of a judicial district presided over by seven judges. The Court of Queen's Bench also hold sittings in the months of February, May, October and December. The section of the Bar of the Province of Quebec located in Montreal numbers about 370 members. The city is the seat of a Roman Catholic Archbishop and an Anglican Bishop.

Montreal claims and certainly deserves the title of the "City of Churches," and, as Mark Twain observes, "is the only city on the Continent where you cannot throw a brick without breaking a church window." It contains some seventy-five churches of all denominations, many of which are magnificent edifices. Among the finest and largest buildings erected of late years may be mentioned the Post Office in St. James Street, erected in 1876, at the cost of $400,000. The new City Hall, which cost close on $120.000. The majestic Cathedral of St. Peter, upon Dominion Square, is to cost when completed $300.000. The Windsor Hotel, built in 1878, at a cost of $1,100,000, and having 434 rooms, and accommodation for 750 guests, is hardly inferior to any establishment of the kind on the Continent. The Bank of Montreal is one of the finest buildings in America, and there are now in course of erection two magnificent

THE POST OFFICE,—MONTREAL.

THE CITY HALL,—MONTREAL.

Railway Depots for the Grand Trunk and Canadian Pacific Railways, a spacious and handsome new Gothic church for the Methodists, and several splendid blocks or buildings for offices, including new offices for two Life Insurance Companies, the New York and the Imperial; while a new building for the law courts, nearly opposite the present building, which has become too small for present requirements, is soon to be erected. Montreal has at present about 145 miles of streets. Between the years 1878 and 1886, no less than fifteen miles 165 yards of sewers were laid down by the city, making a total of ninety miles of sewers existing. One of the most important acquisitions for the city was the purchase by the Corporation, between the years 1872 and 1875, of Mount Royal, and laying it out with drives as a public park, the cost to date being $622,337. The Mountain, which stands alone in the wide river plain, is some 550 feet in height. It is ascended by a winding carriage road, by a series of about 427 steps for foot passengers, and by an elevator. The winding road opens up to the public two very beautiful vistas, one looking down the valley of the St. Lawrence with its many islands, and the other giving a view of the Lake of Two Mountains, whilst in the far distance the Green Mountains of Vermont and a portion of the Adirondacks are plainly discernible on a clear day. This drive is acknowledged by visitors to be by far the most beautiful of any park on this Continent.

GOVERNMENT, POPULATION, REVENUE AND ASSESSMENT.

Montreal is governed by a mayor and city council composed of thirty-six aldermen. It returns three members to the Federal Parliament and three to the Provincial and is the largest and wealthiest city in the Dominion of Canada.

The vast increase in the population of Montreal City goes on with each year, and is stimulated by the accession to he limits of large tracts of territory and thousands of persons who, while residing in suburban municipalities adjacent, are employed during the day at business in the city. In area, the city has increased on every side, the smaller municipalities having yielded to the natural law of gravitation and been absorbed into the larger body. Whereas at her incorporation she covered an area of 3498 acres, she now includes within he borders an area of 5366 acres, including 1230 acres added by the annexation of the municipality of Hochelaga in 1885; 308 acres by the annexation of St. Jean Baptiste in 1886, and 340 acres by that of St. Gabriel in 1887. These accessions to the city limits were severally formed into wards, making with the ward of St. James which had been previously added by the subdivision of the other wards, twelve wards in all into which the city is now subdivided. But it is not in the matter of actual acreage covered that the city has shown the most conspicuous progress. What were, but a few years since, open fields an pastures have become the populous sections of St. Antoine, St. Ann's, St. Mary's and St. James Wards, while the East, Centre and West Wards, constituting the city mercantile, have within the same time been altered by the magnificence and magnitude of their buildings. The population of the city in 1800 was 9000, in 1825 it was 22,000, and in 1831, 27,937.. The last census taken in 1887, added to the annexed ward of St. Gabriel shows the population now to be 200,000.

The Government takes a general census in every tenth year and the following are the figures since 1851, viz. :—

Census		1851	population		57,715
"		1861	"		90,323
"		1871	"		107,225
"		1881	"		140,727
Present population					200,000

The latter figures are very much underdrawn and do not include several large suburban districts which will likely be added to Montreal before the Government takes the census of 1891. The closest estimate of the city's population to-day puts it at 220,000.

The principal source of civic revenue is the tax levied upon real estate, and the following table shewing the assessable value of property within the city during the last seven years indicates the increase in buildings and values :—

1880	$65,199,200
1881	66,483,810
1882	68,157,655
1883	70,478,380
1884	71,583,659
1885	72,877,834
1886	74,786,581
1887	104,758,512

In addition to this assessed value of real estate there is also in the city property of the value of $17,117,340 exempted from taxation under the following heads :—

Government property		$2,419,500
Corporation property		4,282,500
Seminary property		754.750
Churches	Catholic	1,462,000
	Protestant	1,202,500
Personages	Catholic	279,500
	Protestant	190,300
Benevolent	Catholic	4,464,690
Institutions	Protestant	1,289,100
Manufactories		772,500
Total		$17,117,340.

The plan of assessment in New York City is to place and assessed value upon the property and add to this the balance of real or market value to property. If this were done in Montreal on the same principle, the real value of Montreal property would be, $145,000,000 and the assessed value something like $125,000,000. Property is assessed notoriously under the mark of real estate values and no city in Canada escapes with such economical taxation as does Montreal. One bad feature of this part of her machinery is that the churches and much church property are exempt from taxation.

A Board of Assessors appraises the value of the property every year. They are under the control of the City Council, which, however, has no power to do more than make recommendations to them.

The rate of annual assessment is one per cent. on value. There is an additional one-fifth of one cent for school tax which is levied and collected by the city, but handed over for administration to the School Commissioners (a body appointed by the local Government and the city jointly).

In addition to this one and one-fifth per cent. on realty there is a water rate charged to the tenants based on a sliding scale, which amounts to about seven and one-half per cent. on annual rental values, and an assessment of seven and one-half per cent. on the rental of all business premises which is known as the Business Tax; and also specific licenses on certain businesses and the usual taxes on horses, carriages, dogs, etc., which come under the head of Personal Taxes. The city also derives a considerable revenue from the markets and from penalties imposed by the Recorder's Court for infraction of city by-laws. Drains and street improvements are made by special assessments borne in whole or in part by the persons benefitted.

The revenue from all sources in 1886 was $1,908,859, and in 1850, only $150,000, figures which show more clearly than aught else can the material increase of the city. Merchants of to-day, whose fathers reared them in comfortable rooms above the down-town store, now rear their families in palatial residences up town or in the west end. They have grown rich with the city's advance. Their villas lie along the foot of the mountain from which Jacques Cartier first looked upon the then forest of Montreal.

BANKING.

The feature of Montreal's commercial life is her great Banking Institutions. In their working they are after the United States pattern, while the Scottish system is followed as to large capital and numerous branches. The Bank of England's first President was a Scotchman, and so was the first President of the Bank of Montreal, Mr. John Grey. It was established in 1817, and its capital was $350,000. To-day, the Bank has a capital of $12,000,000, and a reserve fund of $6,000,000 besides a large fund for contingencies, and some most valuable property. This Bank is the pioneer of Canadian banks, and in fact there are but two or three other institutions in the world of larger capital. The incorporation of the Bank was in 1818, and as banking was then in its infancy the founders found it no easy matter to induce the confidence of the people, especially the French *habitants* or farmers. They would not at first accept its bills as current money. The directors of the bank were often required to endorse their bank notes, and it was many a year before the prejudice died away. The bank's prosperity was somewhat retarded by the mismanagement of a President who succeeded Mr. John Grey, Mr. Samuel Gerard by name, and also by the panicky feeling caused by the United States threats during the troubles of 1837, when it suspended payment Mr. John Molson became President in 1827. Nearly half of the bank's capital had been sacrificed by bad management previous to that time; but by 1861 it had reached a very forward state, and it was after this period that Mr. E. H. King's master hand appeared in the affairs of the Bank. He knew Wall Street, New York, and had its wants well in his mind. By a series of well considered speculative movements, Mr. King came to the relief of New York merchants and brokers during a great stringency in money, in 1870, which he, of course, did not create, but which he in no wise regretted since it helped him to make his fame and the bank's fortune, at the same time. Loans on call at high rates of interest were the rule ; and here is one of his masterly strokes, a newspaper story of that day :—

" He had a large amount of foreign exchange on hand. New York had very little gold and what it had Mr. King bought up. He then gave out that he had done this in order to ship it to England and loading it in a dray had it carted through the leading streets of New York in sight of the whole population and stored on board an ocean steamer. The natural consequence was that gold at once rose to a high premium He then sold both his gold and exchange at high figures, realizing a handsome profit therefrom. and removed the gold from the vessel for delivery to the purchasers."

At that time the capital of the bank was $6,000,000, but in 1871, on a motion by Mr. Wm. Murray at the annual meeting authority was given to the directors to double the capital at their convenience. On January 15th, 1872, the capital was increased by $2,000,000, and on November 27th of the same year the final $4,000,000 of stock was sold to such shareholders as wanted it at 25 per cent. premium, the remainder being sold in the open market. The bank realized about $1,500,000 which was added to the reserves. Mr. King's resignation followed shortly afterwards and he removed to London, Eng., where he is chairman of the advisory board of the English branch of the Bank of Montreal.

The destinies of the Bank came into the manipulation of Mr. R. B. Angus, after Mr. King went to Europe, and it was in a most troublous time that this handsome Scotchman held the helm. During his *regime* there were failures of the Consolidated and Mechanics Banks, and the most stringent period in finance followed, in course of which there came a reduction of the " rest " or reserve fund taken to pay the dividend of the year, which was ten per cent. Mr. F. C. Smithers succeeded him, and it was under his astute guidance and a return of better times that the bank reached its present excellent position. At the death of Mr. Smithers, Mr. Buchanan succeeded him as

General Manager. The Montreal Bank may be regarded almost as a national institution, for if there should be any trouble in its usually serene chambers, the credit of the country would feel it to its centre.

There are seven other banks in Montreal and eight branches of banks, and financial agencies and correspondents representing every financial centre in the world. The four leading banks, Montreal, Merchants, Molsons and British North America, have sixty-eight branches in Ontario, seven in New Brunswick, five in Manitoba, four in British Columbia, two in Nova Scotia, and live agencies in London, New York, Chicago, and San Francisco.

The smaller banks, People's, Hochelaga, Jacques Cartier and Ville-Marie, have their twenty-four branches all in the Province of Quebec. These figures illustrate the steady growth of the Banking Houses:—

Capital.	Deposits.	Circulation.
1858—13,457,904	6,123,958	6,205,866
1868—18,781,283	20,388,171	2,462,317
1878—33,895,111	30,718,571	10,147,426
1888—27,554,396	43,489,428	13,503,531
Discounts.	No. of Banks.	No. of Branches.
1858—26,803,031	5	39
1868—28.167,554	8	68
1878—58,746,750	11	112
1888—53,245,217	8	118

The statement of deposits does not include those of the Government, except for 1858, at which date the bank returns did not distinguish such deposits.

It will be seen that in 1868 the circulation fell to $2,462,317. This was partly due to the large influx of American silver coin which, to a great extent, took the place of bank notes, and was only removed in 1870, and partly to the use by the Bank of Montreal of Provincial and Dominion notes from 1866 to 1871, at which latter date the total outstanding circulation of the leading bank was only $182,683. The other banks having declined the offer of the Government to pay them a commission to abandon their own circulation and to use that of the Government, the attempt to monopolize the bank circulation was abandoned. The Bank of Montreal resumed its own issues, and by the 30th April, 1872, had an outstanding circulation of $3,116,037. The increase in bank circulation since that date shows how remarkable has been the development of Canadian trade.

The greatest advance, however, is seen in the increased deposits, which have risen from $6,153,958 in 1858 to $43,489,428 in 1888.

Over twenty millions of these deposits bear no interest; adding to this amount the reserve funds, over ten millions, and the circulation, over thirteen millions, it is found that the city banks have (including capital) the use of over seventy million dollars to earn dividends on $27,554,396, to say nothing of the profits on interest-bearing deposits.

To-day, for example, so low has the rate of interest fallen that the Government found it necessary to accept 1¼ for fifteen millions of dollars placed temporarily with banks in Montreal.

The figures above show that while deposits increased in our banks seven times over in thirty years, circulation very little more than doubled and discounts hardly doubled, all facts that show the stability of our banks and banking system.   Dividends paid on the earnings of Banks in Montreal runs from 6 to 10 per cent.   Take this table. It gives the present condition of Montreal Banks in a nut-shell.

STATEMENT OF BANKS ACTING UNDER CHARTER.

For the month ending 31st December, 1885, according to the Returns furnished by them to the Department of Finance.

NAME OF BANK.	Capital Authorized.	Capital Subscribed.	Capital Paid-Up.	Reserve Fund.	Total Liabilities.	Total Assets.	Dividend Declared Rate p. c. per ann'm
Bank of Montreal.............	12,000,000	12,000,000	12,000,000	6,000,000	28,077,748.47	46,749,584.37	10
Bank of British N. America...	4,866,666	4,866,666	4,866,666	1,055,100	6,714,669.00	11,428,842.00	6
Banque du Peuple............	1,200,000	1,200,000	1,200,000	200,000	2,147,430.34	3,676,680.11	6
Banque Jacques-Cartier	500,000	500,000	500,000	140,000	1,251,552.83	1,912,750.25	6
Banque Ville-Marie..........	500,000	500,000	477,530	20,000	958,737.34	1,462,543.94	7
Banque d'Hochelaga.........	1,000,000	710,100	710,100	70,000	1,188,549.75	1,975,811.01	6
Molsons' Bank,.............	2,000,000	2,000,000	2,000,000	675,000	7,959,303.04	10,833,081.98	8
Merchants' Bank of Canada..	6,000,000	5,796,267	5,736,099	1,375,000	14,622,607.89	21,982,369.11	7
Banque Nationale......	2,000,000	2,000,000	2,000,000	Nil.	2,250,341.21	4,390,880.42	Nil.

TRADE OF THE PORT OF MONTREAL.

Having touched upon the heart of our commercial system, on banks let us give the reader a glance at their arteries and feeders. This is the trade of the Port of Montreal has to do with. From the report of Geo. A. Hadrill, Secretary of the Montreal Board of Trade, we find that the total tonnage of sea-going vessels for season of 1885 was 683,854 tons, which exceeds the previous highest record (664,263 tons in 1883). Of this tonnage only 9.39 per cent. was sail, showing how completely steamers have supplanted sailing vessels in the ocean carrying trade of this port. Of inland vessels there arrived 5003, with a total tonnage of 724,975 tons, the aggregate of ocean and inland tonnage being 5632 vessels and 1,408,829 tons.

The lumber trade continues to be a large item in Montreal's shipping business, the exports to South America in 1885 employing 47 vessels, carrying a total of 26,465,-543 feet, the shipments to the United Kingdom being 89,667,407 feet, of which 84,282,-275 feet were by steamers.

There is a large and steady increase in the exports of Phosphate, last year's figures being 24,299 tons; for 1884, 20,461 tons; and for 1883, 17,160 tons.

Receipts of coal by sea in 1885 were, from Great Britain 48,022 tons, from the United States 213,641 tons, and from the Maritime Provinces 215,600 tons, or a total of 478,953 tons.

The port has been lighted with electric lights and the floating elevators and land elevators give great facility to the trade in grain. In 1535, Cartier had to abandon a vessel of 120 tons and reach Montreal in boats. In 1888 ships drawing 27½ feet of water and of 4000 to 5000 tons, ascended and descended the St. Lawrence to Montreal, the deepening of a channel having accomplished the work of rendering the mighty river a purveyor of wealth to Montreal and to the Dominion. The tonnage of 1850 from sea at the port of Montreal was 46,156; in 1877 it was 870,773. The values of merchandise in 1850 was $1,009,256, and in 1887, it was $8,745,526. In 1850 there were exported values to the extent of $1,745.772, and in 1887 they reached $29,391,798. In 1850, the exports were $7,174,180; in 1887, they were valued at $43,100,183. Thus the expansion goes on.

In 1887, some 20,785,976 bushels of grain were received, and 18,701,767 shipped from Montreal's port.

The Cattle Export Trade has largely benefitted the port of Montreal. In 1874-75, the value of imported horses and cattle was $1,008,740; while in 1884-5, it had fallen to $573,690. The exports, however, which were in 1874-75, $2,123,794, increased to $10,668,675. The Port of Montreal, though closed for five months of the year, is the third largest port on the American Continent. It is 250 miles nearer to Liverpool than the other American ports, and is nearer (via the Pacific coast ports and Canadian Pacific Railway) to Asiatic ports by 1134 miles. Take the distance from Chicago to Liverpool *via* Montreal, and it is 4088 miles, against 4480 miles *via* New York, or 392 miles shorter by the Montreal route.

The first ocean mail steamer between England and Montreal, the "Genoa," of 700 tons burden, arrived in port in 1853, and since then the growth of commerce on the St. Lawrence has been such that to-day there are over twenty lines of regular ocean steamships, while the yearly tonnage has increased from 358,000 tons in 1851 to 870,883 in 1887.

At the time of confederation of the Canadian Provinces, the indebtedness of the Harbor of Montreal was about $1,126,000. Since then there has been expended on the harbor proper over $1,520,000, making in all $2,646,000. The present indebtedness is $1,881,000, being a difference of $765,000, which has been paid out of revenue. Much more than this sum, however, has been paid out of revenue, and the total cost of the harbor, embracing as it does nearly five miles of wharfage front and extending from the river St. Pierre to Longue Pointe, is about $3,200,000. All this has been met by tonnage dues and taxes levied upon vessels and their cargoes coming to Montreal.

The cost of excavating the ship channel in 1882 to 1888 was about $5,000,000.

Here is one way that vessels managed to reach their anchorage in 1822, told by a newspaper:—

"There was then only one tow boat on the river, the steamer "Hercules," commanded by Captain George Brush. The "Hercules" was not able to tow the "Favorite," a brig of 276 tons, against the current, and a message was sent to Mr. Hiram Gilbert, a butcher, whose establishment was at the river side and who kept a supply of oxen for

towing purposes, to assist in towing the brig up the rapids.   A hawser was sent on
shore and ten oxen attached to it; but still the united force of steamer and oxen was
not enough.   The " Favorite " had been built by a Mr. Johnstone who carried on his
business at Hochelaga; and he, seeing the plight in which the brig found itself, sent
down forty or fifty of his men to lend a hand.   A second hawser was sent on shore and
to this the fifty men put their strength.   The " Hercules " had just steamed up afresh,
the "Frvorite" carried every inch of available sail, the oxen were whipped up and the
men tugged and pulled as well they could ; and these combined forces enabled the vessel
to get to her anchorage without further trouble.   The aspect of Montreal at that time
was very different from what it is now.   There were no wharves in those days ; to-day
there are over five miles of the finest wharves in the world along the river front.

SHIPPING TRADE.

Montreal's Shipping Trade is a twin brother of the Railway, and plying
between her port and the outside are the steamers and sailing vessels of the Allan Line
Dominion, Beaver, Temperley, White Cross, Hansa, Black Diamond, Furness, Thomson,
Donaldson, and Bossière Lines, and a number of vessels called ocean tramps, all of which
vessels make up a very large carrying capacity.   The Allan Line Fleet comprises thirty
steamers with a tonnage of 96,820 and twelve clipper vessels with a tonnage of 17,432.
This line carries the mail, and was organized by the late Sir Hugh Allan and his brother,
Mr. Andrew Allan, who is at present the head of the Company.   It was the first of the
regular Lines to demonstrate the safety and speed of the new Canadian Lines by the St.
Lawrence route.
    The Dominion Line is a rival to the old Allan Line, and has ten vessels on the
way, aggregating 31,720 tons.   This line carries the mails each alternate week
with the Allans.
    The Beaver Line is purely Canadian, and has six steam vessels running between
Liverpool and Glasgow and Montreal.   The tonnage of the six vessels is about 23,500.
The White Cross Line plies between Antwerp and Montreal and employs three steamers
on the route.   The Hansa Line employs four steamers and does a German trade.   The
Black Diamond Company keeps three coasting steamers between Montreal and the
Provinces of the Prince Edward Island, Nova Scotia and Newfoundland.   The Furness
Line, between London and Montreal, has eight steamships.   The Thomson Line supplies
the Mediterranean Sea trade, and carries large consignments for the Western States, *via*
Montreal.   The line takes back cattle and sheep to Newcastle-on-Tyne.   The Donaldson
Line runs weekly between Montreal and Glasgow and has six steam vessels on the service, which carry general cargoes to Canada and take cattle to Scotland, grain, deals,
butter, cheese and sundries.   This line runs to Halifax in Winter.   The Temperley Line
runs three large steamships between Montreal and London, and do a heavy carrying
business.   The passenger business is done principally by the Allans, Dominion and
Beaver Lines, though the others also carry a fair share of passengers.

Besides these regular lines are the miscellaneous vessels that come consigned to Messrs. Anderson & McKenzie, and also those to Messrs. Robert Reford & Co. They do a large carrying business in lumber to South American ports. Several attempts having been made to induce a French line of steamers, all resulted in disappointment until 1887 when the Bossière Line, comprising five steamers, commenced doing business from Havre to Montreal.

The trade of the whole Dominion for 1887 was, in imports, $112,892,236 and the duty $22,469,705. Of this Montreal took in $43,943,594, which paid a duty of $8,874,-147—nearly two-fifths of the whole imports of the country and more than double that of Toronto.

The export trade shows Montreal's supremacy in trade in even a greater ratio, for while the whole Dominion exported $89,515,811 the port of Montreal exported of that sum about one-third or $29,032,613. Toronto had but $3,192,157, and Quebec $5,318,533. Montreal's export was over nine times that of Toronto, and nearly three millions more than the whole of Ontario.

These figures have relation to Montreal's ocean trade. There are, however, a great many carrying companies on Canada's inland waters. Chief among these is the Richelieu & Ontario Navigation Company. This Company controls the whole river navigation and has a fleet of twenty of the finest steamboats in America. Besides her regular line, which runs from Quebec to Toronto, the Company now owns the Sague-nay fleet and two ferry steamers at Montreal and Longueuil. Besides doing about all the passenger trade of the St. Lawrence the Richelieu & Ontario Company carries immense quantities of freight. Its officers are Alex. Murray, President; Alphonse Desjardins, M.P., Vice-President; J. B. Labelle, M.P., General Manager.

The Montreal Transportation Company does a heavy carrying business in grain and has a lake fleet of eleven vessels with a capacity of 310,000 bushels; also a river fleet of four tugs and thirty-five barges with carrying capacity of 700,000 bushels. The Company also carries coal and has a grain elevating capacity at Kingston of over 20,000 bushels per hour.

The Kingston & Montreal Forwarding Company's vessels have a capacity of 400,-000 bushels of grain per trip and have two floating elevators at Montreal. The barges make ten trips during the year, and so fast has their trade with the Western States ports increased that they are forced to add new vessels each year. Mr. Alex. Gunn of Kingston is President, Mr. J. G. Ross of Quebec, Vice-President, and Mr. Wm. Stewart of Montreal, Managing Director.

The Merchants' Line between Chicago and Montreal, dates from 1836, and is now owned by Messrs. Jacques, Tracey & Co. Their fleet touch points between Chicago and Montreal, and comprises ten steamers and some smaller craft. This line does a very heavy general freight business to and from Chicago and intermediate points.

The Ottawa River Navigation Company supplies one more of the great Cana-dian Waterways, and is a passenger as well as freight line. It is owned by the Shep-pards. Mr. R. W. Sheppards, as early as 1840, commenced the work of this line, and had a splendid fleet of boats upon it by 1860, adding one after the other until to-day there are five splendid boats on the Ottawa River. Comfort is a strong point in this line and there is only one other that excels this good point, and that is safety.

The great lake and river system of Canada has been made continuously navigable for a distance of 2384 statute miles, by a connecting chain of ten canals, comprising 71¾ miles of artificial navigation. This system extends from the Straits of Belle Isle to Thunder Bay, at the head of Lake Superior. The following table of distances indicates also the respective positions of these canals:—

	Miles.
Straits of Belle Isle to Father Point	643
Father Point to Rimouski	6
Rimouski to Quebec	177
Quebec to Three Rivers (or tide-water)	74
Three Rivers to Montreal	86
Lachine Canal	8½
Lachine to Beauharnois	15¼
Beauharnois Canal	11¼
St. Cecile to Cornwall	32¾
Cornwall Canal	11½
River and Farran's Point Canals	16¼
Rapide Plat Canal	4
River and Point Iroquois Canal	7½
Junction and Galops Canal	4⅞
Prescott to Kingston	68⅜
Kingston to Port Dalhousie	170
Port Dalhousie to Port Colborne (Welland Canal)	27
Port Colborne to Amherstburg	232
Amherstburg to Windsor	18
Windsor to Foot of St. Mary's Island	25
Foot of St. Mary's Island to Sarnia	33
Sarnia to Foot of St. Joseph Island	270
Foot of St. Joseph's Island to Sault St. Mary	47
Sault St. Mary Canal	1
Head of Sault St. Mary to Point aux Pins	7
Point aux Pins to Duluth	390
Total	2384

RAILROAD INTERESTS.

Montreal's Railway facilities are but another evidence of her importance, enterprise and riches. The city is the Canadian terminus of the Canadian Pacific, Grand Trunk, Central Vermont, Delaware and Hudson, South Eastern, and branch railways of other lines. In direct communication with Halifax, Portland, Boston, New York, Chicago, Buffalo, Toronto, Winnipeg, Duluth, Ottawa, Quebec, and intermediate points. The lines of railway traced on the map would leave Montreal like a spider in the centre of a web, or the hub of well spread spokes of a large commercial wheel. The Grand Trunk Railway completed its road through from Montreal to Toronto somewhere about 1859, and before that had completed the Victoria Bridge, a wonder in that early day of scientific progress. Since that time this road has covered this part of the Continent of British America, and is now completing a double track over its entire length, while its direct branches extend through the States of Maine, New York, Michigan, Indiana, Illinois and Wisconsin. Its indirect branches reach San Francisco, run through to Mexico, touch Florida and cover the whole Continent. The Trunk line covers to-day about 3000 miles, and while much of its early history is associated with the name of Mr. C. J. Brydges, its former General Manager, Mr. Joseph Hickson's has been the master hand that has created its present importance. His struggle has been against the Vanderbilt and Gould systems in the United States, and his battle against these giants was a noble one, and successful. The report for the year 1851 showed that the number of passengers carried by the Grand Trunk amounted to 117,806 and the tons of freight carried to 116,-571, the receipts being in all $412,590. During the year 1883-4 the same line carried six millions of tons of freight and five millions of passengers. In 1886 its freightage was nearly as large and its passenger list about the same, its earnings being $14,100,000.

Mr. Joseph Hickson's staff comprises men of eminent ability in the railway world, chief among whom is Mr. Wm. Wainwright, Assistant General Manager, who has for many years been associated with the line. Mr. L. J. Seargeant, Traffic Manager. Mr. James Stephenson superintends the division east of Toronto and the north division, the south division being superintended by Mr. Charles Stiff. The Chief Engineer is Mr. E. P. Hannaford, the Mechanical Superintendent, Mr. H. Wallis; the Treasurer, Mr. R. Wright, the Accountant, Mr. H. W. Walker; the Traffic Auditor, Mr. J. F. Walker; the General Freight Agent, Mr. T. Taudy; the General Passenger Agent, Mr. W. Edgar. The accounts of the Company are inspected by a Board of Audit of which Mr. T. B. Hawson, for a considerable period the auditor in chief, is secretary. Mr. S. Barker is the manager of the North and Western divisions, with quarters at Toronto, where Mr. E. Wragge is also local manager. Mr. J. Hobson is the constructing engineer at Hamilton, Mr. A. Burns is the general freight agent in Montreal. The total number of employees is about on an average 16,000 and of these rather more than a third are mechanics. The workshops usually absorb 2000 men in Montreal, 600 or so in Hamilton, 400 in London, and Stratford, severally, 300 in Brantford, 250 in Fort Gratiot, 100 in Gorham, and a small force in Portland, more or less, as required. The balance of the mechanical force consists of engineers and firemen. The workshops always find plenty to do. During the past seven years 150 new locomotives have been built and several hundreds of new cars of all kinds from the palatial order down to the flat car.

The Board of Direction is composed as follows :—President, Sir H. W. Tyler, M.P., Lord Claud Hamilton, M.P., Hon. Frank Smith, Toronto, Messrs. Robert Young,

Robert Gillespie, W. N. Heggate, James Charles, John Mainham, Major A. G. Dickson, M.P.
The Intercolonial Railway was one of the early Government roads and ran to
Halifax as the cementing brick of the Confederation of the Provinces. The North Shore
Road to Quebec afterwards was built in connection with the Montreal, Ottawa and Western to Ottawa.   Then followed the completion of the Montreal, Portland and Boston,
the building of the road of the Grand Trunk along the south shore to Dundee and Fort
Covington, the line to Sorel; and all brought grist to Montreal's Mill.
It was reserved for the greatest tribute of all to be laid at Montreal's feet, and in
1886 the Canadian Pacific Railway was reached completion, to land at Montreal's feet
the grain of a great farming country.   In 1884 the earnings of the Canadian Pacific
were $5,750,521.   In 1887 they were $11,606,412. Thus Montreal reaps benefits that
even her most sanguine sons could not foresee ten years ago.   From Quebec to
Vancouver the distance is 3077 miles, and besides this the railway has acquired nearly
a thousand miles of road in the old Provinces.
The officers of the Company are President, Sir George Stephen, Bart.; Vice-President and General Manager, W. C. Van Horne; who may be looked upon as the guild-
ing spirits in the grand undertaking, whose complete confidence in the future of Canada
and of the ultimate success of Canada's transcontinental road has never for a moment
flagged. Mr. C. Drinkwater, for many years assistant to Mr. Hickson, of the G.T.R., is
Secretary, while Mr. Van Horne has for Assistant Manager, Mr. T. G. Shaughnessy,
whose push and enterprise, coupled with his extended experience in matters of detail
have proved him an invaluable help to the Vice-President. Mr. George Olds, the Traffic
Manager, and Mr. Lucius Tuttle, Passenger Traffic Manager, were both well known in
the railway world of the United States before they came here, and have done good work
in building up the business of the road. The other officers are: Comptroller, I. G.
Ogden; Treasurer, W. Sutherland Taylor; General Superintendent Ontario and
Atlantic division, T. A. Mackinnon; General Superintendent Eastern division,
C. W. Spencer, General Superintendent Western division, W. Whyte; General
Superintendent Pacific division, Harry Abbott; General Freight and Passenger
Agent Western and Pacific division, R. Kerr; General Passenger Agent Ontario
and Atlantic division, D. McNicholl.
At the present moment two great railway stations are in process of erection.
The first is the Grand Trunk's Bonaventure Depot, to cost $300,000. The Canadian
Pacific's new Bonaventure is the second of these and will cost fully $300,000.

ELECTRIC CURRENT.

The Montreal Telegraph Company, Dominion Telegraph Company and Canadian
Pacific Railway Telegraph Company give communication with every part of the known
world. These Companies make use of no less than ten cables. Three from North Sydney, C. B., to Heart's Content, Newfoundland, and thence to Valentia, Ireland; one
from North Sydney, C. B., to St. Pierre, Miquelon, thence to Brest; two from St. John,

N. B., to Canso, N. S., and thence to Penzance; one from Halifax to Ballinskellen, Ireland; one *via* New York to Canso, N. S., St. Pierre, Miquelon; and thence to Brest
two *via* New York to Canso, N. S., and thence to Waterville, Ireland, where it connects
with Weston-Super-Mare, England.

The telephone service is supplied by the Bell Telephone Company. The first
service used was put up in 1878 by Sir Hugh Allan at the suggestion of Mr. Angus
Grant, an electrician and telegraph man well-known in the ranks of telegraphy. This
was used by the Princess Louise to talk to Sir Hugh Allan, and she was delighted to
find that a whisper could be heard 130 miles away. To-day under the energy of Mr.
Sise, of the Bell Telephone Company, there are lines of eight wires running to Toronto
and Hamilton, three to London, two to Sarnia and Detroit, two to Buffalo, two to
Niagara, some 5,000 miles of wire in all.

MANUFACTURING INTERESTS.

Montreal's manufactures form a great and interesting subject in her modern history, and after the inception of the national policy her wealth flowed out in the establishment of mills in every part of the Dominion. Cotton, paper, cigars and tobacco,
boots and shoes, sugar refining, even silk making, each received a very great stimulus
The consequence was that investments in all these departments were so well rewarded
by the result of money making, owing to heavy duties imposed upon outside competitors,
that more money flowed out than the trade of Canada actually warranted; and then
came the inevitable pause in the advance. When the National Policy came into play
there were but seven cotton mills in Canada. To-day there are twenty-three mills, half
a million spindles, 10,000 looms and about 8,000 persons earning their bread from the
product of the looms. Montreal capitalists control more than half the amount of capital put into these mills. They manufacture every class of cottons from the grey
unbleached to the finest qualities of prints and the more ornamental "searsucker," and
curtain goods, plain and fancy shirtings—everything, in fact, that cotton can be used to
manufacture. The annual product is 9,000,000 yards of cotton cloth. Of the twenty-
three mills in Canada the following are controlled by Montreal capital:—

The Hochelaga Cotton Co. with 110,000 spindles and an annual product of 1,500,-
000 yards of cotton cloth, the Chambly Cotton Co., Coaticook Cotton Co., Montreal Cot-
ton Co., Merchants' Cotton Co., Canadian Cotton Co., Stormont Cotton Co., Kingston
Cotton Co., Hamilton Cotton Co., Ontario Cotton Mills, Dundas Cotton Co., and the
Magog Print and Textile Company, are mainly controlled by Montreal capital in
Montreal.

The iron and coal industry was accelerated by the National Policy, and the Montreal Rolling Mill with 500 men and boys in their employ is expected to furnish all the
iron pipe, horse-shoes, horse-shoe nails, etc. The Grand Trunk and Canadian Pacific
Railways shops turn out all the rolling stock and make all the heavy repairs required by

their roads, and the Dominion Car Works make all the chilled steel car wheels for the Grand Trunk and Intercolonial Railways. It employs over 600 men. A large steel axle factory in Hochelaga employs 100 hands. Eight firms of nail and spike makers have $2,000,000 invested in their business, and employ 1600 labourers. There are four horse-shoe factories, five make horseshoe nails, three firms make tacks and ornamental nails, one factory makes iron piping and twelve large foundries supply fittings for stoves, fences, lamps, furnaces, pumps. Three firms manufacture safes, two steel saws, two sewing machines, six wire, four springs, two electric light and two telephone machinery, and so on in a long line the iron and steel trade could be lengthened out. Suffice it to say that fully eight thousand persons earn their bread in this industry. Brass founding is also one of the industries of Montreal and employs nearly half a million of money and about four hundred men. The sugar industry is chief among those that were revised by the National Policy. The Redpath Sugar Refining was closed, but opened again and in a few months was employing 600 or 700 persons and putting out a million and a half pounds of sugar for each year. The St. Lawrence Sugar Refinery is also a Montreal institution and has a capital of $850,000 while the Redpath (or properly speaking Canadian) Sugar Refinery has a capital of $1,000,000. Between them they control the Sugar Trade of the Dominion, the other refiners of Halifax, Moncton and Berthier being smaller concerns. Beet-root sugar making was tried during the past few years; but it was not a success. The cigar and tobacco making industry has grown to immense proportions during the past ten years, and over 1,000 persons are employed in Montreal alone in the cigar business. The tobacco is imported from the West Indies, the United States and from Indian Archipelago. There are twenty-five factories in Montreal.

The silk industry has not proved quite such a bonanza as the cigars and tobacco trade, but trunks and valises, paper hanging leather board, wholesale clothing, are all prosperous and paying.

Paper making is one of the most successful of Montreal's capital. Sought fields and parties in the city control mills in Lachute, Richmond, St. Jerome, Valleyfield and elsewhere where newspaper is turned out for newspaper offices and other departments of printing, and also for the manufacture of paper bags and wrapping paper of all kinds.

EDUCATION.

Montreal Schools have kept pace with her commercial increase. With the Catholics as early as 1535, it was religion and education first, commerce afterwards. With the Protestant English it was conquest and commerce first—religion and education afterwards. The Catholic religion means education also in a sense. The Protestants place secular education alone. The Recollet Fathers commenced the education of the Indians in 1615. Fathers Jamay, D'Olbeau, Le Caron, and Brother Duplessis, better known as Brother Pacific, were the first known teachers in Canada. They taught in St.

Maurice, Tadousac and Quebec in 1614. In Montreal the work was begun in 1692 in a building near Notre Dame Cathedral, long since replaced by commercial houses. The Jesuits did much for education in their day, but were gradually replaced by other methods. The Recollets School in Montreal closed in 1826, and the last Superior of that Order died in the city in 1843, while the last of the Jesuits had died in 1791. The Jesuits estates were confiscated at the conquest; but it was not until 1851 that they returned and founded their present college, called St. Mary's College. The Sulpician Fathers commenced their work in 1657, and after the conquest established a College in Montreal, called St. Raphael's. The Hon. D. B. Viger, L.L.D., the great jurist; Michel Bibaud, the historian; Jean J. Lartigue, first Bishop of Montreal; Sir George E. Cartier; and a number of illustrious men, passed away to their rest now, were educated by the Sulpicians. Of the leading men of this day Judge Coursol, Dr. Hingston the great surgeon and ornament to the profession, Mr. Girouard, M. P., Dr. Beaubien, and others were educated in the Sulpician Colleges, which now provide education in the Classics. Their Montreal College on the slope of the mountain has all the necessary means of education, and is attended by about 300 students. Victoria School of Medicine, a school that has prospered under many drawbacks, is affiliated with Victoria University of Cobourg, and opposed to it is a branch of Laval University, which looks with jealous eye upon all done by it. The Polytechnic School, founded in 1873, by the Hon. Mr. Ouimet, is another step forward of Catholic educational enterprise, and is under control of the Catholic School Commissioners, supported by the tax-payers. It is now associated with Laval University, Quebec, as its Science course. In addition to this, there are a large number of common schools established under the Roman Catholic School Commissioners, and these, supported out of the public purse are very closely watched over by the Catholic Clergy. The advance in these schools from 1878 to 1888 is very gratifying to all who admire the French Canadian race and the spread of knowledge among them.

The Protestant Educational Institutions are more numerous, better equipped, and more serviceable now than they ever have been. As late as 1853 they were poor affairs, compared with what Great Britain could show in her home, national and parish schools. The Common Schools were no worse than the higher schools in this respect, and it was not until a comparatively recent day that there came the general advance all along the line. To-day, Montreal may well be celebrated for her educational schools and universities. In early days the private schools played its part as the pioneers of educational work, and some very curious pioneers they often were, not much progress was made earlier than 1853. In that year there were the National School, on St. Denis Street; the British and Canadian School, under Mr. Minchin; the Colonial Church and School Society, Bonaventure Street, under Mr. (now principal) Hicks; Phillips' School, St. Urbain Street the High School, in Burnside Hall, and one or two other smaller private schools. The strongest of these were the High School, and Mr. Hicks' School, wherein many of the leading merchants of Montreal were educated. Subsequently the Normal School grew to very important proportions as a preparatory school for teachers. Though the Protestant Board of School Commissioners was established in 1846, their real work did not bear fruit until 1870, when the school taxation commenced to supply them with means wherewith to educate the youth of the city. The school tax is a charge upon real property and while the city is bound to collect it, the Commissioners expend it making an annual report of their doings to the City Council which appoints half of the Board, the Quebec Government the other. The Commissioners to-day have established in the city a High School for Boys and one for Girls, a Preparatory High School, Prince Arthur, Berthelot Street, Sherbrooke Street, Ann Street, Luke Street Schools, the British and Canadian School, Grace Church School, the Point St. Charles School, the Hochelaga School, and other schools supplying the common school wants of the city in every particular. The High Schools are self-supporting, from fees. The others as is the case with the Catholic common schools, are supported by taxation.

Protestant Universities, being secular, are more public in their operation than their Catholic confreres. They comprise McGill University, the first endowment of which was by James McGill, now of historic memory, and which has been successively patronized by the late William Molson, Mr. Peter Redpath, Sir Donald A. Smith, and others all of whom gave substantial aid to the University. The Faculties of Medicine, Arts, Science and Law, are all excellent, and the stamp of Sir William Dawson, Principal of the University has made it famous. The Presbyterian, Wesleyan and Congregational Colleges are affiliated with the University, and each has its college buildings in close proximity to the University.

Bishop's College, Lennoxville, has its School of Medicine in Montreal, under Dr. F. W. Campbell, Dean.

The Anglican Diocesan College, which is affiliated with McGill University, is situated on Dorchester Street, near the Windsor Hotel, and has a Principal and five Professors.

THE MAIN BRIDGE.

THE SWING BRIDGE.

THE SAULT BRIDGE.

New York Life Insurance Company, DAVID BURKE, GENERAL
MANAGER FOR CANADA, 23 St. John Street. — The New York Life Insurance Company has come to Canada to stay if we may judge by the amount of business
they have already transacted here and the magnificent building now in course of erection on
Place D'Armes Square.   The Company was founded in New York in 1845, and
in 1868 a Canadian branch was established in this city, under the management of the
late Mr. Walter Burke, who successfully conducted it until the time of his decease in 1878.
In July, 1883, Mr. David Burke, the present General Manager for Canada was appointed and
re-organized the Canadian business.   Mr. Burke was General Agent for the Company in
Ontario, from 1868 to 1878, and thus has a lengthened, practical experience.   To give
some idea of what the New York Life Insurance Company has done, we would quote from
an open letter from the president of the Company to Canadian policy-holders.

" The extent of last years business has never been equalled by any purely Mutual
Company in the history of Life Insurance, and the immense accumulation of invested assets,
which has now reached over $83,000,000.00, and is held for payment of obligations to policy-
holders, can perhaps be better comprehended when compared with the capital of the Bank
of England. which is $70,700,000.00 ; a difference in favor of the New York Life of $12,300,-
000.00.   The investments of the Company are of the highest character, as is shown by the
rate of interest realized annually therefrom, showing conclusively that these investments fully
meet the requirements necessary to the safety and profit of its policy-holders.

"The New York Life is a purely Mutual Company.   It originated Non-forfeiture Policies
in 1860, which feature has since become a part of the Insurance Statues of the country.   The
great saving to policy-holders of the Non-forfeiture system, as originated by the New York
Life, is estimated at several millions dollars per year.   Its policies on the Tontine plan, that
have reached the end of the selected Toutine period, have given the largest profits of any
policies running through the same period of time.   The New York Life is the ONLY Company
that allows grace of one month in the payment of premiums on this class of policies.
The Company's latest contribution to modern Life Insurance is a GUARANTEED (MORTUARY)
DIVIDEND which is applied to all its policies issued on the Tontine plan, as well as to its
Five Year Dividend Policies.   This dividend is equal to 50 per cent. or 100 per cent. premiums
paid, in case of death within the period selected, and comes nearest to giving Life Insurance
for nothing of any system now presented to the public."

The Canadian department of the Company, has, in a period of about four years, produced $10,400,000.00. of insurance in force, yielding an annual premium income of nearly $450,000. The Company has also placed on deposit with the Dominion Government $600,000, in first-class securities for the benefit of Canadian policy-holders. The new building of the Company, of which a cut will be found in this work, and which is expected to be finished in March, 1889, will be the finest and most substantial building in Canada, and will be an ornament to Place D'Armes Square, costing as it will, when completed about $600,000.00. The building will have a frontage of seventy-three feet on Place D'Armes Square and 115 feet on St. James Street. It will be eight stories in height, besides basement and cellar, and will be surmounted by a clock tower, three stories high. The height of the building will be 112 feet from the sidewalk and the clock tower will rise forty feet more, being 152 feet. The basement is constructed of Thousand Island granite and the upper parts of Scotch red sand-stone, especially imported for this purpose and dressed in this city. The forms of architecture will be Italian renaissance, constructed in the most substantial manner, and will be thoroughly fire-proof, the floors and partitions being constructed between iron in such a manner that every room in itself will be absolutely a fire-proof vault. The building will have accommodation for 120 offices each of which being provided with every modern convenience, electric light in every office, the light being produced in the building itself. There will be ornamental iron staircases and marble floors in all the corridors, the building will be heated throughout by steam in winter, and three elevators will be in use for the accommodation of tenants and callers. There will be also a newly-invented patent letter shoot in every office, so that letters can be deposited in the receiving box on the ground floor without the trouble of the tenant leaving his office. There will also be a telegraph office in the building from which messages can be sent to any part of the world without delay. From this brief outline it will be seen that the new building of the New York Life Insurance Company will be the best appointed and most substantial in Canada, and equal to any of its size on the Continent of America. The architects of the building are Messrs. Babb, Cook & Willard, of 55 Broadway, New York, and the work is being constructed under the immediate superintendanc of Mr. G. E. Walters. The contractors for the building, are Messrs. Simpson & Peel, who do the carpenter work, and let the rest of the work to sub-contractors, as follows :—Bricklaying, T. Peel, stone-mason work, Peter Lyall, iron work, E. Chanteloup, Thousand Island granite, Stuart Forsyth.

Mr. David Burke, the General Manager of the Company for Canada, is a gentleman well-known in underwriting circles as well as by the public generally and is held in the highest estimation by all who know him, and under his management the Canadian Department of the Company is assured of success.

Imperial Fire Insurance Company, of London, Eng., W. H. RINTOUL,

PRESIDENT, SECRETARY, HOSPITAL STREET.—Among the most prominent, substantial and old-established fire insurance companies doing business in Canada, the Imperial Fire Insurance Company, of London, England, holds a deservedly high place. Established in London in 1803, it has had a long, honorable and succesful career and has steadily gained its way to public recognition and influence throughout the British Empire. The Canadian business of the Company was established in 1864, when Mr. W. H. Rintoul, became agent and has ever since represented the Company with honor to himself and profit to the Company. The Company has a subscribed capital of £1,200,000, paid up capital of £300,000, and the total invested funds are over £1,550,000. This shows that the Imperial Fire Insurance Company, of London, is in a flourishing and substantial condition. Another proof of this is the beautiful Canadian head office now under process of construction on Place d'Armes Square, and which is expected to be ready for occupancy on the 1st April, 1889. The construction of the building is under the superintendence of Mr. C. W.

Clinton, of New York, the designer of the Mutual Life building in that city. As will be seen from the cut in another part of this work, it will be a handsome structure and will harmonize with the Bank of Montreal and the other noble edifices on the square, and will still further increase the architectural treasures of the city. The building will be seven stories in height. The five lower stories will be of gray stone and upon these other two stories of iron and other fire-proof material, the upper windows is the topmost recess, being circular with extremely handsome stone carving. In the three recesses the columns will be of three orders of architecture, the main recess being of Doric, the second of Ionic, and the third or topmost of Corinthian. The top stories will have dormer windows, with galvanized iron cornices and trimmings, the building terminating in a pointed tower in centre of the roof about 100 feet from the pavement. The roof will be of iron framing with porus slab fillings, which will be the first introduction of this new principle of fire-proof construction into Montreal. There will be an area 19 x 65 feet in the centre of the building, and in the centre of this will be a tower of iron and glass, containing two elevators and an iron staircase with white marble steps. Fire-proof vaults will be attached to each suite of offices, and the floors throughout will be fire-proofed. The entrance hall will be ten feet wide; the floor of marble tiling with terra-cotta centres, and the sides wainscotted in white marble. The building will contain eighty-five offices, the Imperial, of course, occupying the principal part and that best suited to its requirements. The building will be fitted up with every modern improvement, including electric lighting, steam heating, while facilities will be had for telegraphing and telephoning from one office to another in the building as well as with the outside world, while by the use of a "mail tube" on each floor, letters can be deposited in the general letter box below, which will be cleared for the post office every hour. The work has been contracted for as follows:—Mason work, Mr. Peter Lyall; carpenter work, Messrs. Simpson & Peel; iron work, Mr. H. R. Ives; elevators, Messrs. Miller Bros. & Mitchell. It will thus be seen that the new Imperial office will be one of the most complete in the city. The business of the Company is extending rapidly throughout the Dominion, the Maritime Provinces and British Columbia, under the able and efficient management of Mr. W. H. Rintoul, who has given the affairs of the Company his careful and undivided attention for nearly a quarter of a century.

Standard Life Assurance Co., W. M. RAMSAY, MANAGER, STANDARD BUILDINGS, ST. JAMES STREET.—Disease, accident and death are conditions incident to this stage of existence that are certain to come to us all sooner or later. Against the consequences which would in the natural course ensue to our dependants from our being stricken down by death, many assurance companies offer protection more or less ample and effective, and it is the plain duty of every respectable man of good habits while in the enjoyment of his faculties, health and strength to avail himself thereof and throw around his loved ones such safeguards as will secure them from want and dependence. The Standard Life Assurance Co., of Edinburgh, Scotland, has one of the highest reputations and most successful and honorable records of any life assurance companies in existence. Established in the year 1825, it has met with the most phenominal success, which has been due to the strict business principles upon which the affairs of the Company have been conducted as well as its economical management. The Company have invested funds amounting to over $33.000.000, with an annual income of over $4,450.000, and there are deposited with the Government at Ottawa, for the security of Canadian policy-holders, nearly $1.000.000. The amount of claims paid in Canada alone amount to nearly two and a quarter million of dollars. The Company pay all just claims promptly in which respect they have a high reputation. The Company occupy their own building on St. James Street, which is one of the finest architectural structures in the city, and is an ornament to St. James Street as well as a credit to the city. It is a four story building of brown stone front and richly carved and with a central figure of Atlas supporting the globe. The directors of the company are gentlemen well-known in public, financial and mercantile life and are a guarantee of the stability of the institution. Mr. W. M. Ramsay, the Manager, is a gentleman eminently qualified for the position, from lengthened experience and executive ability.

North British and Mercantile Fire and Life Assurance Company,

THOMAS DAVIDSON, MANAGING DIRECTOR, 78 ST. FRANÇOIS XAVIER STREET.— Among the important business interests of Montreal, insurance has such a vital bearing upon all other interests, as to entitle it to special consideration in a review of the resources of the city. Among the many solid and substantial companies doing business here, there are none more worthy of particular mention than the North British and Mercantile Fire and Life Insurance Company, whose head offices for the Dominion are located at No. 78 St. François Xavier Street, of which Mr. Thomas Davidson is the Managing Director. The home offices are located at 64 Princess Street, Edinburgh, and 61 Threadneedle Street, London. This Company was incorporated in the year 1809, and soon took a leading position among British Insurance Companies. It has at all times been noted for careful management, liberal treatment, and a prompt settlement of all just claims. As its name implies both a fire and life assurance business is conducted. It has an authorized capital of $14,600,000 and a paid up capital of over $3,041,666, the Fire Fund and reserves being $8,462,682, the Life and Annuity Funds $20,699,659. The directors of the Company here are gentlemen well-known in business circles and public life. Gilbert Scott, Esq., Hon. Thomas Ryan, W. W. Ogilvie, Esq., and Archibald MacNider, Esq., Thomas Davidson, Esq., being the Managing Director. There are agencies of the Company located in the principal towns and cities of the Dominion, which, during the past year have reported excellent business.

La "Canadienne" Life Insurance Company, 13 ST. LAMBERT STREET,

MONTREAL.—Incorporated by Special Act of Parliament, Authorized Capital, $300,000 ; Government Deposit, $25,000. The Hon. J. G. Laviolette, Legislative Council, President ; F. X. Moisan, Esq., Vice-President; F. N. Belcourt, Secretary and Director ; Dr. Rottot, Medical Adviser ; James Wilson, Chief Agent English Department, at Head Office.

The wise and provident man makes provision against the day of adversity, and, also against the day of his death, when those who are dependent upon him may not be left in adverse circumstances. This can only safely be done in the majority of cases, by life insurance, and it is now acknowledged by every intelligent man, that it is a duty for everyone to be insured. Among the many first-class Insurance Companies in Montreal, is that of La "Canadienne," whose Head Office is located at No. 13 St. Lambert Street. Although this Company was established only one year ago, it has been established upon a solid foundation, and is already giving marked evidences of success. It has an Authorized Capital of $300,000, and issues the following systems of Insurance :—Conjoint, Industrial, Limited Endowment, Endowment, Debenture Policies and Ordinary Life, so that intending insurers have their choice of six different plans, each being first-class in itself. The officers in this Company, are gentlemen well and favorably known in the community, and are, Hon. J. G. Laviolette, President; F. X. Moisan, Esq., Vice-President ; F. N. Belcourt, Esq., Secretary and General Manager, and Dr. Rottot, Medical Adviser. Mr. Belcourt, the General Manager, is a gentleman with large experience in life insurance matters, having been with the Ætna Insurance Company, for two years. He is a gentleman highly esteemed by all who know him, and is a most efficient officer.

The attention of large employers of labor, as well as employees, is directed to this "Industrial Branch," whereby, for a small yearly payment, workmen may secure five dollars per week, when unable to follow their employment, and a substantial sum, for their families, in the event of death.

Windsor Hotel, G. W. SWETT, Manager, Dominion Square.—In writing a brief sketch of the Windsor Hotel, the writer is uncertain whether to treat it as a palace or a public hostelry. Certainly in its architectural appearance and location, its spacious halls, corridors and suites of parlors, it is more on the palatial than the usual hotel plan, either in this country or Europe. When it was first proposed to build the hotel, and in the location where it stands, people cried out, "White Elephant," "Will Never Pay," "Too far from the business part of the city." But the Hotel has certainly become a brilliant success, a source of profit to the stockholders, and an honor to the city. The Windsor Hotel was built in 1877, at a cost of $1,100,000. It covers about two acres of ground and contains over 400 rooms, single and *en suite*. On account of the increasing business, a new wing was built on Stanley Street, in 1882, and this present year it has been found necessary to erect another extension, containing a large banquet hall and concert room, 140 x 60 feet in dimensions, with galleries at each end. The concert and banqueting hall and ball-room will be thirty-seven feet high, with a dome-shaped ceiling and will have side entrances on Peel and Stanley Streets. The rotunda of the Hotel, in which are the business offices, ticket and telegraph offices, is one of the largest and finest of any hotel in the world. The new corridor, on the second floor, is over 225 feet long, and is handsomely furnished, and at night, when the crystal chandeliers are lit up, presents a brilliant appearance. There are three ladies parlors, *en suite*, elegantly and artistically furnished, and giving a beautiful view of Dominion Square. The dining hall, has a seating capacity for 600 guests, with high ceiling and dome in centre, the cornices and dome being hand-painted, the subjects being landscapes and figure pieces, and were executed by an eminent artist. Leading off the dining hall and between it and the Ladies' Ordinary, is the culinary department, where the *Chef de Cuisine* and his numerous assistants may be found busy preparing the delicious *menu*, for which the Hotel has become so justly celebrated on this Continent. By the use of a powerful fan apparatus over the cooking ranges, the kitchen is kept not only comparatively cool, but not the slightest smell can be noticed from the various viands in process of cooking, which is a great consideration to guests. It would be impossible in a short sketch to do anything like justice to a description of this beautiful hotel, so complete in its appointments, its laundry, barber shop, billiard and pool room, and its magnificent bar, hung with costly oil paintings. Lord Stanley, of Preston, the new Governor-General, and a gentleman who has travelled much, expressed his surprise and pleasure at finding such a luxurious hotel on the American Continent, many points in which, he declared to be superior to anything he had seen in Europe. The Directors of the Company are Duncan McIntyre, Esq., President; G. B. Burland, Esq., Vice-President; Philip S. Ross, Esq., Secretary-Treasurer; Directors, Charles Garth, Esq., James P. Dawes, Esq., Wm. Cassils, Esq., Selkirk Cross, Esq., and Henry Joseph, Esq. The Manager, Mr. G. W. Swett, is a gentleman who has had a large experience in hotel management, and has done much in building up the business and the reputation of the Windsor Hotel, and the travelling public trust that he may long be spared to preside over its affairs.

Kingman, Brown & Co., SHIPPING & COMMISSION MERCHANTS, 14 CUSTOM HOUSE SQUARE, MONTREAL.— In reviewing the commerce and manufactures of Montreal, special attention has, of course, to be given to the shipping interests, upon which so much of Montreal's wealth and importance as a distributing centre depends. The Government having assumed the channel debt, it is expected that a great impetus will be given to the shipping trade to this Port during this and the coming years and thus Montreal will be benefitted in a marked degree. Among the shipping and commission houses in this city, is that of Messrs. Kingman, Brown & Co., whose office is located at No. 14 Custom House Square. This business was established fifteen years ago by Robert C. Adams & Co., who were succeeded by the present firm, whose cable address is "Kingman." The firm are managing agents of the Black Diamond Shipping Co. of Montreal, Limited, whose vessels ply between Montreal and Charlottetown, Sidney and St. Johns, New Foundland. The vessels of the line are the "Bonavista," "Coban," and "Cacouna," which are English built, classed 100 A. I. Lloyd's, and are specially fitted for the passenger trade in the Gulf of St. Lawrence. The steamers bring coal from the Lower Provinces to the St. Lawrence Ports, chiefly Montreal, —hence the appropriateness of the Company's name and house flag,—a black diamond in a red ground. The firm are also selling agents for the International Coal Co., Limited, whose colliery is located at Sydney, C. B., and in addition transact a general shipping and commission business. The members of the firm are Mr. Abner Kingman and Mr. Thomas B. Brown.

The Montreal Elevating Co.

The Montreal Elevating Co. ALEX. McDOUGALL, MANAGER, 7 CUSTOM HOUSE SQUARE. -The rapid development that has taken place in the port of Montreal during the past thirty years, has been truly wonderful and is but a slight forecast of what may be expected in the near future, when the increased harbor facilities have been made, and now that the tonnage dues have been removed. In nothing has this development been more noticeable than in the grain elevating trade, a brief sketch of the Montreal Elevating Company, being a good illustration. This business was established in the year 1857 as the "Montreal Steam Elevating Company," with a subscribed capital of $80,000, and with John Esdaile, President ; and H. L. Routh, Andrew Shaw, James Henderson and C. J. Cusack, Directors. The Company started with one elevator in 1858, the amount of grain handled in two seasons being only 500,000 bushels. A second elevator was built for the fall of 1860, another in 1861 and the business had by this time developed such proportions that two other elevators were built for the season of 1863. In 1871, the Company owned seven elevators and 10,000,000 bushels of grain were handled and shipped. In 1872, the Company amalgamated with a new Company then started and known as the " Montreal Elevating Company," which name the amalgamated Companies adopted, and had a capital of $160,000. the following gentlemen being the officers, Andrew Allan, president, Hugh McLennan, Daniel Butters, J. H. Joseph and A. T. Patterson, Directors. To-day the Company own fourteen elevators, having an average capacity of 5000 bushels an hour, and costing $15,000 each, the total fleet costing therefore $210,000. Thus from one elevator in 1857, handling 500,000 bushels in two seasons, the trade has so grown that the floating elevators of this Company are now capable of handling 70,000 bushels an hour and the indications are that the next few years will see a still further heavy increase. The present officers of the Company are Andrew Allan, President, Hugh McLennan, A. T. Patterson, T. A. Crane and Alexander McDougall. Mr. McDougall is the Manager of the Company, a position which he has held since 1861, and under his able administration the business has grown from a single elevator to its present extensive proportions. He is a gentleman of marked push, energy and enterprise, as is amply evinced in the discharge of the duties of his present position.

Mcbride, Harris & Co.

McBride, Harris & Co., IMPORTERS OF FRUIT AND COMMISSION MERCHANTS. 134 McGILL AND 1 TO 21 COLLEGE STREETS, MONTREAL.—Montreal is rapidly building up in commercial and manufacturing importance, as must be readily acknowledged by anyone who takes the trouble to note the many new business houses that have been inceated in this city during the past few years. In fact during the past year a very large number of important houses has been added to the list, and of these, that of Messrs. McBride, Harris & Co., Fruit and Commission Merchants, 134 McGill Street, and 1 to 21 College Street, are deserving of particular mention. The house was established as recently as March 1st of the present year, and yet during that comparatively short space of time a business has been built up that will compare favorably with any in the city, the trade now extending throught the Dominion and considerable export. The firm are heavy importers of foreign fruits from Italy, Spain, the West Indies and South America and California and also do a large business in domestic fruits and produce of every description as well as in imported goods. They receive fruit and produce on consignment, selling the same to the best advantage of the shipper and making the prompt and satisfactory returns in all cases. The premises occupied by them for business purposes consist of two floors each 30 x 120 feet in dimensions, while employment if furnished to ten competent assistants. The members of the firm are Messrs. John Thompson McBride and Irwin Harris, both of whom are natives of Canada and are widely and highly esteemed as enterprising and progressive business men. The members of the firm are both practically experienced in their line, having been in the house of Vipond & McBride for twelve years.

Baylis Manufacturing Co., VARNISHES, JAPANS, PRINTING INKS,

WHITE LEAD, &c., 16 TO 28 NAZATERH STREET, MONTREAL.—The oil and varnish trade of the Dominion, is one of very marked importance, and has made rapid strides in this city during the past fifteen or twenty years. Coach builders and others, now turn out vast quantities of buggies and carriages yearly, selling the same cheap and requiring the best kinds of varnish to make the work look and wear well, and they use large quantities of it, and thus the trade has been developed. There are several important houses in the varnish, japans and oil trade in this city, among the number deserving of special notice, being that of the Baylis Manufacturing Company, whose office and works are located at Nos. 16 to 28 Nazareth Street. The premises occupied, consist of a two-storey brick building, with a frontage of 140 feet, and a depth of ninety-six feet. These are fitted up with every requirement for the successful conducting of the work, and twelve skilled workmen and assistants are given employment throughout the year, while five travellers are kept constantly on the road, the trade of the house extending throughout the Dominion. The Company manufacture and deal in varnishes, japans, printing inks, white lead, paints, machinery oils, axle grease, &c. These goods are all of the very best quality, and have long held a standard reputation in the trade. This business was established twenty years ago, and is one well-known throughout the trade. Mr. Henry Baylis, the Manager of the Company, is the second oldest paint and varnish manufacturer in the city, and is a gentleman well-known and esteemed in trade and social circles.

A. S. & W. H. Masterman, PORK BUTCHERS, 8, 9. 10, 11 AND 12 ST.

ANN'S MARKET, MONTREAL.—Among the many business interests conducted in Montreal, that in the food supplies of the people hold the most prominent place. The baker, the butcher and the grocer, are three important personages, when the necessities of the public are considered. Among those prominently engaged in the pork butchering line in this city, none hold a higher position in the estimation of the people or considered from the extent of business done, than the firm of Messrs. A. S. & W. H. Masterman, whose stalls are at Nos. 8, 9, 10, 11 and 12 St. Ann's Market, the factory being located at No. 2082½ Notre Dame Street. This business was established in 1822, a little more than sixty years ago, by Mr. Christopher Masterman, who was succeeded by Wm. Masterman, who retired in favor of his sons, the present proprietors in 1883, after a successful and honorable business career. The firm deal in all kinds of pork, hams and bacon, these being cured by a special process of their own, which has made the Masterman Brand of Cured Meats famous all over the Dominion. The factory is fitted up with every requisite for the successful prosecution of the business, and nothing is omitted that could possibly aid in success. The firm use from 900 to 1000 hogs a week, the trade being conducted at wholesale and retail, and a specialty is made of supplying the shipping trade with this line of provisions, all orders receiving the utmost care and being promptly attended to. The members of the firm are Messrs. Arthur S. & W. H. Masterman, both of whom are gentlemen of thorough business ability, and fully understand all the details of their trade, and can thus promptly attend to all demands made upon them.

The Montreal Soap and Oil Manufacturing Company, MANUFAC-

TURERS OF TOILET AND LAUNDRY SOAPS, LARD, OILS, ETC., FACTORY, 57 AMHERST STREET, MONTREAL.—Montreal is noted throughout the Dominion for its extensive manufacturing industries as well as its important commercial interests. The outlook at present for the future prosperity of the city is very bright and encouraging, and if present opportunities are properly grasped, Montreal should soon be a Canadian Chicago. Among the important manufacturing industries conducted in this city is that of the Montreal Soap and Oil Manufacturing Company, whose office and factory

THE BAYLIS MANUFACTURING CO'Y.
VARNISH, PAINT, PRINTING INK, AXLE GREASE, &C.

A. S. AND W. H. MASTERMAN, PORK BUTCHERS.

are located at No. 57 Amherst Street. This business was established in the year 1845 by Mr. A. W. Hood, who conducted successfully until the time of his death, seven years ago, since when, the business has been continued by his executors, and was succeeded by the Montreal Soup and Oil Manufacturing Company, in April last. The premises occupied consist of a three-storey building, 138 x 180 feet in dimensions, which is fitted up with all the latest and most improved machinery and appliances, driven by a twenty-five horse-power steam engine, having a sixty horse-power boiler, while employment is furnished to twenty assistants and skilled workmen. The Company are manufacturers of toilet and laundry soaps, of the very best quality, lard and other lubricating oils, such as heavy engine XXX, Stock's X, seal oil, lardine, mineral olive, Arctic seal, neatsfoot, and many other kinds which they manufacture and import. The superintendent of the factory is the most experienced soap-boiler in America, which is saying a great deal, but yet is generally acknowledged, and thus the product of this house is unsurpassed. Mr. Stock was one of the first to put down oil wells in the Pennsylvania region, and has had a lengthened experience and a thoroughly practical knowledge of the oil production and manufacture in all its details. He is a native of England, and is a pushing, active and enterprising business man. The house has had a long and honorable career, and is noted for its straightforward and honorable dealing as well as for the superior quality of its goods.

Kerry, Watson & Co., WHOLESALE & MANUFACTURING DRUGGISTS,

OFFICE AND WAREHOUSE, 351 ST. PAUL STREET, FACTORY, 23, 25, 27, ST. JEAN BAPTISTE STREET.—Montreal, is noted for the character and reliability of its leading business houses, many of which have been established since the beginning of the present century, and have kept steady pace with the development and prosperity of the city. One of the best known houses of this character in the city, is that of Messrs. Kerry, Watson & Co., manufacturing and wholesale druggists, whose office and warehouse are located at No. 351 St. Paul Street, (Nun's Building.) This business was founded in the year 1810, and has passed through several changes of proprietorship in succession, being formerly Carter & McLonald, who were followed by Carter, Kerry & Co., and they in turn by Kerry Bros. & Crathern, the present firm of Kerry, Watson & Co., succeeding to the business in 1872. The house, from the date of its inception, has had an honorable and prosperous career, and its name has been a synonym for straight-forward and liberal dealing with the trade throughout the Dominion, as well as in some parts of England and the United States, where their trade extends. The warehouse consists of five floors 40 x 150 feet in dimensions, and is fully equipped with every convenience for the successful prosecution of the extensive business. The firm manufacture every description of pharmaceutical products, making a specialty of Gray's Syrup of Red Spruce Gum, and they also grind pure drugs for the trade, the factory being located at Nos. 23, 25, and 27 St. Jean Baptiste Street. The products of this house have a standard reputation, and are absolutely pure in every respect. The firm have a manufactory on Lake Street, Rouses' Point, where they manufacture Gray's Syrup of Red Spruce Gum for the United States trade, and they have a depot at 36 and 38 Hanover Street, Boston, which is used as a distributing house for the States, and where all the products of the Rouses' Point factory is sent, and is handled from there. To supply the Western trade of Canada, they have another branch house on Dundas Street, London, Ont., which is known as the "London Drug Company," and in this branch they also manufacture and import. From this brief sketch, it will be seen, that the operations of the house are conducted upon an extensive scale, and that the business is one of the most important in the drug line emanating from Montreal. The individual members of the firm are Messrs. John Kerry, who is an Englishman by brith, David Watson, a native of Scotland, and William Simons Kerry, who claims Canada for his place of nativity, and who is a graduate of the Quebec Pharmaceutical Association.

H. R. Ives & Co., MANU-
FACTURERS OF STOVES,
HARDWARE, ETC., 117 QUEEN
STREET.—The advancement that has
taken place in the tastes of the people during the past twenty-five years,
is a matter that exercises a greater
influence in the prosperity of the
world at large, than the casual
observer takes any cognizance of.
In the demand for articles of ornamentation new industries start into
life, providing profitable employment for countless thousands, thus
contributing to the material welfare
of the country at large. An instance
of this may be seen in the demand
for ornamental iron work, the larger
cities in the Dominion possessing
one or more institutions devoted to
this branch of manufacture. One
of the most important houses in this
line of business, in this Province, is
that of Messrs. H. R. Ives & Co.,
who are also manufacturers of every
description of hardware, stoves, soil
pipes, iron bedsteads, etc., etc. The
office and warehouse of the works are
located at No. 117 Queen Street. The
general foundry, pattern, machine
and finishing shops, as well as the
packing rooms are located in different departments on Duke, Prince,
Queen and Ottawa Streets, the whole
covering about three acres in extent.
A tunnel crosses Queen Street from
the second floor of one building to
the other and an underground tunnel connects the moulding shops
with the yards on Prince Street.
The foundry is fitted up with every
requirement and has three heavy
cranes and an elevator so that all
work can be expeditiously transacted. The hardware and stove
works are located at Longueuil and
are very extensive. The warehouse
is 30 x 100 feet in dimensions and
three stories in height, the office
and pattern shop is two stories in
height, the foundry is 250 x 500 feet
with an L of 100 feet, and the furnishing shop is 40 x 80 feet and two
stories in height. In the Montreal
works the machinery is driven by
a steam engine of 100 horse-power
and employment is furnished to over
200 skilled hands, and in Longueuil

H. R. IVES & CO.

HARDWARE STOVES IRON RAILING & CO.

the engine power is forty horse, and 100 hands are employed. The firm make a specialty of heavy castings, and last winter made about 1000 tons for the St. Lawrence Sugar Refinery. They also make a specialty of architectural iron work and have recently secured skilled pattern makers and workmen from the States for this particular department of the business. The firm received the contract for the iron work for the new Imperial Insurance Building, one of the finest structures in the city. They also make ornamental iron work for buildings and private residences, which includes iron fences, wrought iron gates, crestings and funnels for mansard roof, weather vanes, wrought iron hay racks, window guards, cast iron feed boxes cast iron ramps, etc., etc. The house was established in 1859 and during that lengthened period the business has made steady progress, the works having been constantly improved to meet the requirements of the trade. The firm of Messrs. H. R. Ives & Co. is one of the best and most favorably known in the city, and has been no small factor in building up the commercial importance of the city.

The Canada Wire Co., H. R. IVES, PRESIDENT AND MANAGER, 117 QUEEN STREET.—Messrs. Washburn & Moon, of Worcester, Mass., were the inventors and manufacturers of four point steel wire fencing, and hundreds of thousands of miles of farms throughout the United States have been fenced in by this light, but efficient and comparatively inexpensive article. The Canada Wire Co., of 117 Queen Street, this city, are manufacturing this fencing under license from Messrs. Washburn & Moen, under the Glidden patent, and their annual output is very extensive, the trade extending throughout the Dominion. The works are large and fully equipped with special machinery for this special line of manufacture, while employment is furnished to a large staff of skilled workmen. Stock raisers and farmers speak in the highest terms of this barb wire fencing, and it is in very general use throughout the Dominion, and has received first prizes at many of the exhibitions. Besides this line of barb wire fencing the Canada Wire Co. have an extensive trade in wire stretchers, known as the "Little Hercules," "Little Giant" and others. Also a patented crow-bar and wire stretcher combined which, is very useful for many purposes and also iron posts, post hole augurs, post hole diggers, etc. The President of the Company, Mr. H. R. Ives, is a gentleman well-known in the manufacturing and business circles of the country, and is an extensive manufacturer of hardware, etc., under the firm title of H. R. Ives & Co. Those forming business relations with this house may rest assured of finding all transactions conducted upon the most straightforward and honorable basis.

The Williams Manufacturing Co., MANUFACTURERS OF SEWING MACHINES, C. W. DAVIS, GENERAL MANAGER.—A most wonderful change has taken place in the mechanical industries of the world during the past half century. Nor has this improvement been confined to any particular branch of trade, but has been pretty thoroughly disseminated throughout the various lines of industrial art. No more wonderful invention, however, has been made than that of the sewing machine which has proved an inestimable blessing to toiling thousands, as well as in the homes of the wealthy and in our manufacturing establishments. One of the most important manufacturing houses in the sewing machine line in the Dominion is that of the Williams Manufacturing Co., which, being a purely Canadian Company, is deserving of especial mention in a work of this character. The Williams Manufacturing Company was established in the year 1861, and was incorporated in in the year 1872. It is a joint stock Company having an authorized capital of $1.000.000, and with a paid up capital of $500,000. The President of the Company is Mr. Andrew Allan; Vice-President, Mr. Hugh McLellan; General Manager, Mr. C. W. Davis. The factory, which is located on St. James Street, (St. Henry,) consists of a handsome and substantial brick structure, the main building being four floors in height and with basement, other portions of the works being two and one stories in height, the whole giving 60,000 superficial feet of floor room. The factory is fitted up with all the latest and most improved machinery, driven by a fifty horse-power steam engine. The works are devided into different departments, such as the foundry, machine shop, japanning shop, cabinet shop, factory room, shipping room, etc., etc. The works are equipped throughout with automatic sprinklers, and every other precaution is taken to provide against fire. The Company gives employment to 150 skilled workmen in the different departments in the factory, in this city, in the manufacture of the " New Williams " Sewing Machine. The Company has also extensive works on the Saranac River, at Plattsburg, N.Y., which are somewhat similar in extent and equipment to those in this city, and where employment is also furnished to 150 skilled hands in the manufacture of the " Helpmate " Machine. These machines have a very extensive sale throughout the Dominion, the United States, and in fact in all parts of the civilized world. The trade has been rapidly growing from year to year as the superior qualities of the " Williams " Machines have become more extensively known. The Company has agencies throught the Dominion, the United States, and the principal cities in Europe.

Canada Wall Paper Factory, JOHN C. WATSON, 86, 88 AND 90 GREY NUN STREET.—Montreal has undoubtly a great future before it, if present opportunities as they appear are properly utilized. Judging from the present review of the commerce and manufactures of the city, this will be done, for here we find almost every branch of industry properly represented. In the manufacture of wall papers— which is a comparatively new industry for Montreal—we find the Canada Wall Paper Factory, which is located at Nos. 86, 88 and 90 Grey Nun Street, and of which Mr. John C. Watson, is the proprietor, competing with the products of French, English and American houses, and beating them on their own ground. The goods turned out by this house will compare most favorably with those of any other house in the world and range from the cheapest, costing about 3½ cents a roll up to the most expensive at $3.00 and over. The factory is a four-story and basement structure 90 x 100 feet in dimensions, which is fully equipped with every requisite for the successful prosecution of the work, having four printing machines, from two to eight colors each. Also one grounding machine, two polishing machines, one embossing machine, etc., etc., the machinery being driven by a sixty horse-power steam engine, of the best make. The house manufactures its own rollers as well as having many cut in England and the States, and obtains the designs for the patterns from some of the most celebrated designers in Paris, London and the United States, and thus is enabled to compete successfully with the wall paper factories of those countries in artistic merit. The trade of the house is very large and embraces the entire Dominion, Vancouver, New foundland and the West Indies. Employment is steadily furnished to about fifty clerks, travellers and skilled workmen throughout the year. This business was established by Messrs Watson & McArthur eight years ago and for the past four years, Mr. John C. Watson, the senior member of the old firm, has been sole proprietor. Mr. Watson is a native of Glasgow, Scotland, and is an active member of the Montreal Board of Trade.

W. C. Norman, MANUFACTURER DOMINION WOVEN WIRE SPRING BED, 35½ AND 37 St. ANTOINE STREET.—This nineteenth century is certainly an age of

invention and of luxury. We have palace cars to ride in when journeying from place, we can eat our meals in handsomely furnished dining room cars travelling at the rate of thirty and forty miles an hour and when we reach home we have comfortable woven wire springs beds as a foundation to lie upon. It is an age of mechanical ingenuity and there are every kind of devices for the comfort and convenience of mankind. The Dominion Woven Wire Spring Bed Co., of which Mr. W. C. Norman is the proprietor, has done their share in keeping abreast with the spirit of the times. The factory is located at Nos. 35½ and 37 St. Antoine and consists of a main building 50 x 50 feet in dimensions with other additions. The factory is furnished with steam power; ten weaving machines are in operation and for the purpose of thoroughly seasoning the wood before using, there is a large kiln, capable of drying at one time 12,000 feet of lumber. Employment is furnished to fifteen skilled hands throughout the year. Mr. Norman manufactures the Dominion Woven Wire and Spring Bed in all sizes from the cradle or crib to the largest bedstead. These beds are comfortable, healthful, economical, and impervious to vermin, are perfectly noiseless, adjustable, with wrought iron attachments and are highly recommended by physicians. He also manufactures Norman Patent Combination Iron Bed which is one of the neatest, strongest, simplest and most economical combination beds ever produced. Also the tubular iron combination bed, which is made of one inch tubular iron and can be made in every size. In the manufacture of the spring bed nothing but the best of steel wire, specially prepared and tempered for the purpose, is used and every spring bearing the Dominion Woven Wire stamp is fully guaranteed. The double well interlocked woven wire mattress recently invented by Mr. O. J. Norman, son of the proprietor, is the most neat elastic and serviceable mattress ever produced. These beds are admirable adapted not only for home use but also for convents, colleges, schools, hospitals, steamboat companies, etc., and medals were awarded for them at the Toronto Exhibitions of 1880 and 1882 and at Montreal in 1882 and 1884, and also at Sherbrooke 1886. This business was established in 1881 and ever since the date of its inception has proved highly successful. Mr. Norman, the proprietor, is a native of England and is a thorough going man of business and highly esteemed by all who know him.

R. Henry Holland & Co., IMPORTERS OF FANCY GOODS &c., 340, 342 St. Paul Street, and 177 and 179 Commissioners Street.—There is an old saying, and a true one, that "There is always room at the top." It is as much so in business as in any of the learned professions, and probably harder to reach in business circles. In all lines of commercial industry there are to be found some houses that are thoroughly representative, and leaders in their line. Such must be said of the house of R. Holland & Co., Importers of Fancy Goods, etc. Established as recently as the year 1876, the progress made by this house has been something remarkable, and stands as a bright example of what pluck, enterprise and business ability can accomplish, the trade now extending throughout the entire Dominion, from the Atlantic to the Pacific. The firm were formerly at 266 and 268 St. Paul Street, but finding the premises becoming too small for their rapidly extending business, a palatial structure was erected for their special use at No. 340 and 342 St. Paul Street and 177 and 179 Commissioners Street. This is, without exception, the finest business structure in the Dominion. It has a frontage of thirty-five feet on St. Paul Street and is four stories in height. It has a depth of 165 feet running through to Commissioners Street, where it is five stories in height with sub-cellar, the whole having an area of 34,650 square feet. The building is of limestone and granite with Aberdeen granite, interspersed, and with polished column of the same material supporting the centre double arch to front entrance. The ceilings throughout are of British Columbia pine highly polished, the floors being of British Columbia fir. Two sky lights afford ample light in centre. The windows are all of plate glass, some of them being bevelled. It is heated by two of Gurney's Hot Water Furnaces, and has Hales' (Chicago)Elevator connecting with the different floors, while the offices are fitted up in keeping with the artistic luxuriousness of the entire structure. Entering the basement from Commissioners Street, the visitor finds the receiving, shipping and packing department and also a large stock of vases, glass ware and majolica goods. On the first, or main floor, entered from St. Paul Street, the business and private offices are located in the rear, overlooking the river, with its busy shipping scenes during the season of navigation. On this flat are displayed the more staple goods, such as cutlery, purses, combs, pipes, druggists' and tobacconists' sundries,stationer's supplies and jewelry of which there is a magnificent assortment. On the second flat will be found albums, accordeons, violins, harmonicas, bronze and plush goods, fancy boxes, fans, frames, etc., etc. The third flat is devoted to toys, games, dolls, wood carts, waggons, cups and saucers, china goods, etc. Such is a brief description of this palatial establishment, a front view of which is given elsewhere in this work. The firm issue a large illustrated catalogue of the different goods they handle with the prices attached. The catalogue is called the *Criterion* and is intended exclusively for the trade, and will be found of more advantage to dealers, and to the house than any commercial traveller. The firm have close and direct relations with manufacturers of all the goods they carry, and being familiar with the finest hat are the most saleable in the market, they are enabled to make special arrangements with the best makers, and can thus offer goods, in many cases much lower than are quoted by some manufacturers. Since this firm established their business, twelve years ago, they have built up, not only an enormous business, but a high reputation throughout the Province of Quebec, Ontario, Nova Scotia, New Brunswick, Prince Edward's Island, Manitoba, the North-west Territories and British Columbia Mr. R. Henry Holland, the proprietor, is one of Montreal's most enterprising business men and is a member of the Board of Trade.

R. HENRY HOLLAND & CO., WHOLESALE FANCY GOODS IMPORTERS. (See Page 48)

Wm. Rutherford & Sons, MANUFACTURERS, CONTRACTORS AND LUMBER MERCHANTS, 85 to 95 ATWATER AVENUE.--While the public generally is aware of the fact that Montreal has had, and is having, a phenomenal growth, and that an immense number of new buildings are yearly added, it is only those who have investigated the subject who have any idea of the magnitude of the operations in the building line which have recently taken place, or of the immense amount of money that has been expended in adding palatial mansions, massive business blocks, residences and cottages, to this the metropolis of the Dominion. The plaining mill is one of the most important branches of the building trade, and is well represented in this city, notably by the firm of Messrs. Wm. Rutherford & Sons, whose saw and plaining mills are located at Nos. 85 to 95 Atwater Avenue. Thirty-five years ago Mr. Wm. Rutherford, the founder of the house and senior member of the present firm, started in business in a comparatively small way, as a contractor and lumber merchant. He soon met with gratifying and well deserved success. In 1880 the firm became Wm. Rutherford & Co., and in 1887 that of Wm. Rutherford & Sons. The premises occupied by the mills are substantially built of brick and are two and three stories in height, and occupy 130 x 175 feet in dimensions. These are fitted up with the latest and most improved wood working machinery, driven by an 100 horse-power steam engine, as well as containing every other requisite and convenience for the successful prosecution of the work on hand, while employment is furnished to about 100 skilled and competent workmen throughout the course of the year. The firm manufactures every description of builders material, such as windows, doors, blinds, sash, mouldings, stairs, newel posts. They also manufacture packing cases extensively, and do all kinds of house joiners work, as well as contracting. The work done by this house is unsurpassed in quality and finish, and all orders entrusted to the firm receive prompt and personal supervision, and the best of satisfaction is in all cases guaranteed. Mr. Wm. Rutherford, is a Scotchman by birth, while his sons, and co-partners, Messrs. Thomas J., Andrew and Wm. Rutherford, Jr., are all natives of Montreal and are well-known and highly esteemed in the community. Mr. Rutherford, Sr., is the efficient Vice-President of the Mechanic's Institute of Montreal.

C

Jas. A. Ogilvy & Sons, IMPORT-
ERS OF DRY GOODS, 203 AND 205 St.
ANTOINE STREET AND 144, 146, 148 & 150
MOUNTAIN STREET, MONTREAL.—In a review
of the commerce and manufacturers of Montreal, it is found that the dry-goods trade forms
one of the most important branches of commercial interest, and that its aggregate annual
operations amounts to many millions of dollars.
Among the representative houses in this line
will be found a number established many years
ago and whose success has been in steady con-
sistency with the development of the city.

Holding a prominent place among such,
and deserving of special mention from its
representative character, is that of Messrs.
James A. Ogilvy & Sons, whose handsome
establishment is located at the corner of St.
Antoine and Mountain Streets. Mr. Ogilvy
commenced business in this city in the year
1866, and soon met with gratifying success, but his trade demanded the carrying of a
heavier stock, and so larger premises were obtained, but after a few years the result was
the same and so the present more extensive premises were obtained. These consist of a
handsome brick structure, 30 x 80 feet in dimensions with three floors and basement. The
premises are fitted up in an attractive manner, and the heavy stock of staple and fancy
dry-goods carried is displayed to best advantage, the firm's trade demands the better
quality of goods, and in this respect he has always anticipated the demands of his customers,
and imports heavily from some of the leading houses in England, Scotland, and on the Continent. He carries all lines, such as silks, satins, velvets, dress-goods, laces, trimmings,
hosiery and hosiery notions, and does probably the largest linen trade in the city, having
special advantages for obtaining his supplies, being agent for some of the principal British
manufacturers in this line as well as for plain Jutes and Jute carpets. This firm is sole agent
for the dominion for the celebrated " Rob Roy " fine hose, in use by the fire departments of
all the principal cities in Canada, and for lightness and durability is superior to any hose
introduced. The trade is conducted both at wholesale and retail and is very extensive, and
is still growing to such an extent that the old story of " larger premises required " appears
eminent in the near future. Employment is furnished to nineteen courteous and capable
assistants, as well as operators in the mantle and millinery manufacturing departments.
The Messrs. Ogilvy secure the best help that can be obtained and never discharges any,
even in dull seasons of the year, except for cause, so that customers can always depend
upon being served by experienced clerks. Mr. J. A. Ogilvy is a Scotchman by birth, and
ranks as one of Montreal's representative and progressive business men.

D. & J. Sadlier & Co., PUBLISHERS, BOOKSELLERS AND STATION-
ERS, ETC., 1669 NOTRE DAME STREET, MONTREAL.—The house of D. & J. Sadlier &
Co., is one well-known throughout the United States and the Dominion. Their head
quarters are located in New York, and their Canadian house is located at No. 1669
Notre Dame Street, in this city. The business was established in 1842 and by persever-
ing industry and ability displayed on the part of the firm, it was rapidly extended from
year to year, so that at the present day there is scarcely a city in the United States or
Canada, where their goods are not to be found. The premises occupied here consist of

MONTREAL, ITS COMMERCE AND MANUFACTURES.   51

four floors, each 22 x 80 feet in dimensions, the upper floor being used for shipping goods and for stock. The stock carried is very large and consists of books and stationery, Catholic prayer books and bibles, church ornaments, statuary and religious articles. The stock is an elegant one and very comprehensive. The trade of the Montreal House is very extensive, and covers the entire Dominion. The Dominion series of Catholic school books published by this firm are largely used by schools of every denomination on account of the many valuable improvements they contain, which were never before introduced. For instance, in the Readers and Speller, by a series of *marks* every word and letter has its proper accent, inflection, etc., indicated, and consequently the pupil learns not merely to name letters and words in the same time, but to read according to the best known principles of elocution. This is a vast improvement on the old style of reader which contained a large number of dry rules in the front pages, and nothing to guide the learner to correct pronunciation in the body of the work. Their Ancient and Modern History is admirably arranged, and supplies a long felt want. The enlarge- ment or decrease, the progress or decline of the different countries of the earth are placed before the pupil by series of colored maps of different sizes, for the same countries, all the several periods of their existence treated of. The books also contain many valuable improvements, which space does not permit us to indicate here. The firm publish in New York many Catholic works which are sold by subscription, thus enabling persons to get good works by paying a small amount at a time, so that the expense is not felt, and in this manner they have disposed of hundreds of thousands of dollars worth of books, which have been productive of much good in the homes of the people. Employ- ment is furnished in this city to twelve competent and courteous clerks throughout the course of the year, in the various departments. Mr. James A Sadlier, the resident member of the firm is an American by birth, and is a gentleman of marked business, ability and to his enterprise and energy is due much of the success of the house. He is ably assisted in conducting the business by his manager, Mr. F. McCabe, a gentleman who is a thorough expert in this line, and who is highly esteemed by all classes of the community.

Rice Sharpley & Sons, WATCHES, JEWELLERY, DIAMONDS, CLOCKS, BRONZES, ETC., 225 St. James Street, Montreal.—One of the oldest established, as it is also one of the largest and most important houses in the watchmaking and jewellery business in Montreal, is that of Messrs. Rice Sharpley & Sons. Mr. Rice Sharpley, the senior member of the firm, established this business in the year 1835. It was in rather an unpretentious manner in comparison to the magnificent establishment of to-day, but it was the sound acorn from where grow the stately oak, catered and nourished by persevering industry, enterprise and ability. In the year 1876 Messrs. Wm. E. and Frederick Sharpley, the sons, were admitted into partnership under the above mentioned title. The premises occupied by the business consist of half of Molson's new buildings on St. James Street, and have a frontage of forty by a depth of 100 feet, and are four stories in height, which are fitted up in a luxu- rious manner, and contain a very large and elegant stock of gold and silver English, Swiss and American watches, French and Swiss clocks, diamonds and precious stones in various settings, in necklaces, brooches, rings, earrings, etc. Also sterling silverware, electro-plated ware, bronzes, crystal gasaliers, etc., etc., and all kinds of useful and fancy articles for wedding presents, or gifts on all occasions. The firm are extensive manufacturers of jewellery of every description, their work being highly artistic and beautifully finished. They are the only manufacturers in the city of crystal gasaliers, suitable either for public halls or private dwellings, of which they always keep a com- plete stock on hand. The trade of the house is very extensive, and includes the entire

Dominion and a large portion of the United States. Employment is furnished to thirty-five skilled workmen and courteous assistants in the different departments of the business, throughout the year. Mr. Rice Sharpley, the founder of the house, is an Englishman by birth, while the sons are natives of Canada. The house has had a long and honorable career, and has been closely identified with the development and prosperity of the city.

Geo. T. Slater & Sons, BOOTS AND SHOES, 49 VICTORIA SQUARE, MONTREAL.—One of the oldest trades in existence is that of the manufacture of leather and of boots or shoes, for according to Biblical history shoes were worn about 2000 years B. C.   Of course great changes have taken place in the art of tanning since then as well as in the mode of boot and shoe manufacture.   During the past quarter of a century steam and machinery have completely revolutionized the manufacture of boots and shoes, and immense establishments have been established for their manufacture, giving employment to a large number of people.   In this city there are a number of important establishments in this branch of trade.   Foremost amongst them—not only on account of the volume of business transacted, but also of the excellent quality of work—is that of the firm of Messrs. Geo. T. Slater & Sons, whose office and factory are located at No. 49 Victoria Square.   It is now over a quarter of a century since the business was founded by the late Mr. George T. Slater, the originator of the present firm.   The business was started in a comparatively small way, but by dint of persevering energy and by keeping abreast of the times in all improvements in machinery, and the superior quality of material used, thus producing nothing but the best work, an excellent trade was soon established and a high

PHILADELPHIA 1876.

SYDNEY 1877.

reputation earned. The premises occupied consist of a handsome five-storey building, 50 x 140 feet in dimensions, where employment is furnished to from 100 to 125 skilled operators, the machinery being driven by a twenty horse-power steam engine. The firm employ only the most skilled help that can be obtained either in this country or the United States, wages not being considered so much an object as good work. The line of goods manufactured by the house consist of fine boots and shoes and slippers for men, boys, youths, ladies, misses, children and infants, both hand and machine sewed. Women's bus- toned hand sewed, machine sewed, and turns on opera toe and common sense last, men's hand sewed, French toe lasts, misses' and children's spring heels, machine sewed, men's hand and machine sewed Waukenphasts, which for style, fit and wear have no equal. Nothing but the very best quality of materials is used, and strict supervision is exercised over all workmanship. The trade of the house is very extensive and embraces in the scope of its operations the entire Dominion. Upon the decease of the late Mr. George T. Slater the founder of the house, and one of Montreal's most esteemed members of the business community, a co-partnership was formed between the two sons, Messrs. George A. and Charles E. Slater, who continue the business under the title of George T. Slater & Sons, the new firm coming into existence on the 1st January of the present year. These gentlemen are well trained in the business and the old patrons of the house may rely upon receiving the same attention and satisfaction as in the past. It may be stated in conclusion that the firm took medals for their work at the Centennial Exposition, in Philadelphia, and at New South Wales, the only places where they ever placed their goods on exhibition.

George Barrington & Sons, TRUNKS, VALISES, ETC., OFFICE AND FAC- TORY, 156 AND 158 ST. ANTOINE STREET; SALEROOMS, 1805 NOTRE DAME STREET, MONTREAL.—In a work of this character, calculated to illustrate the commerce and manufactures of Montreal, and its advantages as a business centre, nothing can so well contribute to the end in view as a brief sketch of those houses and business men, who from small beginnings have achieved success. The house of Messrs. George Barrington & Sons, manufacturers of trunks, valises, etc., is known throughout the Dominion. Mr. George Barrington, the founder of the house, and senior member of the firm, was born in Ireland and came to this country at an early age. Having learned the trade of a trunk-maker, with the well-known house of Chambers, of

Whitby, and being frugal and industrious, as well as a most skilled workman, he con-
cluded to go into business on his own account. This he did thirty-five years ago, and
engaged two workmen to assist him. The premises were small, but sufficiently large
for the amount of business done. But gradually Barrington Trunks became known as
being well made and durable, and his trade rapidly increased, and so larger premises
were required and obtained, but with the same result. Four years ago the firm built
their present commodious premises, at Nos. 156 and 158 St. Antoine Street. The
premises consist of a four-storey with basement structure, which has a frontage of
seventy feet with a depth of 206 feet. The factory is fitted up with all the latest and
most improved machinery, driven by two steam engines of thirty horse-power combined, while employment is furnished to 106 skilled hands in the different departments.
The trade of the house extends throughout the Dominion, as well as export, and the
annual output of pieces is, on an average, from 60,000 to 70,000 trunks, bags and valises.
These figures and facts speak for themselves, more eloquently than words can do, of
what well directed energy and ability can achieve in any line of business. The firm
manufacture every size and kind of trunks, valises, travelling bags, as well as blacksmiths' bellows. Their goods are all of the very best quality, and the workmanship is
perfect. The son, Mr. Finley D. Barrington, is a young gentleman of marked business ability, and gives close attention to the business and financial departments of the
establishment. He is a native of Montreal, and is well-known and highly esteemed.
The salesrooms of this concern are located at No. 1805 Notre Dame Street. Such is a
brief record of one of Montreal's representative manufacturing houses. It has had a
long and honorable career, and is a credit to the firm and an honor to the city.

A Canadian Chair & Table

Owen McGarvey & Son, FURNITURE MANUFACTURERS AND DEAL-
ERS IN ALL KINDS OF PLAIN AND FANCY FURNITURE, WHOLESALE
AND RETAIL, 1849, 1851 AND 1853 NOTRE DAME STREET.—In all important centres of

trade and manufacture, there will be found houses in the different lines of business that are pre-eminently leaders in their particular branch, even as there are leaders in the forum, the bar and the church. To lead in business matters requires a vast amount of energy, indomitable perseverance, ability and a thorough understanding of every detail of the special line conducted. Competition is so close and the public so eager and discriminating that " eternal vigilance " is the price of success. Standing in the foremost rank in the furniture trade in Montreal is the old-established and well-known house of Messrs. Owen McGarvey & Son, whose mammoth five-story establishment is located at Nos. 1849, 1851 and 1853 Notre Dame Street. This business was established in 1843, so that it has nearly completed its half century of business success. The premises occupied were built specially for the purposes required, the large windows on each of the five floors shedding a flood of light upon the elegant stock carried. The second flat of this establishment is reached by an elevator which is most handsomely and elaborately upholstered. Here is exhibited the celebrated suites consisting of parlor, dining-room and bedroom furniture, part of which was made for the London, Colonial and Indian Exhibition. The bedroom suite is a gem, being of solid black walnut, statuary marble top and is richly and delicately covered, the whole being of the Louis Fourteenth style, and costing $1500. The dining-room and parlor sets were made to match, and are models of the cabinet-maker's and upholsterer's art. In the front show room may be seen some of the most elegant cabinets to be found anywhere. These consist of cherry, antique oak, black walnut and solid mahogany. Side by side with these are beveled-plate mirrors with massive frames, fancy tables elegantly trimmed, and the display of goods is so rich and varied that a visit to the warerooms would be time well spent. On another flat are displayed leather goods, dining-room furniture, elegant couches, from $40 to $75, and parlor sets, from $35 to $500. The firm are also direct importers of bent goods from Vienna, and make a fine display of these and rattan goods. There are also baby carriages in endless variety, from $10 to $80. A special line of these useful articles is worthy of more than a passing notice. From the ordinary basket sunshade, to the most elaborate and richly upholstered rattan double-seated carriage or perambulator, the stock is most complete. The cut of the chair and table shown herewith, are selected from their exhibit and will speak for themselves. The firm sent goods to the first Paris Exhibition where they received numerous prizes. At the Montreal Exhibition in 1856 they received seven first prizes and a diploma for the largest and best assortment of furniture. In 1880 they received seven prizes and a diploma for the largest and best collection of furniture. In 1882 they received thirty-two prizes and in 1884 twenty-three prizes. There is no doubt that the firm of Owen McGarvey & Son stands pre-eminently in the front rank, and are deserving of every encouragement, for the energy and enterprise manifested in the manufacture of such costly and elegant goods.

Joseph Paquette, MANUFACTURER OF DOORS, SASHES, BLINDS. &C., OFFICE, 286 CRAIG STREET, MONTREAL.—The building trade, together with the auxiliary branches of industry incident to it, prosecuted within the confines of the city of Montreal, still contain, actively engaged in the prosecution of their particular industry, many veterans, the pioneer in fact, in their several departments here, and among these none are more widely known or have engaged a more uniform success than Mr. Joseph Paquette, proprietor of the plaining mill located at No 286 Craig Street. When this gentleman established his first plaining mill a quarter of a century ago, the machinery and appliances for doing the work were in a very crude state, compared to those of the present time, but he steadily kept abreast of the times and to-day has one of the largest and most complete plaining mills in the Province of Quebec. The main building consists of a substantial brick structure four stories in height and 50 x 150 feet in dimensions, the factory on Craig Street being two stories in height and 75 x 90 feet in dimensions. Those are fitted up with all the latest and most improved wood working machinery, driven by a steam engine of 100 horse-power. To properly turn out the work employment is furnished to 120 skilled workmen, on an average, throughout the year. Mr. Paquette manufactures every description of doors, sash, blinds, architraves, house finish mouldings, ceiling, siding, and all other description of builders' wood materials, while all kinds of job work is attended to. The work turned out by this house is unsurpassed, and the trade embraces the city of Montreal and a large section of the surrounding country. A specialty of the house is the manufacture of machine knives for all purposes. These are made from the very best quality of steel, properly tempered and finished in the best manner. Mr. Paquette is a native of St. Vincent de Paul and is a skilled, practical workman and a member of the Chamber of Commerce. His business, from the time of its starting to the present, has been entirely successful.

Lavigne & Lajoie, PIANOS, 1657 NOTRE DAME STREET, MONTREAL.—Very few residences of people in even moderately comfortable circumstances are destitute of pianos. Montreal, notwithstanding her devotion to manufactures and commerce, is rapidly gaining an enviable distinction as a city of home refinement and arts, and not the least of her claims to merit is based upon the encouragement given to musical culture, professional and private. As a consequence, the trade in music and musical merchandise is in a flourishing condition and grows steadily in importance. One of the leading houses here in this line, is that of Messrs. Lavigne & Lajoie of No. 1657 Notre Dame Street. The firm occupy four floors, each 24 x 110 feet in dimensions, where they carry an immense stock of musical goods, including a variety of pianos, organs,&c., of the most celebrated makers, and are the sole agents for the celebrated "Sohmer" and "Kroeger" pianos of New York. Also instruments for fanfare, bands, orchestra, and all other kinds of musical goods, a specialty is made of violins which range in price from $1.25 to $250 each. All instruments handled by the house with the exception of pianos, are imported direct from Paris and made to order for the firm in that city. The house also publish music on a liberal scale, many pieces of which have achieved great popularity. Their works are sold all over the Dominion, and a large trade is done with the sheet music houses of Boston, New York and Philadelphia, and also with A. Leduc of Paris, and Enoch Sons, of London, they also attend to the repairing and tuning of pianos and organs. This business was established in this city by Mr. Lavigne, the senior member of the firm in 1877, and the present partnership was entered upon in 1881. The house has had a prosperous and honorable career, and the success that has been achieved has been eminently deserved. The co-partners are Messrs. Ernest Lavigne and L. J. Lajoie, both of whom are Canadians by birth, and are active members of the Chamber of Commerce. Mr. Lavigne is also well-known to the musical public by his many popular compositions, as well as by the fact of his being leader of the "City Band," which is the leading organization of its kind in Canada.

IMPERIAL FIRE ASSURANCE COMPANY'S BUILDING.

J. Griffin, CONFECTIONER, 155 St. Lawrence Street, Montreal.—Many changes have taken place in Montreal since Mr. James Griffin, Confectioner, of 155 St. Lawrence Street, came to this city. That was in the year 1840. Many reminiscences he can give of those old days and the changes that have taken place from year to year. His own circumstances have also considerably altered since the time he started in business, on his own account, in a comparatively small way, in the year 1857. His present premises consist of a handsome three-story building 24 x 65 feet in dimensions with monsard roof. It is a beautiful structure of the modern style of architecture, and is fitted up in elegant style. The bakery is located in the basement and the two floors over the store are used for the manufacture of candies and confectionery. Mr. Griffin built the structure and consequently it is complete in every respect for the requirements of his business. He makes bread of the best quality, which has a large sale throughout an extensive section of the city. He is also a pastry-cook of high reputation and caters for dinners, breakfasts, suppers, etc., giving entire satisfaction for the excellent manner of conducting those affairs. His candies are noted for their purity, no injurious ingredients being permitted to be used in their manufacture. These facts are well-known to the general public and, hence, Griffin's Confectionery Establishment is a popular place to patronize when wholesome and toothsome articles are in demand. Mr. Griffin, who is a member of the Board of Aldermen, is a native of Ireland, is a practical baker and confectioner, and a most skillful one at that. His pine tar drops having won a high reputation for their speedy cure of coughs, colds, hoarseness, throat affections, lung complaint, asthma and bronchitis. While he has seen many changes in Montreal, he may say with Luke Sharp, that "Montrealer's have seen many changes in him during his fifty-seven years residence in the city." He is ably assisted in the management of his extensive business by his son, Mr. James Powell Griffin, a young man well and favorably known in commercial and social circles.

MODERN PLUMBING.

EDWARD D. WINGROVE, 2418 St. Catherine Street, Montreal.— Modern civilization demands that in each house there shall be a more or less complicated system of pipes and fixtures for the introduction, conveyance and use of water, gas, heat and sound, and for the disposal of refuse matter solid, liquid and gaseous. If such a system be perfect in design and execution, it is a source of comfort, convenience and health ; if it be imperfect it is a constant annoyance and expense, and often the cause of disease and death. What measures to adopt in order to secure perfection in the plumbing of modern houses, and thus protect their occupants, has been, and is the subject of consideration with thoughtful men and municipal governments throughout the world. Sanitary engineering has developed into a science of the first magnitude, especially has this been the case for the past five years, and owing to the rapid and vast strides the city has made in that time, it is the first interests of her citizens to demand that everything that science can supply for the health and cleanliness of their homes should be done, and that by the best and most practical methods, both for the sake of benefit to themselves and to the material interests of the city. Prominently engaged in this business here, is Mr. Edward D. Wingrove, whose workshops are located at 2418 St. Catherine Street. This business was established eight years ago and Mr. Wingrove succeeded to it about twelve months ago, having been manager for the previous firm. He is a practical sanitary engineer, and hot water and steam fitter, and employs a staff of skilled workmen, and personally superintends all their operations, hence, he is enabled to guarantee the perfection of all work entrusted to him. He also makes a specialty of metal roofing, gas cooking stoves and furnaces, and attends to gas engineering in all its branches. The workmanship of this house is first-class in every particular, and is not surpassed by any establishment in the city. Mr. Wingrove is an Englishman by birth, and has resided in this city many years.

John McDougall & Co., MANUFACTURERS OF CAR WHEELS AND PIG IRON, 574 WILLIAM STREET.—Montreal taking, as she does, the front rank among the railway centres of the Dominion, it is according to the law of natural selection that everything relating to railway rolling stock should be manufactured here on a large scale. In the line of car wheel manufacture, the firm of Messrs. John McDougall & Co., of No. 574 William Street, has long held a prominent place in the Dominion. Their product consists of all kinds of wheels for railroad cars and street railway cars. Employment is furnished to sixty-five skilled hands in the shops throughout the year, and the very best of facilities are enjoyed for turning out large quantities of work, there being all the latest and most improved machinery employed in the building, which is driven by a fifty horse-power water wheel. The record of the wheels of this house on a number of the leading railroads has demonstrated the fact that they are equal, if not superior, to any others manufactured in the Dominion, and they obtained a diploma at the International Exhibition in Philadelphia in 1876. Before leaving the shops all wheels are thoroughly tested, so that any flaws or imperfections are readily detected, and back goes the wheel to be cast over again. This business was established here twenty years ago, and ever since the date of its inception it has proved highly successful. The firm manufacture their own pig iron, so that they can thoroughly depend upon the quality of the material they use in their manufacture of wheels, which is an important consideration. The trade of the house extends throughout the Provinces, and quite a large export trade is also conducted.

J. D. Farrow, PAINTS, OILS, ETC., 1822 NOTRE DAME STREET. — Some years ago painters were content with a medium, or inferior quality of paint which could be had at a low price for the work done by them was of a cheap character and was cheaply paid. But in more recent years these matters have been changed, and now the people generally demand a higher quality of work, more artistic taste has to be displayed and the consequence is that the very best quality of paints is now the demand. The manufacturers have recognized this demand and have exerted their abilities and met it with the very best quality of materials that can be procured. Among the more important houses devoted to the paint and oil trade in Montreal, is that known as the " London Paint House," which is eligibly located for business at No. 1822 Notre Dame Street and 30 St. Helen Street. The building is large and commodious, being three stories in height and contains a large and carefully selected stock of paints, oils, varnish, colors, white-lead, artists materials, brushes, etc., all of the best quality and which are obtained from some of the leading manufacturers in this country and Europe. Painters and others requiring anything in the paint, oil or varnish lines will here find an excellent stock from which to select, and the prices will be found to be all right. Since the establishment of this business, six years ago, it has met with the most gratifying success, due no doubt, in a great measure, to the enterprise, push and ability displayed by Mr. Farrow, and his intimate knowledge of all the details of the business.

Drapeau, Savignac & Co., TINSMITHS, PLUMBERS AND ROOFERS No. 120 ST. LAWRENCE STREET, MONTREAL.—The plumber's trade is one of particular importance to the community generally, as upon the perfect or imperfect manner in which their work is done, depends in a great measure, not only the health but even the lives of the inhabitants. Great attention has been paid in recent years to this matter and the results already achieved have been very encouraging. Holding a prominent place among the leading plumbing and steam fitting establishments in this city, is that of Messrs. Drapeau, Savignac & Co., whose establishment is located at No. 120 St. Lawrence Main Street. The premises occupied are large and commodious, being 65 x 160 feet in dimensions, and running through from St. Lawrence Main to St. Charles

Borommee Street. These are fitted up with all the required appliances for the satis-factory prosecution of the work conducted. Here employment is furnished to 125 skilled and competent workmen throughout the year in the different departments of the business. The firm do all kinds of sanitary and general plumbing, fitting up new buildings and making repairs in old ones; also gas and steam and hot water fittings of every description. They also do a large business in roofing in slate, tin, galvanized iron, and all other kinds of work as well as making repairs on roofs, at very moderate prices, they also do all kinds of tinsmithing. They carry a large stock of stoves and ranges, hardware, cutlery, lamps and lamp goods, coal oil, etc., making a specialty of hollow ware. This extensive business was founded a quarter of a century ago by Mr. Drapeau, the senior member of the firm, and eight years since the present firm was formed. The business, since the date of its inception, has been a very successful one, for the work done has been first-class in every particular. The individual members of The firm are, Messrs. F. Drapeau, Practical Tinsmith and Plumber; J. R. Savignac, Business Manager and member of the Chamber of Commerce; and A. Demers and X. Drapeau, both of whom are practical. This is an excellent house with which to form business relations, and those doing so, may rest assured of receiving the best of satisfaction at all times.

J. W. Roberts, IMPORTER OF FINE ENGLISH SADDLERY, 336 St. James Street, Montreal.—Among the active, enterprising business men who have

achieved promi-nence in their respective lines of trade, there are none who enjoy a better reputation as a harness-maker than Mr. J. W. Roberts, of No. 336 St. James Street. This gentleman founded his busi-ness here seven years ago, and during that period, he has made him-self well and favor-ably known, and has secured a liberal and lucra-tive custom. He employs none but the most competent workmen, personally supervises all work, and thus ensures the most satisfactory results in the shape of the best work. Saddles and harness of every description, including the finest, are made to order, and a large assortment kept in stock. He also imports largely of fine English Saddlery, and makes a specialty of nickoline stirrups, bits, spurs and harness furniture. Full lines of horse and carriage furnishings and stable requisites are to be found here, and the rates that prevail are as low as those of anywhere else for first-class goods. The premises occupied by the business, consist of three floors, each 28 x 50 feet in dimensions, and are fully equipped with everything required for the conducting of a first-class business. Mr. Roberts is a native of Canada, and is a skilled, practical harness-maker of many years experience. He has kept fully up to the times in the matter of all modern improvements and styles, and no better or more beautiful goods are to be found in the city than in his establishment. Thoroughly understanding the requirements of the public, he is ever prepared to anticipate their demands.

D. Murphy, SADDLER AND HARNESS-MAKER, 378 AND 380 ST. JAMES STREET.—From time immemorial the trade of the saddler and harness-maker has been prosecuted by all nations, civilized and uncivilized. Of course it was in but a very crude state at first and simply met the exigences of the case. In fact it has only been within the past half century in our own country that the art has been brought to anything like a state of perfection. In our grandfather's days the harness in use were clumsy and heavy and not anything like so beautiful as we have to-day. Holding a prominent position among the old-established houses engaged in this line in this city, is that of Mr. D. Murphy, whose establishment is located at Nos. 378 and 380 St. James Street. This gentleman established his business a quarter of a century ago and he has at all times since then engaged a liberal share of the public patronage and met with gratifying success. Mr. Murphy manufactures all kinds of single and double light and heavy harness, using nothing but the very best of materials and trimmings and exercising the greatest care with regard to the workmanship, so that the most satis-factory results may be obtained. The work done by him is thoroughly reliable and can at all times be depended upon. Repairs of all kinds are promptly attended to and are executed in a neat manner. A good stock is carried of horse furnishings and stable requisites. A specialty is made of "boots" and turf goods—of every description. Employment is furnished to seven skilled and competent workmen throughout the year. Mr. Murphy is a native of St. Scholastique and is a thoroughly skilled, practical workman, and gives all orders entrusted to his care, his careful personal attention.

"Queen's" Restaurant, TIMOTHY KENNA, 231 ST. JAMES STREET.— The tendency of the age is towards or higher state of cultivation and artistic taste and culture marks the progress of the day. In all our surroundings this is very noticeable. In this interior of our dwellings, and especially in some of our leading restaurants all that art and wealth can do to please the cultured eye are lavishly expended. As an example of this in Montreal, we may take the "Queen's," the restaurant, *par excellence*, of the city. This new popular institution was established last fall, by Mr. Thimothy Kenna, who for many years was connected with the St. Lawrence Hall where he formed a circle of friends. The premises occupied by the restaurant are 30 x 90 feet in dimen-sions and are magnificently fitted up in natural wood richly carried and inlaid with beveled plate glass mirrors. The *tout ensemble* of the place is rich and pleasing to the eye. The dining-hall is tastefully furnished and well lighted, and here may be obtained at all times, breakfasts, lunches or suppers that would tempt the palate of the veriest epicure. Fish, game, and all the luxuries of the season that the markets afford can here be procured, the *cuisine* being unsurpassed and the serving all that would be desired. There is an entrance and parlor specially set apart for ladies, who will find here every civility and attention. The bar is stocked with the choicest brands of wines and liquors, and ales and porters as well as Havana and domestic cigars of the favorite brands. Mr. Kenna, the proprietor, is a gentleman who thoroughly understands every detail of the business, and the success that he has already achieved with the "Queen's," has been richly deserved.

A. Chabot, BOOTS AND SHOES, 1449 St. Catherine Street.—Montreal is the great centre of the boot and shoe trade of the Dominion, and thousands of persons are given employment here by this branch of industry alone. While there are many extensive manufacturing concerns, turning out thousands of pairs of boots and shoes a day, there are also some less pretentious houses that are worthy of honorable mention on account of the excellence of their work and the energy and enterprise displayed in conducting their business. Prominent among such is Mr. A. Chabot, boot and shoemaker and dealer, whose store is located at No 1449 St. Catherine Street. The premises occupied by the business are 22 x 50 feet in dimensions, and contain a large and elegant stock of boots and shoes in all weights and grades, from the finest of kid to the most serviceable kip for ladies and gentlemen, misses, youths and children, made up in the latest and most fashionable styles, both on the premises and by other leading manufacturers. Mr. Chabot has a special department for custom work, where those desiring can have their boots and shoes made to order, by measure on short notice, in the highest style of the art, also repairing is promptly and neatly executed. A special department is the repairing of sewing machines. Employment is furnished to twenty skilled workmen throughout the year. Mr. Chabot, who is a native of Montreal, and is a practical shoemaker, established this business eight years ago, and during that time, has built up a large and ever increasing trade.

Leblanc & Paradis, MERCHANT TAILORS, 2093 Notre Dame Street, Montreal.—In deciding upon having a new suit made, the first question that naturally arises in the mind of a man of taste is, "where can I have it well and stylishly made?" There are a number of first-class tailoring establishments in Montreal, where this question can be satisfactorily answered, and among the number, worthy of more than a mere passing notice in a work of this character, is that of Messrs. Leblanc and Paradis, which is located at No. 2093 Notre Dame Street. The premises occupied by the business are 20 x 45 feet in dimensions, and are beautifully and suitably fitted up for the requirements of the trade. Upon the counters and shelves will be found a large and elegant stock of imported and domestic woollens, tweeds, Cassimeres, &c., from some of the most celebrated looms in this country and Europe, and embracing the latest and most fashionable patterns and fabrics, from which an excellent selection can be made. These are made up to order by measure, in the highest style of the art, are perfect fitting and elegantly finished, and in these, and all other respects, are not surpassed by those of any other house in the city. Employment is furnished to fifteen skilled operators, both inside and out of the premises. This business was established five years ago, and it has made very steady progress ever since, the trade having rapidly increased from year to year. The members of the firm are, Messrs. Amedee Leblanc, and Joseph Amedee Paradis, both of whom are natives of St. Denis, and are thoroughly skilled practical tailors, who, giving their personal attention to all orders entrusted to their care, are thus enabled to guarantee their numerous patrons the utmost satisfaction.

Joseph Giroux, DEALER IN PAINTS, OILS, WALL PAPERS, HARDWARE, ETC., ETC., 1732 St. Catherine Street, Between Sanguinet and St. Denis Streets. — The painter's trade has felt the effects of the advanced artistic taste that has been developed amongst the people generally, and the leading houses in the trade have kept abreast of the times in meeting the demands of the public, or rather, in anticipating them. Among the prominent houses in this line of business in Montreal, is that of Mr. J. Giroux, which is located at No. 1732 St. Catherine Street. The premises occupied by the business are 24 x 40 feet in dimensions and contains a large stock of English, French and American wall papers of the latest and most artistic designs, also dados, centre pieces, friinges, borderings, etc. There is also a full stock of oils, paints, putty, glassware, etc., etc. Mr. Giroux attends to all kinds of house and sign painting and decorating, tinting, wall papering, etc. The work done is of the very best quality, none but the best skilled workmen being employed, of whom there are about twenty on an average throughout the year. Mr. Giroux is a skilled, practical painter of many years experience, and giving his personal attention to all orders entrusted to his care, he is enabled to guarantee his customers the most satisfactory results in every case. This business was established ten years ago, and its progress and development since that time has been steady and continuous.

Richard Lamb, IMPORTER AND MANUFACTURER OF HATS, CAPS AND FURS, 2259 NOTRE DAME STREET, MONTREAL.—New business houses, in whatever branch of trade they may be engaged, are to be taken in all commercial communities, as an index of the state and development of trade, and the consequent improvement in business affairs. Montreal has made very marked improvement during the recent years and the outlook for the future is one giving much promise, if present opportunities are taken advantage of. It is always with pleasure, therefore, that we speak of comparitively new houses and, in this connection, we refer to that of Mr. Robert Lamb hatter and furrier, whose store is located at No. 2259 Notre Dame Street. This business was founded in November of last year, and has already met with very gratifying success, the trade having steadily increased from month to month. The premises occupied are 24 x 60 feet in dimensions and are tastefully and suitably fitted up. Here is contained a large and elegant stock of hats and caps in all the latest and leading novelties, from the European and American markets, as well as those of home manufacture. In furs, the stock carried is very fine and embraces everything for ladies' and gentlemen's wear; fur trimmings and the repairing and dyeing of furs being a specialty. Mr. Lamb has recently started to manufacture hats and furs, and employing none but the most skillful of operators, can gaurantee the most satisfactory results. Mr. Lamb is a Montrealer by birth, and is well and widely known here as a go-ahead, active and progressive business man, and one who takes a deep interest in whatever tends to the welfare of the city.

J. A. Denis, DEALER IN PAINTS AND HARDWARE, 206½ ST. LAWRENCE STREET, MONTREAL.—During the past twenty-five years, at least, a very marked improvement has taken place in household decoration, and all the artistic talent of the decorative painter and wall paper manufacture has been brought to bear to meet this demand for the æsthetic in design. This is an excellent indication of the higher culture of the people generally, and it is to be hoped that it will continue. Holding a prominent place among those engaged in the sale of paints, oils and hardware, as well as in the house and sign painting, is Mr. J. A. Denis, whose store is located at No. 206½ St. Lawrence Main Street. The premises occupied by the business are 28 x 60 feet in dimensions and contain a large and carefully selected stock of shelf hardware of every description, as well as paints and oils of the very best quality, also calsomine and ready-mixed paints of all colors. The stock is full and complete and has been selected with accuracy and care. Mr. Denis also attends to all kinds of house and sign painting and decorating, and the work done by him is first-class in every particular, and all orders entrusted to him are guaranteed to be thoroughly satisfactory. This business was established eight years ago, and the success that has attended it has been highly gratifying. Employment is furnished to twenty hands, on an average, throughout the year in conducting the operations of the business. Denis' Step-ladders are also handled in great variety, and in all sizes, from three to ten feet in height. In this specialty, Mr. Denis controls the trade, and his step-ladders are well-known as being superior to any other article of a similar nature in the city. He also sells and has made up to order, refrigerators in all sizes. Mr. Denis is a native of Montreal and is well-known and highly esteemed as an active, energetic and pushing business man.

L. R. Baridon, CHEMIST AND DRUGGIST, CORNER OF ST. DENIS AND ST. CATHERINE STREETS.—The profession of the chemist and druggist is one requiring a deep knowledge of the pharmacopœia, and even watchful care, coupled with experience and practice for its successful prosecution. The standard of requirements has been considerably raised during the past fifteen years at least, and the Colleges of Pharmacy requires a severe and deep course of study from their students, before they can graduate. One of the most careful and proficient of the chemists and druggists doing business in this city, is Mr. L. B. Baridon, whose store is located at the corner of St. Catherine and St. Denis Streets. The premises occupied consist of a double store 48 x 48 feet in dimensions. These are fitted up in a very handsome manner, with plate glass windows, show-cases and cabinets and ornamented fittings, while the stock carried is very large and of the best quality and consists of fresh, pine drugs and chemicals, fancy and toilet articles, imported and domestic soaps, perfumes, etc. Also proprietary remedies of acknowledged merit and standard reputation, druggists' sundries and those articles required by physicians in their practice. A specialty is made of the compounding of physicians' prescriptions and difficult *formula* with care and accuracy at moderate prices, while employment is furnished to seven competent assistants and clerks. Mr. Baridon does a large wholesale business in physicians' supplies and surgical intruments. He is also sole agent for the Dominion for the celebrated French Mineral Waters, *Eau de Pongues,* which acknowledged by the most eminent medical authority of France to be a most valuable remedy in the treatment of kidney diseases, general debility, etc., being specially recommended for ladies. Mr. Baridon is a native of the United States, but has resided in Montreal for the past fifteen years, he is a graduate of the Quebec Pharmaceutical Association, and during the ten years he has been in business, has won a high reputation as one of Montreal's most energetic, pushing and successful young business men.

J. O'Gorman, SHIPPING BUTCHER AND GREEN GROCER, 23 AND 24 ST. ANN'S MARKET, MONTREAL.—There is no business industry of more importance to the public generally or individually, than those that deal in the food supplies of the people, and prominent among these is the butcher trade. In Montreal, there are several butchers who make a specialty of the shipping trade, and of these, none are more deserving of special mention than Mr. J. O'Gorman, whose place of business is located at stall, Nos. 23 and 24 St. Ann's Market. Mr. O'Gorman, has been established in business for eighteen years, and during that time has built up an excellent trade, and met with the most gratifying success. Besides his regular city trade, he does a large shipping business, supplying vessels with meats, vegetables and other shop's stores. He has gained a high reputation for the excellent quality of his supplies, as well as for his upright and honorable business dealings. He does his own killing at the abbatoir, using on an average seven head of cattle and 100 sheep and calves a week, dealing only in beef, mutton and veal. He refers to a long list of captains of vessels whom he has supplied, and they all express themselves as highly satisfied with the manner in which he has filled all orders, being prompt, courteous and attentive. Mr. O'Gorman is a native of Quebec, and is a practical butcher, of many years experience, and thoroughly understanding all the details of his business, is at all times ready to anticipate the requirements of his customers.

Jules Goudron, IMPORTER OF HARDWARE, WOOD, CARRIAGES AND IRONWARE, ETC., 1445 TO 1449 NOTRE DAME STREET.—The mechanical arts are exercising a powerful influence upon the industries of the country. The iron ore, dug from the bowels of the earth, is fashioned into many useful and now absolutely necessary articles. The age of stone and copper has passed away and been replaced by this essentially iron age. The business, therefore, of the hardware and iron merchant is an important one, and forms no inconsiderable portion of the wealth of the country. Among the many important hardware houses in Montreal, it is necessary to classify that of Mr. Jules Goudron, which is located at from Nos. 1445 to 1449 Notre Dame Street. The premises occupied consist of two adjoining stores, 60 x 80 feet in dimensions. They contain a large stock of shelf and heavy hardware, carriage woodwork and carriage hardware, guns and sporting articles, such as fishing rods and reels, fishing tackle, etc., etc., also cutlery and house furnishing goods. The stock is of the best quality, and has been specially imported from some of the leading manufacturing houses in Europe and the United States. Having ample resources and intimate relations with manufacturers at home and abroad, Mr. Goudron is enabled to give his customers the very best of advantages in the shape of excellent goods at low prices. Employment is furnished to fifteen competent assistants in the different departments of the business throughout the year. Mr. Jules Goudron, who is a native of France, has been established in business here for the past fifteen years, during which time he has built up an excellent trade and a high reputation for honorable dealing. He is an active member of the Board of Trade.

Bernard Harkin, BOOTS & SHOES, 1959 NOTRE DAME STREET, MONTREAL.— Among those actively engaged in the boot and shoe trade in this city, is Mr. Bernard Harkin, whose store is located at No. 1959 Notre Dame Street. The premises occupied are large and commodious, being 26 x 70 feet in dimensions and are fitted up in a very neat manner, displaying to excellent advantage the fine stock carried consisting of boots and shoes for ladies and gentlemen, misses, youths and children, also slippers, rubbers, overshoes, &c. The goods handled are of the very best quality and are obtained from some of the leading manufacturers in the Dominion. There is also a special department for custom work, where those desiring can have their boots or shoes made to order. on short notice, and in the very best manner, at reasonable prices, competent workmen being employed for this purpose.

THE MERCHANTS BANK OF CANADA,—MONTREAL.

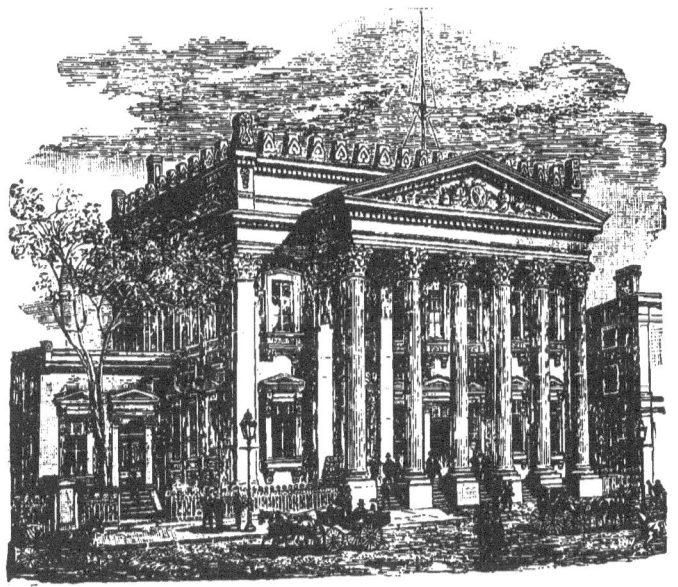

BANK OF MONTREAL,—MONTREAL.

T. A. & A. U. Grothe, WATCHMAKERS AND JEWELLERS, No. 95½ St. LAWRENCE STREET.—The clocks of the ancients, were based upon a uniformity in the velocity, with which a liquid of constant level flows through an orifice. Heron, of Alexandria, composed a treatise upon hydraulic clocks, and Philo, of Byzantium, in a recently-discovered fragment of his Pneumatics, indicates several of the apparatus that were in use, for obtaining a constancy in the level of the liquid motor in cases where there was not at one's disposal a continuous feed which permitted of employing the very simple waste-pipe arrangement. Great changes have taken place in the manufacture of time-keepers since those days, more especially during the past quarter of a century. Holding a prominent place among the watchmaking and jewellery establishments of this city, is that of Messrs. T. A. & A. U. Grothe, which is located at No. 95½ St. Lawrence Main Street. This business has enjoyed an honorable and prosperous career of considerably more than a century, and has descended in regular rotation, from great grandfather to great grandsons. The present firm succeeded Messrs. J. M. Grothe & Co. two years ago. The premises occupied for the store, are 25 x 45 feet in dimensions, and are elegantly fitted up in black and gold, with show-cases and cabinets of the same, giving the place a rich and unique appearance, and showing off to excellent advantage the large and beautiful stock carried, consisting of gold and silver watches, of English, Swiss and American manufacture, also French clocks, rings, chains, brooches, bracelets, setts, and many other beautiful lines in gold, and silver, Whitby Jet, rolled gold plate, &c., as well as a fine line of silver-plated ware. Also a complete collection of spectacles, in gold, silver, nickel and steel. The workshops, which is in rear of the store, is 15 x 30 feet in dimensions, and here employment is furnished to fifteen jewellers, and two watchmakers. The firm manufacture a beautiful line of jewellery, elegant in design and finish of workmanship. The trade of the house is very extensive, and embraces not only the city, but a large section of the surrounding country. The Messrs. Grothe, are natives of Montreal, and are well and favorably known in business and social circles, for their enterprise and progressive spirit, and the interest they take in whatever tends to the welfare of the city.

James Harper, PORK BUTCHER AND CURER, 24 and 25 St. LAWRENCE MARKET; FACTORY, REAR OF 18 St. PHILLIP STREET.—There is no line of business of so much importance to the general community or to its individual members, as that which deals in their food supplies. The butcher, the baker and the grocer, are three very important representatives, therefore, in any civilized community. One of the principal houses in the pork butchering and curing line in this city, is that of Mr. James Harper, whose market is located at Nos. 24 and 25 St. Lawrence Market; the factory being in rear of No. 18 St. Philip Street. This business was established seven

D

years ago, and almost ever since the date of its inception it has met with the most gratifying success, having steadily increased in extent and importance from year to year. Mr. Harper kills, on an average, 150 hogs per week. These are pickled, salted, smoke cured, in bacon and hams, and sausages also are manufactured. The product of this house is of the most excellent quality and a high and widespread reputation has been gained in this respect. Mr. Harper is a skilled, practical pork curer and dry-salter, of many years' experience, and giving his personal attention to all work done, can thus guarantee the most satisfactory results. He gives employment to ten skilled assistants in the different departments of the business. Mr. Harper is a Scotchman by birth, and is a gentleman highly esteemed by all who know him.

Brown Brothers, MEAT MARKET, McGILL COLLEGE AVENUE AND CATHERINE STREET.—The Windsor Market is located at the corner of McGill College Avenue and Catherine Street, which is one of the finest locations in the most aristocratic part of Montreal. The market was established in September 1839, and is therefore nearly half a century in existence. The well-known proprietors, Messrs. Brown Bros. have neither spared time nor expense in making their market what it is to-day, the most elaborate, systematic, and cleanest in the world. Their meats are the best and are prepared, trimmed and cut in the best and most approved manner, and they seem to think that they cannot have anything too good for their very fine *clientelle.* They manufacture to a great extent and select their cattle from the very best feeders. Their beeves are principally bought in and around Guelph and Whitby and from the North-west ranches. Their pork is strictly dairy feed, from which they manufacture their celebrated ham, bacon and English pork sausage, of which they ship to all parts, such is their reputation. Their sheep and lambs are also of the finest grades which are turned into their famous saddles, chops, etc. They are strictly at all times, fighting against frozen meat of any kind, so much so that they will not sell it at any time, as they claim that 90 per cent of indigestion is caused from said cause. Their poultry and game department is a study ; this also comes free from frost and is, without doubt, the best selected from far and near, from the English pheasant to the Illinois' prairie hen, and it is certainly appetising to see how neatly they are prepared and trussed and delivered ready for the fire or cooked if so desired. Next in order is the fish and oyster department of which you can see somewhere between forty and fifty different varieties, among others the celebrated Gaspé Salmon, weighing up in the neighborhood of forty-five pounds. Sizes then come down till they come to the white-bait, of which it takes about seventy-five to make one pound. They import sea and river food from all parts, such as the Florida green turtle, Mississipi prawns, shrimps, etc. Their fruit and vegetable department will show you all through the year, cucumbers, tomatoes, lettuce, strawberries, new potatoes, mushrooms, green peas, and butter beans, etc., etc. Then in their canned goods department you can get all kinds of fruits and vegetables put up in glass expressly for them. The market itself has got to be seen to be appreciated ; suffice it to say that it is the finest in the world, their fresh meat refrigrator, which stands at the rear, is a piece of exquisite workmanship and material measuring on the inside twenty-six feet wide by twenty-two feet deep and nine feet high. The front is of polished cherry wood with two doors, one at each end and have British plate mirrors. There are two large show windows and have the sign Brown Bros., Windsor Market, established 1839 and their crest, which is a stag's head embossed, and in the centre is another beautiful mirror, all this glass has an elegant level of 1¾ inches surmounted by animals beautifully carried in cherry. The verdict of all who have seen it, is that it is a perfect gem and by far the finest ever built, as also are the poultry, fish, vegetable and fruit refrigrators. They are also cold storage men, having large freezers situated on Guy Street.

Mr. Alex. Nelson & Co., HATTERS AND FURRIERS, 107 BLEURY STREET, MONTREAL.—Canada is peculiarly a fur country, and millions of dollars worth are manufactured and imported and exported annually. Russia, Australia and the South Sea Islands, send many of their furs here, and the Canadian fur manufacturers send the domestic articles to England, and many European countries. Among those actively engaged in the fur trade in this city, and deserving of more than a mere passing notice, is the firm of Messrs. Alex. Nelson & Co., who occupy ample warerooms at No. 107 Bleury Street, in this city, and who were established in 1870. In their pleasant showrooms, may be found all choice selections of fashionable fur apparel, dolmans of all kinds and styles, short mantles of the latest designs from Paris, fur-lined circulars in all varieties, fur caps, collars and gloves, and fur trimmings of all descriptions. The concern receive all their goods from the most direct and reliable sources of supply, and they are therefore able to compete with any of the leading furriers of Montreal, as regards price and quality. They are by all odds the best representatives of their line of trade in this city. Mr. Alex. Nelson, visits England and the Continent every year, to purchase goods for the city trade, which includes some of the first families here. The firm also carry an excellent stock of fine umbrellas of all patterns, and of the most reasonable prices. In hats and caps, the stock is one of the most complete in the Dominion, and any style required, can be found in this establishment. The business was established fifteen years ago, and has met with the most gratifying success during those years, which has been due to the perseverance, enterprise and business ability, unceasingly displayed by Mr. Nelson.

The Electric Service Company of Canada, J. H. OAKES, MANAGING DIRECTOR, HEAD OFFICE, 174 ST. JAMES STREET.—The past quarter of a century has witnessed wonderful changes throughout the world. This is the age of electricity and all our ideas seem to have been stimulated into effort to keep pace with the lightnings flash. Electricity has been saddled and bridled and has been made man's obedient servant. It rests not day nor night and is ready at a moments call. The Electric Service Company of Canada, whose head office is located at No. 174 St. James Street, was incorporated by charter on the 8th October, 1887, and commenced operations in January of the present year. They are successors to the Canadian District Telegraph Company, which was established in 1877. The Electric Service Company are doing a good work in the city and their services are being rapidly called into requisition, the more their nature and utility are understood and appreciated. There are a number of special departments connected with this service which we will mention in detail. In the first place there is a system of electtic burglar alarm, for business houses and residences. The houses, stores and offices of subscribers are connected by electrical apparatus with the head office, and on the attempt of a burglar to enter the place an automatic alarm is immediately given and patrolmen are sent at full speed to the scene of operations. There is also a system of night watch for business houses, watchmen being supplied and electrical apparatus furnished. The messenger service is a great convenience to the citizens generally, boys being supplied at so much per message to go to all parts of the city or suburbs. A gentleman wants to send a boquet to a lady, or a husband a bottle of soothing syrup for the baby, and a messenger boy performs the service. Subscribers have small call-boxes in their houses and can call for a cab, a messenger, a policeman or the fire department, the orders being instantly attended to from the head or branch offices. It is the intention of the Company to substitute telephones for the call-boxes and thus valuable time may often be saved by the subscriber being enabled to say what is required of a messenger, without the necessity of his having to go to the house just to find out. Besides it will be useful in many other instances. From the head office also telegrams can be sent to all parts of the world, arrangements having deen effected with the telegraph companies doing business in Montreal. This office is open day and night and the most efficient service is guaranteed. The Company has a capital of $100,000, and the following well-known gentlemen constitute the Board of Directors :—William Cassils, Esq., President, Hector MacKenzie, Esq., Vice-President, R. C. Roome, Esq., and Dunbar Taylor, Esq. Mr. J. H. Oakes, is the efficient Managing Director. This gentleman, who is an Englishman, was Managing Director of the Canadian District Telegraph Company since 1883, and thoroughly understands every detail of the service, and is a gentleman highly esteemed by all who know him. The Company have also branch offices for greater convenience of subscribers at 45 University Street and 2631 St. Catherine Street.

Mr. R. Beullac, 1674 NOTRE DAME, MONTREAL.—Montreal is properly speaking a city of Churches, considering the extent of its population it has more church edifices than any other city on the American Continent. It has been more especially Roman Catholic ever since the days of the first settlers and consequently, the sale of church ornaments is conducted institutions are predominant, and as a necessity, the sale of church ornaments is conducted upon an extensive scale. Holding a prominent position among the different houses engaged in this line of business in the city, is that of Mr. R. Beullac, which is located at No. 1674 Notre Dame Street. The premises occupied are large and commodious, being four stories in height and 25 x 100 feet in dimensions. These contain a very large and magnificent stock of church ornaments of every description, from the smallest to the largest. Mr. Beullac imports his goods direct from some of the most celebrated manufacturers in France, and the lines he carries are unsurpassed by those of any other house in the Dominion. He has a shop on St. Denis Street, which is used for the purpose of manufacturing and fitting up altars, in which branch of the business he has an extensive trade throughtout the city and country, his trade in church ornaments extending throughout the Dominion. Mr. Beullac gives employment to sixteen clerks and workmen steadily throughout the year. Mr. Beullac is a native of France and is a gentleman of marked business ability, and since he established his business here in 1874, he has met with the most gratifying success. He is a member of the French Chamber of Commerce, and the Societe de Geographic of Paris.

Edgar Judge, FLOUR, GRAIN, &c., 444 ST. PAUL STREET.—The completion of the Sault Ste. Marie Railroad, and the relief or the harbor of Montreal from the debt that hung so heavily upon it for many years, will create a boom here in business such as has not been witnessed in the history of the city up to the present time. The Canadian Pacific Railway, it is expected, will carry an immense amount of flour and grain from Minneapolis and the Western States as well as from our own North-west, and Montreal will be the objective shipping point. Prominent among the old-established houses engaged in the flour and grain trade in this city is that of Edgar Judge, whose office is located at No. 464 St. Paul Street. Mr. Judge handles all grades of flour and enjoys special facilities for effecting transactions in coarse grains and feed. Public warehouses are utilized for the storage of goods, and all shipments are made with despatch and orders filled with promptness. Since the establishment of this business it has met with the most gratifying success, and has steadily continued to increase and develop from year to year up to the present time with the brightest prospects ahead. Mr. Judge is one of Montreal's best known citizens and merchants ; he is a member of the Council of the Board of Trade and also a member of the Committee of Management of the Corn Exchange, and has always taken a lively interest in the city's welfare and improvement.

Verret, Stewart & Co., COMMISSION MERCHANTS, 271, 273 AND 275 COMMISSIONERS STREET, COR. ST. NICHOLAS STREET, MONTREAL.—The provision trade of Montreal is conducted upon a very extensive scale and its annual operations amount to several million dollars. There are a large number of first-class houses engaged in this line of trade and among these, one that is deserving of particular mention is that of Messrs. Verret, Stewart & Co., which is located at No. 271, 273 and 275 Commissioners Street, corner of St. Nicholas Street. The head house is located in Quebec and the Montreal branch has been established since 1867. The business is the oldest in the line in Quebec having been establshed in the year 1832 by Donald Fraser, who was succeeded by Thomas Fraser, and he in turn in the year 1872 by the present firm of Verret, Stewart & Co. Mr. Verret is resident in Quebec and has been sitting in the same office since 1851 and Mr. Stewar has been connected with it since 1861. The firm do a large commission business and deal in provisions. fish, oil, salt, etc. They do the largest salt trade of any house either in Que- bec or Montreal, and are manufacturers of Rices' Pure Dairy and Table Salt. This is one of the representative commercial houses of the Dominion and has had a long and prosper- ous career and appear to give their customers every satisfaction, if one may judge by the fact that they are doing business with houses to-day, that their predecessors were trading with over half a century ago. Mr. B. Verret is a member of the Quebec Board of Trade and Mr. J. F. Stewart of the Montreal Board of Trade, and both gentlemen have won the esteem and confidence of all with whom they have business relations.

Montreal Tent, Awning and Tarpaulin Co., W. H. GRIFFIN, MAN- AGER, 42 AND 44 FOUNDLING STREET, FENWICK & SCLATER, GENERAL AGENTS.— A work of this nature could not be complete unless it embraced a full synopsis of all the principal industries, which in a great measure, help to build up the commerce of this city, and which serves to justify its appellation of being styled the "Commercial metropolis of the Dominion." In the varied lines of manufacture, none are deserving of more worthy mention than the Montreal Tent, Awning and Tarpaulin Company, whose offices and factory are situated at No 44 Foundling Street. The building which is especially adapted for this line of manufacture, is admirably situated, being in close proximity to our extensive harbor, quite covenient to the canal, and right in the heart of the business centre of Montreal's very busy city. The firm manufacture all kinds of canvas goods, comprising sails, tents, awn- ings, tarpaulins, horse and wagon covers, bags, aprons, and canvas hose for fire purpo- ses, flags of all nations and to any design, cork feeders, life buoys and belts. They also keep in stock for hire, tents, tarpaulins and flags. They also furnish estimates for con tractors requiring tents and tarpaulins in quantities, and make a specialty of yacht sails and tackle. They do an extensive business in awnings for stores, public buildings, and private residences, and they have been highly complimented on the style, fit and finish of all the goods turned out of their manufactory. A feature of their awning trade, is the taking down and storing of awnings in the fall, insuring them for the winter, and repairing and putting them up again in the spring at a nominal cost. A number of skilled hands are employed, and the factory is fully equipped with all the modern conveniences for success- fully carrying out the requirements of the trade. Mr. W. H. Griffin, the Manager, is well and favourably known in this line in Canada ; Fenwick & Sclater, 42 and 44 Foundling Street, ealers and manufacturers of cotton tackle, asbestos goods, mill, railway, steam- ship and engineers' supplies,—Proprietors of the Phœnix and File Co., Waste Co., 54 Nazareth Street, and the Wolfstown Asbestos and Soapstone Quarries, and General Agents of the Megantic Mining Co.—Proprietors of the Dominion Pipe and Boiler Covering Co. —Are the promotors and Selling Agents for this new enterprise.

Pierre Lemieux, SADDLER, HARNESS, WHIPS AND BRUSHES, HORSES' BOOTS, No. 2200 NOTRE DAME STREET, MONTREAL.—From the very earliest ages, leather goods have been manufactured and have been in general demand among the civilized people of the earth. History does not record the first of harness-making, but it must have been at a very early period in some shape or form, wherever animals were used as beasts of burden. During the past twenty-five years a very marked improvement has taken place in this line of manufacture, which has been in perfect keeping with the development of the times. Among those prominently engaged in the harness trade in this city is Mr. Pierre Lemieux, whose shop is located at No. 2200 Notre Dame Street. The premises occupied are 15 x 40 feet in dimensions where employment is furnished to five skilled and capable workmen throughout the year in the manufacture of light and heavy, single and double harness of the very best quality and make up in the very finest styles. Nothing but the best quality of leather and trimmings is used and the workmanship is all that could possibly be desired. There is also carried in stock at all times a fine line of harness and horse furnishing goods and stable requisites. This business was established thirteen years ago and almost from the time of its inception it has proved very successful, the business steadily continuing to increase and develop from year to year. Mr. Lemieux, the proprietor, is a native of Montreal, where he is well and favorably known. He is a skilled practical harness-maker and thoroughly understanding all the details of the business, is prepared at all times to meet legitimate competition.

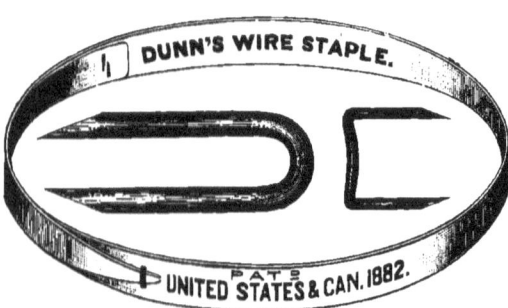

Staple & Machine Factory, Patrick Dunn, COTE ST. PAUL.—Cote St. Paul, is the busy centre of a number of important manufacturing concerns, in the aggregate, giving employment to a large number of skilled hands, and thus building up, and benefitting that section of the city, or what will soon be a part of the city. Among the many industries there represented, that of Mr. Patrick Dunn, proprietor of the staple factory, is deserving of more than a mere passing notice. This business was established thirty years ago and has at all times during that lengthened period, met with the most uniform success. The premises occupied by the works are 45 x 100 feet in dimensions, and are fully fitted up with all the necessary machinery and appliances of the most improved pattern, which are driven by water power derived from the Lachine Canal. None but the best of skilled workmen are given employment. The product of the factory consists of wire staples of all descriptions and sizes, wire tacks, &c. Also machinery of all kinds is built to order, a specialty being made of cut-nail machinery. These are all of the very best quality and are well made and finished in every particular, and have an active demand in the trade. Mr. Dunn, is an Irishman by birth, and is a skilled, practical workman of many years experience, and giving his particular and personal attention to all orders entrusted to his care, is thus enabled to guarantee his customers the utmost satisfaction in all cases.

J. Sloan & Son, BOOTS AND SHOES, 199 ST. ANTOINE STREET, MONTREAL—The manufacture of boots and shoes of whatever form or character they might be, is of very ancient origin. Many changes, however, have taken place in the manufacture of these useful articles of foot wear since they were first worn, but never in the history of the trade has such remarkable changes taken place as during the past quarter of a century. One of the oldest, if not the oldest, merchants in the boot and shoe trade in this city is Mr. J. Sloan, of the firm of Messrs. J. Sloan & Son, whose store is located at No. 199 St. Antoine Street. This gentleman came to Montreal from Ireland sixty-two years ago, and large and interesting is his fund of information respecting the changes that have taken place in the city since those days then the bull frogs, or "Canadian Canaries," as some jocularly called them, exercised their musical voices on the swampy stream that is now Craig Street. He started in business on his own account—not in appreciation to the bull frogs—but in the boot and shoe trade, half a century ago and during all these years he has met with a liberal share of the public patronage and met with uniform and gratifying success, which has been eminently deserved. The premises occupied by the business are 20 x 40 feet in dimensions, and are neatly fitted up and contain a large and judiciously selected stock of boots and shoes, slippers &c., for ladies and gentlemen, misses, youths and children, in all weights and sizes and of the very best quality and newest styles. Mr. Sloan is a practical shoemaker, and a skillful one at that, but his practical work is "awl" over now, for as he says "instep" the large manufacturing houses with machinery and gain the "upper" hand in the manufacturing line, but the sore feeling created by the innovation years ago has long since been "heeled." Mr. William Sloan, the son and partner, is a native of Montreal and is a gentleman of thorough going business habits and ability.

Geo. Tucker, INDIAN HEALER, 86½ ST. LAWRENCE ST., MONTREAL.—An all wise Providence has with a beneficient hand provided by nature for the wants of mankind, but he leaves us to find out for ourselves by our necessities, what the earth contains and their several uses may be. In the bowels of the earth we obtain coal, that black mineral that provides us with heat and steam and yet, by the aid of chemistry, also provides us with colors that rival the colors of the rainbow in brilliancy. Look to the dwellers in the forests primeval, tanned by the summer's sun, supple athletic and noble in learning, when attacked with sickness their "Medicine men" give them decoctions from certain herbs that grow near their wigwams, and thus nature provides a cure ready to the hand of the initiated. In this city, Mr. George Tucker, popularly known as the Indian Healer, whose office is located at No. 86½ St. Lawrence Main Street, and who is proprietor of the Green Mountain, Balm Co., is one of the most successful "Medicine Men" in this country. This gentlemen was born in the United States but was brought up at Three Rivers. His father was an Englishman and his mother an Indian, and from the latter he has inherited his skill in healing which he uses to such good effect for the relief of suffering humanity. Mr. Tucker has nineteen preparations in the market for the cure of the following diseases :—Asthma, Consumption, Bronchitis, Deafness, Gravel, Paralysis, Loss of Speech, Nightmares, Diarrhœa, Dropsy, Epilepsy, Scrofula Hemorrhoids, Swellings, Tumors, Cold Extremities, Nervous Debility, Weak Limbs, Worms, Catarrh, Diseases of the

Kidneys, Deformity of the Limbs, Gout, Neuralgia Sore Eyes, Bilious Complaints, St. Anthony's Fire, St. Vitus' Dance, Dyspepsia, Lowness of Spirit, Constipation, Liver Complaints, Diseases of the Blood, Palpitation of the Heart, Female Weakness, Tumors caused by Fever, Lung Diseases, Swelling of the Joints, Coughs and Colds, Ulcerous Eruptions, Uneasiness, &c., &c.

Special remedies for curing veneral diseases ·—Rheumatism, Cancers and Tape worms always cured radically with the Indian Remedies of Geo. Tucker.

It his Arrapaho Baume, Botanic Syrup, Live Green Mountain Salve possess a reputation for the healing qualities which extends all over the American Continent. Mr. Tucker is well-known throughout Canada where he has been practicing for the past fifteen years, the last four of which he has been established in Montreal, and has won for himself a name and fame that further words of ours can hardly increase.

J. B. Raby, GROCER, 2641 NOTRE DAME STREET, COR. CANNING STREET — There is no branch of business industry conducted in any civilized community in which every individual has such a personal interest, as in those that deal in the food supplies of the people, and next to bread and meat, comes the line of goods generally comprehended under the head of groceries. The grocery trade is conducted upon an extensive scale in this city, and many first-class houses are engaged in it. Among the number deserving of more than a mere passing notice in the pages of a work of this nature, is that of Mr. J. B. Raby, whose store is located at No. 2641 Notre Dame Street, corner of Canning Street. The premises occupied by the business are 25 x 40 feet in dimensions and are tastefully fitted up, and the stock is displayed to the very best advantage. The stock, which is a large one and has been selected with great care, consists of the choicest brands of teas from China and Japan, fragrant coffees from Java, Rio, and South American ports, pine spices, hermetically sealed goods, table delicacies, flour and a fine line of prime provisions, also the finest brands of imported and domestic wines and liquors, specially suited to family trade, while township's butter is made a specialty. This business was established five years ago and has, during these years, met with a liberal share of public patronage, and been built up to quite extensive proportions, the trade being conducted at both wholesale and retail, while employment is furnished to three competent and courteous assistants. Mr. Raby is a native of the Province of Quebec, and is a gentleman well-known and highly esteemed by all classes.

James Currie, MERCHANT TAILOR, 2113 NOTRE DAME STREET, MONTREAL.—It has come to be a recognized fact that the merchant tailoring establishment of Mr. James Currie, which is located at No. 2113 Notre Dame Street, is one of the most popular in Montreal. This has been the result of the aim on the part of the proprietor to produce only first-class garments. The making of gentlemen's wearing apparel to order, by measure, is one of those arts that requires for its successful prosecution the highest degree of artistic skill in every department of the business. Mr. Currie has been nine years in business, three of which he was in partnership with Mr. Inglis, and three with Mr. Saddler. From its inception the principle of the house has been to give full value for money, the best material, fit and excellence, and thus a trade has been acquired among the most exacting of our citizens, and which is annually increasing in volume. The premises occupied by the business consist of a store and workroom 20 x 45 feet in dimensions, the store being fitted up in a very handsome manner and is replete with the finest imported fabrics from the principal looms of Europe, embracing suitings, coatings, trouserings, overcoat goods, etc., of the latest patterns and highest qualities. Employment is furnished to

MECHANIC'S INSTITUTE AND LIBRARY.

ten skilled workmen, and the specialties of the house are correct styles, elegant fits and choice garments. Mr. James Currie, the proprietor, is a native of the Province of Quebec, and is a thoroughly skilled, practical tailor and an enterprising business man, and our readers will find business relations with this house to be of the most satisfactory character.

J. B. G. Perrault, IMPORTER OF HARDWARE, STOVES, PAINTS, OILS, GLASS, ETC., 2315 AND 2317 NOTRE DAME STREET, MONTREAL.—Montreal is well represented in the different lines of commercial interest as well as in her manufacturing industries. The city is admirably located as a distributing centre, not only for the Provinces of Quebec and Ontario but also for the entire Dominion, being situated as it is, at the head of ocean navigation and having ample railroad and water facilities with all points of the interior. The hardware trade is one of the principal lines conducted, here and is well represented by enterprising and progressive merchants. Among those prominently engaged in this line of business here, is Mr. J. B. G. Perrault, whose store is located at Nos. 2315 and 2317 Notre Dame Street. The premises occupied by the business are 60 x 45 feet in dimensions and contain a large and judiciously selected stock of general hardware. of every description, stoves, paints, oils, glass, tinware, varnishes, putty, etc., etc. The line of stoves handled, embrace some of the very best lines manufactured in the Dominion, and all other goods are of the best quality. Mr Perrault imports his stock direct from the leading houses in Europe, as well as his goods of domestic manufacture. This business was established six years ago and has always received a liberal share of the public patronage, and has materially increased in extent and development since the date of its inception. A jobbing as well as retail trade is conducted. Mr. Perrault, the proprietor, is a native of Montreal, where he is well and favorably known in the trade and social circles.

Z. Turgeon, MERCHANT TAILOR. 77 ST. LAWRENCE STREET, MONTREAL.— The first thought of the well-to-do gentleman of good taste, when he decides upon a new suit is, " To whom shall I give my order ?"—a question, usually, much easier asked than answered, for there are tailors and tailors, as there are lawyers and lawyers. Some of these alleged gentlemen's costumers are mere mechanical automatons, another class are true artists and make of every suit they undertake a poem in cloth, an epic in textiles, "a thing of beauty and joy forever," or rather until it is worn out. Of the latter class Mr. Z. Turgeon, whose store is located at No. 77 St. Lawrence Main Street, is an excellent example. This gentleman has been established in business for the past eight years and is a skilled, practical cutter of twenty year's experience. Therefore all orders entrusted to him receive his personal attention and receive the benefit of his extended practice. The premises occupied are 20 x 60 feet in dimensions, and are neatly fitted up and upon the counter and shelves will be found an elegant stock of imported and domestic cloths, tweeds, woollens, Cassimeres, etc., in all the latest and most stylish novelties, from which to make a selection. These are made up to order on short notice in the highest style of the art, and the garments produced by this house are not excelled for perfection of fit, beauty of style and elegance of finish, while the prices charged are very reasonable. None but the most skilled operators are employed, so that entire satisfaction is at all times guaranteed. Mr. Turgeon is a native of the Province of Quebec, and during his business career has built up an enviable and steadily increasing custom, of which he is well deserving.

John Lorigan, MANUFACTURER OF MARBLEIZED SLATE MANTLES, WOOD MANTLES, GRATES AND FIRE PLACES, OFFICE AND WAREROOMS, 2439 ST. CATHERINE STREET; FACTORY, ALEXANDER STREET.—Progress is the watchword of our time, and in no department of business has this been more exemplified than in household interior decoration. A high state of culture has been reached during the past fifteen years at least, and is one of the most encouraging signs of our times. Not least among the lines of mechanical industry that has kept abreast of this demand for artistic work, is that of the manufacture of mantles, grates and fire-places. Mr. John Lorigan, who opened an establishment in this city on the 1st of May of the present year, for the manufacture and sale of these requisites, has had an extensive experience in the business in the United States, and was in business in St. John, N. B., for several years. Desiring a wider field for operations, he severed his connections there and has chosen Montreal as a central point for his enterprise. His warehouse is located at No. 2439 St. Catherine Street, the factory being located on Alexander Street. The object is to build up a first-class connection with builders, inside finishers, and others more or less directly interested, and to that end the latest designs, novelties in patterns, superior material and workmanship and moderate prices are the rule. Mr. Lorigan manufactures and deals in marbleized slate mantles, wood mantles, grates and fire-places, slate wash tubs, urinals, washstand tops, radiator tops, and slate goods of all descriptions. Also, tiles for mantles, hearths, fire-places, etc., etc., as well as brass fenders, frames, fire sets, etc. Employment is furnished to twenty-five skilled hands in the factory, and the trade of the house will embrace in its scope of operations the entire Dominion. Mr. Lorigan, who is a native of the United States, is a thoroughly practical workman and understands the business thoroughly in all its details.

Jas. McCrudden, BOOTS AND SHOES, 86 BLEURY STREET, MONTREAL.— It is now thirty years since this business was first established by the late W.P. Johnston, who was succeeded in March, 1886, by the present proprietor. The premises occupied, which are located at No, 86 Bleury Street, and the stock is a large and elegant one and consists of boots and shoes, balmorals, slippers, etc., for ladies and gentlemen, misses, youths and children, which are of the very best quality and most fashionable styles, and are received from some of the leading manufacturing houses in the Dominion. There is also a special department for custom work, where those desiring can have their boots or shoes made to order on short notice and in the highest style of the art, at very reasonable prices, particular attention being given to the making up of gentlemen's fine boots.

M. Philbin, HOUSE FURNISHING HARDWARE, QUEEN'S BLOCK, 2231 AND 2233 ST. CATHERINE STREET.—The west end of Montreal is being rapidly built up and quite a number of the better class of retail stores are being located here for the accommodation of the residents in this quarter of the city, St. Catherine Street being the principal trade thoroughfare. Among the business houses worthy of special mention, is that of Mr. M. Philbin, hardware merchant, whose store is eligibly located for trade at Nos. 2231 and 2233 St. Catherine Street. The premises occupied are very commodious, being 30 x 110 feet in dimensions. These contain a large and elegant stock of shelf hardware, and house furnishing goods, including, tinware, woodenware, granite ironware, cutlery, brushes, wire mattresses, spring beds, wire goods, refrigerators, iron bedsteads, mangles, clothes, wringers, gas stoves, coal oil stoves, washing machines and many other articles of a similar nature. The stock is full and complete in every particular and all goods handled are of the very best quality and specially suited for a first-class trade. Employment is furnished to four competent and courteous clerks throughout the year. This business was founded by Mr. J. C. Kemp, who was succeeded six years since by the present proprietor. Mr. M. Philbin who has since built up a large and rapidly increasing trade, which now extends throughout the entire city, but the greater bulk of the business being done in the west end. Mr. Philbin is a native of Montreal, where he is widely and favorably known in business and social circles. He has associated in business with him his son, Mr. W. Philbin, a young man of much business ability, push and energy.

Gilmore Augur Works, G. GILMORE, COTE ST. PAUL.—The possibil-. ities for the future of Montreal as one of the most important manufacturing and commercial centres on the North American Continent are very great and encouraging. Having most excellent water power, and being at the head of navigation and with the best railroad and water facilities connecting with the great West and North-west, her position as a great distributing point for the Dominion is unassailable. Among the many and varied lines of manufactures conducted here, that of Gilmore's Augur Works, which are located at Cote St. Paul, on the banks of the Lachine Canal, are deserving of special mention. The premises occupied by the works ar 120 x 50 feet in dimensions which are fully equipped with all the most improved machinery driven by water power, while employment is steadily furnished to twenty-five skilled and competent workmen throughout the year. The product of the works consists of augurs, brace bits, boreing tools and other articles of a similar nature. These are made from the best quality of steel, well tempered and perfectly finished, and each tool being thoroughly examined before packing, all goods are thus guaranteed to be entirely satisfactory. Mr. G. Gilmore, the proprietor of the works is a killed, practical workman and since he started in business here thirty-three years ago, he has met with the most encouraging and well derived success.

Joseph Godin, WOOL HAT MANUFACTURER, COTE ST. PAUL.—Among what may be considered special lines of manufacture that of wool hats is certainly one. In all large business and manufacturing centres will be found nearly every branch of trade represented in some form or other, and Montreal has most assuredly for many years held a high position among the manufacturing centres of the Dominion. In reviewing the various lines of manufacture and commerce in this city, special mention must be made of the wool hat manufactory of Mr. Joseph Godin, which is located at Cote St. Paul. Mr. Godin was formerly located at St. Gabriel Locks, but removed to his present site in April of the present year. The premises occupied by the factory, which is owned and was specially built by Mr. Godin, consist of two adjoining buildings which are 30 x 60 feet in dimensions and three stories in height, and 30 x 60 feet and two stories in height. These are fitted up with the latest and most improved machinery specially adapted to this work, and is driven by sixty horse-power water wheel. There is also a very large boiler for the generation of steam which is used in all the different operations of the manufacture of hats. Employment is furnished to thirty skilled hands throughout the year. The goods manufactured by this concern consist of wool hats for ladies and gentlemen's wear, which are made up in all the latest and most fashionable styles. These goods have an active demand in the market, being of excellent quality and well made in every particular. This business was established eleven years ago, and ever since the date of its inception it has made very marked progress and development until, at the present day the trade extends throughout the entire Dominion. The operations of the house are confined to the wholesale trade entirely and are very extensive. Mr. Godin is a native of Montreal, and is a skilled, practical hat maker. He gives his personal attention and supervision to all work done in his factory and can thus secure the best of results.

Clark's Bell Factory, C. O. CLARK, COTE ST. PAUL.—Montreal is not only metropolitan in the character of its mercantile interests, but also in the extent and diversified character of its manufactures. Here may be found almost every branch of trade successfully conducted. The manufacturing houses are not confined to the city proper, but many are located in the suburbs, Cote St. Paul, being a favorable location on account of the excellent water power derived from the Lachine Canal. Among the many lines of manufacture conducted in Cote St. Paul, none are more deserving of special mention than that of Clark's Bell Factory. This business was established a quarter of a century ago, and has enjoyed a long, honorable and successful career. The premises occupied by the business.

are 40 x 60 feet in dimensions and are fitted up with all the most improved machinery and requirements driven by water power while steady employment is furnished to twelve skilled and competent workmen throughout the year. The product of the factory consists of gongs, hand bells, sleigh bells, house bells, and in fact bells of every description. These are made of sheet and cast metal, a specialty being made of the cast metal bells, there being a much greater demand for them than for the stamped metal article and are excellent in tone and well finished and have an active demand throughout the trade in the Dominion. Mr. C. O. Clark, the proprietor, is a native of the United States and is a thorough going, pushing and enterprising business man as well as a practical workman, and all orders entrusted to his care receive prompt and careful consideration.

Thomas McLeod, BOOTS AND SHOES, 30 CHABOILLEZ SQUARE.—In a country like Canada, having such long and severe winters, the boot and shoe trade must necessarily occupy a prominent position in the commercial and general community, for it is absolutely necessary that people should keep their feet well covered and dry, to prevent colds, consumption and death. Among those engaged in the boot and shoe trade in this city, and who are worthy of more than a mere passing notice in a work of this character, is Mr. Thomas McLeod, whose store is located at No. 30 Chaboillez Square. The premises occupied are commodious and are neatly and suitably fitted up for the requirements of the trade. Here is carried a splendid stock of fine boots and shoes, slippers, rubbers, etc., for ladies' and gentlemen, misses, youths and boys in all weights and grades, from the finest kid to the heaviest kip, and which are made up in the latest and most fashionable styles. Mr. McLeod manufacturers a large part of his own stock, and for this purpose gives employment to twenty skilled and competent hands. He also has a custom department in connection with his business where those desiring boots or shoes made to measure, can have their orders attended to promptly and in the highest style of the art, at reasonable prices. This business was established in 1883 by Mr. D. MacCormack, who was succeeded in February of the present year, by Mr. McLeod, who is a skilled, practical workman and an energetic and enterprising business man.

TRADE MARK

Stanley Dry Plate Co., GEORGE KNOWLTON, MANAGER, 613 LAGAUCHETIERE STREET.—During the past quarter of a century, a most wonderful change has taken place in the art of photography, and from being what many people might term, a "black art," on account of its mysterious manipulations, it has become so simplified by the genius of science that it may be made the pastime of amateurs, and, in fact, the army of amateur photographers is very large at the present day. This result has been brought about in a great measure, by what is known as the dry-plate process. There are several houses on the American Continent manufacturing these dry-plates, and among the number, deserving of particular mention, especially as its Canadian Branch is located in this city, is the Stanley Dry-Plate Co., of Lewiston, Maine. Their office and factory are located at No. 613 Lagauchetiere Street, where a staff of skilled and competent hands is given steady employment throughout the year, in the manufacture of all sizes of these plates, the trade in which, and which is conducted entirely at wholesale, extends throughout the Dominion, and is steadily increasing, a fact, which is a sufficient evidence of the thoroughly satisfactory nature of the goods handled. A year ago last February, Mr. George Knowlton, who was in the Company's employ in Lewiston, was sent to Montreal as Manager, and to open the business here, and during the comparatively short period of time in which the business has been running, it has met with the most eminent success.

W. R. Gardner, MANUFACTURER OF EVERY DESCRIPTION OF HAMMERS AND EDGE TOOLS, Cote St. Paul, Montreal.—In a review of the commerce and manufactures of Montreal, it is made very evident that the city has been rapidly growing in extent and importance as a manufacturing centre, and also that its advantages as such are almost unlimited. Blessed with an abundant water supply, and the very best of transportation facilities, there is no reason why Montreal should not in the near future greatly add to its already large industrial interests. Among the manufacturing establishments located at Cote St. Paul, worthy of honorable mention in a work of this character, is that of the Vulcan Tool Works, of which Mr. W. R. Gardner is the proprietor. This business was established thirty years ago by Mr. Henry H. Warren, who, one year since, retired in favor of Mr. Gardner. The business, ever since the date of its inception, has been a highly successful one, but never so much so as at the present time. The premises occupied by the works are located on the banks of the Lachine Canal, and consist of two floors, each 80 x 120 feet in dimensions. These are fitted up with all the latest and most improved machinery, and employment is furnished to forty skilled and competent workmen throughout the year in the manufacture of hammers and edge tools of every description. These are made from the best of cast steel only and the workmanship is perfect. Mr. Gardner, the proprietor, who is a Scotchman by birth, is a practical workman of many years' experience, and, giving his personal attention to all orders entrusted to his care, can thus guarantee his customers the most perfect satisfaction. The trade of the house is large and embraces the entire Dominion as well as considerable export.

E. Lemieux, MERCHANT TAILOR, No. 3 St. Lawrence Street, Montreal. —A cynic has said that " If it be true that the tailor makes the man," then he has a great deal to answer for. Well, perhaps he has, but it is nevertheless true that many well deserving men would stand unrecognized in the world without a chance to show their ability or sterling worth if it was not for the adventitious aid given by their tailor in the shape of good and fashionable clothes. One of the most popular merchant tailoring establishments on St. Lawrence Main Street, is that of Mr. E. Lemieux, which is located at No. 3 on that thoroughfare. Although it is but five years since Mr. Lemieux founded his business, he has built up an excellent and most lucrative business, his trade being derived from the most critical—in the way of dress—portion of the community. This is on account of keeping nothing but the very best of stock in all the most seasonable and fashionable fabrics, which he makes up to order, by measure, in the highest style of the art. The premises occupied by the business are 28 x 45 feet in dimensions and two stories in height, the upper floor being used as a workshop, where employment is furnished to twelve skilled and competent operators. The store is tastefully fitted up with plate glass front, is lighted by electricity, and presents a neat and attractive appearance, and the stock of goods carried large and elegant, consisting of imported and domestic fabrics, woollens, tweeds, Cassimeres, etc. The garments produced by this house are unsurpassed for beauty of sytle, perfection of fit and elegance of finish, and the prices will be found very reasonable. Mr. Lemieux also carries a fine line of gents' furnishings, including all the latest and most fashionable novelties. Mr. Lemieux is a native of this Province, is an enterprising and progressive business man and an active member of the Chamber of Commerce.

T. Christy, (LATE WITH JOHN DATE) PLUMBER, GAS AND STEAM FITTER, 82 Bleury Street, Montreal.—The scientific and practical attention that has of late years been given to the subject of sanitary engineering and plumbing, has succeeded in vastly elevating in importance and dignity, the plumber's trade. The man who, to-day, would be a successful master plumber must necessarily possess long training and extensive information concerning matters which are purely scientific and yet indissolubly connected with the practical operation of his business. Filling these important requisites in an excellent degree is Mr. T. Christy, whose shop is located at No. 82 Bleury Street. This gentleman has had an extended experience in the plumbing trade and was for a number of years with John Date, of this city, when five years ago he started in business for himself, and by persevering industry and the bringing to bear his well-grounded knowledge of all the requirements of the trade, he has met with the most gratifying success, his trade being constantly on the increase. The premises occupied for store and workshop consist of two floors each 20 x 40 feet in dimensions which are fully equipped with all the necessary apparatus for the proper conducting of the trade, and where employment is furnished to eight skilled and competent workmen, on an average, throughout the year. Mr. Christy attends to all kinds of general and sanitary plumbing ; the fitting up of new buildings with sanitary arrangements, gas and steam fitting, or in making alterations in old buildings in these branches. He also does all kinds of tin and copper smithing. In all these lines he is ever prepared to execute all orders, from the smallest job to the largest contract, and in the most satisfactory manner. Mr. Christy is a native of Ireland and is a gentleman of marked business ability, which, coupled with his practical knowledge of the trade, has ensured his success.

Dr. Dansereau, CHEMIST AND DRUGGIST, 1399 St. Catherine Street.—It may have been well enough in Macbeth's time to say, "Throw physic to the dogs, I'll none of it," for the healing art was then still in a crude condition ; but a vast improvement has been made since those days, and no sane man of the present day would think of disputing the value and efficacy of properly administered drugs. Montreal contains a number of first-class pharmacies, and among these, deserving of special mention, is that of Dr. Dansereau, which is located at No. 1399 St. Catherine Street. The premises occupied, are 20 x 45 feet in dimensions, which are handsomely fitted up, and his stock consists of everything necessary to a first-class drug store, and embraces drugs, chemicals, medicines and proprietary remedies, of standard and acknowledged reputation, elegant fancy goods and toilet articles, fine soaps and perfumery, physicians' supplies and druggists' sundries, &c. It has always been the aim of Dr. Dansereau, to keep fresh and pure drugs, and chemicals. He gives special attention to the compounding of physicians' prescriptions, and family recipes; and being a competent physician himself, is excellently qualified for this branch of the business. Dr. Dansereau, is a graduate of McGill College, and during the three years he has been established in business here, he has received hearty recognition at the hands of the public.

George Roberts, BUILDER AND CONTRACTOR, 597 Lagauchetiere Street ; Stock Yard 57 Drummond Street.—In compiling a record of the rise and progress of a great city, one naturally turns to its builders, they possessing the greatest knowledge as to the indications for the future, and the experiences of the past. They are the men who, from a long and active service in the interests of the people, become intimately associated with them, and, with a sagacity born of a zeal and industry proverbial with the profession, are ever ready with facts and figures. The advantages of a long and successful career make individual leaders in their line of business, and gain for them recognition of the vastness of their work. Holding a conspicuous place among the builders and contractors of Montreal is Mr. George Roberts, whose office and mill are located at Nos. 595 to 611 Lagauchetiere Street. Mr. Roberts, who is a native of London, England, and who learned his business there, and, in conjunction with his father, erected several large buildings, started in business on his own account in this city in the year 1857 and soon took a leading place in the trade, which he has ever since steadily maintained. He is the only builder in the city who manufactures entirely all his own materials, joining and finishing, having an excellently equipped mill furnished with the latest and most improved machinery, driven by a twenty-five horse-power steam engine, and furnishing employment, on an average, to one 100 skilled workmen throughout the year. Mr. Roberts has erected many of the principle structures that have adorned Montreal during the past quarter of a century, and among the number may be mentioned the Standard Life Insurance Building, Molson's Bank, Ewing's Block, Harbour Commissioner's Building, Gazette Building, Hochelaga Cotton Mills, Canada Paper Co's. Building, Canada Paper Co's. Mills at Windsor, Stanley Street Wing of Windsor Hotel, and repairs to St. Lawrence Hall, now erecting J. C. Wilson's mammoth new Building on Craig Street, American Presbyterian Church, St. Martin's Church, Victoria Rink, McDonald's Tobacco Factory, the old Molson College, Redpath's Museum, McGill Medical College, Nordheimer's Block, Hudson Bay Co's. Building, also the beautiful residences of James Johnston, Hon. John Hamilton, Samuel Wardell, Thomas Workman, Sir Hugh Allan, Jonathan Hodgson, Robert Reford, John Redpath, Keenan's Block, corner of Sherbrooke and McKay Streets, for the passed twenty years, also the stores of McKay Bros., Gault Bros., John Ogilvie, and James Hutton, Bank of British North America, Queen's Hall Block, City and District Saving's Bank, Grace Church, Point St. Charles, and Anne Street School, Mr. Dow's residence on Beaver Hall Hill, and many others, but these are sufficient to show the nature and character of his work and the leading position he holds among the representative builders of the Dominion.

Thomas Moll, TINSMITH AND PLUMBER, 2124 Notre Dame Street.— There is probably no trade existing that has made such a marked improvement during the past few years as that of plumbing. It was found that much of the work done was very defective, and promoted the spread of disease, through the admittance into the dwellings of zymotic diseases. An investigation of the causes led to their reform, and now, happily, the errors of the past have been remedied and will be avoided for the future. Among the later additions to the ranks of this trade in Montreal, is Mr. Thomas Moll, whose shop is located at No. 2124 Notre Dame Street. This gentleman started business in March 1887. The premises occupied by the business are ·22 x 50 feet in dimensions, and are fully equipped with all the necessary tools and appliances for the successful prosecution of the work to be done. Mr. Moll attends to all orders for tinsmithing, plumbing, slate and galvanized sheet iron roofing, drainage. He puts up gas, steam and hot water apparatus, and does all kinds of work in galvanized sheet iron, cornices and skylights, extended according to plans. Mr. Moll undertakes all kinds of work in his line, by tender or order, at the lowest possible prices. He gives employment to nine skilled and competent workmen throughout the year. Mr. Moll is a Canadian by birth, and is a skilled, practical workman of much experience, and is an enterprising and progressive business man.

David Brunet, BOOTS AND SHOES, 2125 Notre Dame Street.—Montreal, is one of the most important and substantial business centres on the American Continent, and contains many old-established houses that have grown up and kept pace with the development of the city. In a review of this character, embracing the different lines of business industry here conducted, the boot and shoe trade naturally comes in for a large share of attention, on account of its extensive operations and its importance to the general public. Holding a prominent place among the old-established houses in this line of business in this city, is that of Mr. David Brunet, which is admirably located for business at No.2125 Notre Dame Street. The premises occupied are large and commodious, being 20 x 50 feet in dimensions, and are very tastefully and suitably fitted up for the requirements of the business. Here is carried a large and elegant stock of boots and shoes, in all weights and grades, from the finest of kid, to the heaviest and most serviceable kip, made up in the finest styles for ladies and gentlemen, misses, youths, boys and children. Also slippers, rubbers, &c., of the very best quality. There is a special department for custom work, where those desiring boots or shoes made to order by measure, can have their orders attended to promptly, and in the most satisfactory manner. Employment is furnished throughout the year to eight skilled workmen and courteous assistants. This business was founded twenty-two years ago, and has at all times proved very successful, but never so much so as at present. Mr. Brunet, is a native of Montreal, and is a skilled, practical shoemaker, and a live, active and progressive business man.

W. Tracey, FUNERAL DIRECTOR, 2063 NOTRE DAME STREET, MONTREAL.— The business of a funeral director is one requiring special qualifications for its successful prosecution. The duties devolving upon one in this line are onerous and delicate in the extreme, and it is not everyone that can fulfil the duties in a satisfactory manner. Among those engaged in this line of business, in this city, is Mr. William Tracey, whose shop is located at No. 2063 Notre Dame Street, opposite Dows' Brewery. This gentleman established his undertaking business in 1882, and it has, ever since that time, proved entirely successful, those who have required his services speaking very highly of the satisfactory manner in which he has performed his duties upon all occasions. Mr. Tracey keeps in stock a full line of funeral furnishings, including coffins and caskets, from the plainest and cheapest to the most beautiful and richly finished, so that the requirements of those in any circumstances of life can be attended. He also carries all the minor requisites for funerals and gives his personal attention to all details entrusted to him. Mr. Tracey started in business as a carpenter, in the year 1876, and had a very lucrative and gratifying trade, but he retired from that in order to give his entire attention to his undertaking business, and so far as trade is concerned, he has had no occasion to regret his decision. Mr. Tracey is a native of Ireland but has resided in this country for many years, where he is well-known and highly esteemed by all classes of the community for his many social and business qualifications.

Bush & Read, BOOTS AND SHOES, 2112 NOTRE DAME STREET.—Among the many business enterprises conducted in this city, that in boots and shoes is not by any means the least important. In a climate so severe as that of our Canadian winters, it is absolutely necessary for the preservation of health to have the feet kept dry and warm, and thus it is that the trade of the boot and shoe dealer is a valuable one. Among those actively engaged in this line of business in this city, is the firm of Messrs. Bush & Read, whose store is located at No. 2112 Notre Dame Street. The premises occupied by the business are 18 x 40 feet in dimensions, and contain a large and carefully selected stock of boots and shoes of the very best quality and made up in the latest and most fashionable styles, by some of the leading manufacturing houses in the country. The firm also do custom work, so that those requiring boots or shoes made to measure, can have the same attended to here in the best possible style, and upon the shortest notice, while the prices will be found to meet the views of the most economical. Since this business was established five years ago, it has met with the most gratifying success, and has steadily con-tinued to extend and develop in volume from the date of its inception. Mr. John Bush, the senior member of the firm, is a native of England, and is a thorough business man and understanding all the details of the business, is ever prepared to meet the demands of customers.

CANADIAN PACIFIC RAILWAY STATION, ERECTED 1888.

M. J. Adler, MERCHANT TAILOR, 47 BEAVER HALL HILL.—In all civilized communities of any importance, it is a matter of considerable import how a man dresses, especially those who move in business and social circles, for upon a man's personal appearance depends in a great measure his success in life. The gentlemen of Montreal are proverbially well dressed and this may be accounted for by the fact that the city is favored with a number of first-class merchant tailoring establishments, conducted by gentlemen of marked taste and enterprise. In a review of such, mention must be made of Mr. M. J. Adler, whose shop is located at Nos. 45 and 47 Beaver Hall Hill. The premises occupied by him are neatly fitted up and contain a fine stock of imported and domestic woolens, tweeds, worsteds, etc., in the latest and leading patterns from which to select. Garments or suits are made up to order on short notice in the highest style of the art by competent operators, and in all that goes to make perfection in clothing, will be found in the garments turned out by this house. Since this business was founded five years ago, it has proved highly successful and has steadily increased in extent and importance from year to year. Employment is furnished to twenty-five competent hands on an average throughout the year. Mr. Adler, the proprietor, is a native of Russia, and is a skilled, practical tailor, and giving his personal attention to all orders entrusted to his care can thus assure the best of satisfaction. He has also in connection with his tailoring establishment a first-class cleaning and repairing shop, where all work is satisfactorily turned out at very moderate charges.

Sharpe's City Express and Baggage Transfer, SHARP & CURTIN, PROPRIETORS, OFFICE, 306 AND 308 ST. JAMES STREET, MONTREAL.—This is an age of electricity, telephones, steam engines, instantaneous photography. An age of rush, push and "get there." Those who rest by the wayside will wake up some fine day to realize, like Rip-Van-Winkle, that they belong to a by-gone day. Business is transacted rapidly and with machine precision and the express companies keep with the procession in the rapid, careful and correct transmission of goods. One of the best and most popular express companies in Montreal, is Sharpe's City Express. This business was established in the year 1860 by Mr. John Sharp, and, from a comparitively small beginning, it has become one of the institutions of the city. On the 1st of September, 1887, Mr. Philip Curtin was admitted into partnership, under the firm title of Sharp & Curtin. The office of the firm is located at No. 310 St. James Street, where all orders are received for the removal and delivery of goods to, and from any part of the city, depots and steamboats. Pianos, furniture, baggage and parcels are transferred with promptness and in the most careful manner by experienced men at moderate charges. The stables of the concern are located in rear of No. 306 St. James Street, and has accommodation for twenty-four horses. In summer twenty-four vehicles are in use and employment is furnished to forty-five competent men, and in winter fifteen double and single vehicles are used and employment furnished to about fifteen men, a greater demand being made upon the resources of the firm in the summer than in winter. Mr. Sharp, the founder of the business, is a native of Scotland, and has resided in this country forty years. His partner, Mr. Curtin, is a native of Ireland, and has made Canada his home for over thirty-five years both are thoroughly energetic, prompt and progressive business men, and Montreal is fortunate in possessing such a valuable institution as they own and conduct.

S. A. de Lorimier, GENTLEMEN'S FURNISHINGS, 1700 NOTRE DAME STREET, MONTREAL.—In all business centres it is specially necessary that gentlemen should be well and fashionably dressed, for personal appearance goes a great way towards one's success in this world. Gents' furnishings are an absolute necessity therefore, in all civilized communities. Holding a prominent position among those engaged in this line of business in Montreal is Mr. S. A. de Lorimier, whose establishment is located at No. 1700 Notre Dame Street ; the premises occupied being 30 x 35 feet in dimensions, and elegantly fitted up

D 1

Here is carried a large and elegant stock of the latest and most fashionable novelties in gents' furnishings. Among the specialties may be mentioned Dent's gloves, Lloyd, Attrey & Smith's and Young & Rochester's (of London) haberdashery, Cartwright & Warner's best merino underwear, J. R. Morley (of London) hosiery, Blank and Co.'s flannels, and Irish linens from the County Down Flax Spinning and Weaving Co., and silk hankerchief from Stewart & McDonald of Glasgow. A specialty being made of shirts to order, which are manufactured on the premises, which requires a number of skilled and competent operators to keep up the supply of his large and ever increasing order trade. This business has long been established, Mr. de Lorimier succeeding Kemp & Co. nine years ago. Mr. de Lorimier is a descendant from one of the early French noble families, his grand father being Guillaume Chevalier de Lorimier, author of *Mes Services* (?) and commandant of the Indian allies in 1775 under General Carleton. Mr. de Lorimier is a thorough going business man and enjoys a large trade, extending as it does throughout the Dominion and numbers among his customers the leading families of the city members of the Senate, the two houses of Parliament and other leading officials, and book canvassers.

John A. Peard, PRACTICAL SANITARY ENGINEER, PLUMBER, GAS AND STEAM-FITTER, TINSMITH AND BELL-HANGER, 117 BLEURY STREET, AND 2561 ST. CATHERINE STREET, MONTREAL.—The discussion that has been going on of late, that has led to some very decided action being taken in connection with the plumbing and sanitary arrangement of Montreal, is a matter that is calculated to be of the greatest benefit to the inhabitants, for it is waking up the masses to the fact, which the majority of the people have long known, that unless the sanitary arrangements of a building were perfect, it was impossible for those residing in it to enjoy health ; and by the interest which is being evinced in the matter, it would appear that Montreal should soon become a city of the most perfect sanitary arrangement. Holding a prominent place among the sanitary engineers and plumbers of this city, is Mr. John A. Peard, whose stores are located at No. 117 Bleury Street, and 2561 St. Catherine Street. This gentleman has been established in the business for the past four years, having had a pevious experience in the business of nineteen years, fifteen of which were spent in one of the leading houses in this line in Montreal, and has, during that comparitively short space of time, met with the most unqualified success. The premises occupied by the business are 24 x 65 feet in dimensions where is carried a complete stock of brass goods, house boilers, cast iron sinks, iron pipe and fittings, lead pipe, bath tubs, wash bowls, chandeliers, brackets, and a fancy assortment of gas globes, also an extensive and well selected stock of coal oil lamps, parlor and library hanging lamps and general house furnishing hardware, all of which are imported direct by the house, the advantage thus secured being invariably extended to customers. Mr. Peard does all kinds of house plumbing work on the most approved satisfactory principles known to the craft ; also, gas, hot-water, and steam-fitting, hot-air furnace work, tinsmithing and electrical and mechanical bell hanging. Special attention is given to the sanitary condition of houses, and plumbing arrangements are tested on short notice. Mr. Peard is a thoroughly skilled, practical workman and gives his personal attention to all orders entrusted to his care, and his charges will be found as low as those of any similar house in the city.

Coutlee Bros., MERCHANT TAILORS, 518 NOTRE DAME STREET, CORNER OF CLAUDE STREET, MONTREAL.—Within the past quarter of a century, a very marked improvement has taken place in the ready-made clothing trade, so that now it is possible to get a suit that will be perfect fitting and stylish without the necessity of getting measured and waiting for them to be made up to order. Among the prominent houses that are engaged in both the ready-made clothing and merchant tailoring trade in this city is that of

Messrs. Coutlee Bros., which is located at No. 1518 Notre Dame Street, corner of Claude Street. The premises occupied by the business, consist of two floors 25 x 40 feet in dimensions, where is carried a large and elegant stock of ready-made clothing of all the regular sizes for men, youths, and boys, made up in the most fashionable styles from the leading novelties in fabrics. Also a fine stock of hats and gents' furnishings in the latest styles as well as a fine line of trunks. Mr. A J. Plamondon, a skilled tailor, is attached to this establishment, and those desiring suits made to order, by measure, can have their orders attended to, and the work done in the highest style of the art, being unsurpassed for fit, beauty of style and elegance of finish, suits being made to order in ten hours if required. This business was established by Alfred Meunier fifteen years ago, the present firm succeeding to the business on the 1st February of the present year. The members of the firm are Mr. J. P. Coutlee, formerly of the Great Dominion Syndicate, and Mr. G. Coutlee, both of whom are natives of this Province, and are enterprising and progressive business men.

Felix Mercier, CARRIAGE MAKER, 1260, 1262 AND 1264 NOTRE DAME STREET, MONTREAL.—There is no house in the city, in the carriage building line, that has a higher reputation for excellence of work done and straightforward, honorable business methods, than that of Mr. Felix Mercier. This gentleman's carriage factory is located at Nos. 1260, 1262 and 1264 Notre Dame Street. The premises occupied for the purposes of the business are large and commodious, consisting of four floors each 35 x 100 feet in dimensions. These are fully equipped with every requisite for the successful prosecution of the business, and nothing is omitted that could possibly aid in the accomplishment of high class work. Employment is furnished to twenty skilled and competent workmen in the different departments throughout the year. The factory is divided into different departments, such as blacksmith shop, wood shop, paint and trimming shop, etc., all the work relating to carriage making being done on the premises. Only the best seasoned wood and the finest quality of steel and iron are used in the manufacture of the different vehicles manufactured, consisting of carriages, landaus, buggies, cutters, sleighs, waggons, etc. The house has an excellent record for turning out superior work, and the trade extends throughout the Provinces of Ontario and Quebec while a very large business is done with Ottawa in the manufacture of carters' carriages. Mr. Mercier, who is a native of L'Assumption, is a practical carriage maker of many years experience, and since the time when he started in business on his own account, twenty-six years ago, he has had no occasion to complain of the success that has attended his efforts.

J. A. Nicolle, DISPENSING CHEMIST AND DRUGGIST, COR. BLEURY AND ST. CATHERINE STREETS.—There is no profession conducted that is of more importance to the public generally and individually than that of the pharmacist. The skilled pharmacist has very often to take the place of the doctor and prescribe remedies as well as compound them. In olden times the druggist was barber and leech, all three combined in one, and unlearned at that, but now to be permitted to engaged in this profession one must be a graduate or licentiate of some regularly constituted school of pharmacy. Among the prominent drug stores located is that of Mr. J. A. Nicolle, which is at the corner of Bleury and St. Catherine Streets. The premises occupied are 22 x 30 feet in dimensions and are tastefully fitted up with plate glass show cases, cabinets, etc., for the advantageous display of the elegant stock carried, consisting of fresh, pure drugs, chemicals, fancy and toilet articles, soaps, perfumes, druggists sundries, proprietory medicines of acknowledged merit and standard reputation, etc., etc. A specialty of the business is the compounding of physician's prescriptions and difficult *formula* with promptness and care at reasonable charges. Mr. Nicolle, who is a native of the Island of Jersey, is a graduate of the Ontario College of Pharmacy, and three years ago bought out the insolvent estate of H. H. Curtis, the store being located two doors from where Mr. Nicolle's store is at present. He then fitted up his present establishment and his business efforts have been crowned with well deserved success.

C. Robert & Co., HATTER AND FURRIER, 61 St. Lawrence Street, corner of Vitre Street, Montreal.—Prominent among the many lines of commercial industry is that of the hatter and furrier trade. In a country situated as this is with its long, cold winters, the wearing of furs is an absolute necessity to protect one from the icey blasts of old Boreas. Holding a prominent place among the old-established houses in this line of business in this city is that of Messrs. C. Robert & Co.. whose store is located at No. 61 St. Lawrence Main Street, corner of Vitre Street. The premises occupied by the store are 20 x 45 feet in dimensions, with the workshop in rear, which is 20 x 20 feet in dimensions. A very large and elegant stock is carried, consisting of hats and caps in all the latest and most fashionable styles, received direct from some of the leading manufacturers in this country and Europe, as well as those of the firm's own manufacture. In fine furs the stock is large and elegant and of very best quality, and includes : coats, cloaks, caps, mitts, gauntlets, and such other articles suitables for ladies' and gentlemens' wear. The highest price is paid for raw furs, which are manufactured on the premises by skilled and experienced workmen, and all kinds of hats and furs are repaired at moderate prices. This business was established fifteen years ago, and from the date of its inception it has proved eminently successful, the sign of the big red hat being well-known to the citizens of Montreal as denoting one of the best places in the city at which to obtain hats, caps or furs. Mr. C. Robert is a native of the Province of Quebec, and is a gentleman of marked business experience, taking a lively interest in whatever tends to the welfare of the city, and is an active member of the Chamber of Commerce.

The Terrapin, HENRY DUNNE, Crystal Block, 1681 Notre Dame Street. —If walls could speak what a jolly tale those of the Terrapin Restaurant could tell of the many nights when the leading social and business men of this city have sat around the festive board, the tables groaning with the good things of this life provided by "mine host, Henry Dunne," the prince of caterers and king of right good fellows. The Terrapin has for nearly a quarter of a century been one of the popular institutions of the city. The premises occupied are large and commodious, being 30 x 100 feet in dimensions and two stories in height. In front is a finely fitted up bar containing all the choicest brands of wines and liquors, Havana and domestic cigars, etc., opposite is an oyster bar, where the delicious malpeque, Blue Points, and others of the bivalve species are served on the half-shell or otherwise. In rear is the spacious dining-hall, tastefully fitted up, where can be obtained everythng in the edible line from beefsteak to quail on toast and white-bait, served up in the finest style. This is a favorite dining place for many of our business men and visitors to the city, and as the saying is, "Once a guest, always a guest." Here, on the second floor is a large dining-hall, society and club dinners and banquets are held, and there is no more popular place in the city for this purpose than the Terrapin, nor no more popular host than "Harry" Dunne. Mr. Dunne is well-known in business, social and society circles in this city.

W. P. McVey, BOOTS AND SHOES, 1891 Notre Dame Street.—The boot and shoe trade has, in recent years, made very marked development and is now conducted upon a most extensive scale. Prominently engaged in this line of business in Montreal, is Mr. W. P. McVey, whose store is located at No. 1891 Notre Dame Street. It is now seven years since this business was established and during that time an excellent trade has been built up, which has been the result mainly of the spirit of enterprise displayed on the part of the proprietor, and having a thorough understanding of the requirements and being ready at all times to anticipate their demands. The premises occupied are 27 x 45 feet in dimensions, which are tastefully fitted up and contain a fine stock of boots and shoes and slippers for ladies and gentlemen, misses, youths and children in all weights and grades, and made up in the most fashionable styles by some of the leading manufacturers in this country. There is a special department where ladies and gentlemen can have their boots or shoes made to order by measure, in the highest style of the art, and upon short notice at very reasonable prices. Employment is furnished to four competent assistants throughout the year. Mr. McVey is a native of Montreal and is well and favorably known in business and social circles.

Drapeau & Champagne, PLUMBERS AND TINSMITHS, 1546 ST. CATHERINE STREET, MONTREAL.—A very great benefit has accrued to the general public from the discussion that has been going on of late with regard to the sanitary arrangements of our dwellings and buildings, where many are given employment. It is a well-known fact that unless the sanitary arrangements of a dwelling are perfect it is impossible for those residing therein to enjoy good health. Among the more efficient and prominent of those engaged in the plumbing and tinsmith business in this city is the firm of Messrs. Drapeau & Champagne, whose shop is located at No. 1546 St. Catherine Street. The premises occupied are 22 x 75 feet in dimensions, and here is carried a good stock of house furnishing goods, wicks, brushes, chimnies, lamps, coal oil, etc., etc. The firm also do all kinds of plumbing, fitting up new buildings or making repairs to old ones, with equal care and attention and upon the most scientific principles. They also execute every description of work, such as tin, galvanized zinc, sheet iron and slate roofing and other new work, as well as all kinds of repairs at short notice and in the most satisfactory manner, at moderate charges. The firm give employment to eleven skilled workmen, on an average throughout the year. This business was established fifteen years ago and by the exercise of perseverance, ability and enterprise an excellent trade has been built up. The individual members of the firm are Messrs. J. B. Drapeau and A. Champagne, both of whom are skilled, practical workmen, and members of the Master Plumbers' Association.

A. Lamarche, CARRIAGE MAKER, 1333 ONTARIO STREET CORNER OF ST. ANDRE STREET, MONTREAL.—Among the many business houses engaged in the manufacture of carriages, waggons, etc., there are none who are more entitled to a place in the pages of this work than Mr. A. Lamarche, whose carriage factory is located at No. 1333 Ontario Street. This gentleman has gained a high and widespread reputation for the excellent quality of his work, and the enterprise and energy he has developed in his business. The premises occupied for the purposes of the factory are 50 x 45 feet in dimensions; storage room, 100 x 45 feet, and showrooms 34 x 20 feet; communication being had between the different departments by a carriage elevator. All departments of the work are here done including wood work, iron work, painting and trimming, and employment is furnished to twenty-two skilled and competent workmen in the different departments throughout the year. The best seasoned wood and the finest quality of steel and iron are used in all work. The work of the house is not surpassed, and as regards style, elegance of finish, neatness and general superiority, will compare favorably with that of any other house in the city. Repairs of every description are also attended to promptly and in the most satisfactory manner. This business was founded in a modest way by the present proprietor, eight years ago, and has been steadily built up from year to year since that time, until it now extends throughout the Provinces of Ontario and Quebec. Mr. Lamarche is a practical carriage maker, and gives his personal supervision to all orders entrusted to his care. He is proprietor of his own establishment, is also of the entire block in which it is located, having a frontage of 1200 by a depth of 150 feet. Mr. Lamarche, who is quite a young man, attributes his success largely to his doing business strictly on the cash system, a principle which he has always followed.

Aubut & Barry, GENERAL GROCERS, WHOLESALE AND RETAIL, 1350 NOTRE DAME STREET AND CORNER VISITATION AND ROBIN STREETS, MONTREAL.—In a work of this character reviewing the commerce and manufactures of Montreal, it is always a matter of pleasure, as showing the progress being made in the city, to make special mention of such houses of importance as have been started within a comparatively recent period. In this connection and in this spirit therefore do we refer to Messrs. Aubut & Barry, Grocers, whose stores are located at No. 1350 Notre Dame Street, and corner of Visitation and Robin Streets. These gentlemen, who are Canadians by birth, and natives of this Province, founded this business only one year ago, and yet, during the comparatively brief space of time they have built up a rapidly increasing trade, which is as gratifying to them as it is well deserved. The premises occupied on Notre Dame Street are 28 x 65 feet in dimensions, their other establishment on Visitation and Robin Streets, being about the same size. These are neatly fitted up and suitably arranged for the requirements of the trade, and contain a large and judiciously selected stock of choice family groceries, including the finest of China and Japan teas, aromatic Java, Rio and Mocha coffees, table delicacies, pure spices, hermetically sealed goods, sugars, molasses and all such other articles as come under the head of groceries. Also a fine line of the best quality provisions, and the choicest brands of wines and liquors, specially selected for family trade. An extensive wholesale business is also conducted in the same lines. Employment is furnished to four courteous assistants throughout the year. Both Mr. Z. S. Aubut and Mr. J. B. Barry are thorough going men of business, and understanding all the details of the trade, are ever prepared to meet legitimate competition. Mr. Aubut is also a member of the Chamber of Commerce.

L. C. de Tonnancour, MERCHANT TAILOR, No. 8 ST. LAMBERT STREET, MONTREAL.—Montreal is noted for its merchant tailoring establishments as well as for the marked taste in dress evinced by the inhabitants of the city. who are no doubt indebted to many of the merchant tailors for their style and excellent taste in turning out garments that will fit well and look becoming. One of the most popular merchant tailoring establishments in this respect is that of Mr. L. C. de Tonnancour, which is located at No. 8 St. Lambert Street. Mr. de Tonnancour has been established in business in Montreal since 1867, and during that time he has built up an excellent and ever increasing custom. He has succeeded in doing this by the excellent reputation he has achieved as a skilled artist in his work, the garments turned out by him being perfect fitting in every respect, beautiful in style and elegant in finish, and in these particular points he is not excelled by any other merchant tailoring establishment in the city. He carries a fine stock of English, Scotch, French and American woolens, tweeds, cloths, from some of the most celebrated houses in these countries, and the patterns are all the latest and most fashionable. Besides gentlemen's plain and dress-suits. Mr. de Tonnancour manufactures uniforms for military bands and other work of a similar nature, and in this branch of the business also, he has been entirely successful. Mr. de Tonnancour is a practical tailor of many years experience and gives employment to forty skilled operators and assistants on an average throughout the year.

Scott's INTERIOR DECORATIONS. 2422 ST. CATHERINE STREET, MONTREAL, TELEPHONE NO. 4274.—The rapid extension of the city has necessarily led to great activity in the building trades, a not unimportant branch of which is that of the Painter and Glazier. Amongst those who have come to the front in this line of business is the young and enterprising firm of W. P. Scott, of 2422 St. Catherine Street, who have. by close application to business, and an absolute fulfillment of the many important contracts with which they have been entrusted, earned a reputation second to no other house in the trade.

Of the many large buildings recently completed by the firm, we may mention the Waddell Buildings, the Balmoral Hotel, the magnificent residences of Sir Donald Smith and W. W. Ogilvie, Esq., the new Mountain Street Methodist Church, and the immense building of the New York Life Insurance Co., now in course of completion.

The most important branch of their business, however, is that of the interior decoration of private residences, for which they have special, facilities. At their place of business may be seen samples of all the richest materials employed in the production of those artistic effects which give such an air of refinement and luxury to the homes of some of our wealthiest citizens. High class hand-made wall papers of English manufacture from the designs of such artists as Morris and Walter Crane, can be seen and compared with American productions of a like character, such as the " Birge Velours," a material which is especially attractive both in design and coloring. Novelties are constantly being introduced, both in material and in methods of treatment, and to be successful in a business of this character, requires not only special knowledge of the scope and adaptability of the materials used to produce the desired effects, but, also skillful manipulation, aided by a correct artistic taste. The possession of these qualities in a high degree by Mr. Scott, added to the business tact and ability of Mr. Stevens, the junior partner of the firm, amply accounts for the success which they have achieved in building up a trade and reputation, of which they may well feel proud.

J. W. Lamontagne, MERCHANT TAILOR, 1628 NOTRE DAME STREET, MONTREAL.—The citizens of Montreal are, as a rule, noted for their excellence in dress, and it is a recognized fact in all large communities, if not in every community, that to succeed in life either socially or in business, one must present an attractive appearance in dress and manners. There are many first-class houses engaged in the merchant tailoring line in Montreal, and among the number deserving of more than a mere passing notice in these pages, is that of Mr. J. W. Lamontagne, which is eligibly located at No. 1628 Notre Dame Street. The premises occupied, are 20 x 65 feet in dimensions, and are suitably arranged for the requirements of the trade. Here will be found a fine stock of imported and domestic cloths, woollens, tweeds, &c., of imported goods as well as domestic, in the latest and most fashionable patterns from which to select, which Mr. Lamontagne makes up to order on short notice, in suits or garments by measure in the highest style of the art, and which for elegance of cut, perfection of fit and richness of finish, together with moderate prices, are not surpassed by those of any other house in the city. Employment is furnished to thirteen skilled operators throughout the year. Mr. Lamontagne who is a native of Rivière du Loup, at present known as Louisville, is a practical cutter, and giving his personal attention to all orders entrusted to his care, can thus guarantee his customers the best of satisfaction. He established this business in 1867, and during the years that have passed since then, he has received his share of the public patronage.

 **Lanthier & Co.,** HATTERS AND FURRIERS, 1663 NOTRE DAME STREET, MONTREAL.—In a climate like this, furs are a prime necessary of life, without which comfort is simply unattainable by those  who venture out of doors in winter, particularly ladies, who, accustomed to warm rooms and protection from even the rough winds of spring and autumn, are illy calculated to brave the severe blasts of winter. Holding a prominent place among the hatters and furriers of Montreal, is the firm of Messrs. Lanthier & Co., whose establishment is located at No. 1663 Notre Dame Street. The premises occupied are large and commodious, consisting of three floors, 24 x 100 feet in dimensions. Here is contained a very large and elegant stock of

hats and caps in the latest and most fashionable styles, and of the best quality. The firm manufacture silk hats and pull-overs, which are equal to any imported. In furs, they carry constantly on hand, Russian Furs of the finest quality, personally selected; Royal Russian Sable, Ermine, &c., and Hudson Bay Furs, snowshoes, moccasins &c , &c. The firm manufacture every description of furs, for ladies and gentlemen's wear, both for stock and to order. The workmanship is the very best, and is not surpassed by any other house in the Dominion. The firm exhibited a line of their goods at the Centennial Exhibition in Philadelphia in 1876, and received First Prizes, although there were many exhibitors from all parts of the country. They also received Gold and Bronze Medals at other Exhibitions. Employment is furnished to thirty-five skilled hands and assistants throughout the year, in the several departments of the business. This business was established sixteen years ago, and has at all times proved eminently successful. The members of the firm are Messrs. F. X. Lanthier and A P. Belair, both of whom are Canadians by birth, and the latter gentleman is a member of the Board of Trade.

L. N. Denis, PAINTER, 299½ ST. LAWRENCE STREET.—Where the architect ends, the decorative painter commences, bestowing here some brilliant colors, there some soft predominating tint. It is his promise to modify the entire aspect of a house ; to render it attractive without grandness, and elegant without any pretentious effects. Plain white pine of wainscottings and doors assume, under the manipulations of the grainer, the appearance of fine natural hardwoods. One of the oldest established and most efficient house painters and decorators in this city is Mr. L. N. Denis, whose shop is located at No. 299½ St. Lawrence Main Street. The premises occupied being 25x72 feet in dimensions, with basement and a paint shop 45 x 80 feet in dimensions. There is carried in stock a line of shelf hardware paints, oils, varnish, putty, and wall papers of French, English and American manufacture, in the latest and most fashionable patterns. Mr. Denis attends to all kinds of house painting and decorating as well as paper hanging. The work he has done during the past fifteen or twenty years speaks for itself, being excellent in quality and artistic in design and effect, and it has been by his ability and business enterprise and perseverance that he has been enabled to build up his present extensive business. Mr. Denis conducts his business at both wholesale and retail, and gives employment to ten assistants and skilled workmen throughout the year. Mr. Denis, who is a native of Montreal, established his business here twenty-eight years ago and has earned a high reputation for honorable and liberal dealing. He is a member of the Chamber of Commerce.

T. Fraser, DEALER IN CHOICE GROCERIES, 184 BLEURY STREET, MONT-REAL.—To supply the requirements of the grocery trade all quarters of the earth are made to pay tribute. China and Japan, which at one time, and that not so very long ago either, supplied all the tea, but now India and Ceylon are pressing hard upon them and with a better flavored product. Our compliments came from the West and East Indies, Cuba and the South send their sugars and molasses, Java, Rio Mocha, etc., provide their aromatic coffees, the United States our canned goods, and England and the Mediterranean countries, the table delicacies, and so on. The trade is an extensive and important one. Among the old-established and prominent houses in the grocery trade in Montreal, is that of Mr.T. Fraser, which since the 1st of May of the present year has been located at No. 184 Bleury Street, and previous to that was at No. 1181 St. Catherine Street. The premises occupied by the business are 30 x 60 feet in dimensions and are tastefully fitted up, the large and excellent stock being displayed to the best advantage. The stock consists of the finest quality of fancy and staple groceries, also a prime line of provisions. Employment is furnished to four competent and courteous assistants throughout the year. This business was established twenty years ago by Mr. W. Fraser, brother of the present proprietor, who succeeded to the business eight years since. Mr. T. Fraser was born on Bleury Street, in this city, and is well and favorably known to a large circle of Montrealers, by whom he is held in the highest esteem.

Query Bros., PHOTOGRAPHERS, 10 St. Lambert Street.—Probably there is no art or business calling that has made such continuous progress, and arrived so near perfection during the past quarter of a century, as that of photography. The history of photography during the past twenty-five years is one replete with interest and shows to what an extent inventive genius has arrived during that time. Among the photographers worthy of particular mention in this work, is the firm of Messrs. Query Bros. whose studio is located at No. 10 St. Lambert Hill. Although these gentlemen only started in business, on their own account, on the 15th April of the present year, still they have had a lengthened practical experience in one of the best schools of photography in the Dominion, that of Notman & Co., of this city. Mr. P. A. Query having been with them for fourteen years and Mr. W. G. Query for nine years. During that time they gained a high reputation for their work, and what they have done since being on their own account proves that that reputation was well deserved. They do all kinds of photographic work, enlarging, copying, etc. Also crayon, India ink, water color, oil color and pastel work and guarantee their patrons the best of satisfaction in every case. Their studio and reception room are handsomely fitted up, and every accessory is at hand for the successful prosecution of the work, first-class cameras, back scenes for interiors and exteriors, and every modern improvement that has been made in the art, besides employing only the most skilled assistants. A visit to their studio will well repay all trouble.

The Montreal Moulding and Mirror Manufacturing Co.,

JAMES CUNNINGHAM, Managing Director, 594 Craig Street.—Montreal is fast increasing in extent and importance as a commercial and manufacturing centre, and from the recent advantages given to the port by the removal of the channel debt, and the doing away with tonnage dues, as well as the opening of the Sault Ste. Marie route, the prospects of the future are of the highest character. In a review of the various business interests of the city, mention must be made of the Montreal Moulding and Mirror Manufacturing Company, whose premises are located at No. 594 Craig Street. These premises consist of four floors, each 40 x 100 feet in dimensions, where employment is furnished to forty skilled and competent workmen in the manufacture of mouldings of every description, and also of mirrors. The work turned out by this house is of the very best quality, and is artistic in design and elegant in finish, and the goods have an active demand in the trade throughout the Dominion, where the trade extends. The business was established in 1877 by Messrs. Ewing & Co., who were succeeded in 1880 by Mr. James Cunningham, whose business increased to such an extent that he found it desirable to form a joint stock company, which was done on June 1st of the present year, the officers being Lucien Huot, President; James Cunningham, Managing Director; and C. Robertson, Secretary-Treasurer. All orders entrusted to this house will receive prompt attention, and the utmost satisfaction will be guaranteed in all cases.

F. Smith, PRACTICAL CABINET MAKER AND UPHOLSTERER, 2234 AND 2236 St. CATHERINE STREET, OPPOSITE QUEEN'S HALL BLOCK.—The business of the cabinet-maker and upholsterer is one of much importance in all civilized communities, where evidences of refinement and taste abound in our household surroundings. Montreal contains a number of first-class houses devoted to this branch of trade, among the number deserving of special mention, being that of Mr. F. Smith, whose warerooms are located at Nos. 2234 and 2236 St. Catherine Street, opposite Queen's Hall Block. The premises occupied are large and commodious, being 22 x 110 feet in dimensions, and which contain a fine stock of furniture of artistic design and elegantly upholstered, consisting of fine wire back and other, parlor sets, dining and other easy wire spring back and divan arm-chairs, library chairs, fancy chairs for needle-work, banner chairs, corner chairs, and all other kinds made to order and warranted of the best workmanship. Furniture, both plain and artistic is made to order, and drawings are made and submitted. Hair and other mattresses are made to order at short notice, and old mattresses are re-made and returned the same day. Window and bed draperies are made from the plainest to the most novel designs, as well as window and portiere curtains. Also all other branches of the cabinet-makers' and upholsterers' trade are attended to. Mr. Smith is an Englishman by birth, and is a skilled practical workman, and during the nine years he has been established in business here he has built up a large and ever increasing trade. Mr. Smith was foreman for Messrs. J. & W. Hilton, of this city, for 15 years.

Fred, Lapointe, FURNITURE DEALERS, No. 1447 St. CATHERINE STREET, MONTREAL.—Artistic culture, which has made such rapid strides among the people during the past fifteen years, has shown its good effects in the general surroundings of the people. In their homes, their conceptions of art and music, and even in their furniture and house decoration. The furniture manufacturing trade has kept abreast of this desire for the beautiful and the goods manufactured are elegant in design and finish, as compared with those of an earlier period. Holding a prominent place among those engaged in the furniture trade in Montreal, is Mr. Fred. Lapointe, whose establishment is located at No. 1447½ and 1449 St. Catherine Street. The premises occupied by the business are 45 x 88 feet in dimensions, and occupy four floors in front and three floors in rear. Mr. Lapointe carries a large and elegant stock of household furniture of the finest quality and beautifully designed, and upholstered parlor sets, bedroom sets, dining-room sets and other lines of furniture will here be found in various styles and in different woods, well made and finished. Employment is furnished to from forty to fifty skilled workmen on an average throughout the year. The business is conducted both at wholesale and retail. Mr. Lapointe, who is a native of this Province, and is a cabinet-maker by trade, founded his business eight years ago, and by untiring industry and perseverance and ability, he has met with well deserved success.

Chartrand & Bisson, ROOFERS, 147 St. CHARLES BORROMEE STREET.— The building trade of Montreal is one of its most important branches of business, and furnishes employment to a very large number of hands annually, besides occupying the attention of many of the most expert business men and extensive capitalists among her citizens. But it is more particularly with that department of building known as roofing with which we have now to deal. There are several first-class firms engaged in the roofing trade in this city, among which worthy of special mention is the old-established one of Chartrand and Bisson, which has seen over a century of usefulness and well-merited prosperity. Messrs. Chartrand and Bisson execute contracts for slate and gravel roofs, as well as in tin and rosin cement. A specialty is made of gravel roofs, and repairing of all kinds is promptly attended to. Specimens of their work may be seen all over the city, on many private as well as public buildings. Among the latter may be mentioned the Nazareth Asylum for the Blind on St. Catherine Street, and the new " Beaudry " block on the corner of St. Catherine and St. Charles Borromee Streets. The firm have always gone upon the principle of doing first class work only, hence their reputation A 1 in every particular. A staff of efficient workmen are employed and all orders received at the office, 147 St. Charles Borromee Street, or 483 Laval Avenue, the residence of Mr. Bisson will receive prompt attention. Both Messrs. Charles Chartrand and Frs. Bisson are natives of this Province. The former is a practical roofer and the latter is the business Manager of the concern, both are well and favorably known as active and energetic business men and progressive citizens.

E. Bellavance, 1887 St. Catherine Street, Montreal, Telephone No. 1701.—The marked progress made in Montreal during the past ten years has been something wonderful. Buildings have been erected on every side and new streets have sprung up as if by magic, and while the builders have taken an important part in this result the plumbers, gas and steam fitters, have also taken a prominent position in the result, for with defective plumbing, a building is worse than valueless, so that the plumber exercises a no less influence in the construction of a building than the builder himself. One of the leading houses in this city in this line of business is that of Mr. E. Bellavance, which is located at No. 1887 St. Catherine Street. This gentleman attends to every description of plumbing, gas and steam fitting, employing none but the best of skilled workmen and giving all orders his personal attention, he is thus enabled to guarantee his customers the best of satisfaction. He is also the patentee and manufacturer of the Bellavance Hot Water Boiler and Radiator, which was patented in 1886. It is made of cast-iron and has more heating surface and is easier to repair than any other boiler and radiator on the market. This furnace obtained the first prize and

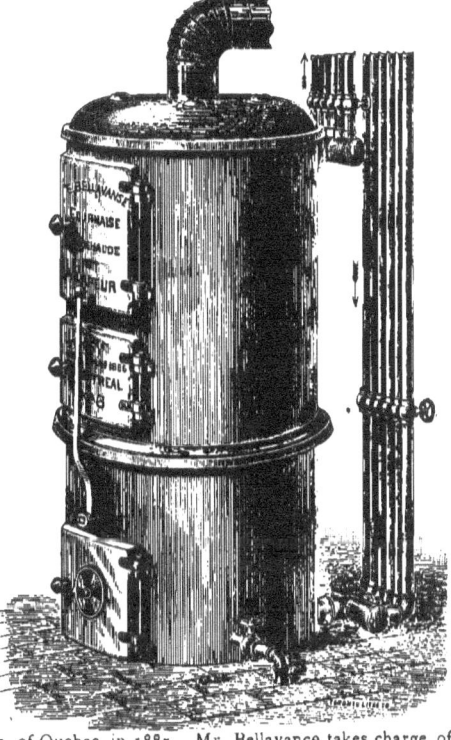

diploma at the Provincial Exhibition, of Quebec, in 1887. Mr. Bellavance takes charge of all work of placing them in churches, religious institutions, public edifices, private residences, nurseries, etc. These furnaces are made in eight different sizes with heating capacity of from 700 to 7000 feet, and are now being extensively used throughout the country.

S. Lachance, CHEMIST AND DRUGGIST, 1538, ST. CATHERINE, MONTRÉAL.—The profession of the chemist and druggist is one demanding deep study and ever careful attention for its successful prosecution, and it must be said that a very marked improvement has taken place in it during the past twenty or twenty-five years, owing to the high grade colleges of pharmacy that have been established in the Dominion. Holding a prominent place among the leading druggists of Montreal is Mr. S. Lachance, whose drug store is eligibly located at No. 1538 St. Catherine Street. The premises occupied are 22 x 50 feet in dimensions and present a beautiful appearance, being artistically fitted up, with plate glass show cases and cabinets for the advantageous display of the large and elegant stock of goods carried, consisting of fresh and pure drugs and chemicals ; medicines and proprietary remedies of acknowledged merit and standard reputation, elegant toilet requisites and fancy goods, physicians' supplies, druggist's sundries, etc., etc. An educated chemist and druggist, Mr. Lachance's prescription department is an important feature of his establishment, and the care, accuracy and skill with which physicians' prescriptions and family recipes are compounded, have gained for him the respect of the medical profession and the confidence of a numerous patronage. Mr. Lachance is a native of Quebec, and is a graduate of the Quebec Pharmaceutical Association and gives employment to six competent clerks and assistants and since he established his business nine years ago he has built up an excellent trade and a high and enviable reputation. Among the special remedies prepared by Mr. Lachance are Dr. Seys' Remedy, the Great French Specific for dyspepsia, and indigestion. " Indigenous Bitters " a most valuable remedy for all disorders of the stomach, loss of appetite, etc. Also the " Father Matthew Remedy " for intemperance, most highly recommended by the medical fraternity and philanthropists all over the Continent of America. Mr. Lachance possesses the sole right for the manufacture of this article in Canada and the United States, having factories for this purpose at Montreal and Rouses Point, N. Y.

M. Saxe, MERCHANT TAILOR, Nos. 1372, 1480 AND 1502 ST. CATHERINE STREET.—It is almost marvellous to contemplate the magnitude which the ready-made clothing trade has attained during the past quarter of a century, when compared with the limit to which it was circumscribed previous to that time. Probably no business has had a more rapid and healthful growth, and this must be largely ascribed to the enterprise and efforts of those long connected with the business. Among the old-established and prominent houses engaged in this line in the city, is that of Mr. Michael Saxe, whose three stores are located at Nos. 1372, 1480, and 1502 St. Catherine Street, the first named being the property of Mr. Saxe. This business was established twenty-two years ago, and during that time it has met with very gratifying success and has steadily advanced in extent and importance from year to year. Mr. Saxe manufactures clothing for men youths and boys in all sizes, and in the latest and most fashionable styles, from the best quality of materials, while the workmanship is all that could possibly be desired. A specialty of the business is the merchant tailoring department, where those desiring can have their suits made up to order, by measure, on short notice and in the very best possible manner, being guaranteed perfect fitting, beautiful in style and elegant in finish. Employment is furnished to a large staff of assistants and skilled operators in the different departments of the business throughout the year. Mr. Saxe is a wide-awake, active and progressive business man, and thoroughly understanding all the demands of the public in the matter of clothing, is ever ready to meet their requirements. Mr. Saxe's long and prosperous business career marks him out as one of the most substantial merchants in the clothing trade in the city, both financially and otherwise.

W. F. Beck & Co., CHINA, CROCKERY AND GLASSWARE, 1509 ST. CATHERINE STREET.—The number and character of the houses which represent the commercial interests of Montreal, show plainly the importance of the city as a purchasing centre. A large section of the surrounding country, as well as her own inhabitants naturally seek supplies here, and the demand has been amply provided for by the enterprise of her merchants. In this connection, mention must be made of the important trade in china, crockery and glassware, in which line of business there are many first-class houses engaged, and among the number deserving of more than a passing mention is that of W. F. Beck & Co., whose store is located at No. 1509 St. Catherine Street. The stock of goods carried here is very large and varied in its character and of the best quality, embracing almost everything in the line required for household use, many of the designs being extremely artistic and beautiful. Employment is furnished to four competent assistants throughtout the year, who take pleasure in showing goods to customers at all times. Mr. W F. Beck, the proprietor, is a native of England, and established this business in Montreal thirteen years ago. From his lengthened experience in this branch of trade, and the enterprise and energy he displays in the conducting of his business may be attributed the gratifying success that has attended his efforts during his business career.

Edmond Leonard, CHEMIST AND DRUGGIST, 113 ST. LAWRENCE MAIN STREET.—The profession of the pharmacist is one that has kept steady pace with the improvements of the times, not alone in medicine, but also in science and the arts. To enter the profession of pharmacy now-a-days, one must have given this subject deep study, and passed a critical examination in some regular college, established for this special purpose, and thus strong safeguards are thrown around the public. Among those who have recently entered upon the practice of this profession in this city, is Mr. Edmond Leonard, whose store is located at No. 113 St. Lawrence Main Street. This business was formerly conducted by Messrs. Laviolette & Nelson, for three years preceeding the first of March of the present year, when they were succeeded by the present proprietor. The premises occupied, are 20 x 55 in dimensions, and are tastefully fitted up with plate glass show-cases, &c. Here is carried a large stock of fresh and pure drugs, and chemicals, fancy and toilet articles, imported and domestic perfumes, soaps, &c., proprietary medicines of acknowledged merit and standard reputation, druggists' sundries, &c. A specialty is made of the compounding of physicians' prescriptions, and family recipes, with care and promptness and at reasonable prices. Employment is furnished to two competent assistants, and of whom is a regular graduated pharmacist. Mr. Edmond Leonard, the proprietor, is a native of Montreal, and is a graduate of the Pharmaceutical Association of the Province of Quebec. He is highly esteemed by all who know him, as a careful and conscientious pharmacist, and a gentleman of marked business ability.

E. A. Gerth, IMPORTER HAVANA CIGARS, PIPES AND FANCY GOODS, 2235 St. Catherine Street.—Sir Walter Raleigh could not possibly have had any idea when he introduced tobacco into Europe, of the tremendous extent to which the soothing weed would be utilized.   In Montreal alone, the value of manufactured tobacco annually amounts to $1,637,403 ; wages to the amount of $392,279 are paid, and employment is furnished to no less than 2300 employees. Prominent among the stores engaged in the retail tobacco trade in this city, is that of Mr. E. A. Gerth, which is eligibly located at No. 2235 St. Catherine Street, in the Queen's Hall Block. The premises occupied by the business are 28 x 30 feet in dimensions, which are tastefully fitted up with plate glass show-cases and cabinets, etc., and a fine stock is carried of Havana and domestic cigars, tobaccos, smoking and chewing, cigarettes and a full line of smokers' articles of the best quality and of great variety, meerschaum pipes, briar pipes, cigar and cigarette holders, cigar cases, tobacco pouches, and many other articles too numerous to mention in detail. Mr. Gerth, who is an American by birth, is a thorough-going and enterprising man of business, and since he established his business here, six years ago, he has met with a liberal share of the public patronage, which has been entirely deserved.

A. M. Allan & Co., MERCHANT TAILORS, 218 St. James Street.—The character and volume of patronage accorded a business man, is a sure test of his merits, and prominent among those concerning whom this is a sure criterion, is the firm of Messrs. A. M. Allan & Co., of the St. James Street Tailoring Emporium, which is located at No. 218 St. James Street. The premises occupied by the business are large and commodious, being 28 x 80 feet in dimensions, and are fitted up with very great taste and are well adapted to the purpose for the proper display of the splendid assortment of the choicest imported fabrics, fine cloths and suitings, English, Scotch, and Irish tweeds, pants' patterns, etc., etc. Messrs. A. M. Allan & Co. have achieved an enviable reputation for the accuracy of fit, perfection of finish, and stylish elegance of all garments leaving their establishment. They bring to bear a judgment, taste, and ability rarely equalled, while their facilities for the prompt fulfillment of all orders—suits being made to order in twelve hours if required—are unsurpassed, employing as they do from forty to fifty skilled operators and assistants. The trade of this house is very extensive, reaching as it does throughout the Dominion and even to British Columbia. The firm name of A. M. Allan & Co. is well and favorably known throughout the country and particularly in Montreal for the past sixteen years, Mr. A. M. Allan being one of the city's most active and enterprising young business men.

L. J. A. Surveyer, DEALER IN HOUSE FURNISHINGS, &c., No. 1588 Notre Dame Street.—Desiring to record for the benefit of the public generally, and business men particularly, the present growth and development of Montreal's commercial and manufacturing interests, we notice in these pages, those houses that are truly representative of their class, of each particular branch of business. In the house furnishing, and builder's hardware trade, we can mention no worthier establishment than that of Mr. L. J. A. Surveyer, which is located at No. 1588 Notre Dame Street, opposite west end of Court House. The premises occupied are very extensive, consisting of a four-storey building, 35 x 100 feet in dimensions, and a warehouse in rear, for the storage of goods. This may well be called a " Novelty Hardware Store," for the stock is so varied in character, and so extensive, consisting as it does of house furnishings, stoves, refrigerators, iron bedsteads, cutlery and electro-plated ware, as well as a carefully selected stock of builder's hardware of the very best quality, also lace curtain stretchers, and the "Patent Can Creamer." Buying in large quantities from first hands, and manufacturers at home and abroad, Mr. Surveyer obtains the best terms, and is thus enabled to offer the trade and general public, advantages not easily to be duplicated. He is also sole agent for the city, for the "Leonard Dry Air Refrigerator," "Geer's Patent Single and Double Acting Spring Beds," extensively used in the United States and Canada, and many other useful articles in the house-furnishing line, too numerous to mention.

Narcisse Beaudry, WATCHMAKER AND JEWELLER, 1580 NOTRE DAME, MONTREAL.—In all civilized countries of the earth and in prosperous communities, the business of the jeweller has been an important one and has given a true indication of the relative prosperity of the people. Workers in gold and silver, and other precious metals, have plied their trade for centuries before the Christian era, a love of the beautiful in nature and art being inherent in human nature. The watchmaking and jewellery trade is conducted upon a large scale in Montreal, and one of the oldest established houses in this line is that of Mr. Narcisse Beaudry. which is located at No. 1580 Notre Dame Street. The business was founded in the year 1832 by Mr. L. P. Boivin, who conducted it alone for many years, and then associated with him Mr. Beaudry, (brother of the present proprietor.) under the firm title of Boivin & Beaudry. Mr. Narcisse Beaudry, succeeded to the business ten years ago. The house has had a long, honorable and prosperous career, and the different proprietors have held a high reputation for straightforward and honorable dealing. The premises occupied are 22 x 40 feet in dimensions, and are very handsomely fitted up with plate-glass showcases and cabinets for the advantageous display of the elegant stock carried, consisting of gold and silver English, Swiss and American watches. Jewellery of every description of beautiful designs and exquisite finish, silver plated-ware, a specialty, being made of optical goods and the filling of optician's prescriptions. Mr. Beaudry manufactures all kinds of jewellery and attends to watch repairing with promptness, giving employment to six courteous assistants and skilled workmen. Mr. Beaudry is a native of Berthierville, and is a member of the Chamber of Commerce.

Dr. A. Thibeault, DRUGGIST, No. 1244 NOTRE DAME STREET, EAST, MONTREAL.—The profession of the pharmacist is one of deep importance to the public generally, as well equally as that of the doctor. Where both professions are combined in one individual practising the pharmaceutical profession, then, of course, the importance of the position is relatively enhanced. Dr. A. Thibeault, whose drug store is located at No. 1244 Notre Dame Street, has been a practitioner of medicine for twenty two years, and is a graduate of the Victoria College. He established his business as a druggist twelve years ago, having graduated from the Quebec Pharmaceutical Association, and is therefore doubly qualified for his position. The premises occupied by the business are 20 x 40 feet in dimensions, and are tastefully fitted up and contain an excellent stock of fresh fine drugs, chemicals, fancy and toilet articles, imported and domestic soaps, perfumes, etc., etc., proprietory medicines of acknowledged merit and standard reputation, druggists' sundries, and such articles as are required by physicians in their practice. A specialty of the business is the compounding of physicians' prescriptions and difficult *formula*, with promptness and care at moderate prices. Dr. Thibeault is a native of Longueuil, and is a gentleman who has won many friends in professional and social circles. and is considered a painstaking, and conscientious pharmacist and physician.

Viau & Bro., MANUFACTURERS OF BISCUITS, CONFECTIONERY AND PREPARED FLOUR, 1288 AND 1292 NOTRE DAME, MONTREAL.—The city of Montreal, among its varied and numerous industries, boasts one of the most extensive manufactories of biscuits and confectionery in the province,—that of Messrs. Viau & Brother, whose elegant four story and basement building at Nos. 1288, 1290, 1292 and 1294 Notre Dame Street, is worthy of special mention. The building is 85 x 104 feet in dimensions, and is fully equipped with the latest and most improved patent machinery for the manufacture of biscuits and confectionery, and which is operated by a fifty horse-power steam engine, while employment is furnished to eighty skilled and competent workmen throughout the year, in the several departments. The firm manufacture every description of biscuits and confectionery from the cheapest to the best that can be found in the market. This firm has the advantage over other houses in a decreased cost of manufacture, and consequently being enabled to place their goods upon the market at lower figures, for same quality of goods than their competitors, from the fact that Mr. Viau owns a farm of 700 acres at Maisonneuve and Longue Point, where he has thirty cows whose milk is received daily and is used in the manufacture of their biscuits. The milk being fresh and pure, the quality of the goods made from it is consequently enhanced. They also use the potatoes raised for the same purpose, and the hay and other products are all used in their business, for feeding their twenty horses, etc. The firm have been awarded first prizes at the Exhibitions in Montreal and Quebec in 1877, 1880 and 1881, for their biscuits, and first prize at the Exhibition in 1881 awarded by a jury of chemists on the strength of their analysis of the prepared flour. The firm manufacture self-raising flour and bread, and as proprietors of the Colonial Company manufacture chocolates of every description. The output of the house averages $250,000 a year, the trade extending throughout the Province of Quebec. This business was established in 1867 by Messrs. Viau & Viger, and for fifteen years it has been conducted under the present firm title of Viau & Brother. Mr. Charles T. Viau is a native of Longueuil and is a member of the Montreal Board of Trade.

J. D. White & Co., GROCERS, 2206 ST. CATHERINE STREET.—In a review of the various business industries and manufactures of Montreal, the grocery trade comes in for a large share of attention, on account of the extensive nature of its operations and the important position it holds with regard to the requirements of the people. Among those prominently identified with this branch of trade, is the firm of Messrs. J. D. White & Co., whose establishment is located at No. 2206 St. Catherine Street. The premises occupied by the business are spacious and tastefully arranged, being 28 x 80 feet in dimensions. Here is carried a very large and comprehensive stock of fancy and staple groceries of every description and of the very best quality, including the finest brands of teas and coffees, pure spices, hermetically sealed goods, table delicacies, sugars, etc. Messrs. J. D. White & Co. succeeded to the business of Cooke, White & Co. in January of the present year, the latter firm having been established three years ago. Messrs. White & Co. have secured the co-operation of several well-known firms in several lines of trade, such as dry goods, drugs, tobaccos, stationery, etc., etc., who are prepared to supply the country trade with anything in their line, through Messrs. White & Co., at lowest prices. In persons, out of town, this is a great convenience; and, even for those residing in the city, it is a matter of time-saving import, and should be taken advantage of. Mr. White was formerly with the Co-operative Supply Association, of this city, and he has retained many of their old customers, who send their orders to him for goods from all parts of the country. Employment is furnished to twelve employees throughout the year steadily, in conducting the operations of the extensive business. The members of the firm are Messrs. J. D. White and Edward Mansfield, both of whom are too well and favorably known in trade and social circles to require any personal notice at our hands.

GRAND TRUNK RAILWAY STATION, ERECTED 1888.

Tees & Co., THE DESK MAKERS, 300 ST. JAMES STREET, MONTREAL.—When the City of Montreal of to-day, is compared with the Montreal of forty years ago, and the wonderful transformation that has taken place is considered, it must be conceded that if the opportunities now offered to the city to grasp the trade coming, not alone from our own west and North West, but also the North-Western States by way of the Sault Sainte Marie Railroad and the Canadian Pacific Railroad, simply by improving our harbor facilities, is extremely reasonable. Montreal of the past was fortunate in the character of many of her citizens, and in the many sterling examples of thrift and enterprise they have given for the example and emulation of others. Some of those men are in business still and of the number must be mentioned Mr. David Tees, senior member of the well known firm of Tees & Co., desk makers and funeral undertakers. Mr. Tees founded this business in 1855 and from a comparatively small beginning he has built it up step by step to its present extensive proportion. The premises occupied consist of office and warehouse and undertaking rooms at No. 300 St. James Street, which consists of four floors 80x40 feet in dimensions. The business offices are in front on the first floor, with the coffin and casket rooms in rear, arranged in the most improved style with lowering cabinets thus keeping the caskets out of sight and free from dust until required to be exhibited. The factory is located on Dowd Street, and is a 2 story structure 48x80 feet and is fitted up with all the latest and most improved wood working machinery and appliances. The firm are extensive manufacturers of office furniture, railroad, bank and office desks, revolving bookcases, parlor and library cabinets, also wood carpet, parquet and inlaid floors, of parquet floors it may be said that they add materially to the sightliness of a room, for they imply either the absence of carpets, or carpets square or oblong, that are complete designs in themselves and only cover a portion of the floor, or with or without these the use of rugs with other brilliant contrasting and usually harmonius colors. The richer interior of recent times have encouraged this art which has existed for centuries in Europe. Those manufactured by Messrs. Tees & Co., are beautiful in design, and rich in color of the natural woods. The firm are also the sole manufacturers of metallic burial cases in the Dominion. Messrs. Tees & Co., give employment to 50 skilled and capital hands in the different departments of the business. They are considered among the leading funeral directors in the city, and provide every miner requisite for funerals of every grade. Mr. David Tees, the senior member of the firm, is a Montrealer by birth and is a practical cabinet-maker and for years worked at the bench until his services became more valuable in looking after the management of his ever increasing business. His son, Mr. William Tees is also a native of Montreal, and visits Europe frequently on business for the house. At the recent Colonial Exhibition held in London England, Mr. Wm. Tees assumed charge of the firms exhibit, and received very flattering notices from the British Press. And more substantial evidence of the popularity of their Desks and Revolving Bookcases in the shape of 320 orders their patrons coming from all parts of Europe. Mr. Tees is a member of the Board of Trade and well known in business circles.

C. B. Lanctot, CHURCH BRONZES, GOLD AND SILVER PLATED WARE, 1664 NOTRE DAME STREET, MONTREAL.—The business that is done in church ornaments, statues, vestments and other religious goods in Montreal is very extensive, and there are a number of first-class houses engaged in this particular line of business. Prominent among the number and deserving of honorable mention in a work of this character, is the house of

D

Mr. C. B. Lanctot, which is located at No. 1664 Notre Dame Street. The premises occupied by the business are extensive, consisting of two floors, each 28 x 100 feet in dimensions. Here is contained a magnificent stock of goods admirably displayed, and consisting of church bronzes, gold and silver plated ware, says, merinos, ecclesiastical vestments, statues, oil paintings, stations of the cross, banners, flags, and all kinds of society regalias. The goods carried are elegant in description and are are not surpassed by those of any other house in the Dominion. Mr. Lanctot imports a great deal of his stock direct from France, and manufactures statues, stations of the cross, banners, flags and society regalia of every description in the highest style of the art. This house was established 12 years ago and the business ever since the date of its inception has been steadily increasing until at the present day it extends throughout the Dominion, Newfoundland and the United States. Employment is furnished to 20 clerks and skilled workers during the year in the different departments. Mr. Lanctot is a native of Three Rivers and is a member of the Chamber of Commerce. He has had many years experience in the church ornament and religious goods business and therefore thoroughly understands the business in all its details. He has associated with him Mr. Albert Gauthier, who is financial manager of the house, and to whose energy and ability much of the success of the establishment is due.

J. M. Fortier, CIGAR MANUFACTURER, 143, 145, 147, 149 AND 151 ST. MAURICE STREET.—According to recent statistics it was found that the people of the United States spent during the course of a year $206,500 000 for cigars and smoking tobaccos, and of this amount $180,000,000 was for cigars alone. Taking it at the ratio of population Canada would figure up nearly $18,000,000 for cigars. This will give some idea of the extent and importance of this one branch of trade. One of the most important houses in this line of manufacture in the Dominion is that of Mr. J. M. Fortier, proprietor of the "Crême de la Crême" cigar factory, which is located at Nos. 143, 145, 149 and 151 St. Maurice Street. The premises occupied by the factory consist of a substantial three story stone structure, 94 x 75 feet in dimensions, wherein about 350 hands are given steady employment throughout the year in the manufacture of cigars, the principal and favorite brands being known throughout the Dominion as "Crême de la Crême," ' Canvas Back," " Noisy Boys," and "Bill Nye." These are well known to the trade and smoking public throughout the length and breadth of the land for their excellent quality and unsurpassed flavor. Mr. Fortier personally visits Havana every year and makes his own selections of tobacco, which upon their arrival in this city, on their route from the cars to the factory, give one an idea that they were in Havana or some other large tobacco centre from the immense number of bales piled up on the numerous Grand Trunk lorries. The business was established here in 1878, and its rapid growth since that time has been certainly wonderful, but at the same time eminently well deserved. Mr. Fortier is a Montrealer by birth and is possessed of all those business and executive qualities so essential to success.

Wilson, Paterson & Co., IMPORTERS OF NAVAL STORES, 5 CUSTOM SQUARE, WAREHOUSE 36 AND YOUNG STREET, MONTREAL.—Holding a prominent position among the important importing houses in this city, is the well known firm of Messrs. Wilson, Paterson & Co., whose office is located at No. 5 Custom House Square, with warehouse at Nos. 36 and 38 Young Street. This firm are heavy importers of naval stores, East India goods, such as cocoanut oil, citronella oil, castor oil, gum copal, gum damar, gum shellac, plumbago, jute cuttings and other goods of a similar nature. They make a specialty of linseed oil and also import largely of chemicals, and general merchandise. They represent the Lehigh Valley Coal Company, doing an extensive business in their coals throughout the country. The members of the firm in this city are Messrs. John T. Wilson and W. S. Paterson, both of whom are well known in business circles and are active members of the Board of Trade, and Mr. R. W. Paterson of New York. The New York house does business at No. 154 Front

Street, under the firm name of Paterson, Downing & Co., in naval stores, and Kundson, Paterson & Co., in East India produce. The firm have also branch houses in Brunswick. Ga. Savannah, Ga. Charleston, S. C. Wilmington, N. C. and Mobile, Ala. Buying in large quantities from producers in the East Indies and in Europe, the firm are enabled to offer the trade advantages difficult to be found elsewhere in the form of best quality goods and bottom prices. The firm have had a long and honorable career and the house has earned a high reputation for straight forward, honorable and liberal dealing.

La Banque du Peuple, S. Bousquet, Cashier, 97 St. James Street,—Upon the solidity of the banking institutions of the country, and their ability to meet the requirements of trade and commerce, depends the prosperity of the country at large, and of the different towns and cities that are units of the same. In reviewing, therefore, the different monetary institutions of Montreal, special mention must be made of the old established and well known La Banque du Peuple, whose head office is located at No. 97 St. James Street. It is over half a century since this business was incepted by Messrs. Viger, DeWitt & Co., who founded a banking house in this city in the year 1835 with a special view of being of benefit to the French Canadian business men. Their enterprise met with success and grew to such proportions that in 1845 a joint stock company was founded under the above mentioned title, receiving a royal charter for the same. The presidents of the bank, from the date of its inception as such, were Hon. Louis Viger, Jacob DeWitt, Hon. F. A. Quesnel, H. B. Smith, John Pratt, C. S. Cherrier, and at the present time the chair is ably filled by Jacques Grenier Esq., a gentleman deeply interested in the business and financial interests of the city, J. S. Bosquet Esq. is the very efficient Cashier, and attends to his duties in the most satisfactory manner, being an able financier. The paid up capital of the bank is $1.200.000 with a reserve fund of $300.000. The following are the branches of the bank in the Province :—Quebec, E. C. Barrow, Manager ; St. Roch, Quebec, P. B. Dumoulin, Managar ; Three Rivers, P. E. Panneton, Manager ; St. Johns, P. Beaudoin, Manager. Agencies :—St. Remi, C. Bedard, agent ; St. Jerome, A. T. Theberge, agent. Foreign Agents :—London, England, The Alliance Bank, (Limited.) ; New York, National Bank of the Republic. The bank conducts a general banking business upon a liberal yet at the same time solid and conservative basis.

James Baylis & Son, CARPETS, 1837 Notre Dame Street, Montreal.— During the past 15 years at least a most marked improvement has taken place in household decoration, not alone in matters of art furniture, papering, printing and glass staining, but also in carpets, oil cloths curtains, rugs and mattings. The designs in these latter articles are most beautiful and artistic, rich in color and with an oriental luxuriousness of appearance. One of the most prominent houses engaged in the wholesale and retail carpet trade in the Dominion is that of Messrs. James Baylis & Son, which is located at No. 1837 Notre Dame street. The premises occupied are large and commodious, consisting of 5 floors each 25 x 100 feet in dimensions. These are replete with a large and most elegant stock of carpets consisting of Brussels, Tapestries, Wiltons, and through all the grades, from the richest and most elaborate drawing room carpets to the plainest and cheapest. The display of rugs is superb and the Orient seems to have given up its treasures, Persia and Turkey being well represented. In some of our more palatial residences of the present day there appears to be a growing taste for parquetry floors, relieved by Oriental rugs which give an excellent effect. There are also fine lines of mattings, mats, oil cloths of English and American manufacture, as well as window shades, curtains, window poles, and other lines of house furnishings. The stock carried by this house is one of the largest and richest in the country and is received direct from some of the leading looms in Europe. The trade of the house extends throughout the Dominion and is very extensive in its operations. This business was established in 1859 and has had a long, honorable and prosperous career. The members of the firm Mr. James Baylis and his son Mr. S. M. Baylis are well known in business and social circles throughout the country.

Great Western Lock and Gun Shop, 83, 85 AND 87 INSPECTOR STREET, MONTREAL. R. DUNCAN, PROPRIETOR, ESTABLISHED 1869.—It is only in large business centres that the different lines of trade and commercial interests are fully represented and the conveniences of modern life secured, Montreal is well favored in this respect for her manufacturing and business interests are many and varied. The history of lock making is an interesting one and a collection of the different devices that have been made in all ages and in different countries for securing doors or receptacles, would be highly instructive and mark the progress of civilization. One of the best known lock and gun smiths in this city is Mr. R. Duncan, proprietor of the Great Western Lock and Gun Shop, which is located at No. 87 Inspector street. It is now 19 years since this gentleman established his business and during that time he has not only built up an excellent trade but a very high reputation as a skilful workman. The premises occupied by the business are 20 x 40 feet in dimensions and are neatly arranged. The assortment of keys carried here one would think should unlock all the locks in Christendom. Mr. Duncan does all branches of locksmithing, manufacturing, repairing, picking locks, etc., etc. There is carried in stock a fine assortment of revolvers and breech loading arms as well as cartridges in all sizes. He also attends to all kinds of gunsmithing in the most satisfactory manner and makes a specialty of stocking and mounting, executing all orders with promptness. He gives employment to 3 skilled and capable assistants throughout the year. Mr. Duncan is a native of the North of Ireland and is a thoroughly skilled, practical lock and gunsmith and thus, giving his personal attention to all orders can guarantee his customers the most satisfactory results. He is the inventor and manufacturer of the alarm drawer with combination locks which has been found so useful in business houses. He does letter cutting in all its branches, grinds skates and all other descriptions of fancy jobbing to order.

E. C. Landon, PHOTOGRAPHIC "DRY PLATES," 643 CRAIG STREET, MONTREAL.—The photographer's art has made most wonderful improvement during the past quarter of a century, and during that time not a year has passed that some important invention has not been made in apparatus that has worked wonders in the *modus operandi* of the profession and brought the art up to a high state of perfection. Among those prominently engaged in the photographic supply business in this city deserving of honorable mention, is Mr. E. G Landon, whose establishment is located at No. 643 Craig street in King's Block. This business was established here 6 years ago and ever since the time of its inception it has met with the most pronounced success, steadily increasing in extent and importance from year to year. The premises occupied are 22 x 65 feet in dimensions, occupying 2 flats which are stocked with an exhibit of photographic goods of every description, imported and domestic, such as perhaps no other house in the Dominion can show, embracing full lines of photographic apparatus, materials, cameras, dry plates, chemicals in short everything relating to the art. Mr. Landon has made a special study of the manufacture of dry plates, his goods having an excellent reputation all over the Dominion, and they are standard in the Photographic Market wherever introduced. This depot of supplies can fit out a complete photographic studio down to the most insignificant item, ready for business, within twenty-four hours. Everything handled by the house is guaranteed as represented, while its reputation for promptitude and reliability is established and secure. Mr. Landon is a Canadian by birth, and is a practical photographer and thus is well qualified to understand the requirements of the trade.

John T. Lyons, DRUGGIST, COR. CRAIG AND BLEURY STREETS.—That there were some good druggists even in Shakespeare's time may be inferred from the fact that discon- solate Romeo after taking the fatal draught, exclaimed " O, true apothecary ! thy drugs are quick." Great changes, however have taken place in the profession of Pharmacy even dur- ing the past quarter of a century, and the pharmacist of the present day, must be a man of culture and deep study in his profession. Mr. John T. Lyons, whose drug store is eligibly located for business at the corner of Craig and Bleury Streets, succeeded to the business formerly conducted by Mr. W. H. Chapman, on the 15th November 1886. Mr. Lyons, who is a native of Quebec city, is a gentleman of marked business ability, push and energy, and is a graduate and gold medalist of the Pharmaceutical Association of Quebec. The prem- ises occupied by the business are 24x50 feet in dimensions and are tastefully fitted up with plate glass show cases, cabinets etc., for the advantageous display of the elegant stock car- ried, and having large plate glass windows facing on Craig and Bleury Streets, the store has a bright and enticing appearance. The large stock carried consists of fresh and pure drugs, chemicals, fancy and toilet articles, imported and domestic soaps, perfumes etc., proprietary medicines of acknowledged merit and standard reputation as well as druggists sundries of every description. A specialty is made of the compounding of physicians prescriptions and difficult formulæ, with promptness and at moderate prices. Employment is furnished to 2 competent and courteous assistants. Since Mr. Lyons has been in business here he has established an excellent reputation as a careful and conscientious pharmacist.

J. O. Wisner & Co., MANUFACTURERS OF AGRICULT- URAL IMPLEMENTS, BRANTFORD, D. F. REAUME, AGENT, 121 COLLEGE STREET.—The Nine- teenth Century has been one of the most wonderful of all cen- turies in the history of the world. Man's ingenuity has been exercised to the highest degree and the result has been that space has been annihilated by the electric telegraph, people converse readily together and their voices are distinguished many miles apart, factories, stores, residences and streets are illuminated by electricity, and machines are made to take the place of from ten to thirty persons at seed time and harvest upon the farms of the country, and that more perfectly than by hand. There are a number of large agricultural implement manufacturing estab- lishments in this country, among the number deserving of special mention in a work of this character being that of Messrs. J. O. Wisner, Sons & Co., of Brantford, Ont. This firm has earned a high reputation throughout the Dominion for the efficiency and excellent quality of their machines, which have taken numerous prizes and diplomas at the different exhibitions and fairs. They manufacture the Wisner Seeders, Tedders, Rakes, Harrows, Cultivators, &c., which are pronounced second to none in the country They have had a branch establishment in this city for the past three years, which has been presided over by Mr. D. F. Reaume for that length of time, and that gentleman has been highly instrumental in building up an excellent trade throughout this province,—a trade that is steadily increas- ing from year to year. Mr. Reaume is a native of Essex County, Ont., and is a gentleman eminently qualified for the position he now holds, on account of his ability and business enterprise.

J. J. Duffy & Co., COFFEE AND SPICE MERCHANTS, CANADA MILLS, 624 CRAIG STREET, MONTREAL.—The coffee tree is a native of Arabia Felix, and Ethiopia, and was first brought to the notice of Europeans by Ranwolfins, in 1573. The Dutch were the first to experiment in transplanting it, which they did successfully at Amsterdam and from there the gardens of the East Indies and Europe were furnished. Its use was prohibited in Syria and also in Turkey as it was alleged that the mosques were deserted and the coffee houses crowded, to the detriment of religion. This was in the early days of its introduction but now it is extensively used in Turkey as well as in Europe and this continent. The firm of Messrs. J. J. Duffy & Co., coffee and spice merchants, proprietors of the Canada Coffee and Spice Mills, of No. 624 Craig street deal extensively in this aromatic and fragrant product and are very successful in its preparation, the roasting process being one requiring great skill and care to preserve the aroma of the bean. The business of the firm was established in 1869 the present firm succeeding Messrs. W. A. Campbell & Co., ten years ago. The premises occupied by the business are large and commodious and are fully equipped with all the necessary appliances, there being 6 mills and 2 roasters, while employment is furnished to 10 skilled and competent hands. Besides coffees and all kinds of spices the firm are manufacturers of the celebrated "The Cook's Favorite" baking powder for which a silver medal was awarded at the Dominion Exhibition in 1884, and again a gold medal and diploma for same goods at Provincial Exhibition in 1887, also Duffy's mustards, for which two diplomas were awarded. A specialty of their business is the manufacture of steam cooked pease meal or flour and for this they were awarded a diploma and bronze medal. The trade of the house is very extensive and embraces the entire Dominion while a large export trade is transacted in steam cooked pease meal and baking powders and mustard. Mr. J. J. Duffy, is a Canadian by birth and a member of the Board of Trade. The house is a representative one in its line and bears a widespread and honorable record.

Geo. W. Reed, SLATE METAL AND GRAVEL ROOFER, 783 & 785 CRAIG STREET. MONTREAL.—Montreal may well lay claim to being the Metropolis of Canada; not only on account of being at the head of ocean navigation and the shipping point for the great grain trade of the West and North West, but also on account of its large business and manufacturing interests. In this, as in all other communities, there are some houses in their particular lines that occupy a prominent position, and are therefore worthy of being classed as representatives. Such a house is that of Mr. George W. Reed, Slater, Metal and gravel Roofer, whose establishment is at Nos. 783 & 785 Craig Street. Mr. Reed, who is a native of New Hampshire, started in business here in the year 1852, and possessed of the American energy and enterprise, by close attention to and thorough execution of his work made a success of his business and secured the confidence of the public. The premises occupied by the business consists of 3 stories and attic, 45 x 85 feet in dimensions. These are used for warerooms. offices and manufactory, and are fully equipped with every requisite for the successful prosecution of the Roofing business, employment being given to about 80 skilled workmen. Mr. Reed does all kinds of roofing, such as slate and metal, pitch, felt and gravel. Reed's Rosin-Cement Roofing is known as one of the best of compositions for flat roofs. &c. He also deals in and supplies the trade with all kinds of roofing materials. He is a manufacturer of and dealer in refrigerators, oil cabinets, coal scuttles, coal sifters, slop pails, and all descriptions of tinware; while galvanized iron cornices, skylights and chimney tops are manufactured to any design. He also deals in slate, and marbleized slate mantles, and grates, table tops, fire walls, shelves, ventilators, registers, &c. Keeping constantly on hand a large assortment of Canadian and American slate of the first quality; also slate nails, zinc, lead, &c., &c. Mr. Reed is a skilled practical roofer, and worked at it from his boyhood days until his increasing business required his personal attention to the supervision and management of its affairs.

N. E. Hamilton & Co., STAPLE AND FANCY DRY GOODS, 1888 AND 1890 NOTRE DAME STREET WEST, (GLENORA BUILDINGS.) MONTREAL.—Holding a prominent place among the leading dry-good houses in this city is that of Messrs. N. E. Hamilton & Co., whose splendid establishment is eligibly located for business in the beautiful Glenora Buildings, Nos. 1888 and 1890 Notre Dame Street. The premises occupied are large and commodious, and are fitted up in modern style, the ceilings being high and the front almost entirely of plate glass, while light is also admitted from windows in the rear and centre, so that the entire place has a light and cheery appearance and the elegant stock of goods is shown to the best advantage. The premises consist of three floors about 45 x 190 feet in dimensions, while the upper floor extends over the adjoining store. The main floor is devoted to the general dry-goods department; the second floor to mantle department; and the ground is utilized as the dress-making and mantle making department, also for the storage of reserve stock and for the packing department. An elevator takes customers from one flat to the other as they may require. The stock carried is very large, is specially imported, and consists of the finest qualities of staple and fancy dry-goods, including, silks, satins, velvets and velveteens, plushes, sealettes, dress-goods of the latest and most fashionable designs, and novelties, laces, trimmings, gloves, linens, damasks, cottons, muslins, prints, hoisery and hosiery notions, underwear, and all such other departments too numerous to mention; but, usually to be found in a first class establishment of this character. To properly conduct the operations of this extensive business, employment is furnished to 33 courteous and competent clerks, and from 30 to 40 skilled operators in other departments. This business was founded 12 years ago, and has proved eminently successful, almost from the date of its inception. Mr. N. E. Hamilton the proprietor, is a native of St. Luc. He has had a lengthened experience in the dry-goods business and thoroughly understands all its details and thus is ever prepared to anticipate and supply the wants of his numerous customers. He has always been in the van in adopting every improvement or invention tending to facilitate his own business operations or benefit the city generally. He was the first merchant in his street to adopt the electric system of lighting, also the first to introduce in Canada the Cash Conductor system of R. H. White Co. of Boston, Mr. Hamilton was also the originator of the project to build the Balmoral Hotel, and to his energy in conjunction with some other gentlemen is the city indebted for that magnificent house His latest enterprise is the De Lobiniere House, at Vaudrieul, near this city, of which he was the principal projector.

The Sparham Fireproof Roofing Co., OFFICE, 309 ST. JAMES STREET, CAMPBELL & CO., ROOFERS.—No matter how well carpenters and builders may erect a building if it is not properly roofed it will be like an umbrella full of holes to permit the rain to enter upon those it was intended to protect and worse than that, possibly, to destroy the structure itself. Therefore roofing is a very important branch of the building trade. Holding a conspicuous place among those engaged in the roofing trade in this city is The Sparham Fireproof Roofing Cement Co., Campbell & Co., whose office is located at No. 309 St. James street, near Victoria Square. This business was established 15 years ago and 6 years since the roofing agency was formed of Campbell & Co., composed of John Campbell and Thomas Gilday. The firm have the exclusive control of the Sparham fire-proof roofing cement for Montreal. This is one of the best cements in the market and is absolutely fire-proof, and impervious to the weather. New roofs are laid and guaranteed for 10 years, old metal roofs are covered with felt and cement and guaranteed for seven years. Old gravelled roofs are re-coated with cement and guaranteed for five years and old flat soldered tin roofs are recoated with cement and guaranteed for 5 years. These are all at different prices per square foot and lower in price in rotation from the first mentioned. The firm give employment to 25 skilled workmen throughout the season. Both Messrs Campbell and Gilday are Canadians by birth and possess all that push, energy and enterprise so essential to success, and their work has been tried and not found wanting.

S. Davis & Sons, CIGAR MANUFACTURERS, 48 COTTE STREET.—The cigar manufacturing trade of Canada is one of a most important character, and very few persons outside of the trade have any idea of its magnitude or extent of its operations. They will scarcely credit that during the year ending June 30th, 1887, there were manufactured in this country alone, 85,587,505 cigars and to make this number required 1,600,780 lbs. of tobacco. Montreal's quotation of this amount was 40,436,190, requiring 760,538 lbs. of tobacco, which is almost half as much as that manufactured in the entire Dominion. Montreal gives employment to 1800 hands in this branch of her manufactures. Standing pre-eminently forth among the cigar manufacturers of the Dominion is the well known firm of Messrs. S. Davis & Sons, whose extensive factory is located at Nos. 43, 45, 47, and 49 Cotte Street, and is one of the most perfect cigar manufactories in the world. The factory proper is a seven story brick structure with stone trimmings and is 106 x 88 feet in dimensions.   It is fitted up in the most complete manner with steam elevators and machinery and six telephones which communicate with the different departments, while a force of about 700 hands are employed throughout the year. The product of this house ranks exceptionally high in the trade and their " El Padre," " Cables," " Madre Hijo," " Mungo " and other brands are known and appreciated from the Atlantic to the Pacific throughout which territory their trade extends.   They use only the best leaf and always maintain their reputation by keeping their grades up to standard. This business was established nearly 30 years ago by Mr. S. Davis, and a few years ago it was changed to the present title, the members of the firm being Messrs. S., E. H., M. E., and N. B. Davis. The firm have a branch house in Toronto for the accommodation of their western traders and the trade, which is conducted by Mr

E. H. Davis. At the present day its output during the year is more than all that of Toronto and Hamilton manufactories combined, which are looked upon as the largest in Ontario. We may also mention that in every instance where this firm has exhibited they have always carried the highest honors, viz., the 1st prize at Paris in 1867 in competition with the world, Medal and Diploma in 1876 at Philadelphia in competition with the world and have always taken the Provincial Medals when they have exhibited including the Dominion Exhibition in 1886 the first and only medal offered as a prize, and were also awarded an additional Gold Medal by the Committee for their excellent display. The reason Messrs. S. Davis & Sons, exhibited in *Sherbrooke* last year, was to let the people see that they were keeping up with the times, though they had not exhibited for several years.

M. Moody & Son, MANUFACTURERS OF AGRICULTURAL IMPLEMENTS. WORKS:—TERREBONNE, OFFICE:—14 ST. CLAUDE STREET.—The inventive genius of this

progressive age has found one of its most fertile fields in devising implements designed to lighten the labors of the agriculturalists, and the progressive farmer of to-day is provided with machines which, to a very great extent, relieves him from heavy manual labor. If some of the farmers of the past generation were to revisit the scenes of their earthy abode and witness a modern harvesting they would scarcely believe their eyes. There are a great many first-class houses engaged in the manufacture of agricultural implements in Canada, and among those deserving of special mention is that of Messrs. M. Moody & Son, whose works are located at Terrebonne and office and warerooms in Montreal at No. 14 St. Claude Street. This is one of the oldest houses in the agricultural implement line in Canada, having been founded by Mr. Matthew Moody 54 years ago. At the works in Terrebonne, which are fitted up with the most improved machinery, driven in winter by steam and in summer by water, and where imployment is furnished on an average to from 80 to 100 skilled mechanics, the Gray Threshing Machine, New Model Buckeye Mowers, Sawyer's Reapers No. 3, Pitt's Horse Powers and Threshers, Tiger Self Dumping Rake, Ithica Hand Dumping Rake, Potatoe Diggers, Triumph Force-Feed Broad-cast Seeder and Cultivator and many other kinds of agricultural implements are manufactured, nothing but the very best of material is used in the manufacture of these implements which are built upon the most scientific principals and have a large sale throughout the Dominion. The present members of the firm are Messrs. Matthew (son of the founder of the business, since deceased) and Henry Moody, both of whom are wide-awake, active and progressive business men and highly esteemed citizens. Mr. Wm. McMillan is the representative of the firm in this city with office and warerooms at No. 14 St. Claude St., facing Bonsecours Market. He is also the efficient superintendant of their vast network of agencies, covering the entire Dominion from the Atlantic to the Pacific, and to his ability, push and enterprise, much of the success of the house is largely due.

G, E. Jaques & Co., GENERAL FOR-
WARDERS, AGENTS OF THE MERCHANTS'
LINE, AND OF THE MERCHANTS' DES-
PATCH LINE, 110 COMMON ST., MONTREAL.—
Situated as Montreal is at the head of ocean naviga-
tion and connected with the West and North-western
Continent by a mighty chain of canals, rivers and
lakes, it is nothing more than natural that it should
be the great commercial metropolis of the Dominion and that its shipping interest should be
one of the most important.   With the *nucleus* of debt removed from the harbor and Montreal
made a free port of entry, the future greatness of the city, may well equal a tale from the
Arabian Nights.   The most important of the inland shipping lines belonging to this port is
that of the Merchants' Line of propellors, the office of the Company being located at No. 110
Common Street.   This Company was originally started in 1835, by Messrs. Henderson and
Hooker, succeeded in rotation by Henderson, Hooker & Co., Hooker and Halton ; Hooker,
Jaques & Co. ; Jaques, Tracy & Co., and since 1868 by G. E. Jaques & Co. Messrs. G.
E. and C. A. Jaques are now the members of the firm. The Company do a large forwarding
business and have the most ample accommodation for all business transacted.
    The Merchants' Line is composed of twelve first-class steamers, and is divided into three
divisions, viz., Lake Ontario line, Chicago and Lake Superior.   The first-class passenger steamers "Persia " and " Ocean " leave Montreal for Toronto and St. Catherines every Friday and
Tuesday respectively, and do a large passenger business They have established a first-class
reputation for efficiency, comfort and speed.   The " Alma Munro," " Cuba" and " Acadia "
perform the Chicago service of the line leaving Montreal every Tuesday, and giving passengers
every opportunity of seeing Niagara Falls, and calling also at Toronto, Cleveland and Detroit
on the way, and giving their passengers a most agreeable combination of sight-seeing and
recreation on the trip.   The line is supplemented by a large number of steam barges for the
carrying of steel rails, iron and heavy freight in large quantities.   Connections are made with
all the principal railways, and freights are forwarded to destination on through bills of lading
from Liverpool, Glasgow, Antwerp, and all the principal ports in Great Britain and the
Continent.   The firm's Liverpool office is at 30, The Albany Old Hall Street, and the agent
there is Mr. Henry J. Cowie, to whose energy and ability much credit is due for the present
satisfactory condition of their European business. Special attention is paid to the comfort
and convenience of passengers and tourists, and all those intending to take a trip for pleasure
or otherwise on the inland waters of Canada will consult their own interests by examining
the facilities afforded by the Merchants' Line. Messrs. Jaques & Co., have also the contract with
the Dominion Government to supply light-houses and naval stations on the inland waters
with stores, &c., by their steamer specially appointed for the purpose, and in this steamer there
is special accommodation for a limited number of passengers, who will find the trip one of
the most pleasant and unique in the Dominion. The firm are also agents for the Merchants'
Despatch Line, composed of the steamers " Welshman," and " Harry Bate " which leave
Montreal on Friday and Tuesday evenings respectively for Ottawa and Newboro, calling at
all intermediate points. The Messrs. Jaques are gentlemen who have long been identified
with the business interests of the city and being natives of Montreal have a natural pride in
seeing it become—what it is surely destined to be—one of the greatest and most beautiful
cities on the American Continent.

FRECHON LEFEBVRE & CIE
ORNEMENTS D'EGLISE

Frechon, Lefebvre & Co., MANU-FACTURERS AND IMPORTERS OF BRONZES & CHURCH ORNAMENTS. 1645 NOTRE DAME STREET, MONTREAL.

—Montreal, ever since the time it was first settled by the French, in the days of Jacques Cartier, has been eminently Catholic, and there is no other city on the American continent that can boast of so many, or such magnificent church edifices and religious institutions. As a natural consequence there are a number of establishments. that are devoted to the sale of church ornaments, bronzes, vestments, &c. One of the leading houses in this line of business here is that of Messrs. Frechon, Lefebvre & Co., which is located at No. 1645, Notre Dame Street. The premises occupied are very extensive, consisting of four floors and basement 24 x 100 feet in dimensions. The stock of goods carried here is magnificent and is well worthy of inspection. The statuary is nearly all manufactured here and, strange though it may appear, it is far better, in artistic design, finish and coloring to the Italian, which nation so long held the monoploy for this line of goods. Messrs. Frechon, Lefebvre & Co. received a diploma for there exhibit of statuary at the Boston Exhibition in 1883, and also received a gold medal for an oil painting. They also manufacture sacredotal vestments on the premises which are very rich and, heavily and artistically worked in gold, and for superiority of workmanship is not surpassed by any imported. The average stock of goods carried by this house amounts to $60,000, so that some idea may be formed of the value of the goods dealt in, while employment is furnished to fifteen hands and clerks throughout the year in the different departments. This business was founded twelve years ago by Messrs. Frechon & Co., and in 1880 it was changed to the present title. The house, from the date of its inception has been highly successful, the trade now being co-extensive with the Dominion. The members of the firm are Mr. Leon Frechon. and Mr. J. B. Lefebvre, both of whom are French-Canadians by birth, and Mr. Frechon is a member of the Chamber of Commerce.

Lyman, Knox & Co., IMPORTERS AND WHOLESALE DRUGGISTS, 374 ST. PAUL STREET, MONTREAL.

—Nothing in the whole catalogue of trade is of so great importance to humanity at large as that of chemicals and drugs, upon their proper compounding and absolute purity depends more than at first sight may appear, health or sickness, life or death. Montreal is highly favored in the character of her drug houses and their reputation. Among those that are thoroughly reliable, and are deserving of special mention in this connection is that of Messrs. Lyman, Knox & Co., whose warehouse is located at No. 374 St. Paul Street, on the corner of St. Sulpice. Although the firm came into existance recently, still the members of it have had a *very extended*, practical experience in this city and are thoroughly competent in every respect and are well and favorably known to the trade throughout the Dominion. The members of the firm are Messrs. Charles and F. G. Lyman, Jas. W. Knox. The premises occupied by them consist of four floors and basement 25 x 150 feet in dimensions, which are completely stored with a very large assortment of drugs, chemicals, and druggists' requisites. The firm import direct from the leading manufacturers both in Euɪope and United States, and can guarantee the absolute purity of all goods handled by them. Their trade which extends throughout the entire Dominion, is gaining rapidly, and promises to be one of the largest as they are now one of the best of our Canadian houses.

Walter Paul, FAMILY GROCER, 2355 ST. CATHERINE STREET AND 98, 100 AND 102 METCALFE STREET; BRANCH, CORNER OF ST. CATHERINE ST. AND GREEN AVENUE. COTE ST. ANTOINE, MONTREAL—St. Catherine Street, West. is the seat of many of the handsome retail stores in the city. Situated, as it is, in the aristocratic residential quarter of city, the custom catered to is the very best and only the finest goods are handled to meet the demand. One of the finest establishments in the grocery business here is that of Mr. Walter Paul, which is located at No. 2355 St. Catherine Street, and Nos. 98, 100 and 102 Metcalfe Street. The premises occupied are large and commodious, with basement of the same size, furnished with elevator for the convenient handling of goods He has also a branch store on Corner of St. Catherine and Green Avenue, Cote St. Antoine, which is 20 x 100 feet in dimensions with basement. These establishment, are elegantly fitted up, and contain large and carefully selected stocks of the finest quality of staple and fancy groceries, consisting of the choicest brands of tea from China and Japan, India and Ceylon, aromatic coffees from Java, Rio, Mocha and other ports, table delicacies from the Mediterranean and the Orient, pure condiments, hermetically sealed goods in tin and glass, and all such other lines as come under the head of groceries and are to be found in a first-class establishment of this character. Mr. Paul imports his own goods direct from Europe and purchasing in large quantities and having the closest relations with first hands and producers he is enabled to offer his patrons the choicest goods that can be found in the market. The business is conducted both wholesale and retail and employment is furnished to sixteen competent assistants in the St. Catherine Street store and five in the Cote St. Antoine branch. Mr. Paul, who is a native of Glasgow, Scotland, established his business ten years ago and by persevering industry and enterprise, coupled with a thorough knowledge of the details of the grocer's trade, has built up a business, both in volume and quality, second to none in the city.

The Montreal Warehousing Co., GEORGE H. HANNA, MANAGER AND SECRETARY, WELLINGTON AND MILL STREETS.—It is not more than thirty years ago that the handling of grain in Montreal was conducted upon the principle known as " bagging," taking hundreds of men to do the work of a single steam elevator of the present day, the cost, of course, being proportionate to the number of hands employed. From the rapid increase made in the grain trade here, it was impossible to continue the old style and the present mammoth elevators and warehousing companies were the result. The most important of these in the city is that of The Montreal Warehousing Co., which is located on Wellington and Mill Streets. The main warehouse on Wellington Street is 500 x 150 feet in dimensions and is seven stories in height at the west end and five stories on the east, and is substantially built of cut stone. In this there are four elevators, operated by a 100-horse power steam engine. The storage capacity of this building is for 400,000 bushels of grain and 80,000 bushels of flour. In the Mill Street elevator the capacity is 600,000 bushels of grain, there being nine elevators operated by a 150 horse power steam engine. Railroad tracks, forming the terminus of the Grand Trunk Railway, connecting with both warehouse and elevators, run along side of the warehouse and cars can be directly loaded and unloaded therefrom. The buildings are all entirely fire-proof, and all the communicating doors and shutters are of heavy iron, while other precautions are taken to guard against fire. The Company was incorporated in the year 1865 with a capital of $600,000, being a joint stock Company with a special charter. The following well-known gentlemen are the officers and directors.—Andrew Allan, Esq., President ; John S. Hall, Esq., Vice-President and Managing Director ; Thomas Davidson, Esq., W. M. Ramsay, Esq., Hon. A. W. Ogilvie, Senator, and Mr. George H. Hanna, Manager and Secretary.

Turkish Bath and Sanitarian, DAVID MACBEAN, M. D , 140 ST. MONIQUE STREET.—Only those who have undergone the operation can have a thorough realization of the health-giving and refreshing properties of the Turkish Bath. It is one of the greatest luxuries introduced into our modern civilization from the Orient and its beneficial qualities, as a cure for chronic diseases, have been duly acknowledged by the medical profession and the public generally. The most complete and important institution of this kind in the Dominion, is the Turkish Bath Institute and Sanitarian, which is located at No. 140 St. Monique Street, foot of McGill College Avenue. This institution was founded here in 1869, but, from time to time it was greatly enlarged and improved. The premises are about 80 x 120 feet in dimensions, the holdings being three and five stories in height. There are fitted up with the most improved appliances and facilities, which are unexcelled on the American Continent, " Hydro-Therapeutic," "Sweedish Movement Cure," and " Massage" treatment are specialties of this institution. A special wing of the institution is fitted up for the reception of guests who here find all the comforts of home combined to the best of medical attention. For chronic cases the treatment here received is unsurpassed. It is good for liver and kidney diseases, rheumatism, impurities of the blood, neuralgia, bronchitis, dyspepsia and many other cases of a similar nature, too numerous to mention. Dr. MacBean, the founder and manager of the Baths, is a gentleman of ability and under his judicious care, the institution has won a high reputation.

J, & R. Weir, ENGINEERS AND MACHINISTS, 25 TO 29 NAZARETH STREET.—. Although the invention of the working steam engine—the king of machines—belongs, comparatively speaking, to our own epoch, the idea of it was born many centuries ago. Like other contrivances and discoveries, it was effected step by step—one man transmitting the result of his labors, at the time apparently useless, to his successors, who took it up and carried it forward another stage—the prosecution of the inquiry extending over many generations. The steam engine was nothing, however, until it emerged from the state of theory and was taken in hand by practical mechanics. Among those engaged in this line of business in this city is the well-known firm of Messrs. J. & R. Weir, whose works are located at from No. 25 to 29 Nazareth Street, the premises occupied being 40 x 95 feet in dimensions. Here employment is furnished to about thirty-five skilled and competent workmen throughout the year in the manufacture of marine engines and boilers, stationery engines, pulleys, shaftings, etc. The works are fully equipped with all the latest and most improved machinery, and nothing has been omitted that could possibly add to the successful prosecution of the work in hand. Since this business was established in 1875, the firm have met with the most gratifying success, and steadily has the business increased from year to year. Both Mr. James and Mr. Robert Weir are practical engineers and machinists, having had over thirty years active experience in marine and general engineering work. They give their personal supervision to all work entrusted to them, and can thus guarantee their customers the best of satisfaction, while their prices will be found as reasonable as anywhere else in the Dominion, while their work is unexcelled.

Wm. Clendinneng & Son, MANUFACTURERS OF STOVES, RANGES, RAILINGS, ETC.,

OFFICE AND WORKS, 145 TO 179 WILLIAM STREET.—"There is a tide in the affairs of men, which, taken at the flood, leads on to fortune " So also is it the case with cities and nations, even as it is with individuals. At the present time it would appear as though the flood-tide in the affairs of Montreal had arrived and should be grasped. At the headwaters of sea-going navigation and with the finest system of railroad connections with the Pacific washed shores of British Columbia ; the new Sault Sainte Marie connection of the Canadian Pacific Railway to Minneapolis and the fertile States and Territories of the American North-west which offer to send their products for shipment from our port, it would be a crime to posterity not to grasp the golden opportunity and make our facilities equal to the demand, and thus build up the trade and prosperity of the city. In reviewing the manufacturing resources and development of Montreal, it is entirely safe to venture the opinion that no one establishment has done more to enhance the high repute of this city as an important productive centre, than that of the firm of Messrs. Wm. Clendinneng & Son, Iron founders and Machinists. This business was established in a moderate way and upon a moderate scale at a time when some of our present business men were still at school, but through untiring industry and perseverance, on the part of Mr. Clendinneng it has grown to be probably the most extensive industry of its kind in the Don : ion, furnishing employment to over 300 skilled workmen and assistants, and turning out a vast amount of work of of a very superior character. The buildings constituting their plant of the works and office, are located at from Nos. 145 to 179 William Street and the corner of Inspector Street, and cover over three acres of ground. These are equipped with the very best machinery, tools and appliances that modern ingenuity could invent. The scope of the work includes all kinds of light and heavy castings, stoves and ranges, including the celebrated "Leader" sectional circular fire pot cook stove which is of beautiful design and is acknowledged by all to be a most excellent baker. Also a full line of coal and wood-cooking and heating stoves, hot air furnaces, hot water boilers, machinists, railway and builders' castings, railings, funnels, crestings, balconies, brackets of which they carry the best selection of patterns in the country. Also iron-bedsteads, sinks, tea kettles, and many other lines too numerous to mention. In all departments of the works the most skilful workmen are employed, the best of materials obtainable used, and the most excellent work turned out. So extensive has the trade of this house become that it covers, in the scope of its operations, not only the entire Dominion from the Atlantic to the Pacific, but also many foreign countries. The salesrooms of the house are located at Nos. 664 and 666 Craig Street, 524 Craig Street, and corner of William and Inspector Streets where very large stocks are carried and the trade conducted at both wholesale and retail. Mr. Wm. Clendinneng, the senior member of the firm, is one of Montreal's most representative and progressive business men. He was born in Cavan, Ireland, in 1833, and came to Montreal at fourteen years of age. In 1852 he became a clerk in the employ of Mr. Rodden, and by his ability and valuable qualities was afterwards taken into partnership. He takes a deep interest in the welfare of all his employees and exercises a fatherly care over them and many a boy and man has been led to live a useful and honorable life through his influence. Mr. Clendinneng has been Governor of the House of Refuge and Industry since the inception of that institution, and was at one time Governor of the Montreal General Hospital and is a member of its committee of management. He represents St. Antoine Ward in the Board of Aldermen, and is a prominent member of the Board of Trade. There are few enterprises inaugurated for the benefit of the city in which he is not associated. Mr. Clendinneng, Jr., is one of Montreal's best known young business men and to his talents and push most of the success of the establishment is largely due.

W. Mc Nally & Co,, CEMENT, DRAIN PIPES, TILES, &c.. OFFICES: 46 TO 52 McGILL ST., COR. WELLINGTON. YARDS AND WAREHOUSES : McGILL, WELL-INGTON, GREY NUN AND 3 YOUVILLE STREETS.—The manufacture of Portland cement was not begun until about the years 1844 and 1845, and it was until 1858 that Messrs. Sir Wm. Armstrong & Co., the hydraulic and ordinance engineers brought it into general use. Concrete is now used greatly by engineers, architects, contractors and others in laying the foundations of important buildings, as well as in the contruction of pier works, breakwater, quay-walls, tanks, reservoirs, streets, foot paths, yards, railway platforms, warehouse and cellar floors, &c., &c., and is therefore an important article of comerce ; or, more correctly speaking, its ingredients are, Portland cement being the principal. Among the more prominent houses engaged in the Portland cement, drain pipes, fire bricks, fire clay, calcined plaster, and builders' and contractors' supplie business, in this city is the well known firm of Messrs. McNally & Co., whose offices are located at Nos· 46 to 52 McGill Street, and their yards and warehouses at McGill, Wellington, Grey Nun, and Youville Streets. The premises occupied cover nearly one acre of ground, and contain a very heavy stock of the goods dealt in, from 28 to 30 hands being employed to properly conduct the operations of the business, the trade extending over every section of the country, This business was established in the year 1875, and during the years that have passed since then it has met with the most gratifying and continuous success. Mr. W. McNally, the proprietor, is a Canadian by birth and is a gentleman of large experience in the line in which he is engaged ; he is thorough going and progressive, and is a member of the Montreal Board of Trade. He is a large importer of drain pipes and connections, Portland cements, best brands, Keen's parian cement, Roman cement, Canada cement, fire bricks, square and shaped, best brands, furnace blocks, tiles, chimney linings, flue covers, fire clays, gas retorts, cast iron pipes for water and gas works, sewer bottoms, stable bricks, calcined plaster, floor tiles, porcelain sinks, terra cotta, and navvy, steel body, coal and garden wheel-barrows, and railway and road scrapers. The house is a well known one to the trade and has always held a high reputation for liberal and honorable dealing.

W. Drysdale & Co., BOOKS AND STATIONERY, 232 ST. JAMES STREET, MONTREAL.—It is said, and with no little degree of truth, that in the homes of the cultured "books and pictures come next to bread and butter." In a cultivated and refined mind nothing can give greater delight than the perusing of some standard author of the past or present age, or the pleasure to be derived from viewing beautiful pictures. Holding a prominent and popular place among those engaged in the bookselling and stationery line in Montreal, is the firm of Messrs. W. Drysdale & Co., whose store is located at No. 232 St. James Street. The premises occupied by the business consist of 4 floors 20x112 feet in dimensions. Here is contained a large and elegant stock of books in every description of binding, from paper covers to full russia, and including the standard authors in science, art, history, poetry, theology, light literature &c., also magazines and periodicals, tourists guide books, maps, views of Montreal and other parts of Canada, as well as fancy goods of almost every description. In stationery the stock is very large and complete, including school books, and school stationery, counting house requisites, and beautiful paper and envelopes for ladies use with all the desk requisites. This business has been established nearly 16 years and from the date of its inception has proved very successful, steadily increasing in extent and importance from year to year. Mr. Drysdale commenced his business career in the Witness Office under the late John Dougall, founder of that great paper, afterwards serving as clerk and business manager for one of the principal book and stationery stores in this city. He has been nearly a quarter of a century before the public so that he is well known in business and social circles, and is held in the highest esteem by all as an upright, honorable and conscientious merchant.

W. Strachan & Co., SOAP AND OIL, 36 JACQUES CARTIER STREET, MONT-REAL.—In commenting on the trade and manufactures of Montreal, there are certain indus-tries that have been found to have developed to a very marked degree and to have attained such proportions as to call for more than the usual allotment of space in describing them and their operations. For instance in the manufacture of soaps Montreal is the seat of several establishments in this line of business, the quality of whose products is equal to any on the American continent. Among the specially prominent manufacturers of soap is the old-established and well-known firm of Messrs. Wm. Strachan & Co., whose office and factory are located at No, 36 Jacques Cartier Street. This business was first established by Wm. Christie in 1830, and was succeeded 13 years ago by Mr. Strachan. The business at its inception was, comparatively speaking, small, but by adopting the policy of manufactur-ing nothing but the best it has been built up to its present extensive proportions, and "Strachan's Gilt-Edge Soap" is "familiar in our mouths as household words"—that is, the name, not the compound—which is used for cleansing and beautifying the skin and com-plexion. The factory is a large, commodious and substantial brick structure, three stories in height and 150 x 200 feet in dimensions. It is amply equipped with a full complement of machinery, driven by a 16 horse power steam engine, and is supplied with all the requisite and various paraphernalia of soap making, while 18 skilled workmen are given steady em-ployment. The laundry soaps manufactured by this house are sold throughout the Dominion and have been universally and particularly commended for special purity and excellence, qualities that make these goods of staple value to the trade wherever introduced. The firm are also manufacturers of lubricating oils, and are only one of three in the Dominion that make a specialty of pressed lard oil, large quantities of these oils being exported to England. Mr. W. Strachan, the proprietor, is a Scotch-Canadian by birth and a gentleman of marked push and enterprise, and it is to the progressive character of such men that Montreal must look for that vast future development to which her citizens so confidently look forward. Mr. Strachan is an active member of the Montreal Board of Trade.

Lucien Huot, GENERAL IMPORTER, 466 ST. PAUL STREET, MONTREAL.—Montreal, from its geographical position, in being at the head of ocean navigation, and having the very best of railway, river and lake transportation with the West and Northwest, has gained the enviable position of being the metropolis of Canada. But geographical position alone would not have done it, had it not been for the enterprise and ability of her merchants, who send their travellers and merchandise throughout the Dominion, Among the business houses of importance in this city must be mentioned that of Mr. Lucien Huot, who is inti-mately connected with many different lines of commercial industry, being a general importer, his office being located at No. 466 St. Paul Street. This business was established in 1862 by A. Giberton, who was succeeded in 1878 by the present proprietor under the name of A. Giberton & Co., it has been carried on since 1881 under the present name. During the quarter of a century that has passed since then he has built up an excellent connection with the business houses of the Dominion, and many of the leading houses of Europe. Mr. Huot imports all kinds of French wines, liquors, and in fact anything and everything that is re-quired in the commercial way. He also makes a specialty of dried fruits from the Mediter-anean and other European ports, passes all goods through the Customs, paying all freights and charges and thus relieving merchants of all troubles in such matters. Mr. Huot is a French Canadian by birth, and is a progressive business man, being largely interested in some of Montreal's most wealthy, monetary, mercantile, and manufacturing institutions. He has been for 9 years a director of the Jacques Cartier Bank, is President of the Montreal Moulding and Mirror Manufacturing Company, and has been prominently identified with most of the leading enterprises of Montreal's most busy city. He is highly esteemed in busi-ness and social circles, and is a member of the Montreal Board of Trade.

N. E. HAMILTON & CO., DRY GOODS. (See page 103.)

John Cowan, MANUFACTURER OF SUNDRIES, LIQUOR AND CAR-
BONATE AMONIA, AGENT FOR THE BROCKVILLE CHEMICAL AND SUPERPHOSPHATES
COMPANY, [LIMITED.] No. 3 DALHOUSIE STREET, MONTREAL. P. O. BOX 319.—A
review of the various commercial and manufacturing industries of Montreal gives plain
evidence of the metropolitan character of the city, from the multiplicity of
interests conducted here, and it is not unreasonable to suppose that the coming
ten years of its history will be the highest and most prosperous ever known
if proper advantage are taken of the opportunities offered. The drug and
chemical trade forms a very important factor in the city's make up and is deserving of special mention. Among those prominently engaged in the chemical line in this city is Mr.
John Cowan, whose warehouse is located at No. 3 Dalhousie street. This gentleman has
been established in business for the past 15 years and during all that time he has met with
a market degree of prosperity, which has been commensurate to the energy, enterprise and
ability he has displayed in the business. The premises occupied are 40 x 100 feet in dimensions and consist of 2 floors. Here is carried a large and excellent stock of the purest quality of oil of vitriol, muriatic acid, nitric acid, tin crystals, tin spirits, nitro-muriate of tin,
nitrate of iron, muriate of iron, iron liquor, oxy-muriate of antimony, Glauber's salt, red
liquor, etc., etc. Mr. Cowan being agent for the Brockville Chemical and Superphosphates
Co., Limited, the trade can be supplied from stock at any time and the best of advantages
are afforded them. The trade is quite extensive and embraces in the scope of its operations
the entire Dominion.

R. C. Jamieson & Co., OFFICE, 12 AND 13 HAMILTON CHAMBERS, 17
ST. JOHN STREET, FACTORY AND WAREHOUSE, 23 TO 29 ST. THOMAS STREET,
MONTREAL.—This is undeniably an age of improvement and culture. Artistic taste is being
diffused throughout the people, and in nothing is this more observable than in the painting
and decorating of private residences. The painters' trade has undoubtedly kept pace with
this cultured demand, and the manufacturers of painters' requisites have been fully alive to
their requirements, and the leading houses have equipped themselves to meet this demand
by the production of the best class of goods, knowing full well that competition is keen, and
that "to the victors belong the spoils." One of the most important and best known houses
in the varnish and Japan manufacturing trade in the Province is that of Messrs. R. C.
Jamieson & Co., whose office is located at Nos. 12 and 13 Hamilton Chambers, 17 St. John
Street, in this city. This business was established in a comparatively small way as long ago
as the year 1858. Owing to persevering industry on the part of the proprietors, and
a determination to place upon the market nothing but the very best, a reputation was soon
made in the trade which has been steadily maintained during the passing years. The
factory—which comprises a number of buildings—is located at Nos. 23 to 29 St. Thomas
Street, where is also the warehouse. These buildings cover over 80 x 210 feet, and are
fully equipped with all the latest and most improved machinery specially invented for the
line of work here conducted. In fact, there is nothing better in machinery of this kind
in the United States and Europe. Employing nothing but the best of skilled help under
experienced supervision, the most satisfactory results are at all times obtained, and the
"Jamieson" varnishes and Japans are implicitly relied upon. The product of the house
consists of varnishes of all kinds and Japans for coach builders, railroad car builders, cabinet
makers, picture frame makers, and others requiring the finest grades. The firm also boil
oils for their own use and for selling to the trade. The output of the factory amounts to
2,000 barrels a year of varnish and 7,000 barrels of oil, which is put up in cans and barrels.
The firm are also heavy importers of and dealers in oils, paints, colors, spirits of turpentine
and other goods of a similar nature. The trade of the house is very extensive and its
operations extend throughout the Dominion, from the Maritime Provinces to British
Columbia. Mr. R. C. Jamieson, the senior member of the firm, is a gentleman of marked
business ability and is a member of the Council of the Board of Trade, and his partner, Mr.
A. T. Higginson, is also a member of the same body.

J. E. Townshend, 334 ST. JAMES STREET, MONTREAL.—The manufacturing industries of Montreal are many and varied in their character, and in the aggregate have made the city what it is, not only the commercial but the manufacturing metropolis of the Dominion. Among those establishments deserving of special mention in a work of this character is that of Mr. J. E. Townshend, sole manufacturer and patentee of the Stem Winder Wove Wire Mattress and the Duguay (or improved Wilder) Steel Spring Bed, and every description of bedding. The store and factory are located at No. 334 St. James Street. The store is 25 x 75 feet in dimensions and two stories in height, and the factory in rear is two floors in height and 40 x 60 feet in dimensions. Mr. Townshend gives employment to 10 skilled and competent hands in his manufactory throughout the year, his scale of wages averaging for males from $7.00 to $16.00 a week and for females from $7.00 to $8.00 a week. which must certainly be considered good pay, but the work they do is the best, and consequently the goods manufactured by this house are of a very superior quality. Among the line of beds manufactured are common wove wire beds, No. 2 stem winders, No. 1 stem winders, Hartford stem winders, Duguay or improved Wilder ; also, palliasses, pillows, flock matts, fibre matts, seabeds and pillows, hair mattresses, feather beds, bolsters and pillows are made to order. Mr. Townshend is a native of London, England, and is a gentleman of an inventive turn of mind, having taken out at different times 23 different patents, among the number being for a boot jack that not only can you take off your boots, but you can put them on by it. It is simple in construction but "it gets there" just the same. For this he received a medal and diploma at the Colonial Exhibition in London. His patent stem winder mattress is one of the best of its kind ever made and has a very large sale throughout the Dominion. Mr. Townshend began business for himself in London in 1847, and established his business in Montreal in 1870, and ever since that time he has met with the most gratifying success, which has been entirely owing to his own individual push and energy and holding to the motto that "What is worth doing at all is worth doing well."

Charles Alexander, CONFECTIONER, 219 ST. JAMES STREET.—The business conducted by Mr. Charles Alexander at No. 219 St. James street, was established in the year 1842 and may well be said to be one of the constitutions of the city. The Canadians, especially the rising generation, are probably the largest consumers of candy and confectionery in the world, with probably the exception of those in the United States and the productions of our manufacturers can compete favorably with those of France, which country, for a long period has been considered the most successful in this particular line. Mr. Alexander has long enjoyed a high reputation for his candies, confectionery and the productions of his culinary department. The premises occupied by him are large and commodious and are fitted up in a most artistic manner indicating at once taste and culture. Plate glass, show cases and cabinets contain fine assortments of confectionery, cakes, pastry, etc., at once tempting and appetizing to look at. His refreshment rooms are fitted up, in an elaborate and tasteful manner and here may be obtained at all hours of the day tempting lunches and elaborate dinners including every description of fish and game in their season, cooked in the highest perfection of culinary art and served with Parisian grace such as has made the cafés of that capital of civilization the delight of travellers. Mr. Alexander also supplies wedding breakfasts, supper and dinner parties with everything requisite in the line of which he has an elaborate assortment of the richest quality. Mr. Alexander is to Montreal what Delmonica was for so many years to New York, he may be said to have been the inceptor of the catering business in this city and the benefit he may have reaped from his extensive business has also been enjoyed by the elite of the city through his valuable services. Mr. Alexander has during nearly half a century of a business career enjoyed the esteem and confidence of the public and earned a high reputation of which he is eminently deserving.

Thompson & Co., MANUFACTURERS OF FINE BOOTS AND SHOES, 712 to 716 CRAIG STREET, MONTREAL.—The manufacture of boots and shoes is of very ancient origin, for foot wear of some description was worn in the early centuries of the world's history. Shoes—particularly women's shoes—have their romance as well as the glove, for history tells us that the Egyptian King Psammetich, in the year 630 B. C. while holding court in the market place of Memphis, attended by his nobles, espied an eagle circling in the air above his head, which, upon gradually coming closer to the earth dropped a shoe into the monarch's lap, it was of exquisite shape, and like the prince in the tale of Cinderella, the king sought out the owner and found it to be the beautiful Rhodope, whom he married and made queen of his empire. That was the first "shoe fly" on record. But from poetry we must come to prose in a work of this character and speak of the leading houses engaged in the manufacture of boots and shoes at the present day in Montreal. Among the more important houses in this line in this city is that of Messrs. Thompson & Co., whose extensive factory is located at No. 712½ Craig street extending through to Fortification street. The premises occupied by the business consist of a 4 story building having 40,000 feet of flooring. These premises are fitted up with all the latest and most improved machinery specially adapted for this line of business, which is driven by a 40 horse power steam engine. Employment is furnished on an average from 450 to 500 skilled hands throughout the year in the manufacture of boots and shoes of fine quality for men and women, misses, youths and children. These are made up in the most fashionable styles and are well finished in every particular, the finest quality of materials only being used, two thirds of the stock used being imported from some of the most celebrated European and American houses. A specialty of the manufacture of this house is turned slippers and shoes, technically known to the trade as "turns". The manufactured output is from 25 cases of 60 pair to the case, the capacity of the factory being 400,000 pairs a year, averaging in value between $400,000.00 and $500,000.00. The trade of the house is very extensive and covers the entire Dominion and orders are being received so fast from all parts that many have to be refused as it is impossible to meet all demands. That this house is an important factor in computing the wealth and advantages of the city may readily be seen from the large number of hands employed whose wages amount to one eighth of a million dollars a year, which is distributed amongst the store keepers for necessaries, for rents, etc. This business was established only 5 years ago and the figures just quoted speak more eloquently than any words of ours can of the success that has been achieved. The members of the firm are Mr. Edwin Thompson, who is a native of England and is a practical boot and shoe maker and Mr. Edward James Savage, who was born in the Eastern Townships, and attends to the financial part of the business. Both gentlemen are active members of the BOARD OF TRADE.

C. J. Covernton & Co., DRUGGISTS, BLEURY ST., COR. DORCHESTER ST.— There is no more important profession to the community generally, than that of the pharmacist. One of the best known houses in this line of business in Montreal, and one that has gained a high reputation for care and accuracy in the compounding of physician's prescriptions and family receipts, is that of Messrs. C. J. COVERNTON & Co., whose store is located at the corner of Bleury and Dorchester Streets. The stock embraces fresh and pure drugs, chemicals, fancy and toilet articles, imported and domestic soaps, perfumes, etc., druggist's sundries, and those articles required by physicians in their practice. The firm also compound a number of specialities which have proved very efficacious for the different purposes for which they are designed, and have received the commendation of many physicians. Those requiring anything in the drug line, (and that is the general lot of frail humanity,) will find everything that they require at Messrs. COVERNTON & Co's of the purest quality and the prices reasonable two very desirable qualities, not only in drugs, but also in all other lines of commodities. The firm have established an excellent trade during the years they have been in business, and also an excellent reputation for skill and accuracy.

J. E. Doyle & Co., No. 434 St. James Street, Montreal.—The cork tree rarely exceeds from thirty-five to forty feet in height and from two to three feet in diameter. It is found in abundance in Portugal, Spain, Italy, the southern parts of France, and in the Barbary states. Spain and Portugal supply the greater portion of the cork which is used in Europe. The outer bark of this tree grows unusually large, and when removed is speedily again renewed by the biber or inner bark. This process, so far from injuring it, is said to prolong the life of the tree; for when this excess of bark is not artificially removed the tree seldom lives longer than fifty or sixty years, while the barked trees flourish for upwards of a hundred and fifty. It is not till after ten years that the bark has all the qualities for making good corks; and from this period a tree is regularly barked every eight or ten years. Cork is manufactured into many useful articles besides corks for bottles, such as shoe soles, life preservers, belts, &c., &c. There are but two manufacturers in the Dominion of whom the firm of Messrs. J. E. Doyle & Co., of No. 434 St James Street, are worthy of particular mention. This business was established 10 years ago and from the date of its inception, it has met with the most marked success and has rapidly increased in extent and patronage from year to year. The operations of the business now covering the entire Dominion. The firm have an extensive manufactory in Toronto at the corner of Queen and Shumach Streets, which is fitted up with all the most improved machinery and appliances for the successful prosecution of the work in hand, and where employment is furnished to 50 skilled hands, in the manufacture of corks, belts, and all other articles that are usually made from this useful product. The Western and North-Western trade is attended to from the Toronto factory. In this city the office and store is 60x30 feet in dimensions with a new warehouse in rear, three stories in height and 60 x 75 feet in dimensions where the goods are stored and packed for shipment. The firm are also importers of and dealers in capsules, corking machines, tinfoil, bottling wax and wire etc. All goods handled by this house are of the very best quality and have an active demand in the market. The members of the firm are Mr. J. E. Doyle, who is a native of New York city, and is a member of the Montreal Board of Trade, and Mr. P. Freyseng, who is a native of Germany, and attends to the affairs of the Toronto house. Those forming business relations with this house will find all transactions conducted upon the most satisfactory basis.

B. D. Johnson & Son, BOOTS & SHOES, 1855 Notre Dame Street.—The boot and shoe trade, as at present conducted, is one of the most prominent of any of the branches of commercial industry. Mammoth establishments have been established for the manufacture of these most useful articles of wearing apparel, and employment is furnished to hundreds of thousands. Machinery has worked wonders in this line of manufacture, and the cost of boots and shoes is now almost 50 per cent. less than it was 25 or 30 years ago. Actively engaged in the retail boot and shoe trade in this city is Mr. B. D. Johnson, whose store is admirably located for business, at No. 1855 Notre Dame Street, near McGill Street. It is now 23 years since this business was founded, it having been carried on at wholesale for fifteen years on McGill Street, and eight years since was opened as retail in its present location. During that time a very large trade has been established and is still steadily on the increase. The premises occupied are 26 x 90 feet in dimensions, and are tastefully fitted up and neatly arrayed, while the stock is displayed to excellent advantage. The stock of goods carried is of the very best quality and is extensive in its character, embracing all kinds of boots and shoes and slippers for ladies and gentlemen, misses, youths, boys and children, which are obtained from some of the leading manufacturing houses in the Dominion and are sold at prices that must meet the views of the most economical. There is a special department for custom work where ladies and gentlemen can have their boots or shoes made to order by measure on short notice and in the best style of the art by skilled workmen. Mr. Johnson, the senior partner, is an American by birth, and is a gentleman who has a thorough knowledge of all the details of the boot and shoe trade, and those forming business relations with him may rely upon entire satisfaction.

Edward Auld, MANUFACTURER OF PREMIUM MUCILAGE AND LIQUID GLUE, 759 CRAIG STREET, MONTREAL.—If there is one article more than another, apart from our food supplies, about which people are most particular, it is mucilage. There is a good deal of this sticky stuff put upon the market that is very inferior and has not the strength to stand up for its own reputation. Montreal, however, has one house, at least, engaged in this line of manufacture, that has earned a well-deserved reputation for their goods, and that is Mr. Edward Auld, whose factory is located at No. 759 Craig Street. This business, although it was established only 3 years ago, has already been built up to very extensive proportions, its operations now covering the entire Dominion. Mr. Auld manufactures the " Premium " and " Anchor" brands of mucilage, which are put up in different size packages from 2 oz. to gallons ; also, the " Excelsior " brand of liquid glue, which is also put up in similar sizes. Nothing but the very best and purest of materials are used in the manufacture of these articles, so that their genuiness and excellent qualities can be at all times relied upon. He also manufactures Auld's Lithographic Composition, which is also highly spoken of by the trade. Mr. Auld made it a business principle when starting in business to build up a trade on the character of his goods, and he is already reaping the benefits of this wise policy. There is a less margin of profit on the stated quantity, but the public are demanding his goods, and the increasing sales tell in the long run. Mr. Auld is a Montrealer by birth and is a wide awake, active and enterprising business man and is eminently deserving of all the success he has, or will achieve.

Dominion Brass Works, ESTABLISHED 1860, CUTHBERT & SON, 23 AND 25 COLLEGE STREET, MONTREAL, TELEPHONE NO. 1300.—It was only as recently as the year 1830 that the first iron steamship was built and now they are traversing every ocean, sea, lake and river in the civilized and uncivilized parts of the world. It has been a wonderful half century of progress in the mechanical arts, and in this respect the brass founding branch, has of necessity kept abreast of the times, the demand for brass and copper work having rapidly increased. One of the best known and oldest established houses in this line of industry in the city is that of the Dominion Brass Works, of which Messrs. Cuthbert & Son, are the proprietors, the works being located at Nos. 23 and 25 College street. This business was established in the year 1860 and from a comparatively small beginning, has, by steady industry and perseverance on the part of the proprietors, coupled to excellence of quality in work, been built up to its present extensive proportions. The premises occupied by the works consist of a 3 story stone building, 75 x 120 feet. These are fitted up with all the latest and most improved machinery and appliances, the machinery being driven by a 20 horse power steam engine while employment is furnished to 25 skilled and competent workmen on an average throughout the year. The firm do all kinds of brass founding and finishing, and are also copper smiths, plumbers, gas and steam fitters. A specialty of the house is steamship work in which line of work they have gained a high and wide spread reputation, for its superiority and quality. All orders entrusted to this firm are attended to promptly and the utmost satisfaction in all cases is guaranteed, so that those forming business relations with them may rest assured of liberal treatment and conscientious work. The members of the firm are Messrs. Robert D. Cuthbert and Mr. Wm R. Cuthbert, who are natives of Perthshire, Scotland, and are both skilled, practical workmen and enterprising and progressive business men.

D. Parizeau, LUMBER MERCHANT, Head Office, Corner of Craig and St. Denis Streets; Yards, Corner of Craig and St. Denis Streets and 430 Lagauchetiere Street.—In treating of the growth of Montreal, the gathering together of the statistics reveals a condition of affairs, interwoven with her growth, that is a matter of surprise to one even who is accustomed to stumbling over the greatest surprises in this direction and that is, the magnitude to which some of the industries prosecuted within its borders have been developed simultaneously with the growth of the city, and of this the lumber trade is a striking example. In this respect no better illustration could be found than the business at the head of which is Mr. D. Parizeau. This gentleman established his business in this city in the year 1870 and from the time of its inception it has been steadily increasing and been added to, both in the extent of its operations and facilities from year to year up to the present time. The head office and yard is located at the corner of Craig and St. Denis Streets, opposite Viger Garden. This yard is 132 x 128 feet in dimensions. The following are the other yards owned by Mr. Parizeau in different parts of the city, with their dimensions: On Lagauchetiere Street 92 x 185 feet, in Hochelaga 150 x 300 feet, on the canal bank 150 x 150 feet, and on corner of Craig and Amherst Streets 50 x 90 feet. It will thus be seen that Mr. Parizeau has ample room and facilities for conducting his extensive business, which has an output of from 6,000,000 to 7,000,000 feet of lumber a year. He deals in all kinds of dressed lumber and timber for builders' use, keeping constantly on hand a very large stock. In conducting his business he gives employment to seven clerks, salesmen and book-keepers, six carters and four pilers. Mr. Parizeau is a native of Boucherville and is a thoroughly enterprising and progressive business man, of pleasant manners, and those who have formed business relations with him have always found all transactions conducted in a straightforward and liberal manner. Mr. Parizeau is a member of the Council of the Chamber of Commerce.

Henry R. Gray, (established 1859,) CHEMIST and DRUGGIST, 144 St. Lawrence Main Street, Montreal, Physicians' prescriptions carefully prepared, Hospitals, Dispensaries, Convents, and Physicians, supplied with genuine Drugs and Chemicals.—The English, as a rule, are proverbially conservative, especially in business matters and there are many old English houses that are looked up on as being, in a comparative degree, as solid as the Bank of England. It is this conservatism and stability that has given England and English business houses such a prestige the world over. Englishmen going to foreign countries carry these principles with them and act upon their surroundings like the leaven that leaveneth the entire lump. The old established and well known drug house of Mr. Henry R. Gray, which is located at No. 144 St. Lawrence Main Street, was established in the year 1859. Not only that but it has continued at the same place since the first day it was started with the exception that extensions were made to the premises from time to time to accomodate the ever increasing business. Mr. Gray does a regular chemist and druggist business, but has also had a specialty for many years that of supplying physicians, hospitals, dispensaries, and other public institutions with pure drugs. He has also 151 regular physicians upon his books whose offices are scattered throughout Canada, whom he supplies with their requirements in the drug line, and he also supplies professional lecturers with chemicals for the demonstration of their experiments. He has achieved a high and widespread reputation for reliability and the entire profession has the utmost confidence in his ability and carefulness in filling their orders. He also makes a specialty of compounding physicians prescriptions and family recipes. Mr. Gray is a native of England, and is a licentiate of the Pharmaceutical Association of the Province of Quebec, and of the Ontario College of Pharmacy and served his term of apprenticeship in England, and is one of the most esteemed members of the profession.

He was appointed a member of the Provincial Board of Health last year and served as a member of the Central Board during the epidemic of 1885-86.

Fee & Martin, 357, 359 & 361 St. James Street, Montreal. — Few people give any heed to or imagine the extent of the furniture trade in this city. From a close computation it is estimated that over one million dollars worth of furniture—not manufactured in the city—is sold here by the regular dealers, not to speak of the large quantities that are consigned to the auction rooms by outside parties. Now that the enterprising men of the city are agitating increased harbor facilities, this is a good point, to show what a field there is for the manufacture of furniture here, as well as there is for the other lines of manufacture. Only pessimists look with gloomy forbodings upon Montreal, and lend their clammy influence to the half-awakes, but the enterprising men, the " get-up-and-gets," will be at the top of the ladder, while they are still trying to find out if the bottom rung is strong enough to hold them. One of the most enterprising firms in the furniture line to-day is that of Messrs. Fee & Martin, whose handsome establishment is located in Bishop's Block, Nos. 357, 359 and 361 St. James Street. The premises occupied are three stories in height and with fine high ceilings and basement. It is fitted up in excellent style and displays the elegant stock of furniture carried, to excellent advantage. There is an extension in rear of 11½ x 15 feet and three floors in height. Although this business was established only in November of 1887, the success already attending it has been remarkable and gives the most flattering assurances of a bright and prosperous future. The firm employ 25 men all the year round fitting up and upholstering. In February of the present year the firm took a $6,000 contract for fitting up the new hotel at Vaudreuil. Mr. Wm. R. Fee, the senior member of the firm, is a native of this province and there is no pessimist about him. He fully believes in Montreal and its destiny, and it is only a pity that there are not more like him than there are. What he does not know about the furniture trade in Canada is not worth knowing. For 17 years he has travelled from Dan to Beersheba, or more correctly speaking, from the Atlantic to the Pacific, and knows every furniture man of any importance throughout the country. He has been in the business in Boston, New York and Chicago, and travelled this country for an American house. He was with H. J. Shaw & Co., of this city, for some time, and later with the Montreal Furniture Company, so these statements speak for themselves. His partner, Mr. Martin, is also a native of the Province of Quebec and is a thorough-going, active and enterprising business man.

James Wilson, Jr., 66, 67, 68 and 69 Common Street, Montreal. P. O. Box 1835, Telephone 639.— The city of Montreal is a very prominent railroad and shipping centre, being at the head of ocean navigation and the terminus of the inland lake and river navigation. Consequently there are a number of houses that make a specialty of supplying the wants of those engaged in this traffic. Among those most prominently engaged in the railroad, steamboat and mill supply business in this city is Mr. James Wilson, Jr., whose warehouse is located at Nos. 66, 67, 68 and 69, Common street. The building occupied, which, is owned by Mr. Wilson, has a frontage of 105 ft. 11 in. x 117 feet depth and consists of 3 floors in height, with basement. Here is carried a very heavy and varied stock of railroad, mill and steamship supplies of every description which are of the very best quality and are obtained direct from the manufacturers in this country and Europe. Mr. Wilson is also a manufacturer of oils and cotton waste of which he keeps a large stock constantly on hand. Having ample resources and the best of facilities for obtaining supplies and purchasing in large quantities, he is enabled to give his patrons the benefit of the very lowest market prices, for similar quality of goods. Mr. Wilson furnishes supplies to nearly all the railroads in Canada as well as many of the steamship and steamboat lines and mills throughout the country. This business was established 14 years ago and from a comparatively small beginning it has been built up to its present most extensive proportions while the trade is still steadily increasing. Mr. Wilson is a native of Ireland and has resided in this country since early youth. He is one of Montreal's representative business men and a member of the Board of Trade.

D. Drysdale, 645 CRAIG STREET, MONTREAL.—The progress made in the building operations of Montreal during the past five years has been very marked, and the building trade has been considerably benefited thereby, as well as the sister branches thereof, wherein the builder's hardware trade forms an important adjunct. One of the well known houses in the builders' and general hardware line in this city is that of Mr. D. Drysdale, which is located at No. 645 Craig Street. The premises occupied by the business are 24 x 60 feet in dimensions, and contain a large and carefully selected stock of builders' supplies, hardware, mechanics' tools, etc., etc. The stock is large and comprehensive and is all of the very best quality, being obtained from some of the most celebrated manufacturers in this country and Europe. This business was founded three years ago, and during that comparatively short space of time it has met with remarkable success, and has steadily grown up from year to year, the prospects for the future being exceedingly encouraging, both a retail and jobbing trade being conducted. Mr. David Drysdale, the proprietor, who is a Montrealer by birth, and is widely and favorably known here, was in the employ of Mr. Walker, hardware merchant, for 20 years, so that he thoroughly understands every detail of the business and is at all times prepared to meet the demands of the trade and the public. He is a progressive business man and a member of the Montreal Board of Trade.

Raoul Dufresne, OFFICE: 537 B. CRAIG STREET, MONTREAL; FACTORY: BEDFORD, QUEBEC; TELEPHONE 1380.—The colors used by the old Italian painters were the very purest that could be obtained, and thus it is that the Italian paintings are so remarkably well preserved to the present day. During recent years the demand for the best quality paints has greatly increased, and manufacturers are using their best endeavors to satisfactorily meet the market in this respect. Among the more reliable manufacturing houses in this Province in the paint line is that of Mr. Raoul Dufresne, whose factory is located at Bedford, P.Q. This gentleman manufactures the Pacific brand of pure white lead which is so well and favorably known to the trade throughout the country for their purity and excellence. A speciality is made of coach colors, which, as everyone knows, are the most difficult kinds of paints to be obtained that will give satisfaction. Mr. Dufresne has met with the most gratifying success in this respect. A branch of the house was established in this city two years ago, being now located in handsome and elegantly fitted up premises at No. 537 B Craig Street. Mr. A. Frappier is the efficient agent, and has succeeded in building up an excellent and ever increasing trade. All goods manufactured at the factory are shipped to purchasers from the warehouse here. Besides these paints Mr. Frappier deals in all kinds of dry colors, which he specially imports from some of the leading manufacturing houses in Europe and the United States. The trade of the house extends throughout the Provinces of Ontario and Quebec. The premises occupied by the warehouse are 22 x 45 feet in dimensions, with an extension in rear of 30 feet. These are heavily stocked with the goods dealt in, which are put up in tins, cans and bulk. Mr. Frappier is a native of the Province of Quebec and is a pushing, energetic and successful business man.

Sackville S. Bain 48 BEAVER HALL HILL, MONTREAL. NURSERIES: AT "VERDUN," AND ST. CATHERINE STREET, MONTREAL.—An all wise Providence has furnished to mankind in the flowers that shed their fragance on the air and delight the eye, a source of keen enjoyment to refined natures. Flowers are ever acceptable either in the house of mourning or of joy. We place upon the brow of the bride the orange wreathe and upon the casket and grove of our beloved dead we give our best tribute of love in the form of flowers. Montreal has several first class houses engaged in the nursery and florist business and among these deserving of special mention, is Mr. Sackville S. Bain, whose store is located at No. 48 Beaver Hall Hill. He has also a greenhouse on St. Catherine street for decorative plants, for house decoration. the terrace or reception. The nursery is situated at Verdun, about 2 miles from Montreal, and covers 10 acres of ground. There are 4 glass houses, 20 x 100 feet in dimensions. These are heated by hot water from 3 boilers and there is a pump for pumping water from the river for use in the grounds and nothing is omitted that could tend to the successful prosecution of the business. The nursery is richly stocked with some of the choicest plants and flowers to be found in the Dominion and Mr. Bain, who is a native of Scotland, and learned the business of a nurseryman in that country is one of the best line in the country and has proved highly successful as a power and also as a business man, for since he established his business here 10 years he has built up a trade that now extends throughout the entire Dominion.

Goldie & McCulloch, GALT SAFE WORKS, ALFRED BENN, MANAGER, ST. JAMES STREET.—" The bold, burglarious burglar is a burgling" at all times whether we have detectives and police or not and the only safe guard for ones valuables is a burglar proof safe. For many years the burglar kept a head and neck race with the safe manufacturer and as soon as a safe was made said to to withstand all attempts made upon it, around came the bold burglar and, presto ! it was opened and the contents abstracted. The manufactureres however have been gaining on their antagonists of late years. The Goldie & McCulloch safes, are acknowledged to be superior to all others in the Dominion as to burglar and fire proof qualities. The Goldie & McCulloch, Galt Safe Works were established in the year 1844 and from a comparatively small beginning have been built up to their present extensive proportions. The firm manufacture all kinds and sizes of safes for all purposes and they have supplied the Dominion Government, Bank of Montreal, Canadian Bank of Commerce, Bank of London, Bank of Ottawa, Imperial Bank of Canada, Quebec Bank, Ville-Marie Bank and many other prominent institutions both at home and abroad. Their safes have stood many severe tests and have upon all occasions come out successfully Their record is well known to the business men throughout the Dominion and orders are daily being received by mail and otherwise from all parts of the Dominion for their safes. Messrs. Goldie and McCulloch have been awarded Gold medals both for their Fire and Burgler Proof Safes at the exhibitions held in Toronto, Ottawa, Quebec and St. John, N. B., also first prize at Montreal and all the principal exhibitions throughout the Dominion. Mr. Alfred Benn the General Manager for this city whose office and warerooms are located at 298 St. James St., is a gentleman eminently qualified for the position, both by experience, ability and enterprising characteristics.

R. J. Inglis, MERCHANT TAILOR, 31 BEAVER HALL HILL, MONTREAL.—The gentlemen of Montreal are particularly noticed for their fashionable style of dress and other cities in the Dominion take their copy from here. That is not to say, that Montreal sets the styles, for that emanates from the parliament of tailors, even as the laws of the country are emanated from our legislative halls, but people are prone to copy after others and what attracts the eye, generally influences the decision. Montreal is well favored in possessing a number of first-class merchant tailoring establishments, among the number worthy of honorable mention being that of Mr. R. J. Inglis, which is located at No. 31 Beaver Hall Hill. The premises occupied are 22x48 feet in dimensions and are the most elegantly fitted up of any similar establishment in the Dominion. The wood-work being in stained cherry and the walls covered with Japanese leather paper, while mirrors of beveled glass reach from floor to ceiling, the whole presenting a rich and unique appearance. A magnificent assortment is kept in stock of imported woollens, tweeds, cassimeres, coatings, which are imported direct from some of the most celebrated looms in Europe and embrace the most seasonable and fashionable styles, from which gentlemen can select to suit their taste. These are made up to order by measure in the highest style of the art and for beauty of style and finish, as well as perfection of fit, the garments turned out by this house are not surpassed by those of any other establishment in the city. Mr. Inglis does the work of making the uniforms for the C. P. R·, employees, and goes twice a year as far as the Pacific coast, having customers throughout the Dominion. These facts speak for themselves, more plainly than words of ours can do, of the excellence of the work done by Mr. Inglis and the satisfaction given his numerous patrons. He gives steady employment throughout the year to about 35 skilled operatives. Mr. Inglis is a native of Toronto and is a gentleman of marked ability, push and energy.

Lymburner & Matthews, 485 St. James Street, Montreal.—Few outside of the regular branch of the trade know to what an extent that branch of business known as brass moulding and electro silver plating is conducted. It is a specialty in itself but forms an important factor in the general make-up of the manufacturing industries of the city. One of the most prominent houses in this line of business in Montreal is that of Messrs. Lymburner & Matthews, of No. 485 St. James Street. This business was established by Mr. Lymburner 20 years ago, and from a comparatively small beginning it has been built up to its present extensive proportions. The premises occupied by the business consist of the plating department on St. James Street, which is 30 x 70 feet in dimensions, and the foundry which is located at St. Cunegonde. In the electro plating department is contained the latest and most improved machinery and appliances specially adapted for this class of work, which is driven by 10 horse steam power. To successfully turn out the work to supply the trade, employment is furnished to 25 skilled hands throughout the year. The firm do all kinds of brass moulding, harness and carriage trimmings, oreide, nickel, close and electro silver plating and gilding. The trade of the house is very extensive and embraces in its scope of operations the entire Dominion, the sale being principally with wholesale saddlery hardware houses in their carriage trimmings, which are beautiful in design and elegant in finish.

Montreal Quilting Co'y., King's Block, 643 Craig Street, Montreal.—In these modern days there is a marked tendency to specialties in all general branches of manufacture, and by thus confirming the efforts to one special branch, better work can be done and cheaper than when the operations are extended over a larger field. Thus we see that in furniture manufacturing, some houses devote their energies entirely to chairs and others to tables, &c. Among the special lines of manufacture in this city must be mentioned that of the Montreal Quilting Company whose factory is located at No. 643 Craig Street, in King's Block. The premises occupied are commodious and are fitted up with all the most improved machinery specially manufactured for this line of work, while employment is furnished to a large staff of skilled operatives throughout the year, in the manufacture of quilted linings for fur goods, mantles, clothing, skirt lining &c., &c. The work turned out by this house is first-class in every particular, being artistic in design and the materials used of the very best quality. This is in itself well worthy of honorable mention. The members of the firm are Messrs. Wm. Koch, who is a resident of New York, and Th. Messmer, who attends to the business operations here. The trade of the house is very extensive, embracing as it does in the scope of its operations, the entire Dominion. This business is conducted entirely at wholesale with the furriers, clothiers, &c. This house was established 2 years ago and from the time of its inception it has proved entirely successful.

Hill & Forbes, 427 St. James Street, Stephens' Block, Montreal; Telephone No. 982 —Within recent years a very marked improvement has taken place in the tastes and culture of the general public, and this is especially seen in the decoration of their homes. The house painter has of course been obliged to keep up with this desirable tendency of the times and bring his best efforts into play by harmonious coloring and artistic design. The painter, in his turn, has demanded from the paint manufacturers the best that can be procured, for unless the colors are rich in tone and pure in quality good and lasting work would be an utter impossibility. Holding a prominent position among those engaged in the paint and oil trade in this city is the firm of Messrs. Hill & Forbes, whose establishment is located in the Stephens' Block, 427 St. James Street, into which they moved on the 1st May of the present year, their former location being at 430 St. James Street, nearly opposite. This business was established seven years ago, and one year since was purchased by Mr. William Hill, the senior member of the present firm, he having had a previous experience in the business of a quarter of a century in the well known house of S. H. May & Co. On January 1st of the present year Mr. Forbes was admitted into partnership under the above mentioned title. The handsome premises occupied consist of three floors with basement 25 x 60 feet in dimensions. These are well adapted to the business conducted, and in the different floors the large stock is admirably and conveniently arranged. The firm are heavy importers and dealers in paints, oils, varnishes, brushes, window glass, glue, bronzes, kalsomine, artists' and coach painters' materials, etc., and they are also general agents for the Alabastine Co., of Paris, Ont. All goods handled by this firm are of the very best and purest quality and are procured direct from manufacturers in this country and Europe, so that customers can fully and implicitly rely upon whatever they obtain here as being according to sample or representation. The trade of the house is very large and is conducted both at wholesale and retail, and its operations extend throughout the entire Dominion. Mr Hill is a native of Ireland and Mr. Forbes is a Canadian by birth. They are both "workers" in the business in every sense of the word, and the success that has attended the efforts of the house has been eminently deserved.

SEELEY'S HARD RUBBER TRUSSES.

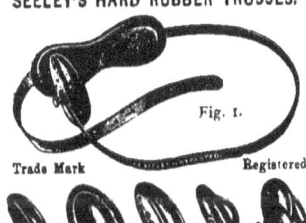

Fig. 1.

Trade Mark   Registered

Montreal Truss Factory, J. Hudson Proprietor. 686 Craig St., Montreal—Frail humanity is subject to a great many ills and infirmities, either hereditary or caused by accident or neglect and the best endeavors of mankind have been devoted to devising means to counteract, if not permanently cure the deformity or defect. In no branch has human ingenuity been more beneficially extended than in the manufacture of deformity apparatus, artificial limbs, &c. Among those prominently engaged in the manufacture of such articles in this city, there are none bearing a higher reputation than Mr. J. Hudson, proprietor of the Montreal Truss Factory, which is located at No. 686 Craig Street. This gentleman manufactures all kinds of deformity apparatus, trusses, supporters, braces, crutches, artificials limbs &c. The articles he manufactures are all of superior quality and are constructed upon the most scientific principles, being in every respect specially suited for the requirements. Special attention is given to the cases of children and a lady is in attendance for those of her sex. A very large and varied stock of goods is carried embracing everything in the truss, supporter, brace, and artificial limb line, while orders for special articles are attended to promptly and in a satisfactory manner. During the 4 years that Mr. Hudson has been engaged in business here he has built up an excellent trade that is steadily on the increase. Mr. Hudson is a native of Montreal and is a practical truss and artificial limb manufacturer of many years experience.

B. E. McGale, CHEMIST AND DRUGGIST, 2123 NOTRE DAME STREET.—There is an old saying and a true one, that "There is always room at the top." In all lines of business as well as in the professions, this is the case, and there are very few that reach there, and those who do so, only succeed by the exercise of hard work and indomitable energy and industry. Among those engaged in the profession of pharmacy in this city, Mr. B. E. McGale may truthfully be said to have reached that commanding height of success. Mr. McGale is a native of Saint Roch de l'Achigan, Montcalm county, but has resided in Montreal since his childhood. He received his early education at Mr. Doran's Commercial Academy, and afterwards at the Montreal Business College. He began the study of pharmacy at Gray's drug store on St. Lawrence Main Street, and graduated with high honors from the Montreal College of Pharmacy. Twelve years ago Mr. McGale started in business for himself and ever since the date of its inception his success has been rapid and assured. The premises occupied by him at No. 2123 Notre Dame Street, are elegantly fitted up in natural woods, beautifully carved, plate glass show cases and cabinets for the advantageous display of the splendid stock carried. The store is one of the finest in the city as it is one of the most popular. A very large and elegant stock is carried, consisting of fresh and pure drugs, chemicals, fancy and toilet articles; imported and domestic soaps, perfumes, &c., also proprietary medicines of acknowledged merit and standard reputation, as well as all such articles as are required by physicians in their practice. Employment is furnished to 3 competent and careful assistants throughout the year. The store at night is brilliantly lighted by electricity and presents a very attractive appearance, and is well worth a visit.

John E. King, SADDLE HARNESS AND TRUNK MANUFACTURER, 302 ST. JAMES STREET, NEAR VICTORIA SQUARE), MONTREAL.—Montreal has many old-established and substantial business houses, the names of the owners of which are as "familiar in our mouths as household words." They have done much to build up—not only the commercial prosperity—but the good name of the city and they are deserving of the thanks of our citizens. Some businesses have descended from father to son in regular rotation. Among such houses worthy of special mention in a work of this character is that of Mr. John E. King, saddle, harness and trunk manufacturer, whose store is located at No. 302 St. James street. This business was established by Mr. William King in the year 1850 and was successfully conducted until 1873, when the present proprietor Mr. John E. King succeeded to it and the reputation of the old house has been steadily maintained. The premises occupied by the business are 25 x 60 feet in dimensions and contain a fine stock of saddlery and harness, horse furnishing goods and stable requisites, as well as a fine line of trunks of every description. Mr. King manufactures single and double light and heavy harness of the best description nothing but the very best quality of materials and trimmings being used, while the workmanship is scrutinized thoroughly so that the most satisfactory results are obtained. The house has long held a high reputation for the work turned out, and it has stood the test of years, which should be a sufficient guarantee. Mr. King is a Canadian by birth and is a skilled, practical workman and an energetic business man.

D. Campbell & Son,, 36 DALHOUSIE STREET.—Contained among the many manufacturing industries of Montreal, is the important factor of cooperage. The numberless kegs, barrels and casks that are used in vinegar factories, flour mills, paint works, etc., have all to pass through the coopers' hands. The business is actively prosecuted in this city, and among the most prominent of those engaged in this line is the firm of Messrs. D. Campbell & Son, whose cooperage is located at No. 36 Dalhousie street. The premises occupied by the cooperage are commodious and are 2 stories in height, employment being furnished to 20 skilled workmen throughout the year. The firm manufacture all kinds of barrels, casks and kegs, and their trade is very extensive and embraces in the scope of its operations the city and a large section of the surrounding country. This business was established 35 years ago by Mr. John Campbell, and the present firm succeeded to the business 10 years ago. From the date of its inception it has proved highly successful and has been steadily built up from year to year. The firm do also an extensive warehousing business, having adjoining premises, 3 stories in height for this purpose. The entire buildings occupied cover 90 x 120 feet in dimensions, the cooperage being built of brick and the warehouse of stone. The members of the firm are natives of Glasgow, Scotland, and are practical coopers and give their personal attention to all orders entrusted to their care. They are straightforward and honorable men of business and both are members of the Montreal Board of Trade.

D. Nicholson & Co., (Successors to R. Alexander,) GRAVEL and GENERAL ROOFERS, 41 St. Antoine Street, Montreal.—Leaking roofs have at all times been the bane of life of landlord and tenant alike, and as well as being inconvenient, do considerable damage to property. It is an old saying and a true one, that "a stitch in time saves nine," and this is most forcibly applicable with regard to a leak in a roof. If repaired immediately, it is noticed that it saves considerable expense and damage in the future. One of the best known firms of roofers in this city is that of Messrs. D. Nicholson & Co., whose office is located at No. 41 St. Antoine Street. This business was founded 20 years ago by Dr. Cowan, who in time was succeeded by Mr. R. Alexander, and upon the decease of that gentleman 8 years ago, the present proprietors came into possession. The firm do all kinds of gravel, rosin cement and general roofing, gravel roofing being a specialty. They also repair gravel and rosin cement roofs, tin, iron and shingle roofs are repaired and painted. The work done by this firm is of the very best quality, and all orders entrusted to them are guaranteed to be satisfactory and promptly attended to at reasonable charges.

On an average 12 competent men are given employment throughout the year. Messrs. Nicholson & Co. do one of the best lines of business in the city as their work can at all times be relied upon. They keep for sale roofing felt, pitch, rosin cement, etc. The individual members of the firm are Mr. D. Nicholson who is a native of the Isle of Skye, Scotland, and is a thoroughly skilled practical roofer, and Mr. John Smith who is also a Scotchman by birth, and an enterprising business man.

Both members of the firm are practical to the trade in which they are engaged, and personally supervise all work entrusted to them, thus ensuing perfect satisfaction. The business department is ably conducted by Mrs. D. Nicholson, in whose efficient hands it is carefully and successfully administered.

J. W. Paterson & Co., MANUFACTURERS AND DEALERS IN ROOFING MATERIALS, 47 Murray Street, Montreal, and 217 Front Street, East, Toronto.—Consequent on the growth of the country, the various branches of business conducted have been divided and sub divided into certain sections, until to day, when work is needed to be done that comes under a generic head, it is necessary to call upon one who practices that special branch of the given industry. In the mechanical branches there can be no question but that this sub-division has been productive of the greatest good, especially is this the case in the building trade. In the manufacture and dealing in roofing materials the house of Messrs. J. W. Paterson & Co., which is located at No. 47 Murray Street in this city, is one of the most important in the line. The business was established here in 1872 and so rapidly did their trade extend that 7 years ago a branch establishment was founded at No. 217 Front Street, East, Toronto, under the title of J. W. Paterson & Bro., Mr. W. L. Paterson being the manager there, and attends to the western trade. The firm manufacture and deal in all kinds of tarred felt, tarred sheathing, hard and soft dry felt for lining and carpets, rosin sized sheathing &c. Also coal tar, American and Canadian shingle varnish, roofing pitch and cement, gravel for roofs and walks, rosin, pine, pitch, tar, oakum &c. The manufactory is fitted up with all the most improved machines and appliances for the successful prosecution of the business and only the most skilled workmen are employed. The trade of the house is conducted at both wholesale and retail and its scope of operating extends throughout the Dominion and Newfoundland in which latter country it was introduced only a year ago but has already made the most satisfactory showing even in the face of American competition. Mr. Paterson is a Scotchman by birth and in his line of business he occupies a prominent place, a position that has been won by energy and enterprise, and that strict attention to detail in filling all orders, that is always sure of attracting a large patronage.

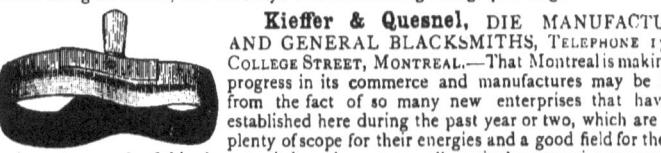

Kieffer & Quesnel, DIE MANUFACTURERS AND GENERAL BLACKSMITHS, Telephone 1724, 27 College Street, Montreal.—That Montreal is making rapid progress in its commerce and manufactures may be learned from the fact of so many new enterprises that have been established here during the past year or two, which are finding plenty of scope for their energies and a good field for their operations. In a work of this character it is a pleasure to call particular attention to some of the more important of these houses of comparatively recent establishment. In this connection the firm of Messrs. Kieffer & Quesnel, die manufacturers and general blacksmiths, of No. 27 College Street, are deserving of special mention. This house was founded only one year ago at No. 31 McGill Street, and during that short time it has been doing business it has met with such success that larger premises became necessary, and so the works were removed to 27 College Street in May of this year. The premises occupied are 30 x 55 feet in dimensions and are fitted up with all the latest and most improved machinery and appliances for the successful conducting of the work in hand, a 15 horse-power engine furnishing the motive power, while employment is furnished to 10 skilled and competent workmen throughout the year. The trade of the house is increasing very rapidly and the scope of its operations embraces the entire Dominion. The firm manufacture all kinds of dies for boots and shoes, envelopes, gloves and anything else in the die line. They also do a general blacksmith business, and all orders entrusted to them are attended to promptly and the best of satisfaction is guaranteed. Mr. Louis Kieffer, the senior member of the firm, is an Alsatian by birth, and Mr. Alphonse Quesnel is a native of Chateauguay. Both are practical workmen and energetic business men.

Alfred Eaves, IMPORTER OF WATCHES AND JEWELLERY, 1679 Notre Dame Street, Montreal. — In estimating the value of the commercial interests of Montreal it is found that the watchmaking and jewellery trade forms a very important factor and is an indication of the prosperity of the city at large. There are a large number of first class houses engaged in this business here, prominent among them being that of Mr. Alfred Eaves, whose establishment is located at No. 1679 Notre Dame Street. The premises occupied are large and commodious, being 30 x 80 feet in dimensions, and are handsomely fitted up with plate glass show cases and cabinets, wherein is displayed to excellent advantage an elegant stock of English, French and American watches in gold and silver, clocks, rings, chains setts, pins, a fine assortment of jet jewellery, spectacles, glass eyes for birds and animals, watch tools and materials, and many other beautiful articles of jewellery too numerous to mention in detail. Mr. Eaves imports his own stock direct from some of the leading houses in Europe and the United States, and purchasing in large quantities on the most favorable terms is enabled to give his customers the benefit of bottom prices for best quality of goods. The business is conducted at both wholesale and retail and a large jobbing trade is done with the retail merchants throughout the Provinces of Ontario and Quebec. This business was established 15 years ago and almost ever since the date of its inception it has proved eminently successful and has steadily increased in extent and importance. Mr. Eaves is a native of England, and having had many years experience in the watchmaking and jewellery trade thoroughly understands all its details and the requirements of the trade and public.

James M. Aird, 1877 NOTRE DAME STREET, MONTREAL.—It has with truth been said that "Bread is the staff of life." It is one of the articles of food of which one never tires, even if served at every meal ; at the same time it is nourishing and wholesome. It is necessary, however, that it should be made of the best materials, and that no injurious ingredients should be used in its manufacture. One of the most important houses in this line of business in this city is that of Mr. James M. Aird, whose store and office is located at No. 1877 Notre Dame Street, near McGill Street. The store is large and commodious, and is tastefully fitted up. In rear is a refreshment room containing fifteen tables, where lunches and refreshments can be obtained. There is a handsome soda water fountain in front and all the appointments of the store are in excellent taste. Mr. Aird has just built a new bake house at No. 101 St. Urbain Street, which is two stories in height and 50 x 55 feet in dimensions. This contains three brick ovens and one continuous baking oven, and is fully equipped with all the latest and most improved appliances for the successful prose-cution of the work. Mr. Aird makes more varieties of bread than all the other city bakers combined, having 35 kinds to choose from. He also manufactures choice cakes and can-dies. He does not do business with the trade, as his family custom is all that he can attend to, having 1500 families whom he serves regularly, besides his transient custom in the store. In the prosecution of his business he gives employment to 35 skilled hands and courteous assistants, and has six teams constantly on the road delivering goods to his customers throughout all parts of the city. Mr. Aird is a native of Outremont, and since founding his business in 1877 he has met with the most flattering success, which has been due to his untiring efforts to supply his customers with the best that could be produced.

Montreal Optical and Jewellery Co. [Limited]. MANUFACTURING OPTICIANS, 1685 NOTRE DAME STREET, MONTREAL.—None save those who have lost it can fully appreciate the value of good eyesight, nor can anyone outside the profession measure the difficulties that lie in the way of successful treatment of diseases of the eye and even partial restoration of impaired sight. Diseases of the organs of vision, too, are on the increase, as may be seen by the constantly augmenting number of those who are compelled to resort to the use of glasses at a comparatively early age, and skilfully fitted glasses present the only practical hope for those whose eyes exhibit symptoms of deterioration. The Mont-real Optical and Jewellery Co., Limited, whose establishment is located at No. 1685 Notre Dame Street, are manufacturing opticians and importers, and manufacturers of every description of spectacles, eyeglasses and cases. The premises occupied by the business consist of two floors, each 15 x 68 feet in dimensions, and which are fitted up with every appliance for the successful prosecution of the work in hand, while employment is steadily furnished to 12 skilled and competent workmen throughout the year, while three commercial travellers represent the house in all parts of the Dominion. The goods manufactured by this company are of the very best quality and the most perfect workmanship, and have a high standard reputation throughout the trade, which embraces in the scope of its opera-tions the entire Dominion. This business was established in the year 1883, and has made rapid progress since that time and been at all times highly successful. The Montreal Optical and Jewellery Co. is a joint stock concern, having for its officers the following well-known gentlemen : C. A. Vallee, President ; M. Schwob, Vice-President , Charles Grant, Secretary-Treasurer. The company has won an enviable reputation for straightforward dealing and excellent quality of goods.

Arcand Brothers, 111 ST. LAWRENCE STREET, MONTREAL.—Holding a conspicuous place among the retail dry-goods establishments of Montreal is that of Messrs. Arcand Brothers, which is located at No. 111 St. Lawrence street, corner of Lagauchetière street. The premises are admirably adopted to the business conducted, being 28 x 70 feet in dimensions and are fitted up in an attractive manner, the large stock being displayed to excellent advantage. The stock handled embraces staple and fancy dry goods of every description, silks, satins, velvets and velveteens, plushes, dress goods in all the latest novelties, and most fashionable patterns, smallwares, linens, laces, trimmings, hosiery and hosiery notions and many other departments too numerous to mention in detail. A specialty is made of the manufacture of ladies' mantles, and there is also a tailoring department connected with the business, which is under the personal supervision of Mr. W. Arcand, who is a practical tailor of many years experience and has now an enviable reputation for the perfection and beauty of the garments turned out. The firm have only one price and that is the lowest they can possibly afford consistent with a safe and honorable business and it has been upon this policy that they have, during the six years they have been established in business, built up so excellent a trade, as well as to their liberal and straightforward dealing. Employment is furnished to 20 courteous assistants and operatives in the different departments. The individual members of the firm are Messrs. J. A. ; J. Z. ; and W. Arcand, gentlemen well known in commercial circles, for their business qualification, push and enterprise.

(FORMERLY MOLSONS COLLEGE)

Colin McArthur & Co., MONTREAL WALL PAPER FACTORY, 15 VOLTIGEUR ST., COR. NOTRE DAME ST., MONTREAL.—There is a recognized connection between all branches of design, some of these being intimately associated, so that knowledge gained in one art is partially transferable to another. Textile patterns in connection with wall papers afford an instance. Many of these textile patterns are repertones for suggestive applications of graceful lines, harmonious disposition of colors and symmetrical spacing for walls of rooms. Thanks to the wall paper manufacturer's art, the palaces of the rich, and the cottages of the poor alike, are rendered luxurious, beautiful, and more homelike than ever before, while skill and invention are more than ever stimulated to new and pleasing combinations of patterns, colors and effects. The Dominion of Canada was, for many years, dependant upon England, France and the United States for its wall papers, but progress is the motto of the age and to-day there are three wall paper factories in the Dominion, chief among which is the Montreal Wall Paper Factory, which is located in the old Molson's College. The building is a substantial brick structure, 3 stories in heighth with basement and also two towers, the dimensions of the building being 225 x 35 feet. The basement is utilized for the color room, the raw stock, and also for the engine room; on the ground floor are the business offices, the stock room and packing room, and also the most expensive part of the works —the making of the brass pattern rollers ; as a great many patterns of paper are turned out twice a year, and as in some cases it takes as many as eight rollers for one pattern of paper, it will readily be seen that a great many are required ; upon the wooden rolls is pasted a paper pattern in outline, and this is followed by indenting brass into the wood, in a similar manner to what the Japanese make thin gilt lines in satsuma ware. These must present an even surface, otherwise the printed design would be imperfect, so only the best of skilled help is employed; as this work is not intended as a technical authority on the process of manufacture of the different branches of trade in the city, but simply as an outline of the various manufactures, intricate details are uncalled for. The second floor is used for the manufacture of " regulars," " metallic's," and "micas." " Regular " papers contain 7 yards to the roll, and from 5000 to 6000 rolls can be manufactured in a day. Bronze papers :— as it takes about 24 hours for these to dry, a special flat is devoted to their manufacture, containing every facility for the proper execution of the work,—contain 8 yards to the roll, and about 2000 rolls are manufactured in a day. The first process of manufactured wall paper was entirely by hand stamping, and for the most expensive kinds of paper, this is continued to the present day, one of the towers is devoted to this purpose, and of these the average manufacture is 100 pieces a day. The other tower is used for general carpenter work. This factory gives employment to 50 skilled and competent workmen, and the five printing machines are driven by a 25 horse-power steam engine. The line of papers manufactured by this house are unexcelled by any manufactured in the country ; and many lines are equal to any imported ; the trade of the house extends throughout the Dominion. This business was established 5 years ago, and almost from the date of its inception it has proved eminently successful. Mr. Colin McArthur, the senior member of the firm, is a practical workman and was manager of the works of Wylie & Lochead, of Glasgow, Scotland for many years. He is a member of the Montreal Board of Trade. Mr. James Worthington, the other partner is manager of the Dominion Bolt Factory of Toronto, and was the celebrated contractor of the Canadian Pacific Railroad ; also, of part of Lachine Canal, &c., and is a member of the Toronto Board of Trade. The representatives of the house are, for Toronto and western Ontario, W. Williamson ; Ontario, east of Toronto and Eastern Townships, O. W. Ellis ; Nova Scotia and New Brunswick and Prince Edward Island, A. S. Kemp ; Quebec and District, W. M. McDonald ; Manitoba and North West, Tees & Persse of Winnipeg, and Montreal and District, D. J. McArthur.

Morris & Reynolds, METROPOLITAN BOOT AND SHOE STORE, 2015 NOTRE DAME STREET, MONTREAL.—Among the more important of the manufacturing and business industries conducted in this country is that of boots and shoes. Since the introduction of machinery in this branch of trade, this industry has assumed gigantic proportions and has given employment to thousands. Engaged in the retail branch of this business in Montreal, and situated in the centre of commercial activity at No. 2015 Notre Dame Street, is the well known firm of Messrs. Morris & Reynolds, proprietors of the Metropolitan Boot and Shoe House. Established twelve years ago, it has enjoyed a long, honorable and prosperous career. The premises occupied are commodious and well adapted to the business, and are stored with a complete stock of goods, embracing ladies', misses', gentlemen's, youth's, boys' and children's boots, shoes and rubbers of all kinds, from the principal manufacturing establishments of the Dominion. In addition to dealing in the above goods, the firm makes a specialty of ladies' and gentlemen's boots and shoes to order, and they are enrolled in this branch of the trade to turn out as handsome, well-fitting and durable goods as can be produced. Employment is furnished to 14 skilled and competent assistants throughout the year. A distinction specially is made of fitting deformed feet, and the possessors of such are always sent away happy from the "Metropolitan" as the house guarantees satisfaction in every case. The house possesses every known facility for the successful prosecution of the business, and owing to the experience of the proprietors and their widespread and intimate relations with manufacturers and producers, they are enabled to offer to the public reliable goods in the way of first-class reliable goods at low prices, not surpassed by any boot and shoe house in the city. Mr. George J Morris, the senior member of the firm, is a native of Montreal, and his co-partner, Mr. James E. Reynolds, is a Torontonian by birth.

Vulcan Boiler Works, W. C. WHITE, Proprietor, Corner Nazareth and Brennan Streets, Montreal.

—For many years man's ingenuity was exercised to find a way to manufacture a boiler that would not explode, but just as soon as success had been supposed to have been achieved away went the result of their labors in the air, and lucky it was if a number of lives did not go with it. The papers contained almost daily accounts of explosions of boilers in different parts of the country, either on the rivers, lakes, or on land. Now, however, accounts of such occurrences are but rare, which is a sure indication that non-bustible boilers have been brought as near perfection as possible. Among the most prominent and successful boiler makers in Montreal is Mr. Wm. C. White, whose works are located at No. 46 Brennan Street. This gentleman has been established in business since the year 1860, and from a comparatively small beginning has built up an excellent and ever increasing trade as well as a high reputation for the superior quality of the work turned out by him. He manufactures all kinds of boilers for marine and stationary engines. Another branch of the business is the manufacture of iron and steel steamers for lake and river navigation. He has built many of these that have given the most satisfactory results with regard to speed and stability. The works, which are 110 x 180 feet in dimensions, are fitted up with all the latest and most improved machinery. driven by two steam engines of 25 horse power combined, while employment is furnished to from 50 to 60 skilled workmen on an average throughout the year. The trade of the house is very extensive and embraces the entire Dominion from the Atlantic to the Pacific. Mr. White is a native of Paisley, Scotland, and is a practical boiler maker of many years experience and is a progressive and enterprising business man and citizen. Mr. Hugh Vallance, nephew of Mr. White, is business manager of the concern, and to his ability much of the success of the present establishment is due.

J. D. Bennett, CABINET MAKER AND UPHOLSTERER.

—There are few lines of business of more importance to the public generally—with the exception of those dealing in food supplies—than the furniture trade. This business has made very marked improvement during the past fifteen or twenty years, both in extent of operations and the style and quality of goods made. Holding a prominent place among the old established houses in this line in Montreal is that of Mr. J. D. Bennett, whose establishment is located at No. 562 Craig street. The premises occupied by the business consist of 2 floors each 45 x 90 feet in dimensions. Here is contained a fine stock of household furniture of every description, artistic in design and beautifully upholstered. Mr. Bennett makes a specialty of the manufacture of show cases for jewellery stores, millinery stores, gents furnishings stores and in fact for all purposes. He also manufactures plate chests, glass cases, gun, pistol, jewel and fancy cases of all kinds and descriptions.

He also does picture and mirror framing and neatly repairs papier mâché and leather work. His work is first class in every particular and the trade of the house extends throughout the city and vicinity, employment being furnished to 8 skilled and capable workmen throughout the year. Mr. Bennett, who is a native of Ontario, is a practical workman of large experience, and during the 22 years he has been established in business in this city he has built up a trade of which he may well feel gratified and a high reputation for straightforward and honorable dealing.

J. E. Manning, GROCER, 1, 3, 5 St. Antoine Street, Montreal.

—There is scarcely any line of business in which neatness and taste in display of the goods is of so much importance to success as in that of groceries. If the store is kept in a slovenly manner and the goods and fixtures look dusty there is nothing to tempt the eye or win a customer. On the other hand cleanliness, neatness and taste have their desired effect. Among the many grocery stores in this city worthy of special mention for its general appearance and excellent quality of stock carried, is that of Mr. J. E. Manning; which is located at No. 1, 3, 5 St. Antoine Street. The premises occupied are 26 x 80 feet in dimensions, with high ceiling and are fitted up in an excellent manner and the large stock handled is shown to the best advantage. The stock includes the finest brands of China and Japan teas, coffees from Java, Mocha and Rio, table delicacies, hermetically sealed goods in glass and tin, as well as all other articles usually to be found in a first-class grocery establishment of this character. There is also a fine line of prime quality provisions and the choicest brands of wines and liquors, imported and domestic, and specially suited for fine family trade. This business was established six years ago and ever since the date of its inception its progress has been steadily onward, and is still increasing. The trade is conducted at both wholesale and retail and embraces the city and vicinity. Employment is furnished to four competent clerks and two teams are used for the delivery of goods. Mr. Manning, the proprietor, is a Canadian by birth, and is thoroughly acquainted with all the details of the grocery business, by long practical experience.

Michel Lefebvre & CO., MANUFACTURERS IN BOND OF VINEGARS AND METHYLATED SPIRITS, 23 GOSFORD STREET, MONTREAL.—Montreal contains many old established and reliable houses in the several branches of manufacturing industries. These have been incepted and conducted by men of marked business ability, push and enterprise, and it is to their efforts, in a great measure, that the present status, as a commercial and manufacturing centre, the city of Montreal is now due. Among the old-established and prominent houses, in the manufactory line, is that of Messrs. Michel Lefebvre & Co., manufacturers of vinegars and methylated spirits. Their office and warehouse are located in the old Dominion theatre, Nos. 21 to 25 Gosford street, the works being located at No. 80 Papineau road. The works are located in a substantial 4 story building, 200 x 56 feet in dimensions. These are fitted up with every known requirements and facilities for the successful prosecution of the business while employment is furnished to 30 skilled workmen and assistants in the various departments. The firm manufacture vinegar and methylated spirits and these products have for many years been held as standard throughout the trade in the Dominion and received a medal at the Paris Exhibition of 1878 in competing against many of the most celebrated manufacturers of Europe. This, in itself, is a strong recommendation of the excellent quality of their goods. This business was founded in the year 1849 and from a comparatively small germ has arisen the present wide spreading oak. The trade of the house, which is on an extensive scale, is co-extensive with the Dominion. The Messrs. Lefebvre are Canadians by birth and are active members of the Montreal Board of Trade. The different brands of vinegars manufactured by this house are Imperial, triple strength, Côte D'Or, Crystal pickling, Bordeaux, Orleans, White Wine XXX, XX, X, Cider XXX, XX, X, Malt XXX, XX, X, and Port Wine Vinegar, all of which brands are well known as standard throughout the trade.

A. T. Pratt, MERCHANT TAILOR, 64 BEAVER HALL HILL, MONTREAL.— The establishment of new business houses in any community, especially if those houses are of importance in their special line, is a sure indication of progress and development. From the number of business establishments that have been located in Montreal during the past year, it is very evident that the city is rapidly growing as a commercial centre. Among those that have recently been incepted here, is that of Mr. A. T. Pratt, which is eligibly located for business at No. 64 Beaver Hall Hill. Mr. Pratt, although he only commenced business for himself on the 1st of March of the present year, is well known in tailoring circles and to the citizens of Montreal. He learned his business, practically, with Mr. J. E. McEntyre, with whom he was for ten years, and he was head cutter for Mr. R. Charlebois for four years, so that he has had an extended experience in the very best of schools in the city. The premises he occupies for the business are 24 x 50 feet in dimensions, and are handsomely fitted up, and contain an elegant stock of the most seasonable and latest fabrics from the leading

European houses, all goods handled are of the best quality. Mr. Pratt makes up suits to order on short notice in the highest style of the art and for excellence of fit, elegance of finish, and beauty of style these are not surpassed by any other first class house in the city. Employment is furnished at present to about 30 skilled operaters, and the business, considering the short time it has been established has met with marked success.

Thos. Allan & Co., JEWELLERS, &c., 2219 ST. CATHERINE ST., QUEEN'S BLOCK, MONTREAL.—The Watchmaking and Jewellery trade is a sure indication of the prosperity, or otherwise, of any particular community. Where it flourishes there will be found a large class of well-to-do people, who can afford to indulge their tastes for the beautiful in the precious metals. Montreal is of course the commercial metropolis of the Dominion, and here the Watchmaking and Jewellery trade is prosecuted on a large and important scale. Prominent among the old established and popular houses in this line of business here is that of Messrs. Thos. Allan & Co., whose store is eligibly located in the Queen's Block, 2219 St. Catherine Street. The premises occupied are large and commodious, being 30 x 110 feet in dimensions, and which are fitted up with marked taste and suitable for the requirements of the trade, having plate glass show-cases and cabinets, &c. for the advantageous display of the elegant stock carried, consisting of gold and silver watches of English, Swiss and American manufacture, clocks, rings, chains, setts, sleeve-buttons, scarf pins, bracelets, and a beautiful line of Canadian Jewellery ; also, choice bric-a-brac, electro plated ware, and many other beautiful lines that must be seen to be admired. The firm manufacture all kinds of Jewellery to order, and do watch and jewellery repairing on short notice and in the very best manner, giving employment to 5 competent jewellers, 1 watchmaker, and 3 boys. The business was established 20 years ago, and has at all times proved highly successful. The firm were formerly on St. James and Notre Dame Streets. Mr. Allan is a native of Scotland, and learned his trade in this country, he is well known and highly esteemed in business and social circles.

Smith & Co., MERCHANT TAILORS, 364 ST. JAMES STREET, MONTREAL.— Nowadays it is almost absolutely necessary with every man engaged in mercantile life to be well dressed; The world goes largely by appearances, and to the natural dignity of the man, tasteful dress adds great impressiveness. The importance of the art of the tailor was never so well understood or so heartily appreciated as at the present day, and the fact constitutes one of those features of modern civilization which an accurate journalist cannot conscientiously overlook. Hence in presenting a faithful picture of the business interests in Montreal, the merchant tailor must necessarily occupy an honorable position. One of the best and most popular houses in this line is that of Messrs. Smith & Co., which is located at No. 364 St. James Street. The premises occupied are 24 x 45 feet in dimensions and are fitted up in handsome style and the large and elegant line of goods carried is displayed to the best advantage. The stock consists of cassimeres, woollens, tweeds, suitings, vestings, and a vast variety of fashionable goods from which to make selection. The newest patterns and most attractive styles are always on hand as soon as put on the market. Custom-tailoring is done in all its branches, and the most stylish, well-fitting and durably made garments are here turned out to order at the shortest notice. As the members of the firm are practical cutters and tailors of extensive experience and attend to the cutting department themselves, and as rents are not so high in their location as in the more central portion of the city, it stands to reason that what they can save on these two important items, they can give their customers the benefit of and thus draw a large trade, which they have already done during the seven years they have been in business. Mr. Irving L. Smith, is a gentleman of marked business ability of courteous manners and straightforward in a his dealings.

Edmund Eaves, IMPORTER OF WATCHES AND JEWELLERY, 1683 NOTRE DAME STREET, MONTREAL—It is only in prosperous communities that the jewellery business can amount to any great proportions, for in new countries and settle-ments where the struggle is hard for the necessaries of life, luxuries are unthought of. Canada has passed the struggle stage and now contains many prosperous towns and cities, where as fine lines of goods can be found as anywhere on the American continent. Among those engaged in the wholesale watch and jewellery trade in the Dominion, none hold a higher or more important position than Mr. Edmund Eaves, whose establishment is located at No. 1683 Notre Dame Street. This gentleman established his business 15 years ago, and from a comparatively small beginning has built up a most extensive trade that now comprises the entire Dominion. The premises occupied by the business are large and commodious, being 24 x 90 feet in dimensions, and are finely fitted up and con-tain a very large and elegant stock of gold and silver English, Swiss and American watches, clocks, jewellery, watch tools and materials, fancy goods, bird's eyes, etc. Having ample resources and purchasing direct from some of the leading manufacturing houses in Europe and the United States he is enabled to give his numerous patrons advantages not readily to be obtained elsewhere. He gives employment to eight competent assistants throughout the year. Mr. Eaves is an Englishman by birth and is a thorough going man of business, and those forming business relations with him may rest assured of liberal and honorable treatment.

George Payne, GUN MAKER, 687 CRAIG STREET, MONTREAL.—A collection of different kinds of fire arms that have been manufactured in different countries and in different ages since the discovery of gun powder would make a very interesting exhibit and be a good indication of the progress and civilization made by the different countries. Even during the past half century, a remarkable improvement has been made in fire arms, and these have completely changed the methods of warfare. Among those prominently engaged in the manufacture of guns in this city, is Mr. George Payne, whose shop is located at No. 687 Craig Street. Mr. Payne manufactures guns and does gunsmithing in all its branches, choke-boring, repairing, etc., etc. He also manufactures racing skates after the most ap-proved models, from the finest quality of steel, which are finished up in the most perfect manner, and, are not surpassed by those of any other manufacturer in the Dominion. Among the prominent skaters who patronize Mr. Payne are: O'Brien, of New York; Dowd, of Montreal; and Black, of Fergus, Ont. He also deals in fishing tackle and all kinds of sporting goods. This business was established here thirty-five years ago and has at all times met with the most satisfactory success, which has been due no doubt in a great measure to the excellent quality of work done and the enterprise and ability displayed by Mr. Payne in the conducting of his business. Mr. Payne, is a native of Birmingham, England, and is a sk...ed, practical gunsmith of many years experience.

V. T. Daubigny, FRENCH VETERINARY SCHOOL, 378 AND 380 CRAIG STREET.—With the increase of the population of Montreal, and the developement of her business interests, comes the opportunity, nay necessity, for the establishment of those branches of industry which can only be prosecuted in a populous city ; because where there are few inhabitants, a sufficient support could not be provided for them to justify, their establishment, and in no business is this so true as in that of the veterinary surgeon. What the Montreal Veterinary College is to the English speaking races, so is the French Veterinary College, of which Mr. Victor Theodule Daubigny, is the proprietor, and professor, to the French. This school is in connection with the Laval University at Montreal, and is located at Nos. 378 and 380 Craig Street, in a substantial 3 story brick building 50x105 feet in dimensions, which are fitted up in the most approved manner in different departments. Mr. Daubigny, is well qualified for his profession being a graduate in 1879 of the Montreal Veterinary

College, and is Honorary President of the French Medical and Veterinary Association of Montreal. He is an enthusiast in his profession, and, as his services were called into requisition, so great was the success attending his treatment as a veterinary surgeon, that he immediately rose into popularitary, and a large practice came to him, which called for the possession of thorough hospital premises to successfully attend, and these are in connection with his school, where there is accommodation for 14 horses. Mr. Daubigny teaches the veterinary science in all its branches. There is also in connection with this establishment a school of horse-shoeing, in which this very essential department of veterinary knowledge is taught in the most scientific manner, and has proved a highly successful teacher. He is a Canadian by birth and is a gentleman highly esteemed both inside and out of the profession.

Norman Fletcher, BOOKS, STATIONERY AND FANCY GOODS, 146 ST. LAWRENCE MAIN.—During the lifetime of the present generation a wonderful advance has been made in the matter of education and it might truly be said that "The school-master is abroad. Our splendid system of common schools has done much to remove the demon of ignorance, and the good effect has been very observable. Another great aid to elevating the masses in the educational and moral scale is the publication of standard works at nominal prices so that they are kept within the reach of all. The booksellers and stationers are therefore reaping the benefit from this new order of things. Among those who are actively engaged in the bookselling and stationery trade in this city, is Mr. N. Fletcher, whose store is located at No. 146 St. Lawrence Main Street. The premises occupied are 15 x 40 feet in dimensions, and are completely fitted with a fine stock of books in general literature, newspapers and periodicals, including Century, Scribner's, St. Nicholas Bow Bells ; also, stationery for the home, the counting house, and the school. In fancy goods the stock is full and complete, and contains many beautiful articles both useful and ornamental. This business was established five years ago and Mr. Fletcher succeeded to it on the 1st February, of the present year. Mr. Fletcher is a native of Canada and is a gentleman of excellent business qualifications, being energetic, enterprising and progressive, and there is every indication that his efforts to build up a good trade will be fully crowned with success.

S. Goltman, MERCHANT TAILOR, 2226 ST. CATHERINE STREET. OPPOSITE THE QUEEN'S HALL.—Among the many vocations followed in Montreal, that of Merchant tailoring may be regarded as of the greatest importance to the community in furnishing those evidences of refinement and taste in dress that are represented in fashionable and well-fitting garments. One of the houses in this line of business which has been foremost in promoting the standard of excellence in dress, that of Mr. Samuel Goltman, established over 20 years ago, is of special importance, and demands more than a passing mention in review of those places most desirable in Montreal as purchasing points. The premises occupied, which are large and commodious, and handsomely fitted up, are located at No. 2226 St. Catherine Street. Here is carried a very large and elegant stock of imported and domestic cloths, woollens, tweeds, cassimers, &c., in the latest and most fashionable novelties from some of the most celebrated looms in this country and Europe. These are made up to order by measure on short notice in the highest style of the art, and in respect to perfect fit, beauty of style and elegance of finish are not surpassed by those of any other merchant tailoring establishment in the Dominion. The trade of the house is derived from among the most critical class in the country, and it is sufficient guarantee of the excellence of Mr. Goltman's workmanship to say that his custom is very extensive. Mr. Goltman is thoroughly skilled in all the details of the tailoring trade and at all times guarantees his patrons perfect satisfaction.

Thousand Island Granite Company, R. FORSYTH, Proprietor; Sole Agent for the Dominion of Canada for "Stuart's Granolithic;" Office, 130 Bleury Street; Factory, 552 William Street, Montreal.—The growth of Montreal in late years has been very rapid, not alone in the increase of her population but in the advancement in the character of the buildings erected, so that what was once a city without pretension to adornment has become the location of buildings noted for their architectural beauty over the entire continent, and this advancement in the taste exhibited is by no means confined to the public buildings, but is seen in many of our private residences. Polished granite and marble enter largely into the building operations of the present day, and the old wood and flagstone pavements on the principal streets and avenues are being replaced by Granolithic. The Thousand Island Granite Company of this city, of which Mr. Robert Forsyth is the proprietor, is one of the most important concerns engaged in the granite and marble trade in the Dominion. The office is located at No. 130 Bleury Street, and the factory at No. 552 William Street. This business was established here about 30 years ago, but in its inception it did not give promise of the extensive proportions to which it has since grown. The granite manufactured by this company is quarried at Thurso, on Grindstone Island, Jefferson County, New York, and at Gananoque, Ont., and also grey granite quarries at Stanstead, Que. This granite is admirably adapted for fine work on buildings and for monumental purposes, being impervious to damp and not liable to be effected in color by age or exposure to the weather. It is also well suited for interior decorations, giving a beautiful effect. The factory here covers about two acres of ground, there being a number of buildings upon it, which are fitted up with the most improved machinery for sawing, grinding and polishing the stone and marble, which is driven by water power of 75 horse, while employment is furnished to 75 skilled hands in the works and 50 men on an average are employed in the quarries. Mr. Forsyth manufactures the granite and marble for building purposes and also for monumental work. In the latter branch of the business he has a beautiful collection of specimens worthy the attention of the trade. Mr Forsyth also imports largely of Italian and foreign marbles from some of the most celebrated quarries in Europe. He is also sole agent for Canada for Stuart's Patent Granolithic, which is now so extensively used for street flagging, railway platforms, steps and landings, stable and coach house floors, etc., etc. He has also an agency for the same in Toronto. The trade of the house is very extensive and embraces the entire Dominion and a large section of the United States. Mr. Forsyth is a native of Caithness, Scotland, and is a civil engineer by profession, and was harbor engineer of Montreal for years. He is pushing, active and progressive and is looked upon as one of Montreal's representative citizens.

The Canadian Cork Cutting Co., JOHN AULD, Proprietor, 642 Lagau-gauchetiere Street, corner Chenneville and St. George Streets, Montreal.— The cork tree is formed in abundance in Spain, Portugal, Italy, the South of France, and the Barbary States, but the Spanish cork is considered the best for commercial purposes. Cork was well known to the ancients and is mentioned by Theophrastus, Pliny and other authors as being in use among the Greeks and Romans for floats to fishing nets, buoys to anchors, etc., and during the seige of Rome by the Gauls, when Ramillus was sent to Rome through the river Tiber, he had a cork life preserver under his dress. Cork is now extensively used for commercial purposes and its manufacture is an important industry. One of the most important houses in the Dominion in this line of manufacture is that of the Canadian Cork Cutting Co., of which Mr. John Auld is the proprietor. Recently a handsome 4 story brick structure 55 x 97 feet in dimensions was built by Mr. Auld at No. 642 Lagauchetiere street, corner of Chenneville and St. George street for factory purposes, the old factory having been located on College street. This business was established a quarter of a century ago by Evans, Mercer & Son, who in turn were succeeded by W. J. Matthews, S. S. & A. H. Ewing, and then in 1872 by the present proprietor, Mr. John Auld. The business during the past ten years at least, has made rapid development and now stands second to none in the Dominion either in quality of product or extent of operations. The factory is fitted up with the latest and most improved patent machinery, specially constructed for this line of business, and is driven by a steam engine of 30 horse power, while employment is furnished to 25 skilled hands throughout the year. Mr. Auld manufactures every description of corks, of which he keeps a large stock on hand, and cuts to order on the shortest notice. Also cork wood and cork life preservers, wood bungs, tops, spiles, caps, bottling wax and wire, cork driving and capping machines, tin foil, capsules, cane bottle baskets and many other lines of a similar nature. The trade of the house is very extensive and embraces in its scope of operations the entire Dominion and New Foundland. Mr. Auld is a native of Montreal and is well known in business and social circles.

James Fowler, FINE CUTLERY, 639 CRAIG STREET, (KING'S BLOCK,) MONTREAL.—Among the many lines of business conducted in Montreal will be found almost every branch of trade and manufacture represented, thus making Montreal a truly representative commercial centre and an important distributing point for the entire Dominion. Among those houses worthy of particular mention in a work of this character is that of Mr. James Fowler, manufacturer and importor of fine cutlery, whose establishment is located at No. 639 Craig Street, in King's Block. The premises occupied are 22 x 60 feet in dimensions and contain a fine stock of goods, consisting of hones, razor strops, brushes, combs, razors, and barbers' supplies generally, which he is prepared to furnish to the trade in large or small lots at lowest prices, quality considered. In the manufacturing department special attention is given to the making, repairing and grinding of fine cutlery, the concave grinding of razors, the manufacturing of moulders' and plasterers' tools being a leading specialty for which the house is celebrated. Mr. Fowler is agent for the celebrated tailors' shears manufactured by R. Heinish, of Newark, N.J., and devotes particular attention to this line of goods. The factory is fitted up with the most improved machinery, driven by steam power, and only the most skilled workmen are given employment. This business was established here 20 years ago by Mr. James Fowler, father of the present proprietor, who succeeded to the business three years ago, upon the decease of the founder. The business has at all times proved eminently successful.

R. N. McCallum, IMPORTER OF FANCY GOODS AND STATIONERY, 2217 ST. CATHERINE STREET.—Under the general head of fancy goods is embraced a great variety of articles, both useful and ornamental for the household, and a very large business is conducted in this line in Montreal. Among the houses devoted to this branch of trade here, none are more deserving of special mention in this work than that of Mr. R. N. McCallum, whose store is located at No. 2217 St. Catherine Street, Queen's Block. The premises occupied by the business are large and commodious, being 30 x 110 feet in dimensions, wherein is displayed to excellent advantage a large and comprehensive stock of fancy goods of every description, as well as stationery and toys, Christmas gifts, New Year's presents, wedding presents, birthday gifts, etc. In plush goods the stock contains the latest designs and colors, plush shaving cases, plush toilet sets, plush workboxes and jewellery cases. Also games, tea sets, horses, waggons, building blocks, stables, doll houses, dolls, toboggans, sleighs, tool boxes, doll sleighs, and many other lines too numerous to mention in detail. Since this business was established twelve years ago it has met with the most gratifying success and has constantly increased and developed in extent and importance from year to year. Employment is furnished to a number of competent and courteous assistants throughout the year. Mr. McCallum is a business man of marked push and enterprise, and the success that has attended his efforts has been well deserved.

Wm. Farquharson, MERCHANT TAILOR, No. 135 St. Peter Street,. Montreal.—Among the many lines of business followed in Montreal that of merchant tailoring may be regarded as of the greatest importance to the community, in furnishing those evidences of refinement and taste in dress that are represented in fashionable and well-fitting garments. For often the world is apt to judge a man by his clothes when his personal qualities are unknown. It is therefore necessary to success in life that one should be well dressed. As one of the houses in the merchant tailoring line, here, deserving of more than a mere passing notice in a work of this kind on the commerce and manufactures of Montreal, that of Mr. W. Farquharson is worthy of consideration. The premises occupied by the business are located at No. 135 St. Peter Street, and are 24 x 40 feet in dimensions and two stories in height, the upper floor being used as a workshop. This business was established 12 years ago, and soon a widespread and high reputation was built up on the excellence of the work done, and the result was the formation of an excellent trade. Mr. Farquharson, who is a native of Scotland, is highly proficient in the several details of the business, and has acquired an enviable name as a master of the art of fine tailoring. He is also noted for his marked good taste displayed in the selection of his stock, which is not to be surpassed in the city as regards quality and style of goods, and being thus enabled to give his patrons assortments from which to choose for either dress or business suits. At the same time the workmanship, style and fit of the garments produced are beyond adverse criticism and are made to order at short notice and at moderate prices, a specialty being made of military uniforms. In the various departments of the business employment is furnished to 15 skilled and competent operators throughout the year. With a complete knowledge of the business, Mr. Farquharson is in a position to meet all legitimate competition he may be called upon to withstand. He is ably assisted in the management of his business by his son, Mr. W. J. Farquharson, a young gentleman to whose ability much of the success of the business is due.

John B. Young, TINSMITH, IRON AND TIN-PLATE WORKER, 44 Bleury Street, Montreal.—The secret of manufacturing tin-plate from which so many useful articles of house furnishings are now made, was long and jealously guarded by the discoverer, but at last it was surreptitiously obtained and its manufacture became general. Half a century of a career for any business is a long and honorable record, and such is that of the house now represented by Mr. John B. Young, tinsmith. This business was founded by Mr. Dedman, fifty years ago, and then it was succeeded to by Messrs. Dedman & Young, and latterly Mr. John B. Young became the sole proprietor, and for a quarter of a century it has been located on Bleury street, the present number being 44. The premises occupied are 20 x 40 feet in dimensions, the workshop being in the rear where employment is steadily furnished to seven skilled hands. Mr. Young manufactures every description of tinware for house-furnishing goods and other articles, is an iron and tin-plate worker, and does all kinds of metal roofing. It is scarcely necessary for us to say anything about the quality of the work done by this house, it is too well known to the people of Montreal of the past and present generation. The house has always kept abreast of the times and held a prominent place in the trade. Mr. Young, the proprietor, is a native of Scotland, and came to this country in early life. He is a thoroughly skilled practical workman, and all orders entrusted to him receive his personal attention, are executed with promptness, and the utmost satisfaction guaranteed in all cases.

W. H. Hope, MANUFACTURER OF PICTURE FRAMES &c., 2253 and 2254 St. Catherine Street, Montreal.—Art in all ages and in all climes exercised a powerful influence in refining and civilizing communities. It has only been during the past half century however that the masses of the people have had such an opportunity of studying art in sculpture or the works of the engraver or painter. In such a high state of perfection has the lithographic art been brought in the present day that beautiful specimens of this art are now brought within the reach of all at a nominal price. Mr. W. H. Hope, whose store is located at Nos. 2253 and 2254 St. Catherine St., imports largely in steel engravings, chromos, water colors, oil paintings, photographs &c. The stock he carries in these lines is large and has been selected with excellent judgement and taste and will be found well worthy of inspection, there being many choice works of art in the collection. Mr. Hope also does an extensive business in the manufacture of gilt and walnut frames, photograph frames, gilt, antique, oak and bronze mouldings, wholesale and retail, and easels of all sizes. Also picture framing, re gilding and and all other work of a similar nature. Those desiring any thing of this kind done should call upon Mr. Hope who guarantees perfect satisfaction both as regards the quality of work done and moderate prices. Mr. Hope has been established in business during the past 10 years during which time he has built up an excellent and steadily increasing business. He is a Scotchman by birth and is well known in business and social circles in which he is high-ly respected for his many intrinsic qualities.

R. Cochenthaler, ROYAL CIGAR PARLOR, 63 BLEURY STREET, MONTREAL— There are some people who are strong opponents to the practice of smoking, and in their self-importance believe they have a right to control the opinion and habits of the world in this respect. Do such people stop to think that they are in a very insignificant minority, or what the figures for smoking show. During the year 1886, in the United States alone $180,000,000 worth of cigars were consumed, besides $6.500,000 for cigarettes and $20,000,000 for tobacco for pipe use, and for chewing tobacco $50,000,000. These figures prove that the army of smokers and chewers is a very powerful one. One of the neatest cigar stores in this city is that of Mr. R. Cochenthaler, which is known as the Royal Cigar Parlor, and is located at No. 63 Bleury Street. Although this business was established only 2 years ago it has during that comparatively short space of time succeeded remarkably well and has steadily increased in patronage from month to month. The premises occupied, which are 15x45 feet in dimensions are tastefully and uniquely fitted up with plate glass show cases and cabinets and ornamental fittings in dark woods, the whole giving a very inviting and comfortable appearance. Here will be found a fine stock of specially imported genuine Havana cigars of the favorite brands, Egyptian, Turkish and American cigarettes, cut plug and perique mixture, meerschaum and briar pipes, and a large and fine assortment of tobaccos and smokers sun-dries. Mr. Cochenthaler is a native of Montreal and is well known in the community and being thoroughly progressive and enterprising is assured of a successful future.

City Ice Company, R. A. BECKET & CO. 21 VICTORIA SQUARE, MONTREAL— Canada is a splendid ice manufactory during three months in every year, nature is lavish in her supply and it only remains for capital and energy to take advantage of the provision made for the use of man against the time when "old sol" takes the place of Jack Frost. Holding a prominent position among those engaged in the ice business in this city is the City Ice Company, of which Messrs. R. A. Becket & Co., are the proprietors, the office being located at No. 26 Victoria Square. This business was established many years ago by Messrs. D. Morrice & Co., who were succeeded by the present firm. This business has always been a very successful one on account of the energy, enterprise and foresight displayed in its oper-ations. The firm have ice houses at No. 461 William Street and at Basin St. corner of Richmond Street and back of the Rolling Mills, near Cantin's ship yards. The firm have made many improvements, and use the latest appliances for the successful prosecution of the business. They have 25 horses, 8 wagons, besides hotel waggons and carts, as well as a "flote" for supplying the steamships with ice. The average output of ice during the season is 25,000 tons. The ice served by this company is the purest that can be obtained, and for their family trade is procured from the St. Lawrence above the Victoria Bridge where the water is clear. Mr. R. A. Becket, the proprietor, is a native of Ayrshire Scotland. and was manager of the ice department of D. Morrice & Co., for many years and latterly on his own account, and although having reached his majority in the ice business, he is not by any means of a cold disposition.

James Scott, GRAIN, HAY, MILL-FEED, &c., 132 St. Antoine Street, Montreal.—Canada is par-excellence, a grain growing country, and the operations of this trade are conducted upon a scale commensurate with its importance. The Canadian Boards of Trade and Corn Exchanges have done much to facilitate this business, and if the contemplated improvements in Montreal are carried out, this city will before long rank as a second Chicago. Its possibilities are great, it only requires the spirit of enterprise to make it so. Among those prominently engaged in the grain trade in this city is Mr. James Scott, whose store is located at No. 132 St. Antoine Street. This business was established 12 years ago by Mr. J. St. Jean, who was succeeded six years since by the present proprietor, Mr. Scott. The premises occupied by the business are large and commodious, being 26 feet frontage on St. Antoine Street and with a depth of 105 feet on Windsor Street, the building consisting of two floors and cellar. These are fitted up in the most approved manner for the convenient handling of the commodities dealt in, consisting of grain, hay, mill-feed, etc. The business is conducted both at wholesale and retail, and embraces the city and vicinity in its scope of operations. Mr. Scott also does a very large commission business, both in car lots and otherwise, receiving consignments and selling the same to the best advantage of the consignor and making prompt and satisfactory returns upon all sales. Mr. Scott is a Scotchman by birth and is possessed of their proverbial business ability and shrewdness. He is well and favorably known in business and social circles, and is an active member of the Montreal Board of Trade and the Corn Exchange.

M. T. Sarault, MERCHANT TAILOR, 1909 Notre Dame Street, Montreal.— In a city like Montreal great attention is paid to matter of dress, not only in the social circles but also in business, and to be well received within those social circles men must depend in a great measure upon their tailors. It is therefore necessary to go to a first-class one, whose reputation for taste and skill is assured. There are many first-class merchant tailoring establishments in this city, among the number deserving of special mention in a work of this character being that of Mr. M. T. Sarault, whose store is eligibly located for business at No. 1909 Notre Dame Street, opposite Balmoral and City Hotels. This business was established in the year 1865 and almost ever since the date of its inception it has met with the most pronounced success, the trade having steadily increased from year to year. The premises occupied are large and commodious, being 26 x 75 feet in dimensions, and are tastefully fitted up and contain a fine stock of imported and domestic fabrics, including tweeds, woollens, cassimers, coatings, etc., in the most fashionable and seasonable novelties. These Mr. Sarault makes up to order by measure in the highest style of the art, and for perfection of fit and beauty of style, coupled with elegance of finish, are not surpassed by those of any other merchant tailoring establishment in the city, while the prices will be found to suit the views of the most economical. These is also a fine stock of gents' furnishings, including all the latest novelties in neck wear, handkerchiefs, underwear, etc. Mr. Sarault is a native of the Province of Quebec and, thoroughly understanding all the details of his business, is at all times prepared to meet the public requirements.

George Brown & Sons, MERCHANT TAILORS, 21 Bleury Street, Montreal.—It has long been a recognized fact that the merchant tailoring establishment of Messrs. George Brown & Sons, at No. 21 Bleury Street, is one of the most prominent and popular in the city. This has been the result of the aim of the proprietors to produce only first-class garments. The making of gentlemen's wearing apparel to order by measure is one of those arts that requires for its successful prosecution the highest degree of artistic skill in every department of the business. This house was founded 20 years ago on Bleury Street, and has at all times been in the enjoyment of a liberal patronage, while the trade has steadily increased from year to year. From its inception the principle of the house has been to give full value for money, the best material, fit and excellence, and

thus a trade has been acquired among the most exacting of our citizens.   The premises occupied by the business on Bleury Street are 25 x 65 feet in dimensions, wherein is contained a
large and elegant stock of imported and domestic woollens, tweeds, coatings, etc., in all the
latest and most fashionable patterns from which to select, and which are made up to order on
short notice and at reasonable prices.   The stock of men's furnishings has been selected with
the utmost solicitude, as being especially of a ready selling character, and is procured direct
from first hands and manufacturers.   The firm also do a large business in the manufacture of
shirts and collars, which for perfection of fit and quality are not surpassed by any other house
in the city.   The members of the firm are Messrs. George James and Robert George Brown,
who have continued the business under the old firm title since the decease of their father,
Mr. George Fraser Brown.   They are natives of Montreal, and are young gentlemen of
excellent business qualities and are well and favorably known to all classes of the community

   R. Charlebois, MERCHANT TAILOR, 1879 NOTRE DAME STREET, MONTREAL—
Merchant tailoring, as it is conducted at the present day, is a fine art and requires for it
successful exponents, gentlemen of natural taste, acquired skill, and practical experience.   It
is no easy matter to make to order by measure a garment that, while it perfectly fits the body
will be pleasing to the eye.   Holding a prominent place among the merchant tailoring establishments in this city is that of Mr. R. Charlebois, which is eligiby located for business at No.
1879 Notre Dame Street, near McGill Street.   Founded just 6 years ago, this business has
been built up upon a solid foundation, deriving its patrons from among the most cultured
portion of the community.   While an excellent custom has been established, and also has a
high and widespread reputation for the work produced.   The premises occupied are large and
commodious being 24x60 feet in dimensions and consisting of 3 floors.   These are fitted up
in a very neat and tasteful manner and upon the counters and shelves is carried a large and
elegant stock of the finest woollens, tweeds, cassimeres, coatings &c., of foreign and domestic
manufacture embracing the latest and most fashionable novelties and fabrics.   These are
made up to order in the highest style of the art, and which, for beauty of style, perfection of
fit and elegance of finish are not excelled by those from any other merchant tailoring establishment in the city.   Employment is furnished on an average to 35 skilled operators and
assistants throughout the year.   Mr. Charlebois is a native of Montreal and is a practical
cutter giving his personal attention to all orders entrusted to his care, he ensures his
patrons the best satisfaction.

   L. Laurin, MERCHANT TAILOR, 3133 NOTRE DAME STREET, ST. CUN-
EGONDE.—The gentlemen of Montreal have the reputation of being the best dressed of any
in the Dominion, and this has been due no doubt in a great degree to the fact that there are
quite a number of first-class merchant tailoring establishments here, conducted by gentlemen
of marked skill and taste in this special line who produce garments that might be called
"poems in cloth."   Among the more popular houses in this line is that of Mr. L. Laurin,
which is located most eligibly for business at No. 3133 Notre Dame Street.   The premises
occupied are 24x65 feet in dimensions, the workshop being in the rear.   These are fitted up
in a very tasteful manner and upon the counters and shelves is carried an elegant stock of
imported and domestic woollens, tweeds, serges, tricots, cassimeres &c., in the latest and most
fashionable patterns from some of the most celebrated looms in Europe and this country
These are made up to order on short notice in the very finest styles and are not surpassed
by any other house in the city in respect to perfect fitting, beautiful style and elegance of
finish.   Employment is furnished to 25 assistants and skilled operatives throughout the
year.   There is also carried a beautiful stock of gents furnishings, embracing all the latest and
most seasonable novelties from Europe and this country.   This business was established 8
years ago and ever since the date of its inception it has met with the most pronounced
success.   Mr. Laurin, the proprietor, is a native of St. Eustache, and is a practical tailor
of marked ability and an enterprising and progressive business man.

Eagle Foundry, GEORGE S. BRUSH, 14 TO 34 KING STREET AND 43 QUEEN STREET.—One of the most strongly marked features of the Anglo-Saxon race is their spirit of industry, standing out prominent and distinct in their past history, and as strikingly characteristic of them now as at any former time. It is this spirit that has laid the foundations and built up the industrial greatness of the Empire. This rigorous growth has been mainly the result of the free energy of individuals, and it has been contingent upon the hands and minds from time to time actively employed within it. The Eagle Foundry, on King Street, of which Mr. George S. Brush is the proprietor, gives an illustration of the above principle. It is over half a century since this business was first established in a comparatively small way by Mr. John D. Ward and his brothers, who were afterwards joined by Mr. George Brush, under the title of Ward & Brush. After a number of years Mr. Brush became the sole proprietor and so continued until his death. Since the decease of Mr. George Brush his son—Mr. George S. Brush—has conducted the business of the foundry. The Eagle Foundry has long held a high reputation for the excellent quality of the work done there, which consists of marine engines, hoisting engines, steam boilers, steam pumps, circular saw mills, bark mills, shingle mills, shafting, hangers and pulleys, hand and power hoists for warehouses. Mr. Brush is also the sole maker of Blake's Challenge Stone Breaker and is agent for Waters' Perfect Steam Engine Governor, and also does jobbing and repairs of every description for shops and factories. A large staff of skilled workmen are given steady employment throughout the year, and several of the employees of this house have died in harness after long years of service, while others are well established in business of their own, which speaks in the highest terms for the amicable relations existing between employer and employed. All orders entrusted to Mr. Brush will receive prompt attention and perfect satisfaction is guaranteed in all cases. The trade of the house is very extensive, orders being received from all parts of the Dominion. Mr. Brush is one of Montreal's progressive business men, taking a deep interest in its affairs and he was for a number of years a captain in the Montreal Garrison Artillery.

J. E. Deslauriers, HATTER AND FURRIER, 2031 NOTRE DAME STREET, MONTREAL.—The hat and fur trade has at all times been an important one in Canada ever since the first settlers sent beaver skins to France and were compelled to take their pay for them in hats made out of the skins. With long, cold winters the wearing of furs has been a necessity and so for home use and for export, the trade has been an important and profitable one. Among those engaged in the hat and fur trade in this city is Mr. J. E. Deslauriers, whose store is located at No. 2031 Notre Dame Street. Established as recently as 1886 this business has during that comparatively short space of time been built up to quite satisfactory proportions and the prospects for the future are of an encouraging nature. A fine stock is carried of hats and caps, in all the latest and most fashionable styles. In the line of furs the stock is excellent and embraces almost everything in ladies and gentlemens wear in that material, such as coats, caps, mitts, gloves, capes, &c., &c. in beaver, mink, seal-skin, astrachan, Persian lambskin &c., also straw hats, lined kid gloves and umbrellas. Mr. Deslauriers also manufactures silk hats and pull overs for stock and to order in the very highest style of the art and at very reasonable prices. Orders left with him receive prompt attention and the most perfect satisfaction is guaranteed in all cases. Mr. Deslauriers is a native of St. Scholastique, P.Q. and is a thorough going man of business full of push, and business ability, and if these qualities are deserving of success, he will achieve it.

Great London and China Tea Co'y., 1987 NOTRE DAME STREET, MONTREAL.—What the people did for a refreshing beverage before tea was introduced into European countries, it is hard to say. Of course the old adage holds good that "Where ignorance is bliss ' tis folly to be wise," and so not knowing the exhilirating qualities of this now universal beverage, they did not feel its want. Among the prominent houses engaged in the grocery business in this city is that of the Great London and China Tea Company, of which Mr. A. P. Torrens, is proprietor. This establishment is admirably located for business at No. 1987 Notre Dame Street, the premises occupied being 70 x 32 feet in dimensions ; with a tea room on the second floor. The store, which is painted red on the outside, is tastefully fitted up in the interior, the stock being displayed to excellent advantage and presenting a very enticing appearance. The Great London and China Tea Company are heavy importers of and dealers in the choicest brands of teas from China and Japan, fragrant coffees from Rio and Java, also of pure spices, and canned goods of the best quality and all such other articles coming under the head of general groceries usually to be found in a first-class establishment of this character. Employment is furnished to five competent assistants. The company have branch stores at the following places : 191 Barrington Street, Halifax, N. S. ; 139 Argyle Street, Halifax, N. S. ; 33 King Street, St. John, N. B. ; 45 Main Street, Portland, N. B. ; and 86 Queen Street, Charlottetown, P. E. I. Mr. Torrens, the proprietor of the store here, is a native of Ireland, and is a thorough-going and enterprising business man, understanding fully the wants of the public and how to supply them. Mr. J. F. McLean, the manager, is a Nova Scotian by birth, and is a gentleman eminently fitted by ability and experience for the position he holds.

F. Duclos, TINSMITH AND PLUMBER, 463 ST. JAMES STREET, MONTREAL— Among the manufacturing and business interests of the community that of the roofer, plumber and tinsmith is not by any means the least important. The plumber in a certain sense may carry life or death into a house, for if his work is not well done and defective drainage occurs, disease is sure to follow. Among the most reliable in the plumbing and tinsmith trade in this city is Mr. F. Duclos, whose shop is located at No. 463 St. James Street. The premises occupied are 20x60 feet in dimensions and are fitted up with every requisite for the successful prosecution of the business conducted, and here steady employment is furnished to 12 skilled and competent workmen throughout the year. Mr. Duclos does all kinds of tinsmithing, plumbing, roofing, gas and steam fitting, and also all kinds of cornice work. What he does he does well and in all cases guarantees the utmost satisfaction. Those requiring any work done in his line will have their orders attended to with promptness and at moderate prices. Sanitary plumbing is specially attended to, and all work done upon purely scientific principles so that no danger need be apprehended from defective work. Mr. Duclos, who is a native of Beloeil is a thoroughly skilled and practical workman of many years experience and gives his personal attention to all orders entrusted to him.

Dr. Gustave Demers, CHEMIST AND DRUGGIST, 2193 NOTRE DAME STREET, MONTREAL.—Of late years a very marked improvement has taken place in the profession of pharmacy, and although it has at all times held a high and honorable position, more recently the qualifications for those professing it have been raised to a great degree, by the requirements of high graduation either from the medical or pharmaceutical colleges. Among those who have lately entered upon the practice of this profession in this city is Dr. G. Demers, whose store is located at No. 2193 Notre Dame Street. This gentleman established his business in June 1887 and during the comparatively short time he has been engaged in it he has met with the most gratifying success, while his future prospects are all that could possibly be desired. The premises occupied are most handsomely fitted up with plate glass show cases and cabinets, displaying to advantage the excellent stock carried, consisting of fresh and pure drugs and chemicals, fancy and toilet articles, imported and domestic soaps, perfumes &c. as well as proprietary medicines of acknowledged merit and standard reputation, also druggists sundries of every description, the celebrated St. Leon Waters are always kept on hand. A specialty of the business is the compounding of physicians prescriptions difficult formulæ, with care and accuracy at moderate prices. A specialty is also made of

" Dr. Demers Tamarac Cough Syrup," an excellent preparation for coughs and colds. Dr. Demers is a graduate of the Laval University Medical Department, and is a skilled medical practitioner and pharmacist. He is a native of Montreal, and was born in the same place now occupied by his store, the building having been erected by his grandfather in 1848, so that Dr. Demers is well and favorably known to the entire community.

|**Wallace Dawson,** CHEMIST AND DRUGGIST, 169 St. Lawrence Main.— With all due respect to our esteemed friend Macbeth we think he erred in judgment when he said, "Throw physic to the dogs ; I'll none of it." Certainly drugs are not pleasant to take, but they are good for the body when taken in time. In those old days of course physicians were not men of remarkable erudition and patients suffered more than need be. We are living in a more intelligent and enlightened age, and now those who practice medi-cine or pharmacy must be gentlemen who have passed regular examinations after long and mature study. Among those prominently connected with the profession of pharmacy in this city is Mr. Wallace Dawson, whose store is located at No. 169 St. Lawrence Main Street. This gentleman has been established in the business since the 1st May, 1887, in this city, but was established in business in Sorel for some time previous to coming here. He is a graduate of the Montreal College of Pharmacy and has a high reputation as a thor-oughly skilled and careful pharmacist. The premises occupied by him are fitted up with much taste in cherry wood. with plate glass show cases and cabinets, for the advantageous display of the stock, and contain a fine assortment of fresh and pure drugs and chemicals, fancy and toilet articles, imported and domestic soaps, perfumes and proprietary medicines of acknowledged merit and standard reputation, as well as druggists' sundries of every description. A specialty is made of the compounding of physicians' prescriptions and family recipes with care and accuracy at reasonable prices. The dispensary department has been recently renovated and all prescriptions are put up under the personal supervision of Mr. Dawson, whose reputation for accuracy and reliability has already secured for him an excellent patronage derived from the leading families of the city. Employment is fur-nished to two courteous and competent assistants throughout the year. Mr. Dawson is a Canadian by birth and is a gentleman highly esteemed by all who know him.

L. Blanchet, CLOTHING, 19 St. Lawrence Street, Montreal.—During the past quarter of a century a very marked change has taken place in the clothing trade. Pre-vious to that time ready made clothing was not very stylish in cut and could readily be dis-tinguished from custom made and at the same time the prices were comparatively high. Now however, large concerns make a specialty of manufacturing clothing, their cutters being the most skilled and experienced men that can be obtained and the prevailing fashions are scrupulously followed, while the fabrics are of excellent quality. In March of 1887 Mr. L. Blanchet, whose store is located at No. 19 St. Lawrence Main street, established his present business, and during that comparatively short space of time he has built up an excellent trade which has steadily increased from month to month. The premises occupied are 26 x 40 feet in dimensions and are heavily stocked with as fine a line of clothing as can be found in the city. They are in the most fashionable styles and are in all sizes to suit men, youths, boys and children. These are sold for cash as low, if not lower, than anywhere else in the city and the most perfect satisfaction is at all times guaranteed. In gents furnishings the stock is full and complete and embraces all the latest and leading novelties in neckwear, underwear, etc. A special branch of the business is that of tailoring where those desiring can have suits made up to order by measure, on short notice, and in the highest style of the art at reasonable prices, there being a fine stock of fabrics to select from. Employment is furnished, on an average throughout the year, to from 12 to 15 competent assistants and skilled operators. Mr. Blanchet, the proprietor is a native of Quebec Province, and is a gentleman who has now the esteem and confidence of the trade and public.

T. C. O'Brien, BOOTS AND SHOES, 209 ST. LAWRENCE MAIN STREET.—The trade in boots and shoes is one of the most extensively conducted in Canada, and this is naturally so on account of the long cold winters when it is an absolute necessity for rich and poor alike to keep their feet warm to preserve their health, if not to loose their feet. Montreal is an important centre for the trade there being a number of large concerns engaged in this line and the retail trade is conducted on an extensive scale. Among those actively engaged in this line here, is Mr. T. C. O'Brien, whose store is located at No. 209 St. Lawrence Main Street. The premises occupied are 12 x 40 feet in dimensions and are neatly fitted up, and contain a large and elegant stock of boots and shoes for ladies and gentlemen, misses, youths and children, in all weights and grades from the finest Kid balmoral, to the heavy and servicable Kip. The goods are made up in the very best style and in the latest fashion, and the material used are the best procurable, so that a high reputation has been gained for goods he handles. He also keeps slippers, rubbers, &c. Since the business was established, it has proved highly successful and steadily increases in extent and development. Mr. O'Brien is a Canadian by birth and is a live, active and progressive business man, fully understanding all the details of his business, and being at all times ready to meet whatever demands may be made upon him.

De Zouche & Atwater, PIANOS AND ORGANS, 63 BEAVER HALL HILL, MONTREAL.—Most refined people are more or less musical; consequently, the more intelligent and refined the community, the more inclined it is to be musical and inclined to musical pursuits. Hence Montreal, while making no noisy pretensions to extraordinary musical culture, is, nevertheless, as the home of a well-to-do, educated people, really a musical centre of no small merit, and its people liberal patrons of all that tends to encourage and elevate the art. Consequently the vocation of the dealer in pianos, organs, and musical goods takes high rank here, and is generously supported by the public at large, and more especially by those whose social and pecuniary position is such as to require and justify the necessary outlay. The firm of Messrs. De Zouche & Atwater whose handsome music emporium is located at No. 63 Beaver Hall, is one of the most prominent houses in the music line in the city. This firm are agents for the celebrated pianos of Decker Bros., (Behr Bros., Emerson, Ivers & Pond, Morris and the organs and pianos of the famous Mason & Hamlin, as well as for the pianos and organs of other well known American manufacturers. It is unnecessary to say much regarding the merits of the Mason & Hamlin or Decker Bros.' instruments, their fame is already too well known to require extended words of comment. Messrs. De Zouche & Atwater are well known citizens of Montreal and their splendid establishment is the resort of the musical culture of the city and those in, or out of the city requiring anything in their line will meet with every courtesy and attention by calling upon them.

Singer Manufacturing Co.,—The first sewing machine was patented by Elias Howe, Jr., in the year 1846, but since that time wonderful developments have been made in the sewing machine trade as well as in the improvements upon the machine, so that the sewing machine of Elias Howe in 1846 bears about the same resemblance to the sewing machine of the present day as Watts' or Fulton's steam engine does to the steam engines of the Atlantic liners of the present period The largest and most important sewing machine manufacturers in the world is the Singer, whose machines are now in use throughout the civilized world. The head offices of the company are located at New York, and their works are in Elizabeth, N.J.; South Bend, Indiana; Glasgow, Scotland, and this city. The factory in this city is located at No. 2710 Notre Dame Street, and is about 450 feet in length by 45 in width. These are fitted up with all the latest and most improved machinery, and employment is furnished on an average to over 300 men. The latest and best family machine made by the company is known as the new "Improved Family," which has an oscillating shuttle, and is specially adapted to all kinds of family sewing. It has a high arm, is self-threading,

B. E. McGALE'S DRUG HALL, 2123 NOTRE DAME STREET. (See Page 124)

and has a self-setting needle and a shuttle that can be threaded without removing it from the machine. They also manufacture machines for heavy work, such as for clothiers, boot and shoe makers, harness makers, etc. It is hardly necessary to sing the praises of these machines, they are Singers that the public can best appreciate for their own intrinsic and well known value which has been proved by many years experience.

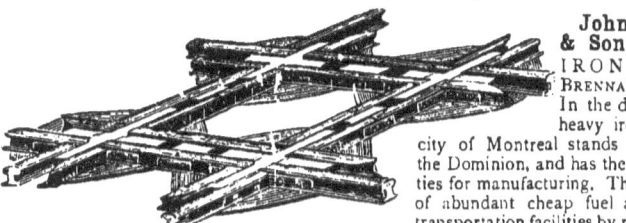

John McIntosh & Son, VULCAN IRON WORKS, BRENNAN STREET.— In the department of heavy iron work, the city of Montreal stands unrivalled in the Dominion, and has the best of facilities for manufacturing. The advantages of abundant cheap fuel and excellent transportation facilities by rail and water, both for receiving the raw material and delivering the manufactured article, are used to the fullest extent. In the manufacture of railroad and general castings the firm of Messrs. John McIntosh & Son take a leading position. Their establishment is located on Brennan Street and covers 100 x 200 feet in dimensions. These are fitted up with all the latest and most improved machinery and appliances for the successful prosecution of the special line of work conducted, the machinery being driven by a 20 horse power steam engine. Their facilities are unsurpassed, for everything required for castings for railroad and general purposes and for years this house has done a large railroad trade. This business was established 30 years ago by Mr. John McIntosh, the senior member of the firm, and 12 years since, his son, Mr. Thomas McIntosh, was admitted to partnership under the above mentioned firm title. The house, since the date of its inception has proved highly successful and has steadily developed in extent and importance from year to year. The firm manufacture frogs, switches and diamond crossings, and do all other kinds of general wrought iron work. The trade of the house is very extensive and extends throughout the Dominion with the different lines of railroads and railroad agents, employment being steadily furnished to 24 skilled and competent workmen. Mr. John McIntosh is a native of Perth, Scotland, and his son is a Montrealer by birth. Both are skilled, practical workmen, and have a well-established reputation for the general superiority of all classes of work turned out by them.

A. Lesperance, No. 47½ BLEURY STREET, MONTREAL.—If there is one line of business more than another where cleanliness and neatness in the display of the goods dealt in, is indispensable to success, it is in the butchering trade. Some butchers, in there places of business, display more taste that others, and it is a pleasure to visit their markets. In compiling the business statistics of Montreal, our reporter called at Mr. A. Lesperance's market, at No. 47½ Bleury Street, and was highly impressed with the general of the place, the wholesome air pervading it and the excellent quality of the meat displayed. The market is 25 x 55 feet in dimensions, and is fitted up with every requisite for the successful prosecution of the business : large refrigerators, chopping blocks, &c., &c. Mr. Lespesance does all his own killing and thus knows exactly the condition and quality of the stock he handles. His trade is derived from some of the leading families in the city, and having been established here for fifteen years, he is well known and highly esteemed in the trade and business community, and customers can at all times rely upon the goods they obtain here, orders are received by mail or telephone No. 1512, and all goods are delivered promptly while great care is taken to fill such orders as satisfactory as though the customers themselves made their selection. Mr. Lesperance deals in beef, lamb, veal, pork, poultry,

F

game, oysters, fish, canned goods, fruits, vegetables, &c., in their season.   Employment is furnished to 6 courteous assistants throughout the year.   Mr. Lesperance is a native of the Province of Quebec, and being a thoroughly skilled practical butcher and understanding all the details of his business, is at all times ready to meet the demands of the public.

Mongeau & Baker, PRACTICAL JEWELLERS AND OPTICIANS, 140 St. Lawrence Street, Montreal.—Long before the days when Greece and Rome were in their glory, or the Pyramids of Egypt pointed towards the zenith, the workers in gold and silver and other precious metals plied their trade.   Many changes have passed over the world since then, and the march of civilization has advanced all the arts and sciences. The cost of all Mark Antony's galleys as he went to meet the lovely Cleopatra could not have purchased a watch that can now be obtained for a few dollars.   Holding a prominent place among those engaged in the watchmaking and jewellery trade in this city is the well-known firm of Messrs. Mongeau & Baker, whose store and factory are located at No. 140 St. Lawrence Main Street.   The premises occupied are 20 x 60 feet in dimensions and are neatly fitted up with plate glass showcases and cabinets for the advantageous display of the elegant stock carried, consisting of watches, clocks and a general assortment of jewellery. The firm are practical jewellers, opticians and general engravers, and manufacture all kinds of jewellery to order in the most satisfactory manner, and repairs are neatly executed. They do lettering of all kinds, crests, and monograms are engraved at the lowest rates, and also make a specialty of diamond setting.   The work done by this firm is of the very best kind and is not excelled by that of any other house in the city.   This business was established three years ago and has already far exceeded the expectations of the members of the firm, while the trade is still steadily increasing.   Employment is furnished to 10 skilled and competent workmen throughout the year.   The members of the firm are Mr. Adolphe Mongeau, who is a native of the Province of Quebec, and Mr. C. H. Baker, who is an Englishman by birth.   Both are practical workmen and progressive business men.

"Acme" Ornamental Wire Works, J. J. ULLEY, MANUFACTURER, Office and Works: 34 Bleury Street, Montreal.—The past quarter of a century has witnessed a most remarkable improvement in the arts and manufactures of the country as well as in its scientific attainments.   The use of metal has entered largely into the construction and ornamentation of our houses and business establishments, as well as for articles of household use &c.   Among the manufacturing establishments in this city devoted to the manufacture of wire work is the "Acme" Ornamental Wire, Brush and Iron Works, of which Mr. J. J. Ulley is the proprietor, the works being located at Nos. 34 and 34½ Bleury Street.   This business was established in the year 1878 and ever since the date of its inception it has met with the most gratifying success.   None but skilled workmen are employed, and Mr. Ulley, who is a practical workman of 22 years experience, personally superintends all orders entrusted to him and thus guarantees his customers entire satisfaction.   He manufactures signs to order of any size or shape in wire work, also window guards, wire fencing, flower stands, coal screens, riddles and sieves, wire cloth of copper, brass, tinned iron and steel wire, twilled locomotive and miner's cloth, and in fact wire work of every description. He uses only the best quality of materials and the goods manufactured are well finished and unsurpassed by those of any other house in the Dominion.   His prices will also be found as low as any in the market.   He also manufactures and largely imports steel and hair brushes, and general mill brushes, including such brushes as are required for woollen cotton and paper mills, boot and shoe factories &c.   Also all kinds of brushes and feather dusters for household use.   Goods are made to order, as well as supplied to the trade.   Mr. Ulley is a native of the Isle of Wight, England, and has resided in this country many years.   He is a thorough going man of business and is well deserving of the success he has attained.

Alfred Blais, TINSMITH, PLUMBER, STEAM & GAS FITTER, NEW CONTRACT WORK AT MODERATE RATES, A SPECIALTY, No. 105 ST. ANTOINE STREET, MONTREAL.—The art of plumbing has been brought to a large state of perfection during the past 10 years. Medical men and sanitary engineers recognized the fact that a large percentage of sickness and death was attributable to defective plumbing, and so measures were taken for remedying of the evil and they have met with a marked degree of success. Among the most skilful and popular plumbers, steam and gas fitters in this city is Mr. Alfred Blais, whose premises are located at No. 105 St. Antoine Street. The premises occupied consist of a store 38 x 20 feet in dimensions with workshop up stairs 45 x 20 feet in dimensions, Mr. Blais attends to all kinds of tinsmithing, plumbing, steam and gas fitting, slate and metal roofing, bell hanging, &c. All orders are executed promptly and the utmost satisfaction is guaranteed in all cases. Mr Blais being a skilled and practical plumber and tinsmith, gives his personal attention to all orders entrusted to his care and thus ensure the best of results. He gives employment to from 10 to 26 skilled workmen according to the season of the year and the pressure of business. He is the sole manufacturer of the patent railway milk can which is fitted with a patent liquid proof cover of his own invention, and is by far the most safe and convenient milk can ever invented in the market. He also carries a fine line of hot air and hot water heating apparatus ; also, stoves and ranges, house furnishing goods, cutlery paints and oils, glass, putty, &c. Since he started in business 4 years ago he has met with the most gratifying success, and his prospects for the future are of the brightest.

A. M. Craig, HOUSE, SIGN AND DECORATIVE PAINTER, 8 BLEURY STREET.—In a publication of this character, devoted to the business and manufacturing interests of Montreal, those who, by reason of the length of time they have been established, are looked upon as pioneers in their department, are certainly entitled to special mention in these pages, and it is therefore with a great deal of pleasure that we refer to Mr. A. M. Craig, house, sign and decorative painter, whose shop is located at No. 8 Bleury street. This gentleman, one of the oldest engaged in this line of business in the city, established himself here thirty years ago, and from the time of his advent he has always occupied a prominent position in this branch of trade. He gives employment, on an average throughout the year, to 14 skilled and competent hands. He does all kinds of house, sign, decorative and fresco painting, and the evidences of his skill may be observed in a large number of the leading residences and business establishments throughout the city. The work done by him is artistic in a high degree and the utmost care is taken to ensure the most satisfactory results. All orders entrusted to him receive his personal attention and supervision and the consequent benefit of his extensive experience. Mr. Craig is a Scotchman by birth and is endowed with that persistent energy and perseverance that is proverbial in that race. He has built up his reputation and his business on the thoroughness of his work and thus the success that has attended his efforts has been well earned and deserved.

N. Kearns, GROCERIES & PROVISIONS, 36 BLEURY ST. AND CORNER CITY COUNCILLOR AND MAYOR STREETS,—So long as people have to eat to live, and that will be till the end of time, so long will those lines of business that deal in the food supplies of the people have a particular interest for every man, woman and child in every community. The grocery trade is one of the most important of all lines of business conducted, and gathers its supplies from all quarters of the earth. Among the old established and prominent houses in this branch of trade in Montreal is that of Mr. N. Kearns, whose stores are located at No. 36 Bleury Street, and one which he opened one year ago at the corner of City Councillor and Mayor streets. It is now 30 years since Mr. Kearns first started in business, and by persevering industry and enterprise and thoroughly understanding the requirements of the public he has succeeded in building up an excellent trade. His stores are large and commodious and are tastefully fitted up and present an inviting appearance. Large stocks are carried of choice family groceries, including the finest brands of teas from China and Japan, fragrant coffees from Java and Rio, pure spices, table delicacies, hermetically sealed goods in glass and tin, also a fine line of provisions and the choicest brands of wines and liquors, imported and domestic, specially suited for family use. A policy of the house has been to sell the best quality of goods at the lowest reasonable advance above cost consistent with a safe business, and this the public well aware of have been liberal in their patronage. Mr. Kearns, who is a native of Ireland, came to this country in early life. and here he has won the confidence and esteem of all with whom he has had business or social relations.

Berard & Major, CARRIAGE MAKERS, 1947 ST. CATHERINE STREET, MONTREAL.—Of manufactures having direct reference to local wants, none are of greater importance to the citizens of Montreal than the building of light business and pleasure vehicles. Among the most successful and popular houses engaged in the branch of industry in this city, is that of Messrs. Berard & Major, whose carriage factory and warerooms are located at No. 1947 St. Catherine Street, and is one of the most complete and best appointed in Montreal. The premises occupied, which are owned by the firm, consist of 2 and 3 story buildings, covering 50 x 150 feet in dimensions, these are fitted up with the latest and most improved machinery and appliances and nothing is omitted that could possibly add to the successful conducting of the work, while employment is furnished to from 20 to 24 skilled and competent workmen throughout the year. The firm employ only the most skillful men in their shops, and are prepared to execute promptly and satisfactorily all orders with which they may be favored for the manufacture of buggies, carriages, business waggons, sleighs and cutters and light vehicles generally. Being practical carriage makers of many years experience, they can guarantee all work from their establishment, and those who have once patronized them have no hesitation in recommending them to others. They do work in French, English, and American styles, and were awarded 5 prizes at the Exhibition in Montreal in 1880. The business was established 14 years ago and has steadily improved from year to year since that date, their trade now extending throughout a large section of the province. The members of the firm are Messrs Alfred Berard and E. Major, both of whom are natives of the province of Quebec, and are skilled workmen and progressive business men.

Wm. M. Briggs, PRACTICAL PLUMBER AND SANITARIAN, 40 ST. ANTOINE STREET.—There is scarcely any subject in matters of domestic economy that has received so much attention of late as that of sanitation and scientific plumbing. This was a necessity, for it had become a recognized fact that a great deal of so-called plumbing was simply a system of disease and death breeders. Happily a great change has been effected in this respect, and the majority of plumbers are fully qualified for the work required. Holding a prominent position among the old-established and reliable houses in the line in this city is that of Mr. Wm. M. Briggs, whose shop is eligibly located at No. 40 St. Antoine street. This gentleman established his business 16 years ago, and by close attention, persevering industry and a thorough knowledge of the business, he soon succeeded in building up an excellent trade, which has been steadily maintained. The premises occupied by the business are 22 x 55 feet in dimensions, and are fully equipped with all the requisite appliances for the successful prosecution of the business. Mr. Briggs attends to every description of plumbing. sanitary matters, steam and gas fitting and hot water fitting. He is an Englishman by birth and is a skilled, competent workman in all the branches enumerated and giving his personal attention to all orders entrusted to him and supervising all work done by his 14 skilled workmen he is enabled to give his customers the utmost satisfaction. Mr. Briggs is an active and energetic business man and a member of the Master Plumbers Association

Grignon & Levesque, OFFICE AND WAREHOUSE: 230 ST. LAWRENCE STREET, FACTORY: 159 ST. CHARLES BOROMMEE STREET, MONTREAL.—Montreal is the Canadian Metropolis of business and manufactures, and the industries conducted here are many and varied and give employment to a large majority of the people. Among the many lines conducted, that in tinware and plumbing, forms a very important factor. Holding a prominent place in this line of business is the firm of Messrs. Grignon & Levesque, whose store and factory are located at No. 159 St. Charles Borromee Street, and the office and warehouse at No. 230 St Lawrence Main Street. The premises occupied by the warehouse are 24 x 45 feet in dimensions, and the factory is a 3 story building, 30 x 30 feet in dimensions, and is fitted up with all the most improved machinery and appliances for the successful prosecution of the work, while employment is furnished to from 18 to 20 skilled and competent workmen. The firm are importers' and manufacturers' of plain, stamped, and japanned tinware, square oil cans, biscuit tins, confectioners' supplies, &c., &., also, pieced tinware for the cheap counter trade, they are also plumbers, roofers, gas and steam fitters. The work done by this house is unsurpassed and in all cases the best of satisfaction is guaranteed. The firm were previously with Mr. Jos. Delorme. This business was established 2 years ago and from that date of its inception has been entirely successful. The members of the firm are Messrs. A. Grignon and A. E. Levesque, the former being a practical workman and the latter business manager of the concern.

E. C. Mount & Co., PLUMBERS, IRON PIPE AND TIN PLATE WORKERS, No. 16 VICTORIA SQUARE, MONTREAL.—The agitation that has been going on in relation to sanitation and sanitary plumbing for the past few years has been productive of much good and has undoubtedly prevented a great deal of sickness and possibly death by the improved scientific method of plumbing which have been inaugurated. Holding a prominent place among the practical sanitarians and plumbers of Montreal, is the firm of Messrs. E. C. Mount & Co., whose establishment is located at No. 16 Victoria Square. This business was founded by Mr. Mount in 1884, and the present firm is composed of that gentleman and Mr. J. P. Pierce. The premises occupied by the business are 22 x 75 feet in dimensions, the office being in front and workshops in rear and basement, employment being furnished on an average to from 20 to 30 skilled and capable workmen. The firm are practical sanitarians of high and acknowledged ability ; also, plumbers, iron pipe and tin plate workers, gas and steam-fitters, tin and metal roofers. They attend to all matters of drainage and ventilation and put in electric call bells, &c., all orders entrusted to their care are attended to promptly and all work is guaranteed entirely satisfactory, lead burning being a specialty of the business. The firm are agents for the *Lee's* patented *Gas Governor* which saves from 15 to 40 per cent. of gas, and these are put on on trial for those desiring. They have also the Combination Cook-Stove which has a circular fire grate, the same as a heating stove which saves fuel and will maintain a uniform heat for 24 hours without attention, it is also very useful for heating upper tenements and single flats with hot water. Heating by hot water is a distinctive specialty of the house, the cost having been by special study reduced to such a low rate that this beautiful and satisfactory system of heating is placed within the reach of even those in very moderate circumstances. They carry in stock, sanitary earthenware, plumbers' supplies, gasaliers, brackets, &c. Mr. Mount is a native of England, and a practical workman, a member of the Master Plumbers' Association. His partner, Mr. Pierce, is a Canadian and attends to the financial portion of the business, he was for many years chief clerk of the largest plumbing establishment in Canada.

P. Poulin, LUMBER MERCHANT, OFFICE AND YARD, 469 WILLIAM STREET, CORNER RICHMOND, MONTREAL.—The lumber trade of Montreal is one of its leading commercial industries, and luckily, is in the hands of an enterprising, long-headed and liberal class of men who permit no obstacle to withstand their energy or discourage their spirits. Prominent among those engaged in this line of business in this city is Mr. P. Poulin, whose office and yards are located at No. 469 William Street, corner of Richmond Street. The yards are 154 x 154 feet in dimensions and there is another yard leased from the Government on the canal basin which has an area of 4600 square feet. These have a capacity for storing about 12,000,000 feet of lumber. There is every facility for receiving lumber by way of the Lachine canal as well as by the railroads. Mr. Poulin established his business 10 years ago last August ; and has, during that time, built up a very gratifying trade which is constantly increasing. Mr. Poulin deals in every description of lumber and dimension timber for builders' and others, both at wholesale and retail, a speciality being made of pine. He also deals in cedar of all lengths and sizes as well as tamarack, hemlock, laths and shingles. Builders and others requiring anything in this line would do well to call upon or write to Mr. Poulin, as they may be assured of liberal and satisfactory treatment. There are 15 competent hands employed in the business on an average throughout the year and 5 teams, the trade of the house extending throughout the city and surrounding section of county. Mr. Poulin, the proprietor, is a native of the county of Terrebonne, and is an active member of the Chamber of Commerce.

James Pearson Jr., NEW YORK MEAT MARKET, 533 CRAIG STREET, MONTREAL.—Of all lines of business conducted in any civilized community where neatness and cleanliness are important and necessary accessories, it is in the butcher trade. Where one sees the meats displayed tastefully and no refuse matter lying around, and the clerks neat in attire, there is a strong attraction for the purchaser and a good trade is the result. Among the meat markets in Montreal answering these requirements is the New York Meat Market of which Mr. James Pearson Jr., is the proprietor. This market is eligibly located for business at No. 533 Craig Street, it is 40 x 22 feet in dimensions and is fully equipped with every requirement for the satisfactory prosecution of the business, refrigerator room, office &c. Everything about the place has a neat and clean appearance, and the stock of meats handled is displayed to the best advantage. Mr. Pearson deals in all kinds of fresh and salt meats, beef, mutton, lamb, veal, corned beef, pork &c., also poultry and game in their season, and butter, eggs, fruit and all kinds of vegetables. Nothing but the very best and most wholesome of meats and produce is handled and customers can at all times rely thoroughly upon what they obtain here. Employment is furnished to 5 competent assistants throughout the year in helping to conduct the operations of the business. Mr. Pearson, who is a Canadian, is a practical butcher and during the 15 years he has been established in business has built up an excellent and ever increasing trade.

C. A. Briggs, HATTER & FURRIER, 2097 NOTRE DAME STREET, MONTREAL— Among the oldest established of the business houses in Montreal engaged in the hatter and furrier trade is that of Mr. C. A. Briggs, which is located at No. 2097 Notre Dame St. The hat and fur trade is one of the most important in Canada and its operations are conducted upon a very extensive scale. The premises occupied by Mr. C. A. Briggs, are 20x75 feet in dimensions and are fitted up in an excellent and very tasteful manner, and contain a large and elegant stock of furs for ladies and gentlemens wear, of every description. Also a fine stock of English, French and American hats, as well as those of his own manufacture. The stock carried is full and complete in every particular is of the very best quality, and made up in the latest and most fashionable styles. Mr. Briggs manufactures every description of fine furs for ladies and gentlemen's wear, the work being perfect in every particular and the goods elegantly finished. He also manufactures silk hats and pull-overs in the latest leading styles. This business was established 22 years ago from a comparatively small beginning has been built up to its present extensive proportions. Mr. Briggs, the proprietor. is a native of Montreal, where he is well and favorably known in business and social circles. He is a skilled; practical hatter and furrier and giving his personal attention to all orders entrusted to his care can thus guarantee his customers the best of satisfaction.

"Au Bon Marche," ALPHONSE VALIQUETTE, 1869 AND 1871 NOTRE DAME

STREET.—Engaged in the dry-goods trade of Montreal are many enterprising merchants, whose establishments are the scenes of busy industry from morning until night. One of the most popular and best known in this branch of trade here is that of Mr. Alphonse Valiquette proprietor of the "Au Bon Marche," which is located at Nos. 1869 and 1871 Notre Dame Street. This business was founded in the year 1873, and ever since the date of its inception it has proved eminently successful and has steadily continued to increase and develop from year to year. The premises occupied consist of a double store of three floors, each 100 x 45 feet in dimensions. Here is contained a very large and comprehensive stock, consisting of staple and fancy dry goods, including silks. satins, velvets and velveteens, dress goods in the latest and most fashionable novelties, linens, tablings, cottons, smallwares, laces, trimmings, kid gloves, hosiery and hosiery notions and underwear in great variety, also black and colored silks and satins in all styles and in any variety required. In the line of black goods the house has no superior in this city. A distinctive specialty is made of carpets, English oilcloths, and linoliums, one of the commodious stores being devoted entirely to this department, the extensive trade of which is carried on both at wholesale and retail, samples being sent free to any address. It would be impossible within the limits of a brief sketch like this to enumerate and describe even a portion of the varied and magnificent stock carried at all seasons. Suffice it to say that everything new, tasteful and useful in carpets, draperies, upholstery goods, English oilcloths, mattings, etc., can be found here in endless variety, quantity. quality, style and price. There are also separate departments for the manufacture of mantles, millinery, dressmaking and tailoring, a competent staff of operators being engaged for these departments. A prominent feature of this house is its discount of *ten per cent.*, which is always made to colleges, religious institutions and communities. Employment is furnished to 50 skilled operators and courteous assistants throughout the year. The courtesy of the large staff of salesladies is a marked feature of the establishment, the patrons being attended to with the utmost dispatch and politeness. Mr. Valiquette. who is a native of the province of Quebec, is a gentleman of marked business ability, tact, push and enterprise, and is a highly esteemed member of the business community.

Patterson Bros., WATCHMAKERS AND JEWELLERS, 45 BLEURY STREET,

MONTREAL.—In a review of the business interests of Montreal particular mention must be made of the watchmaking and jewellery trade, as one of the important factors in computing the wealth of the city. It is a well-known and easily understood fact that the greater the amount of wealth and refinement there is in any particular community there will be found a greater love for the beautiful exhibited, and jewellery has at all times been given a high place in such matters. Actively engaged in this line of business here is the firm of Messrs. Patterson Bros., whose store is located at No. 45 Bleury Street. The premises occupied by the firm, and are tastefully fitted up, and contain a fine stock of gold and silver watches in English, Swiss and American manufacture, clocks, chimes, rings and many other lines of jewellery, beautiful in design and finish but too numerous to mention in detail. A specialty of the house is the repairing of the finer grade of watches. Mr. Patterson has had an extended experience in this class of work, and all orders enstusted to his care will receive the utmost attention and be executed with prompt ness and at very reasonable prices.

Dominion File Works G OUTRAM & SON, ST. GABRIEL LOCKS. MONTREAL— In reviewing the various manufacturing industries that have done so much to build up the trade and commercial interests of Montreal and placed it in front of all cities in the Dominion, there are bound to be a number of special lines that derive their trade from the entire Dominion and among such must be mentioned the Dominion File Works of which Messrs. George Outram & Son, are the proprietors. This manufacturing house is one that is well known, not only in the city, but throughout the entire country, having been established by Mr. George Outram, the senior member of the firm, in 1869. In the year 1875 his son, Mr. Frederick Outram, was admitted into partnership under the above mentioned firm title. The premises occupied by the works are large and commodious, consisting of 3 buildings, located at St. Gabriel Locks. These are divided into separate departments such as the forging, annealing, grinding, cutting, finishing and packing branches of the business, while employment is furnished to 30 skilled and competent workmen throughout the year. The works are fitted up with the latest and most improved machinery driven by 15 horse water power. The firm manufacture all kinds and sizes of files and rasps such as mill saw, flat, round and square, and hand files, taper saw, slim taper, pit or frame saw half round, band saw blunts, &c., &c. Also, horse and shoe rasps, tanged horse rasps, half round shoe rasps, flat and half round wood rasps, cabinet files and rasps. Files and rasps are made to special pattern and for all kinds of metal. The goods manufactured by this house have a standard reputation as being of the very best quality in every particular. The trade of the house is very extensive and embraces the entire Dominion. Mr. George Outram is a native of Sheffield, England, where he learned his trade of file making, Mr. Frederick Outram is also an Englishman by birth and is a skilled, practical workman and gives personal supervison to the work.

Joseph Levesque, 112 BLEURY STREET. MONTREAL.—There is no more important line of business conducted in any community or country than that which deals in the food supplies of the people, and in this connection the butcher business is certainly the foremost, not only on account of its extensive operations, but of the necessary character of the stock dealt in as a supporter of life. Conspicuous among those engaged in this line of business in this city and deserving of more than a mere passing mention in a work of this character, is Mr. Joseph Levesque, whose market is located at No. 112 Bleury Street. This business was established in the year 1866, and it has been steadily built up from year to year until it is at the present day one of the most important in the line in the city. The premises occupied are 26 x 48 feet in diminsions with a large and well equipped refrigerator room in rear, which proves of incalculable advantage in keeping the meats fresh and pure in summer. There is also a neatly fitted up business office and other accessories to a well appointed establishment, while employment is furnished to eight competent assistants. Mr. Levesque deals in the choicest qualities of meats, such as beef, mutton, lamb, veal, etc., which he kills himself, and thus can guarantee their wholesomenesss and quality. He also, in their season, deals in vegetables, fruit, game, poultry, fish, etc. The trade, which is very extensive, is derived from some of the leading families in the city. and special prices and arrangements are made with ship owners or masters, restaurant and boarding house keepers. Mr. Levesque is a native of the Province of Quebec and is a representative of the business enterprise of Montreal.

John Martin, PLUMBER, GAS AND STEAM FITTER, Nos. 25 AND 27 ST. ANTOINE STREET, MONTREAL.—Within the last few years particular attention has been given to the matter of sanitary plumbing. It has become a recognized fact that a very large amount of sickness has been caused by defective plumbing, and a marked improvement in in the methods has been the result. One of the oldest established houses in this line of business in this city is that of Mr. John Martin, which is located at Nos. 25 and 27 St. Antoine Street. This gentleman, who is a native of Scotland, learned his trade and worked in some of the best shops in Edinburgh and Glasgow, and then coming out to this country started in business for himself 35 years ago. Starting in a comparatively small way he gradually built his business up to its present proportions. The premises occupied by the business consist of 3 floors 35 x 100 feet in dimensions which are fully equipped with all the necessary appliances for the successful prosection of the work. He employs none but the most skilful workmen and personally superintending all orders entrusted to him, can thus guarantee his customers the best of satisfaction. He does all kinds of plumbing, gas and steam fitting, and manufactures and deals in English and American gas fixtures, plumbers', gas and steam fitters' goods, all kinds of gas burners &c Also deals in machinery of all kinds new and second hand. He manufactures the "Underground Gas Machine" which is used for lighting dwellings, churches, factories and public buildings. It is buried in the earth, and has no gas house, vault, fire or danger, and is warranted reliable in winter as well as in summer, a specimen of these machines may be seen in operation at his establishment. He also carries a fine line of gas stoves for cooking, heating shoemakers irons, rooms &c. Those forming business relations with this house may be assured of every attention and satisfaction.

James Moffat, STAPLE AND FANCY DRY GOODS, 155 & 157 ST. ANTOINE STREET, MONTREAL.—In scarcely any line of industry is there so much capital invested or so many people given employment as in that of dry-goods. It is one of the important factors in computing the commercial wealth of the country and the status of trade. Among those actively engaged in this line of business in this city deserving of more than a mere passing notice in a work of this nature, is Mr. James Moffat, whose store is located at Nos. 155 and 157 St. Antoine Street. The premises occupied are 22x65 feet in dimensions and are fitted up in a tasteful manner, the large stock being displayed to the best advantage, which consists of staple and fancy dry-goods including velvets, laces, trimmings, dress goods, prints, cottons, linens, smallwares and many other departments too numerous to mention but usually to be found in a first-class establishment. There is a special department for the manufacture of pinafores, aprons, skirts, and underwear to order, while babies requisites are constantly carried in stock. Since this business was established 3 years ago it has met with the most gratifying success and has constantly increased in extent and importance from year to year. Employment is steadily furnished to 7 competent and courteous assistants in the different departments throughout the year. Mr. Moffat, the proprietor, is a native of Scotland and has had a lengthened experience in the dry-goods trade so that he thoroughly understands all its details and thus is enabled at all times to meet the demands of his customers promptly and in a satisfactory manner.

Alexander Watt, BAKER AND CONFECTIONER, 173 St. Antoine Street— Nature has made ample provision for the wants of mankind, and in nothing is this better seen than in our food supplies. While quail are not extremely plentiful it has been fully demonstrated that the average stomach will rebel against this bird if given as food too frequently. Wheat however is plentiful and bread is a staple article of food, and is enjoyed at every meal from childhood to old age. This being the case it is necessary that it should be of the best quality and that no injurious ingredients should be mixed with it in its manufacture. One of the oldest established and most popular bakers and confectioners of this city is Mr. Alexander Watt, whose store and bakery are located at No. 173 St. Antoine Street. It is 35 years since Alexander Watt, the father of this gentleman, started in business on his own account, the present proprietor acquiring possession on the death of the former in 1877, and during this time has been built up an excellent and ever-increasing trade, which in its scope of operations embraces the entire city. The premises occupied consist of a a handsomely fitted up store, 22 x 30 feet in dimensions, containing plate glass show cases, etc., for the advantageous handling of the stock of pastry and confectionery. The bakery is in a brick building in rear and contains three large ovens and all other improved apparatus and appliances for the successful prosecution of the work. Throughout the year employment is furnished to 12 skilled hands and competent assistants. The goods manufactured by this house are of the very best quality and have won an enviable reputation with consumers. The trade is conducted both at wholesale and retail, and, as previously mentioned, is very extensive. Mr. Watt is a Canadian by birth and of Scottish descent, and is a member of the Montreal Board of Trade.

A. Harris, Son & Co., (Limited.) Manufacturers of Agricultural Implements, Brantford, Ont., George T. Vincent, General Agent, 125 College St.—If agriculturists, who passed to their rest over thirty years ago, should arise from their graves and look upon our immense farms of the west and north-west during seed time and harvest, they would be as much surprised as old Rip Van Winkle after his memorable sleep on the the Catskill mountains. A wonderful change has taken place in farming methods during the past twenty-five or thirty years, through the instrumentality of machinery, not a year has passed during the past quarter of a century but what some marked improvement or notable invention has taken place in the manufacture of agricultural implements, one of the most prominent houses in this line of manufacture in the Dominion being that of Messrs. A. Harris, Son & Co., of Brantford, Ont. They are the manufacturers' of the Brantford Steel Binders, which are acknowledged to be the best in the market. Their latest styles of these machines will be constructed almost entirely of steel and malleable iron. They do invariably good work, and of light draft and great durability. The firm also manufacture mowing machines and reaping machines. They sold during the season of 1887 over six thousand machines and could have sold many more had their supply been equal to the demand. They also deal extensively in the Blue Tin Tag Binding Twine, which is one of the best and most reliable for the purpose in the market. Besides the extensive trade conducted throughout the Dominion, large numbers are exported to England, Scotland, Ireland, and South America. The general agent for the machines in Montreal and Quebec Province, is Mr. George T. Vincent, whose office and warehouse are located at 125 College Street. This branch has been established in this city for 7 years, and during that time, Mr. Vincent has built up a very large and steadily increasing business. Mr. Vincent is a native of Montreal where he is widely and favorably known as a wide awake and enterprising business man.

P. O'Donoghue, SADDLE AND HARNESS MAKER, 30 BLEURY STREET, MONTREAL.—Who the first harness maker was or when the first harness was made are matters lost in the mists of antiquity, but it must be assumed that it was at a very early period of the world's history that beasts of burden were used for carrying people and goods, either across the plains of Egypt, throughout the lost Atlantis, or for dog sleds in the frozen regions of the North. But it is not of antiquity that we have now to deal but of the business interests of the present day. Actively engaged in the saddle and harness making line in this city is Mr. P. O'Donoghue, whose shop is located at No. 30 Bleury Street. The premises occupied consist of two floors, 20 x 65 feet in dimensions, where employment is furnished to four skilled and competent workmen in the manufacture of single and double light and heavy harness, saddlery, etc. Nothing but the best quality of materials· is used and every portion of the work is executed with the greatest care. Repairs of every description in leather work are executed on short notice, and in the most satisfactory manner A fine stock of horse furnishing goods, whips, brushes, curry combs and other stable requisites is always carried. Since Mr. O'Donoghue started in business here 13 years ago he has built up an excellent trade, as well as a widespread reputation for first-class work and moderate prices. Mr. O'Donoghue is a native of the county of Kerry, Ireland. He is a skilled saddle and harness maker and is of that genial disposition for which Irishmen at home and abroad have for ages been famed, in fact, long before the Kings of Kerry reigned in their ancestral halls.

S. Myers, WATCHMAKER, JEWELLER AND STATIONER, 2261 NOTRE DAME STREET.—Centuries ago the workers in gold and silver plied their trade under the shadow of the pyramids and along the banks of the Nile, in ancient Egypt. It has always been a valuable and honorable trade, and in all civilized communities is prosecuted successfully. Among those actively engaged in this line of business in this city, of whom special mention should be made, is Mr. S. Myers, whose store is located at 2261 Notre Dame street. Mr. Myers was formerly at No. 153 St. Antoine street but on the first May of the present year he removed to his present more eligible location. The premises occupied are commodious and are tastefully fitted up with plate glass show cases, etc., for the advantageous display of the fine stock of goods carried, which consists of English, Swiss and American articles in gold and silver, clocks, chains, rings, setts, earrings and many other beautiful articles of jewellery too numerous to mention. Watches, clocks and jewellery are also cleaned and repaired with promptness and in the most satisfactory manner. There is also a fine stock of books, stationery and periodicals as well as fancy goods of every description. Mr. Myers, who is a native of Canada, started in the jewellery business 5 years ago and 2 years since added books, stationery and fancy goods to it and thus drew more custom and increased his jewellery trade as well as building up both branches in a most satisfactory manner. Mr. Myers is a gentleman of thorough going business habits and is well deserving of every success.

G. Rosser, PLUMBER, 2139 ST. CATHERINE STREET, MONTREAL.—There has probably been no branch of trade that has been subjected to so much criticism, or that has undergone so marked an improvement during the past few years as that of plumbing. Sanitary experts and medical men have devoted much time and attention to sanitary plumbing, and from the improved methods and scientific principles now in vogue by our experienced plumbers, the danger of the admittance of zymotic diseases into our dwellings by defective plumbing, has been greatly removed. Among the old established houses in the plumbing and steam-fitting line in this city, is that of Mr. G. Rosser, which is located at No. 2139 St. Catherine Street. This business was established 10 years ago, and Mr. Rosser soon built up a high and wide spread reputation for the excellent quality of the work done by him, so that business soon met with rapid increase, both in extent and developement, its operations now embracing the city and a large section of the vicinity. Mr. Rosser attends to all orders for plumbing, gas and steam-fitting, and gives the same attention to small orders as to the largest contracts. He also does bronzing of every description and also repairs chandeliers. Mr. Rosser is a native of Swansea, Wales, and is a practical plumber and steam-fitter of many years experience, and giving his personal attention to all orders entrusted to him can thus guarantee his patrons the most satisfactory results. Mr. Rosser is also agent for the "Gleason Incandescent Gas Burner" in all styles and sizes. This Burner produces a pure white light and effects a saving of forty per cent. in the amount of gas consumed and is by far the best article of its kind ever introduced.

Leclerc & Cusson, 211 McGILL STREET, MONTREAL.—The more an individual or community advances in civilization the greater attention do they pay to matters of art, whether it be music or painting or sculpture. Within late years a marked improvement has taken place among the masses, and art in paintings, etchings, engravings, chromos, etc., have been brought more into their notice and their tastes have become educated and refined. Among those prominently engaged in the picture trade in this city is the firm of Messrs. Leclerc & Cusson, whose store is located at No. 211 McGill Street. These gentlemen were formerly at No. 317 St. James Street, but removed to their present more eligible quarters on the 1st May of the present year. The premises occupied are large and commodious, consisting of three floors, each 50 x 25 feet in dimensions. They are manufacturers of gold, bronzed and imitation mouldings for picture frames and mirrors, cornices and curtain poles, while regilding is done equal to new. They are importers of steel engravings, chromos, lithographs, photographs, albertypes and albums; also British and German mirror-plates. The work done by this house is of the best quality, and is not surpassed by that of any other house in the Dominion, while employment is furnished to 30 skilled and competent workmen. The advantages accruing to those of our citizens who are in moderate circumstances from the installment system of doing business are very great, as they are thereby enabled, by a very small weekly outlay, to furnish their houses comfortably and even elegantly, which otherwise would have been an utter impossibility. This house is one of the most reliable in the city in this line of business. This business was established 10 years ago by Mr. Joseph Leclerc, and three years since Mr. Cusson was admitted into partnership under the above mentioned title. These gentlemen are thoroughly conversant with all the details of their trade, and will be found straightforward and honorable business men.

Charles E. Scarff, CHEMIST AND DRUGGIST, 2262 ST. CATHERINE ST., MONTREAL.—The profession of the pharmacist is one of the most important and effects the general community to a great extent. If it was not for the drug store how many of the ills and troubles, peculiar to the human race, would go unrelieved or grown into serious maladies. As a rule, the gentlemen following this profession, are among the most upright and conscientious of our citizens, and deserve and receive the respect of the community. Among those who have lately started, in this line of business in this city is Mr. Charles E. Scarff, whose handsome drug store is located at 2262 St. Catherine. This business was established in May, 1888 and it has already given gratifying evidence of a successful future. The store is a large and commodious and is handsomely fitted up with plate glass show cases and cabinets and is well filled with an elegant stock, including fresh and pure drugs, chemicals, fancy and toilet articles, perfume, imported and domestic soaps, druggists sundries and articles required by physicians in their practice. A specialty is made of the compounding of physicians' prescriptions and difficult formules, with care and accuracy and at moderate prices. The latest and most improved appliances for securing safety in the handling and compounding of drugs are used. Mr. Scarff, who is an Englishman by birth is a graduate of the Ontario College of Pharmacy and also of the Quebec College of Pharmacy and is considered a most careful and reliable pharmacist.

Andrew Baillie, THISTLE BOOT AND SHOE STORE, 161 St. Lawrence Main St., Montreal.—Montreal contains a number of old-established and reliable business houses which have been well tried during many years of a business career and have not been found wanting. It is to such substantial houses that a city owes much of its reputation as a commercial centre. Among those houses deserving of special mention in a work of this character on account of those qualities just mentioned is that of the Thistle Boot and Shoe Store, of which Mr. Andrew Baillie is the proprietor and which is eligibly located for business at No. 161 St. Lawrence Main street. Mr. Baillie has been established in business for 22 years and during 18 years of that period he has been in his present location. The premises occupied by the business are 18 x 40 feet in dimensions and are neatly fitted up and contain a fine stock of boots and shoes, slippers, etc., for ladies and gentlemen, misses, youths and children. These are in all weights and grades from the finest of kid to the heaviest kip, and are made up in the latest and most fashionable style, being obtained from some of the most prominent manufacturing houses in the Dominion. Mr. Baillie handles only the very best quality of goods so that his numerous patrons could at all times depend upon what they were getting. Mr Baillie is a native of Fyfeshire, Scotland, and came to this country in the year 1854. He has always retained his old love for the land of the thistle while at the same time he has taken a deep interest in all that had for its object the wellfare of Montreal and Canada.

Chartrand & Bisson, ROOFERS, 147 St. Charles Borromee St., Montreal.—The building trade of Montreal is one of its most important branches of business, and furnishes employment to a very large number of hands annually, besides occupying the attention of many of the most expert business men and extensive capitalists among her citizens. But it is more particularly with that department of building known as roofing with which we have now to deal. These are several first-class firms engaged in the roofing trade in this city, among which worthy of special mention is the old established are of Chartrand and Bisson, which has seen over a quarter of a century of usefulness and well merited prosperity. Messrs. Chartrand and Bisson executes contracts for slate and gravel roofs, as well as in tin and rosin cement. A specialty is made of gravel roofs and repairing of all kinds is promptly attended to. Specimens of their work may be seen all over the city, on many private as well as public buildings, among the latter may be mentioned the Nazareth Asylum for the blind on St. Catherine St., and the new "Beaudry" block on the corner of St. Catherine and St. Charles Borromee Sts. The firm have always gone upon the principle of doing first-class work only, hence their reputation is a 1 in every particular. A large staff of efficient workmen are employed and all orders received at the office, 147 St. Charles Borromee St., or 483 Laval avenue, the residence of Mr. Brisson will receive prompt attention. Both Messrs. Charles Chartrand aud Frs. Bisson are natives of this province. The former is a practical roofer and the latter is the business manager of the concern, both are well and favorably known as active and energetic business men and progressive citizens.

E. Lemieux, MERCHANT TAILOR, No. 3 St. Lawrence Main St, Montreal. A cynic has said that "If it be true that the tailor makes the man," then he has a great deal to answer for. Well, perhaps he has, but it is nevertheless true that many well deserving men would stand unrecognized in the world, without a chance to show their ability or sterling worth, if it was not for the adventitious aid given by their tailor in the shape of good and fashionable clothes. One of the most popular merchant tailoring establishments on St. Lawrence Main Street is that of Mr. E. Lemieux, which is located at No. 3 on that thoroughfare. Although it is but five years since Mr. Lemieux founded his business, he has built up an excellent and most lucrative business, his trade being derived from the most critical—in the way of dress—portion of the community. This is on account of keeping nothing but the very best of stock in all the most seasonable and fashionable fabrics, which he makes up to order by measure in the highest style of the art.   The premises occupied by the business are 28 x 45 feet in dimensions and two stories in height, the upper floor being used as a workshop, where employment is furnished to 12 skilled and competent operators. The store is tastefully fitted up with plate glass front, is lighted by electricity and presents a neat and attractive appearance, and the stock of goods carried large and elegant, consisting of imported and domestic fabrics, woollens, tweeds, cassimeres, etc.   The garments produced by this house are unsurpassed for beauty of fit, perfection of fit and elegance of finish, and the prices will be found very reasonable.   Mr. Lemieux also carries a fine line of gents' furnishings, including all the latest and most fashionable novelties.   Mr. Lemieux is a native of this Province, is an enterprising and progressive business man and an active member of the Chamber of Commerce.

Edmond Leonard, CHEMIST AND DRUGGIST, 113 St. Lawrence Main Street.—The profession of the pharmacist is one that has kept steady pace with the improvements of the times, not alone in medicine but also in science and the arts.   To enter the profession of pharmacy now-a-days one must have given this subject deep study and passed a critical examination in some regular college established for this special purpose, and thus strong safeguards are thrown around the public.   Among those who have recently entered upon the practice of this profession in this city is Mr. Edmond Leonard, whose store is located at No. 113 St. Lawrence Main Street.   This business was formerly conducted by Messrs. Lavoillette & Nelson for three years preceding the first of March of the present year, when they were succeeded by the present proprietor.   The premises occupied are 20 x 55 feet in dimensions and are tastefully fitted up with plate glass show cases and cabinets, etc.   Here is carried a large stock of fresh and pure drugs and chemicals, fancy and toilet articles, imported and domestic perfumes, soaps, etc., proprietary medicines of acknowledged merit and standard reputation, druggists sundries, etc.   A specialty is made of the compounding of physicians' prescriptions and family recipes with care and promptness and at reasonable prices.   Employment is furnished to two competent assistants, one of whom is a regular graduated pharmacist.   Mr. Ed. Leonard, the proprietor, is a native of Montreal and is a graduate of the Pharmaceutical Association of the Province of Quebec.   He is highly esteemed by all who know him as a careful and conscientious pharmacist and a gentleman of marked business ability.

Elmwood Floral Nurseries, 2508 St. Catherine Street, A. Martin, Proprietor.—The human heart is drawn towards flowers as naturally as the bee in looking for the sweets to make its honey.   The Persian delights in their perfume and denotes his love by them.   Orange blossoms are with us a bridal crown, while flowers garlanded the Grecian altar, and hung in native wreaths before the Christian shrine.   Flowers deck the brow of the bride and are entwined around the tomb.   The business of the florist is therefore one of the most delightful of occupations.   Among those prominently engaged in this line of business in this city is Mr. A. Martin, whose office and floral nurseries are located at No. 2508 St. Catherine Street.   The nurseries are 120 x 200 feet in dimensions, half of which is under glass.   Every requisite is on hand for the successful prosecution of the business, and the greenhouses are heated by hot water.   Here will be found a beautiful assortment of rare and choice plants, as well as table and bedding plants in their season. Mr. Martin keeps constantly a splendid assortment of cut flowers and makes up floral designs of every description at short notice, for weddings, receptions and funerals in the highest style of the art.   Mr. Martin is a native of England, and learned his business in that country, being thoroughly skilled in all its details.   He established his business here on his own account five years ago, and during that time has met with the most gratifying and well deserved success.

Hecla Iron Works, ROBERT DONALDSON, SMITH AND MACHINIST, 29 McGILL STREET, MONTREAL.—The machinery trade of Montreal is conducted upon an extensive scale, which is due in no small degree to the number of manufacturing establishments located here, requiring machinery of various kinds and also on account of the number of ocean and inland steamers that visit this port during the season of navigation. Apart from this there is a general trade at all times throughout the city. In reviewing those houses engaged in the machinist business in this city, mention must be made of the Hecla Iron Works, of which Mr. Robt. Donaldson is the proprietor, and which is located at No. 29 McGill Street. The premises occupied are 35 x 50 feet in dimensions and are fitted up with all the latest and most improved machinery driven by a 6-horse power steam engine, while employment is steadily furnished to six skilled and competent workmen and four apprentices. The work done by this house consists of the manufacture of engines and machinery, steamfitting, contractors' tools, shipsmithing, heavy forgings under steam hammer, and all other kinds of a similar nature. The work done by this house is first class in every particular, being of good quality and the best of finish and perfect in design and application. Mr. Donaldson, the proprietor, is a Scotchman by birth, and is a thoroughly skilled and practical workman of many years experience. He founded the business twelve years ago and during that time has met with the most encouraging success, and has built up a trade of which he may well feel gratified.

Ι. Dr. F. L. Palardy, CHEMIST & DRUGGIST, 396 ST. JAMES ST. MONTREAL—There is no profession practised that requires more constant care and attention for its successful prosecution or for the avoidance of mistakes than that of the pharmacist. The wonder is, not that any mistakes should occur, but that so few do. The law has guarded this profession with zealous care in the interest of the public and now only those who have passed through a severe course of study, and passed a successful examination at colleges established for this purpose, are permitted to practice. Holding a prominent position among the pharmacists of this city is Dr. F. L. Palardy, whose store is located at No. 396 St. James Street. Dr. F. L. Palardy, is a graduate of the Victoria College of Ontario, and is a thoroughly skilled and able physician, and is careful and conscientious to a marked degree. He established his business here 7 years ago, and almost from the date of its inception it has proved eminently successful. The commodious premises occupied are 35 x 60 feet in dimensions, with the dispensary in rear, making the largest retail drug store in the city. It is fitted up in beautiful style, leading in black and gold, with plate glass show cases and cabinets, soda water fountain and every accessory for the successful prosecution of a business of this character. The stock carried is large, and consists of fresh and pure drugs, chemicals, fancy and and toilet articles, imported and domestic soaps, perfumes &c., proprietary medicines of acknowledged merit and standard reputation, druggists sundries &c., &c. A specialty of the business is the compounding of physician's prescriptions and family recipes with care and accuracy. The store is opened on Sundays from 9 to 10 A.M', 12 to 1, and 7 to 8 P.M. when all orders will receive strict attention. As a specialist Dr. Palardy has achieved to an enviable position in his treatment of diseases of the skin. He also manufactures and sells at both wholesale and retail the following well known articles, Specific against intemperance, Dr. Palardys Compound Syrup, Syrup Iodo Bromo Quinique, Cod Liver Oil with Hypophosphites, and with Hypophosphites and Iron, and Quinine Wine. He is a native of Vercheres, and his successful business is the best evidence of his ability in the profession of his choice.

J. C. Beauvais & Co., DRY GOODS & MERCHANT TAILORS, 1529 NOTRE DAME STREET, MONTREAL.—The above house was established in 1870, and constitutes a very important addition to the retail dry-goods houses in this city. From its inception it has enjoyed an unbroken career of success, which is attributable to the honorable methods of conducting business, which were adopted from the first, and which have been adhered to in all its transactions, reflecting alike credit on its proprietors and the community in general. The firm carry out their business at No. 1529 Notre Dame Street, three doors east of the City Hall, the premises accupied consisting of 3 floors 24 x 60 feet in dimensions. Here a large and complete stock of imported and domestic fancy and staple dry-goods is carried, which stock for careful selection and variety, cannot be duplicated in city. The firm purchase direct from the manufacturers all their British and Foreign goods, and their large and varied stock comprises contributions from many of the manufacturing centres of Europe. Operating all departments on the most economical basis, they are enabled to offer their goods to the public at lowest prices. There is a special department for merchant tailoring, where will be found an excellent line of imported and domestic tweeds, woolens, cashmeres, in the latest and most fashionable patterns, which are made up to order in short notice in the highest style of the art. Also direct importers of Gent's Furnishings of which the stock is full and complete. This business was formerly conducted by Messrs. Beauvais & Perrault, but now Mr. J. C. Beauvais, has the entire control. He is a French Canadian by birth and a member of the Chamber of Commerce.

Robert H. Bryson, CHEMIST & DRUGGIST, 2391 St. Catherine Street, Montreal.—The past quarter of a century has witnessed a remarkable improvement in the profession of pharmacy, and the care and attention that has been devoted to students in this branch of the profession, has been the means of turning out from the colleges of pharmacy, gentlemen of undoubted ability as well as high and conscientious principles. Among those prominently identified with this profession in Montreal, none are more deserving of special mention than Mr. Robert H. Bryson, whose store is located at No. 2391 St. Catherine Street. The premises occupied for the purposes of the business are 18 x 45 feet in dimensions, and are fitted up with much taste, having plate glass show cases and cabinets, well stocked with a fine line of goods, including all the various drugs and chemicals, pharmaceutical preparations and proprietary remedies. Also toilet and fancy articles, imported and domestic soaps, perfumes &c., and those articles required by physicians in their practice, and druggists sundries generally. As a practical druggist and chemist, Mr. Bryson makes a specialty of the compounding of physicians prescriptions and difficult formulæ, with promptness and accuracy. He also prepares cough syrups, remedies for chapped hands and other like specialties which are highly beneficial for the purpose designed. Employment is furnished to three competent and courteous employees throughout the year. Mr. Bryson, who is a native of Montreal, is a graduate of the Quebec Pharmaceutical Association, and is a thoroughly skilled pharmacist, and during the six years he has been established in business on his own account he has met with the most encouraging success.

O. Courtemanche, FURNITURE, 1519 Notre Dame Street, Montreal.— Among the many different lines of business conducted in Montreal that in furniture and house furnishings holds a conspicuous place and among those engaged in this line none are more deserving of special mention than Mr, O. Courtemanche, whose stores are located at No. 1519 Notre Dame street. The premises occupied on Notre Dame Street consists of 3 floors and basement 40 x 114 feet in dimensions ; and the warehouse on Dorchester Street, consists of 2 floors 50 x 50 feet in dimensions. The stock of goods carried is very large and varied, and consists of household and general furniture, both new and second hand. Also stoves and ranges of all kinds and a great variety of hardware, crockery, carpets, and a general line of house furnishing goods, as well as pianos from several of the leading manufacturers of the continent. The stocks are full and complete in every descriptions and those requiring anything in this line would find it to their advantage to inspect it before purchasing eleswhere, as Mr. Courtemanche is in a position to offer advantages not easily to be obtained elsewhere. Employment is furnished to 4 competent and courteous assistants in the different departments throughout the year. Mr. Courtemanche, who is a native of the Province of Quebec, established his business here 16 years ago during which time he has met with very much success and has built up a trade that is steadily on the increase.

CANADIAN PACIFIC RAILWAY BRIDGE OVER THE ST. LAWRENCE RIVER, NEAR MONTREAL.

T. M. Bell, CROCKERY, CHINA, GLASS, EARTHENWARE, LAMPS, &c., 259 St. LAWRENCE MAIN STREET, MONTREAL.—That Montreal is rapidly increasing in extent and importance as a commercial centre may readily be observed by the large number of business houses that have been recently established here. It is by this infusion of new blood into any business community that a spirit of enterprise is installed or kept active. Among the business houses, therefore, coming under this head and deserving of more than a mere passing notice is that of Mr. T. M. Bell, importer of and dealer in crockery, china, glass, etc. This gentleman founded his business here in August of 1887, at No. 42 Bleury Street, and meeting with such marked success that he required more room for the operations of his business, he, on the 1st of May of the present year removed to his more commodious premises at No. 259 St. Lawrence Main Street. The premises occupied are 40 x 60 feet in dimensions, which are neatly and suitably fitted up for the requirements of the trade, and where is carried a large and elegant stock of crockery, china, glass, earthenware, lamps, etc., a specialty being made of chamber sets. Purchasing direct from some of the leading manufacturers in this country and Europe and thus avoiding the commissions usually paid to middle men, Mr. Bell is enabled to give his customers the advantage of low prices, which defy competition and certainly warrants the assertion of this being "the cheapest house in the city" in this line. Mr. Bell is a native of Liverpool, England, and has had an extended experience in his line of business, and can thus meet any of the demands of the public in a satisfactory manner.

Francois Godin, MANUFACTURER OF WASHING MACHINES, 2192 NOTRE DAME STREET, MONTREAL.—This is an age of invention and the best efforts of man have been put forth to produce labor saving machinery. We look around and in the harvest fields find agricultural implements doing the work that would have formerly taken 20 men to do. We look into the household and into the clothing, shirt and other factories and find sewing machines lightening the labor of women. And now we look into the kitchens and and wash-rooms and find the washing, plague to tired womankind, being done by wonderful working though simply constructed and easily managed machines. Mr. Francois Godin, of No. 2192 Notre Dame Street, is the manufacturer of one of the best washing machines in the market. It was patented March 18th 1879 and many improvements have been made upon it since that time. At the Provincial Exhibitions it took first prize in 1880, diplomas in 1881 and 1882, and a medal in 1884, also 1st prize and diploma at Provincial Exhibition at Quebec 1887. These machines will wash in one day as much linen as a woman could wash in three days with their hands only. In using the machine, soak your linen in water all night and the next day make good warm suds, and put 3 or 4 buckets of boiling water into the washing machine with the linen, stir for ten minutes and then take it out. These machines have received high recommendations from institutions and individuals who have used them. Mr. Godin is the sole manufacturer for the Dominion. At his store on Notre Dame Street, he also carries a fine stock of toys and woodenware of every description. Mr. Godin is a native of the Province of Quebec, and is a live, active and progressive man of business, and is eminently deserving of the success he has achieved.

J. G. Michon, MERCHANT TAILOR, 3111 NOTRE DAME ST. ST. CUNEGONDE—. The great question with gentlemen who are about to get a new suit is. "where is the best place to go, where the garments will be well and fashionably made and the prices moderate?" It is absolutely necessary in these modern days that a man should be well and fashionably dressed if he would make a good impression in the world and meet with business and social success. Among those merchant tailors doing business in Montreal there are none more deserving of honorable mention than Mr. J. G. Michon, whose shop is located at No 3111 Notre Dame Street. The premises occupied are commodious and are neatly fitted up and contain a fine stock of imported and domestic cloths, woollens, tweeds, cassimeres &c., in the latest and most fashionable patterns from which to make a selection. These are made up to order on short notice and in the highest style of the art, and in respect to perfect fit, elegance of finish and beauty of style are not surpassed by those of any other house in the city, while the prices will be found very reasonable, and must meet the views of the most economical. Employment is furnished to 5 skilled and competent operators throughout the course of the year. Mr. Michon, who is a Canadian by birth, is a practical and excellent tailor of many years experience, and gives his personal attention to all orders entrusted to his care, and since he established his business here 2 years ago he has met with the most eminent and well deserved success.

Carroll Bros., PLUMBERS, GAS & STEAM FITTERS, 795 CRAIG STREET, MONTREAL.—The agitation which has taken place in recent years respecting sanitary plumbing and the evils arising from defective work, has been productive of much good. It has caused an enquiry into the causes and the proper remedies, and the efficient plumbers have been the gainers. Among those prominently engaged in the plumbing business in this city is the firm of Messrs. Carroll Bros., whose shop is located at No. 795 Craig Street. This business was founded 7 years ago and has at all times proved highly successful, and has steadily increased in extent and importance from year to year. The premises occupied are 45 x 70 feet in dimensions, and are fully equipped with every requisite for the successful prosecution of the work done. Employment is furnished on an average throughout the year to from 10 to 12 skilled and competent workmen. Mr. Patrick Carroll, now the sole proprietor is a practical and skilled sanitarian and thoroughly understands the work in all its phases. He also does plumbing of every description, fitting up new buildings, making repairs and also gas and steam fitting, as well as tin and sheet iron working. All the work done by this house is of the very best description, being personally superintended by Mr. Carroll, guaranteed to be entirely satisfactory, while the charges are moderate. Mr. Carroll is a native of Ireland, and came to this country in early youth. He is an active and energetic business man, full of energy and enterprise, and is a member of the Master Plumbers Association of Montreal.

Pierre Demers, HARDWARE, PAINTS, & OILS, 2191 NOTRE DAME STREET, MONTREAL.—There is possibly no city on the American continent that contains more solid, old-established business houses than Montreal. In almost every branch of the trade will be found representative houses that have grown with the city's growth and kept steady pace with the improvements of the times. Among such houses in the hardware trade deserving of special mention in a work of this character, is that of Pierre Demers, which is eligibly located for business at No. 2191 Notre Dame Street. This house was founded 28 years ago, and by the exercise of persevering industry and untiring energy, coupled with a thorough knowledge of the business on the part of the proprietor has been built up steadily to its present extensive proportions. The premises occupied by the business are large and commodious, being 24 x 70 feet in dimensions, with a storehouse in rear for heavy and surplus stock The stock carried is very large and varied in character, and includes almost everything coming under the head of shelf and heavy hardware, builders' and mechanics' requisites, cutlery &c., &c. Also all kinds of carriage wood bent stuff, and paints, oils, varnish, brushes, glass, putty &c., &c. All goods handled are of the very best quality, and are received direct from first hands and manufacturers in this country and Europe. The business is conducted both at wholesale and retail and embraces, in the scope of its operations, not only the city of Montreal, but a large section of the surrounding country. Employment is furnished to 5 competent and courteous assistants in the different departments. Mr. Demers, is a native of Pointe Claire, and is a gentleman of extended experience in the hardware trade and fully understanding the requirements of the public is ever prepared to anticipate their demands.

Wm. F. Smardon, FINE BOOTS AND SHOES, 1665 NOTRE DAME STREET, AND 2337 AND 2339 ST. CATHERINE STREET, MONTREAL.—In reviewing the commerce and manufactures of Montreal, many facts of interest are elicited with regard to the personality of those engaged in the different lines of business. It is not always those who "fall into their father's shoes," so to speak, that succeed the best, but in many cases it is those who have to carve out a way for themselves. Mr. Wm. F. Smardon, dealer in boots and shoes, at Nos, 2337 and 2339 St. Catherine Street, and No. 1665 Notre Dame Street, started to work at the shoemaker trade when only 12 years of age. He was made of the right material and by persevering industry, energy and enterprise he has carved his way to permanent success and gained an enviable reputation as a straightforward and honorable business man. The stores he occupies are large and commodious and are handsomely fitted up, and contain a large and elegant stock of the finest quality of boots and shoes for ladies and gentlemen, youths, misses and children. These are all specially marked, according to the particular size and make, so that any person can have their boots or shoes duplicated at any time without fitting on, and in fact Mr. Smardon is filling orders every day for boots and shoes for customers all over the Dominion. He does a large city and country trade and his business is still steadily increasing. He started in business for himself on February 1st, 1876, and opened his Notre Dame Street store, which was formerly the retail department of T. & J. Bell, two years ago. Employment is furnished to nine courteous assistants and skilled workmen throughout the year, and Mr. Smardon makes a specialty of ladies, misses, and children's fine goods, a large family trade being done in this department, also the making up of boots and shoes to order in the highest style of the art, and secures the most satisfactory results by giving his personal attention to the cutting of all stock for orders.

George J. Sheppard, MUSIC DEALER, 2282 ST. CATHERINE STREET, MONTREAL.—Most persons of refinement and culture have a love if not the talent, for music, and there are very few houses of the "well-to-do" classes in which either a piano or organ is not to be found. In a community like Montreal a taste for music is widespread and the business of the music dealer is therefore an important one. One of the most enterprising and progressive houses in this line of business in the city, is that of Mr. George J. Sheppard, which is located at No. 2282 St. Catherine Street. The premises occupied occupy two floors. On the ground floor is contained an elegant stock of sheet music, musical goods, pianos and organs, Mr. Sheppard being agent for George Steck & Co. and Stultz & Bauer, of New York, and Mason & Risch, of Toronto, (who made such an impression at the Colonial Exhibition, in London, Eng., last year for the superior quality of their pianos,) and also for Mason & Hamlin, of Boston, manufacturers of organs. These instruments require no comment at our hands, they are too well known throughout the North American continent for their excellence. Mr. Sheppard has had the enterprise and culture have a love if not the talent, for music, his success—of originating in Montreal something that professors of music and music students in certain circumstances have long desired without knowing how to accomplish On the second floor of Mr. Sheppard's establishment are fitted up five music studios, where professors can make arrangements to hold their classes and where students, who probably board out and have no music conveniences, can have set hours for practice. Even New York has been behind hand in this respect, and the musical press is just beginning to agitate the question so Mr. Sheppard deserves the thanks of the musical fraternity of Montreal for his forethought and enterprise. Mr. Sheppard is a native of Montreal and has a thorough talent for music, which of course is of great value to him in his present business, which he established only one year ago, but which has already far exceeded his most sanguine anticipations.

A. A. Beauchamp, WATCHMAKER AND JEWELLER, 1692 NOTRE DAME STREET, MONTREAL.—A very remarkable improvement has taken place in the manufacture of watches during the past quarter of a century. The intricate and delicate machinery that has been invented for the manufacture of watches, enables manufacturers to turn out hundreds of these perfectly finished and correct time-keepers, where previous thereto only one could be turned out by hand in the same space of time. Consequently the price of these necessary articles has been so reduced that they are now brought within the reach of all. Among those actively engaged in the watchmaking and jewellery trade in this city is Mr. A. A. Beauchamp, whose store is located at No. 1692 Notre Dame Street. The premises occupied are 20x45 feet in dimensions and are tastefully fitted up with plate glass show cases and equipments, and contain a large and elegant stock of gold and silver, English, Swiss and American watches, clocks, rings, chains, brooches, earrings, sleeve buttons, scarf pins, lockets and many other beautiful articles of jewellery in gold and silver, jet &c., too numerous to mention in detail. Mr. Beauchamp makes a specialty of the manufacture of jewellery, and also of watch repairing, giving employment to 12 skilled and competent workmen throughout the year. His work is of the very best quality and being a practical jeweller himself he gives his personal attention to all orders and thus secures the most satisfactory results. This business was established in 1827 by the late D. Smillie and has been carried on by Mr. Beaudry for the last 24 years, perseverance and enterprise, has built up a business of which he may well feel proud. He is a progressive citizen and is a member of the Chamber of Commerce.

Picault & Contant, CHEMISTS AND DRUGGISTS, 1475 NOTRE DAME ST MONTREAL.—The profession of the pharmacist is one of the most important of any conducted and during the first quarter of a century a very marked improvement has taken place in it, and on account of the necessity of those professing it, having to be graduates of regularly constituted pharmaceutical associations, the profession is hedged around with safeguards for the public safety. Among the best known and oldest established houses in this line of business in the city is that of Messrs. Picault & Contant, whose store is located at No. 1475 Notre Dame Street. The premises occupied are 25 x 45 feet in dimensions, and are handsomely fitted up with plate glass show cases and cabinets for the proper display of the fine stock of goods carried, consisting of fresh, pure drugs, chemicals, fancy and toilet articles, imported and domestic soaps, perfumes; &c., &c., proprietary medicines of acknowledged merit and standard reputation, as well as all such articles are required by physicians in their practice. A specialty of the house is the compounding of physicians prescriptions and difficult formulæ, with care and accuracy. The firm manufacture a number of proprietary medicines that have proved highly efficacious and have met with a strong demand. Employment is furnished to 10 competent assistants and other help throughout the year in the different departments of the business. This house was founded by Dr. Picault, in the year 1833, while Montreal was still a small place. Mr. Picault is since deceased and Mr. Joseph Contant, has conducted the business alone for the past 4 years. Mr. Contant, is a native of Montreal and a graduate of the Pharmaceutical Association of the Province of Quebec, and is a member of the council of the Chamber of Commerce.

A. M. Featherston, BOOTS & SHOES, No. 1 ST. LAWRENCE MAIN STREET, AND COR. OF ST. CATHERINE AND VICTORIA STREETS.—St. Lawrence Main Street is one of the most important of the retail thoroughfares of Montreal; and upon it are located many first-class establishments in the different branches of trade. It is the artery of business, joining the north and south sections of the city. Holding a prominent place in the boot and shoe trade on this street is the establishment of Mr. A. M. Featherston, which is located at No. 1 and the corner of Craig Street. It is now 10 years since this business was founded and during the time it has proved very successful owing to the enterprise and energy displayed on the part of the proprietor. The premises occupied are 28 x 40 feet in dimensions and are suitably fitted up for the requirements of the business. Here will be found a large and first-class stock of boots and shoes, slippers, rubbers, &c., for ladies and gentlemen, misses, youths, boys and children in all weights and grades, from the finest of Kid to the heaviest of Kip, made up in the most fashionable styles by some of the leading manufacturing establishments in the country. Those desiring to have their boots or shoes made to order by measure can be accommodated here and their orders executed with promptness and in the most satisfactory manner at very reasonable prices. For the accommodation of residents in this section of the city Mr. Featherston has a store agency of the Canadian Pacific Railway for the sale of tickets, and all information respecting routes, &c., may be here obtained. A similar establishment is conducted by the proprietor at the corner of St. Catherine and Victoria Streets. Mr. Featherston is a native of Canada and a gentleman of marked business ability, push and energy, and the success that has attended his efforts so far has been justly deserved and is but an augury of what the future has in store.

Henri Larin, PHOTO-ARTIST, 18 St. Lawrence Street, Montreal.—If one of our modern photographers had suddenly appeared in the midst of the people one hundred years ago and practised his vocation, he would have been looked upon as a manipulator of the "black arts" and would have been in danger of forming a central figure in a barbecue. That pictures could be taken instantaneously by the aid of the sun's rays would have been beyond belief; but this past quarter of a century has been a wonderful one in the world's history and in the history of photography. Amongst the most popular of the photographic artists in this city is Mr. Henri Larin, whose studio is located at No. 18 St. Lawrence Main Street. The premises occupied for reception room, studio. dark room, &c., cover 38 x 75 feet in dimensions and are handsomely fitted up and contain the most modern and improved apparatus, thus ensuring the successful prosecution of the business. Mr. Larin does every description of photography, such as taking from life, copying, enlarging, &c. He also executes work in water colors, crayon, India ink, pastel &c. His work in all the different branches is excellent and is well worthy of inspection by those who have any intention of leaving their "counterfeit presentment" to their friends and posterity. Since this business was established 8 years ago it has proved highly successful and has steadily continued to increase and develope. Employment is furnished to careful and capable assistants. Mr. Larin is a native of Lachine, and is a thoroughly skilled, practical photographer who has well merited his success.

W. J. Clark & Co. No. 50 Beaver Hall Hill.—The booksellers' and Stationers' trade has for many generations been a most highly honored one, in this country as well as in England. Some of the old London book stores were the resorts of many of the greatest literary and scientific celebrities of their time, and many a story has been passed down from generation to generation of their sayings and doings. But it is of the present we have now to speak and not of the past,—of Montreal book stores and not those of London. One of the most prominent and popular houses in this line in this city is that of Messrs. W. J. Clark & Co., which is located at No. 50 Beaver Hall Hill, midway between the residential and business quarters of the city. This business was established by Messrs. G. & W. Clark 15 years ago, the present proprietor succeeding to the entire business 6 years since, the premises occupied are 24 x 50 feet in dimensions and are handsomely fitted up and contain a large and elegant stock of books in standard, general and light literature, and in the different styles of binding, also stationery of all kinds, from the ordinary commercial to the finest and most expensive for ladies' use. In fancy goods the stock is very large and contain a most elegant and varied assortment of articles useful and ornamental. This is also a headquarter for views of Montreal, Indian curiosities, and Canadian souvenirs ; also, sheet music from the leading publishers of Great Britain the United States and Canada, for both vocal and instrumental use. Visitors to the city, as well as residents will find this one of the best and most satisfactory places at which to obtain their supplies. The firm have sole right of Mount Royal Park for the sale of their goods, and during the summer season a well stocked establishment is conducted on the mountain for the sale of books, curiosities, photos and travellers and tourists' requisites generally. Mr. Clark is a native of Montreal, and is widely and favorably known in business and social circles.

S. Nightingale, TEAS AND COFFEES, 143 St. Lawrence Main Street.— It is claimed that Arabia is the home of coffee and it is known that the most fragrant kinds come from that country, But when Arabia held the monopoly coffee sold in England for $25,co a pound, so it may well be imagined that it was not to be found on every boarding-house breakfast table. After the berry had been cultivated in other countries the price came down until now rich and poor alike enjoy the fragrant aroma. Among those promi-nently engaged in the tea and coffee trade in this city is Mr. S. Nightingale, whose store is located at No. 143 St. Lawrence Main Street. This business was successfully conducted by his brother, Mr. E. A. Nightingale, for six years previous to the 1st of May of the present year, when Mr. S. Nightingale succeeded to it. The premises occupied are 24 x 38 feet in dimensions, are neatly fitted up and contain an excellent stock of the choicest brands of teas and coffees. Competent judges affirm that these beverages lose their flavor when they are carried in stock with cheese, ham, pepper, etc., and therefore to obtain them in their native purity they should be kept separate and apart from all such articles. At Mr. Nightingale's they will be found of the very best quality, and handling these goods alone and purchasing direct from shippers, he obtains his goods under the most favorable terms and can thus give his numerous customers the benefit, not only of low prices but of beautiful presents as well. Employment is furnished to three competent assistants in conducting the business. Mr. Nightingale, who is a native of Montreal, has a thorough and comprehensive knowledge of the business, and his customers can thus be assured of obtaining the best the market affords at all times.

Arthur Bourdon, GROCER, No. 127 St. Lawrence Main Street, Montreal.— So long as people live by eating so long will the grocery trade hold a paramount place in the estimation of every individual in the land. All quarters of the earth are made to con-tribute of their products to meet the demands of this trade. It was under the regime of Louis XV of France that tea was first introduced into Canada and was then enjoyed only by the wealthy. But now, rich and poor alike can enjoy the fragrant beverage. Among those prominently identified with the grocery trade in this city, and deserving of more than a mere passing mention in these pàges, is Mr. Arthur Bourdon, whose store is located at No. 127 St. Lawrence Main Street, near Lagauchetiere Street. The premises occupied are 22 x 50 feet in dimensions and are tastefully and suitably fitted up for the requirements of the trade. Here is carried a large and carefully selected stock of staple and fancy groceries, including the choicest brands of China and Japan teas, fragrant coffees from Java and Rio, pure condiments, table delicacies, canned goods, butter, cheese, hams and other provisions of the very best quality, as well as the finest brands of wines and liquors specially suited for fine family trade. The stock has been selected with the utmost care and will be found first-class in every particular. This business, which was established in the spring of 1887, has proved very successful indeed, and this has been due in a marked degree to Mr. Bourdon's extended knowledge of the business, he having been for 15 years a clerk with Mr. Dodd. Mr. Bourdon is a native of Montreal and is widely and favorably known in business and social circles.

Henry Birks & Co., WATCHMAKERS, JEWELLERS, ETC., 235 AND 237 St. James Street, Montreal,—That Montreal is the centre of the wealth and culture of the Dominion may be judged not alone by her palatial residences and public buildings, but from the number of excellent establishments devoted to art goods and jewellery. Beyond all question the house of Messrs. Henry Birks & Co., at Nos. 235 and 237 St. James Street, is the best equipped and most liberally patronized of any in this section of the Dominion. The premises occupied are 30 x 120 feet in dimensions. The store is a truly elegant and inviting place, the resort of the best people of Montreal and vicinity—the class who recognize and appreciate artistic taste, genuine value and the highest grade of workmanship. All of the latest and most improved machinery and special tools used in the trade are provided, and a vast quantity of superior goods are produced, the specialties of the house embracing choice diamonds, rubies, sapphires, pearls, emeralds, rich jewelry in original and standard designs, English, Swiss and American watches and clocks, solid silver and silver plated ware, brass and optical goods, gold and silver headed canes, and all the latest and most attractive novelties of the trade as fast as introduced. This business was established in the year 1879 and soon took a leading place among the representative houses of the country, the trade now extending from the Atlantic to the Pacific. Of course, the aggregate annual sales are very large and the business a prosperous one. Mr. Birks, the proprietor, is a Montrealer by birth, and is a gentleman well-known and highly esteemed.

Anderson, McKenzie & Co., STEAMSHIP AGENTS, FORWARDERS AND COMMISSION AGENTS, 227 COMMISSIONERS STREET.—Conspicuous among the old established and reliable steamship agents in the city of Montreal is the firm of Anderson, McKenzie & Co., whose office is located at No. 227 Commissioners Street. They charter steamers and sailing vessels for the conveyance of freight to all parts of the world. They are considered among the most prominent forwarders in this city, and their reputation for business methods and honorable dealing stands high throughout the country, so that the utmost confidence is placed in their judgment and foresight. They receive consignments, and are engaged in the forwarding and freighting in the phosphate, lumber and deal trade, probably doing a heavier export trade in these products as forwarders than any other house in the city. They are agents for the Furness Line of steamers, running between Montreal, London and Liverpool in summer and Portland and Liverpool in winter. The steamers of this line are the "Durham City," 3092 tons; "Boston City," 2324 tons; "Madura," 2315 tons; "Washington City," 2296 tons; "Gothenburg City," 2526 tons; "Katie," 2795 tons, and others. Messrs. Anderson, McKenzie & Co, receive goods on commission and sell the same to the best advantage, making prompt settlements upon all sales, and guaranteeing the best of satisfaction in every case. With the harbor relieved from debt and the opening up of the Sault St. Marie Railway, the shipping business of the Port of Montreal must be enhanced to a very considerable extent during the coming years, and Mr. Anderson will be sure to have at least his share of the increased business, for if push and enterprise will obtain successful results he will obtain them.

Bowes & McWilliams, COMMISSION MERCHANTS, 1836 NOTRE DAME STREET, MONTREAL.—The wholesale fruit trade is one of the important branches of commercial industry conducted in Montreal, and as this is the distributing point for a large section of the Dominion, several leading houses are engaged in this line of trade, among which none hold a higher reputation or do a more extensive business than the firm of Messrs. Bowes & McWilliams, whose store is located at No. 1836 Notre Dame Street. These gentlemen established the business 8 years ago, and during that time they have built a very enviable trade that now embraces the provinces of Ontario, Quebec, New Brunswick and Nova Scotia. They are direct importers of foreign fruits from Italy, Spain, Sicily, Florida and California, and deal largely in Canadian fruits. As importers and commission merchants the firm stands high and controls one of the largest trades that comes into Montreal, and are considered one of the largest and most reliable houses in the city. The members of the firm Mr. Archibald Bowes and Mr. John McWilliams, both of whom are Canadians by birth, and are thorough going and enterprising business men thoroughly alive to the wants of the trade and knowing how best to meet the requirements of patrons. They are well known and highly esteemed in business and social circles.

R. Nicholson Sons, BUTCHERS, 16, 17, 18 St. Ann's Market.—The commercial interests of a large city would be incomplete without the extensive element made up by the provision trade, an important branch of which is the trade in fresh meats.   In this line we find a number of leading firms doing a large and prosperous trade, the majority however confirming themselves to the city business.   There are several that make a specialty of supplying the shipping with meat and other shop stores and of these Messrs. R. Nicholson Sons are deserving of special mention.   Their market is located at Nos. 16, 17 and 18 St. Ann's Market.   This business was established by Mr. R. Nicholson — now deceased — 47 years ago, and 4 years since, the Sons Messrs. George C. and John S. Nicholson succeeded to the business.   The house has had a long and honorable as well as successful career. The firm use on an average 30 head of cattle and 100 calves and sheep a week, dealing as they do entirely in beef, mutton and veal.   Besides their regular city trade they supply vessels that enter the port and have gained a high reputation for the excellent quality of their supplies and for their prompt attention to all orders.   The Messrs. Nicholson are young gentlemen of marked business ability, push and enterprise and are highly esteemed by all who know them.

The Davis & Lawrence Co., Limited, PROPRIETORS, MANUFACTURERS AND GENERAL AGENTS, St. Antoine Street, corner of Chatham Street.—The whole range of the wonderful commercial history of Canada records few more brilliant and deserved business successes than that which has marked the progress of this house, and which will constitute a lasting and honorable memorial to the distinguished business talent and persevering efforts of Mr. W. V. Lawrence, the President of the Company, who in the year 1866 started the business here described in a little 8 x 10 store on St. Paul Street, which in a few months was found too small, and it became necessary to remove to larger quarters. These quarters, which were also upon St. Paul Street, after two or three years also were found too crowded, and in 1875 a large factory building was erected by the Company on Plymouth Grove especially for their use, which at the time was thought great enough for all future requirements, but this too at the end of five years was found too small for the rapidly growing business, and then it was that the Company decided to erect the present magnificent building, a picture of which we give below :—

We cannot enter into a description of it in the limited space at our disposal here, further than to give a general idea of its size and uses. In extent it covers three sides of a square, having a total frontage on three streets of 404 feet, with an inner court in which is built the engine and boiler house. It is four storeys high with the basement, and is built entirely of brick and stone, the St. Antoine Street front being handsomely faced with sandstone. For substantial structure and architectural beauty it is not excelled by any factory building in Montreal. Every modern improvement that would facilitate the business has been adapted, such as steam elevators, hand railways, machines for bottle washing, bottle filling, bottle corking, &c. Steam and gas are carried to all parts of the building.

Commencing at the top floor, which is set apart entirely for laboratory purposes, it is here where are manufactured their world-renowned preparations, which are so well and favorably known to the people of Canada.

Descending to the next floor we find the bottling department and store rooms for finished goods. Again descending we come to the finishing apartments, shipping department, sample rooms and offices.

The basement is used for the storage of cased goods, and as a bonded warehouse.

The Company have spared no pains or expense in elevating their business to its present high position. Their travelling agents visit periodically every city, town and village in the Dominion and their preparations are household words everywhere. Who is not familiar with Perry Davis' Pain Killer. Allen's Lung Balsam, Fellow's Syrup of Hypophosphites, Wyeth's Beef, Iron and Wine, Campbell's Cathartic Compound, Murray & Lanman's Florida Water, and other preparations of this order, which are made exclusively in this great factory, the largest and most perfectly equipped in Canada if not in the world

Hudon, Hebert & Co., IMPORTERS AND WHOLESALE GROCERS, 304 AND-306 ST. PAUL, AND 143-145 COMMISSIONERS STREETS, MONTREAL.—Montreal is the great distributing centre of the Dominion, and here of course it is natural to look for the centre of the importing and wholesale trade. Situated at the head of ocean navigation and at the foot of inland communication, by rail, canal river and lake, no position could be better adapted for the commercial metropolis of the Dominion. Among the old established houses in this city devoted to the wholesale grocery trade, that of Messrs. Hudon, Hebert & Co., stand pre-eminent in many respects. The premises occupied are in a handsome and substantial 6 storey building 109 x 150 feet in dimensions, and running straight through from St. Paul to Commissioners Street. These are fitted up with every modern convenience for the proper conducting of the business, and each floor from basement to attic, is heavily stored with a fine line of imported staple and fancy groceries, wines and liquors. The choicest goods from China and the West and East Indies, Mediterranean countries and the south, are all here represented, as well as choice lines of provisions. The firm deal largely in the best brands of wines and liquors, and make a specialty of altar wines which are warranted absolutely pure and have been selected with the most critical judgment. The trade of this house is very extensive, its customers hailing from all parts of the Dominion. Hudon, Hebert & Co., have enjoyed a long, honorable and prosperous career, and built up a high reputation for straight forward and liberal dealing, which has been fully appreciated by the trade.

W. Scott & Son, IMPORTERS & DEALERS IN OIL PAINTINGS, ETCHINGS &c., 1739 NOTRE DAME STREET, MONTREAL.—A goodly proportion of the people of Montreal are of cultivated taste and indulge their pleasures in the arts of painting, music and poetry.   There is no city in the Dominion where art is so appreciated as in Montreal, and consequently those who deal in paintings and objects of art have a good field for their operations.   One of the most important houses in the oil painting, water color and etching line in this city is that of Messrs. W. Scott & Son, whose establishment is located at No. 1739 Notre Dame Street.   Established over a quarter of a century ago, this house has had a long, honorable and prosperous career and has increased in extent and importance from year to year.   The premises occupied, which are 28 x 70 feet in dimensions and 4 stories in height contain a choice collection of oil paintings by foreign masters and home talent, aquarielle studies, etchings, engravings, oriental carpets, rugs and mats, artistic furniture and countless other lines that must be seen to be understood or appreciated.   Mr. W. Scott the senior member of the firm has a keen taste for works of art and his good judgment in such matters is seen in the elegant and artistic stock collected.   Mr. W. A. Scott, the son, is a gentleman of marked business ability and also takes after his father in love for art, so that purchasers may rest satisfied with the judgment of these gentlemen.

W. Scott & Son, have lately added to their business another branch, which under their acknowledged good taste in selection of Tiles and Grates together with excellent designs and workmanship is assuming large proportions, we allude to the now popular Hardwood Mantels, Grates and Tiles, the late tombstone looking mantels are fast becoming a thing of the past, the only wonder is that such hideous things survived so long, this firm now keep the largest and best assorted stock in the Dominion, and their trade in this line is rapidly developing.

Northern Assurance Company, of London England, ROBERT W. TYRE, MANAGER FOR CANADA, 1722 NOTRE DAME STREET, MONTREAL.

—Fire and life assurance has for many years been given deep study by business men and has been reduced to one of the sciences in its methods and application.   When conducted by substantial companies it is not ephemeral in its character, but is as reliable as any institution can be made by wise laws and judicious management.   Holding a prominent place among the old established and substantial assurance companies doing business in this city is the Northern Assurance Company, of London England.   The Canadian Office is located at No. 1724 Notre Dame Street, and is under the management of Robert W. Tyre, Esq.   The company has a subscribed capital of $15,000,000.   It has accumulated funds of almost $17,000,000, an annual revenue from fire premiums of $2,910,000, an annual revenue from life premiums of $990,00, and its annual revenue from interest upon invested funds is $690,000. It is prompt in its settlement of all losses and liberal in its dealings with the insured.   Since the company was established it has earned a high and enviable reputation for its excellent management and the pronounced success that has attended its administration, placing it in a high rank with the leading assurance companies in the world, so that intending insurers need have no hesitancy in placing their risks with it. Mr. Robert W. Tyre, the manager for Canada, is a gentleman possessed of a deep knowledge of assurance in all its phases and is eminently qualified for the responsible position he holds in the company.

Guardian Fire and Life Assurance Company, ROBERT SIMMS & CO.,

& GEORGE DENHOLM, GENERAL AGENTS, 45 St. SACRAMENT St. MONTREAL.— During the years that have passed since insurance was first made a business institution, able statistitians have given the subject so much thought and actual experience has demonstrated the correctness of their reasoning that insurance might now almost be placed as one of the exact sciences, so far as figures are concerned. Prominent among the old established insurance companies doing business in this city, is the Guardian Fire & Life Assurance Company, of England, whose head office for Canada is located at No. 45 St. Sacrament Street, the general agents being Robert Simms & Co., and George Denholm. This company was founded in the year 1821, and owing to the sound principles upon which it was established, combined with judicious management it has been entirely successful and its business has been extended to very large proportions, not only in England but throughout the Dominion. It has a paid-up capital of one million pounds sterling, the largest paid-up capital of any company in existence, and has total funds amounting to $20,000,000, while the amount deposited with the Canadian Government for the security of Canadian policy holders is $100,000. Fire risks are accepted at current rates and all losses, settled in a prompt and liberal manner. The company have branch agencies in all of the principal towns and cities throughout the Dominion, all of which report good progress.

Miller Brothers & Mitchell, MACHINISTS AND MILLWRIGHTS, 110

TO 122 KING STREET, MONTREAL.—Among the many and various business manufacturing industries conducted in Montreal, there are none that have tended more in building up the reputation and prosperity of the city than that of its engineering and machinists establishments of which there are a large number of representative firms. Holding a prominent position among these is the well known firm of Messrs. Miller Brothers and Mitchell, whose office and works are located at from 110 to 122 King Street. The premises occupied by the works are 200 x 110 feet in dimensions and 2 stories in height. These are fully equipped with all the latest and most improved machinery and appliances driven by a 35 horse-power steam engine. The firm manufacture all kinds of machine work, especially for mills, and mill fittings ; also rock drill plant, and cordage machinery. They also manufacture and put up safety passenger and goods elevators of the most approved pattern. Using nothing but the very best of materials and employing none but the best of skilled workmen, of whom there are over 100 and giving their special supervision to all orders entrusted to their care, it is no wonder that the reputation of the house is as high and widespread as it is, or that their trade extends throughout the entire Dominion. Both members of the firm are skilled, practical workmen of many years experience, and are justly entitled to the marked success that has attended their efforts.

The Royal Canadian Fire and Marine Insurance Company, G. H.

McHENRY, MANAGER, 157 St. JAMES STREET, MONTREAL.—There are a number of first-class insurance companies doing business in Canada, companies that will rank with any in the world for solidity and thorough business principles of management, among such must be mentioned the Royal Canadian Fire and Marine Insurance Company, whose head office is located at No. 157 St. James Street in this city. This Company was incorporated in the year 1873 and during the 15 years it has been in existence it has met all engagements promptly and honorably. It has a capital of $500,000, assets of $708,328. It transacts both a fire and marine insurance and in the interests of its patrons is very careful of the character of the risks it assumes, while at the same time dealing liberally with the insured and meeting all.

losses promptly and in a satisfactory manner. The officers of the Company, are Andrew Robertson, Esq., President, Hon. J. R. Thibaudeau, Vice-President, Henry Cutt, Secretary, Archibald Nicoll, Marine Underwriter, G. H. McHenry, Manager. The Company has branches in the principal towns and cities in the Dominion which are under the management of competent agents, and those wishing to insure will find in the Royal Canadian all that they could possibly desire, for safety, promptness in settling claims and liberal treatment. The manager Mr. McHenry, is a gentleman of marked ability as an underwriter, and much of the success of the company is due to his executive ability, painstaking efforts and well directed enterprise.

A. Roncari, BOSTON, FRENCH AND AMERICAN CONFECTIONERY, 101 AND 309½ ST. LAWRENCE STREET.—Canadians, as well as the people of the United States and France and Italy are great lovers of confectionery and eat more of it than all the other countries of the world combined. Some years ago there were a number of people engaged in this line of manufacture who, for the sake of increased profit, adulterated their materials and put in compounds injurious to health. But two powerful agencies were at work against such people—the law, and a cultivated taste—and they found their occupation gone, so that now only those can hope to succeed in business who produce only the purest and best goods. One of the most reliable houses in this line of business in Montreal is that of Mr. A. Roncari, who is the owner of two stores, one at No. 101 and another at No. 309½ St. Lawrence Main Street. This gentleman established his business in April of 1887, and very soon succeeded in building up a flattering trade, both wholesale and retail, which is still steadily on the increase. Mr. Roncari manufactures all kinds of Boston, French and American confectionery, using nothing but the purest sugars and other materials, and nothing whatever of an injurious nature is permitted in their mixture. On the strength of this reputation is due, in a great degree, the excellent success which he has already met with. He intends, in the near future, to add to his business that of bread and pastry baking. Mr. Roncari is a native of sunny Italy, and is a skilled practical candy maker of many years experience and was in this same line of business in his native land for some years previous to coming to Canada.

D. Schwersenski, FANCY FURS AND FUR TRIMMINGS, 29 ST. LAWRENCE MAIN STREET, MONTREAL.—Ever since the day when the free traders settled in Quebec after its discovery by Jacques Cartier, down to the present time, Canada has been pre-eminently a fur trading country. A large trade is done, not only in the exportation of raw furs, but also in the manufacture of foreign and domestic furs. Holding a prominent place among those engaged in this line of business is Mr. D. Schwersenski, whose store and factory are located at Nos. 27 and 29 St. Lawrence Main Street. This gentleman has been established in business in this city for the past nine years, five of which he has been in his present position. The premises occupied are 50 x 26 feet in dimensions, and consist of two floors, the upper floor being used as the factory, where employment is furnished to 16 skilled and competent hands in the manufacture of fancy furs of every description, such as cloaks, mantles, capes, muffs, caps, mitts, etc., etc. All work done by this house is of the very best quality and the finish is elegant and perfect. He also manufactures fur trimmings of every description. Mr. Schwersenski is a practical hatter and furrier of many years experience and giving personal attention and supervision to all work turned out, he can guarantee his customers perfect satisfaction in every respect, both as regards quality of work, material and price. The trade of the house is very extensive and embraces not only Montreal but a large section of the Dominion. This gentleman also pays the highest price for raw furs. Mr. Schwersenski is a native of Germany, and is thorough-going, active and enterprising in all his business transactions and is entirely deserving of all success.

Ant. Beaudoin, PAINTS, WALL PAPERS, ETC., No. 49 St. Lawrence Main Street, Montreal.—It has very truly been said that nothing can be more favorable to the progress of house painting in its best style, than improved artistic culture on the part of the public, as well as the growth of the feeling to enjoy art. People appeared to be too much absorbed in business years ago to pay much attention to, or give any great encouragement to the painter artist, and, in fact, very indifferent or rather plain house painting formerly satisfied the owners of large mansions. Now all this is changed and the best is demanded. Wall papers are manufactured with high artistic taste, for nothing else will satisfy the demand. Holding a prominent place among the old-established houses engaged in the paints, oil and wall paper trade is that of Mr Ant. Beaudoin, whose store is located at No. 49 St. Lawrence Main Street. The premises occupied are 28 x 50 feet in dimensions and contain a very large and excellent stock of paints, dry and ground in oil and Japan for house painters and coach builders, etc. Also oils, varnishes and brushes of every description for all purposes. There is also a fine line of artists' materials, containing the product of some of the most celebrated makers in Europe. In wall papers the stock is full and complete and embraces beautiful specimens of the work of English, French and American makers, and being particularly adapted to the artistic taste of the present day. The trade of the house is conducted both at wholesale and retail and embraces in its scope not only the city but a large section of the surrounding country. Since this business was founded 18 years ago it has received a liberal share of the public patronage and proved lucrative to a satisfactory degree. Mr. Beaudoin, the proprietor, was born near Terrebonne and is an enterprising man of business and a much respected citizen.

John Lee & Co., SHIP LINERS, CARPENTERS, CAULKERS AND SPAR MAKERS, Montreal.—It appears to be an indisputed fact that the future of Montreal, as a great commercial and manufacturing centre—a Canadian New York, in fact—is well assuerd. The Board of Trade, Chamber of Commerce and Citizens Committee have been indefatigable in their efforts to have the necessary improvements made in the transportation facilities of the city, and one result of their endeavors appears to be that the Government assumes the harbor debt and that the tonnage dues on shipping will be removed from this part. This will encourage trade in a marked degree and greatly increase the number of vessels visiting this port during the season of navigation. One important branch of trade connected with the shipping interests is that of the ship liner and carpenter in which line the firm of John Lee & Co. of No. 207 Commissioners street stands pre-eminent. This business was established 20 years ago and steadlly through those years it has progressed and developed. The firm attend to all kinds of ship's carpentry fitting up vessels for horses, cattle, sheep and hogs, lining ships, caulking and making spars. Having a large force of workmen constantly on hand, during the season, numbering from 150 to 300, they are enabled to attend to all orders with the utmost promptitude and in the most satisfactory manner, so that vessels need not be delayed. The work done by this house is first-class in every particular as has been well attested. The members of the firm are Messrs. John Lee and John C. Murray. John Lee, who came to this country from Ireland when a child has been fully identified with all that has been for the city's welfare and is one of the most popular members of the Board of Aldermen. Both gentlemen are highly esteemed in business and social circles and are active members of the Board of Trade.

W. A. Dyer & Co., PHARMACEUTICAL CHEMISTS, 14 AND 16 PHILLIPS SQUARE, Montreal.—One of the most prominent, as it is also the most popular drug stores in Montreal is that of Messrs. W. A. Dyer & Co., which is eligibly located for business at Nos. 14 and 16 Phillips Square, corner of St. Catherine street. The premises occupied are large and commodious, being 50 x 65 in dimensions and 3 stories in height. These are fitted up with much taste, with plate glass show cases, cabinets, etc., for the advantageous display of the excellent stock carried, consisting of fresh, pure drugs, chemicals, fancy and toilet articles, proprietary medicines of acknowledged merit and standard reputation and all such other articles as are used by physicians in their practice.   The firm also possess the sole right in the Dominion for the manufacturing of the preparations of Messrs. Caswell, Massey & Co., including emulsion of Cod liver oil, pepsine and quinine.   They receive vaccine points every few days from the celebrated farm of Dr. H. A. Martin & Son, Roxbury, Mass. This firm was the first in Canada to make a specialty of Antiseptic Dressings and they have at all times considered quality in these goods to be the most desired point, not price.   The medical profession throughout the country, has recognized their efforts in this direction and give them liberal support.   Messrs. W. A. Dyer & Co. among many other well known preparations manufacture Jelly of Cucumber and Roses ; Quinine and Iron Wine ; English Lavender Water, etc., etc., giving employment in their establishment to 13 skilled hands and competent assistants.   Mr. W. A. Dyer, who is a native of England, is a graduate of the British Pharmaceutical Association, and was for 16 years manager of the present store when it was conducted by Messrs. Kenneth, Campbell & Co., 5 years ago Mr. Dyer assumed the proprietorship of the place and his success at all times has been eminently deserved.

J. H. Chapman, Wholesale and Retail SURGICAL INSTRUMENTS, 2294 St. Catherine Street and 14 McGill College Avenue, Montreal.—Montreal is undoubtedly the commercial metropolis of the Dominion, for here are to be found nearly all branches of trade, commerce and manufactures represented.   That the future of the city will far outshadow, in the near future, the progress made during the past ten or fifteen years, is beyond all question if present indications are any criterion.   Among the many business houses here located, worthy of particular mention as truly representative, is that of Mr. J. H. Chapman, dealer in surgical instruments and supplies of every description. This is the only establishment of the kind making a specialty of this business in the city, and is located at No. 2294 St. Catherine Street, corner of McGill College Avenue, being fitted up in a very tasteful and suitable manner, and carries a very large and comprehensive stock of physicians' and surgeons' supplies of the very best quality.   Mr. Chapman imports his goods direct from the principal manufacturers in Europe and the United States

Although established only since January, 1888, he has already built up the nucleus of what promises to be a most successful business, extending throughout the Dominion and neighbouring states. Mr. Chapman, has a thorough and comprehensive knowledge of every detail and requirement of his business, having had eight years practical experience in this line before going into business on his own account, and was induced to open this establishment on the earnest solicitation of many of the most eminent medical men throughout Canada, including all the medical college professors in the city, and the success that has attended his efforts thus far is a good indication of the satisfaction which his patrons find in procuring their supplies from this source.

Credit Foncier Franco-Canadian. E. J. BARDEAU, DIRECTOR, M. CHEVAL-IER, Gen. Secretary, 30 ST. JAMES STREET.—In all business communities, as well as in farming districts there are times when many thrifty and well-to-do people require more ready money than they have at their disposal. It may be either to take advantage of a bargain in stock or buy improved implements with which to work their farms to greater profit. In whatever legitimate case it may be, a little money obtained at a time when most required pays itself back with more than re-doubled interest. Conspicuous among the institutions in Montreal that have been established for loaning money on good security, is the Credit Foncier Franco-Canadian, whose office is located at No. 30 St James Street. This institution was founded in this city in 1881 and has, ever since the date of its inception proved not only highly successful in its management but of great benefit to many of our citizens The capital of the concern is $5.000.000, of which $4.000.000 has been loaned. The Credit Foncier gives loans on mortages, on improved farms, also on houses, stores and other real estate in the city. It lends money to corporations and school corporations. It makes its loans with or without amortization at the option of the borrower. By amortization the borrower is assured the benefit of the interest at the same rate as that charged upon the loan. The concern also permits of reinbursements before the due date, which in many instances is of much benefit to the borrower. E. J. Barbeau, Esq., the director of the company is a native of this province and is a gentleman well known and highly respected in business circles. The general secretary M. Chevalier, Esq., is a Frenchman by birth, and is eminently fitted by experience and ability for the responsible position he holds.

Hugh Ross, SUCCESSOR TO J. D. ANDERSON, MERCHANT TAILOR, 206 ST. JAMES STREET, MONTREAL.—Montreal has, in recent years, become a recognized centre of fashion second to none on the continent, and our leading merchant tailors have achieved an enviable reputation for their skill, taste and superior qualifications. One of the most popular and enterprising houses in the trade in this city is that of Mr. Hugh Ross, successor to J. D. Anderson,—so long and favorably known this in city. The establishment is located at No. 206 St. James Street ; the premises being 40 x 84 feet in dimensions, and are handsomely and suitably fitted up for the requirements of the business, the large plate glass front, not only lighting up the store but showing to advantage the fine display of goods. The spacious premises contain one of the largest and finest stock of imported fabrics, fine cloths and suitings, Scotch, English and Irish tweeds, trouserings, &c., in the latest and most fashionable patterns. These he makes up to order by measure on short notice and to those who desire the highest grade of custom tailoring, Mr. Ross' establishment commends itself as one that can be implicitly relied on to furnish faultless garments. that shall, in a word, rank superior in all respects. Employment is furnished to 45 assistants and skilled operators on an average throughout the year. Mr. Ross is a native of Rosshire, Scotland, and succeeded to Mr. Anderson's business here 3 years ago since which time he has built up an excellent and ever increasing custom.

Robin & Sadler, MANUFACTURERS OF LEATHER BELTING, DEALERS IN COTTON AND RUBBER BELTING, 2518, 2520 AND 2522 NOTRE DAME STREET.— With the development of the country and the establishment of new manufacturing enterprises the demand for all classes of machinery and equipments is constantly augmenting, and with experience, owners of industrial plants learn that in the purchase of supplies, as in other matters the best is the cheapest and always makes the best returns for the outlay. The same rule holds true in the transmission of power, and the broad, strong and reliable belt, constructed upon correct principles and capable of withstanding any strain, has replaced the crooked, unsafe and exasperating devices with which our progenitors were forced to be content. The most important house in the manufacture of leather belting, fire engine hose and lace leather, in the Dominion, is that of Messrs. Robin & Sadler, whose office and factory are located at Nos. 2518, 2520 and 2522 Notre Dame Street. The factory is fitted up with the latest and most improved machinery and none but the best of skilled help is given employment so that the product turned out is first class in every particular and is not surpassed by that of any other house. The leather belting manufactured by this house is made from carefully selected leather, the centres of hides being used, and are of the same thickness throughout. The trade of the house has steadily increased ever since the date of its inception. It is not so many years ago that most of the machinery used in this country was imported from Europe, and with it also come the belting for driving purposes. The belting imported was, as a rule, clumsy and heavy, with heavy rivets put in the centre where joined. These proved very unsatisfactory and it required Canadian push and energy, coupled with the protection afforded by the National Policy to meet the requirements of the present age, and produce belting that was made upon scientific principles, and capable of not only replacing the imported article but also of overcoming the prejudice in its favor. Messrs Robin & Sadler are manufacturing belting that has no superior on this continent. It is made from short laps only and the butt lap is joined to the shoulder lap, which equalizes the strength throughout, and is very uniform and smooth running. Messrs. Robin & Sadler have gained a widespread reputation for the superior quality of their belts and with it of course has extended their enormous trade, their goods being classed as standard throughout the Dominion.

And 3 years ago it was found necessary to open a branch at 129 Bay Street, Toronto, for the purpose of bringing goods nearer the consumer in Ontario, where a large stock is carried.

Hearn & Harrison, OPTICAL, MATHEMATICAL & SURVEYING INSTRUMENTS, 1640 & 1642 NOTRE DAME STREET, MONTREAL.—The business interests of Montreal are conducted upon an extensive scale and are comprehensive in their character fully justifying the city's claim to be the business and manufacturing metropolis of the Dominion. Among the important lines of commercial industry that in optical goods, mathematical instruments, &c. holds an important position, and one of the oldest established and best known houses in this line is that of Messrs. Hearn & Harrison which is located

THE GEORGE BISHOP ENGRAVING AND PRINTING COMPANY, MONTREAL.

at Nos. 1640 and 1642 Notre Dame Street. The premises occupied consist of 4 floors 30 x 30 feet in dimensions, which are heavily stocked with a large and elegant line of goods, consisting of optical, mathematical and surveying instruments, magic lanterns, photographic cameras and supplies, nautical and philosophical instruments, &c., galvanic batteries, telegraph instruments, electric machines, air pumps, magnesiun lights, electro-plating apparatus, stereoscopes, opera glasses, eye glasses, spectacles, field and marine glasses, thermometers, barmometers, chronometers, builders' and drainage levels, levelling rods, land chains, ship compasses, and many other articles too numerous to mention in detail. The firm manufacture optical instruments employing the best of skilled workmen for the purpose, and have received medals at the French and Philadelphia exhibitions for the superior quality of their work. This business was established by Mr. Charles Hearn, in 1857 and Mr. T. H. Harrison, father of the present proprietor, entered into partnership in 1871, Mr. Thomas L. Harrison has now been manager for the past seven years. He is an Englishman by birth and is a thorough going and enterprising man of business. The trade of the house is very extensive and embraces in its scope of operations the entire Dominion and Newfoundland.

Henri Jonas & Co., MANUFACTURERS OF FLAVORING EXTRACTS, ETC., 10 De Bresoles Street.—Besides being a metropolitan city Montreal is metropolitan in regard to its manufactures. Here nearly every branch of industry is prosecuted, and that successfully. The different lines are very numerous and their products find an active market throughout the Dominion. Among what may be called the specialties is that conducted by Messrs. Henri Jonas & Co., manufacturers of flavoring extracts and grocers sundries, the office and factory being located at No. 10 De Bresoles street. Established in the year 1870, the house has had a long and prosperous career, the trade extending throughout the Dominion. The firm manufacture concentrated extracts of almost every description, for confectioners, druggists, grocers, caterers, &c. They are also agents for French pickles, potted meats, and fancy groceries, as well as a prime quality of wines and liquors of the most celebrated brands These goods are sold to the trade and being imported direct by the firm, the advantages thus secured are invariably extended to their customers. All the goods handled are standard on the markets of the Dominion. The firm also manufacture pure fruit syrup and confectioners' supplies. Also, essential oils, essences, flavoring extracts and colorings for grocers and wine merchants, and also make a specialty of cod liver oil, castor oil and olive oils. These goods are manufactured with the greatest care and from the purest materials, and on this account have gained the great favor they meet with from the trade. Mr. Jonas is a gentleman of large business experience, and is well known in business and social circles, and his partner, Mr. Jessie Joseph, Jr., is one of the most enterprising and progressive of Montreal's younger merchants.

Louis Fortin, COAL AND FIRE WOOD, 3090 NOTRE DAME STREET, WEST MONTREAL.—Nature has been bountiful in the provisions it has made for the comfort and necessities of man. This may be seen in no small degree in the abundant supply of fuel spread throughout the earth's crust in her coal fields and the timber in her mighty forest. A very large business is done in coal and wood in this city many important houses being engaged in this branch of trade. Among those specially worthy of mention in these pages is Mr. Louis Fortin, whose office and yards are located at No. 3090 Notre Dame Street, which was formerly Grier's wood-yard. The premises occupied are 100x120 feet in dimensions where is carried a large stock of coal and wood. The annual output of coal amounts to 3000 tons and of wood 1500 cords. Employment is furnished to 15 hands throughout the year, and 12 teams. The trade of the house is very extensive and extends throughout the city and vicinity. Mr. Fortin has the contract to supply the Montreal Rolling Mills Company, and does the cartage to and from the works of the raw and manufactured material. This business was established 22 years ago and has at all times proved very successful, but never so much so as at the present time. Mr. Fortin is a native of Montreal and is a gentleman of marked business ability, push and enterprise, and is a highlg respected citizen and a member of the Chamber of Commerce.

Dr. Leduc & Co., CHEMIST AND DRUGGIST, 2033 AND 2035 NOTRE DAME STREET.—The times have long since passed, and, happily forever, when the barbers used to cup and bleed people under the term of surgery. A more enlightened era has dawned upon the human race and now physicians and surgeons, as well as pharmacists, must have given their professions deep study in properly constituted colleges and received their diplomas to practice. Prominent among the well-known physicians and pharmacists of this city is the firm of Messrs. Dr. Leduc & Co., whose office and drug store are located at Nos. 2033 and 2035 Notre Dame Street. The drug store was established 20 years ago, and Dr. Leduc succeeded to the business 14 years since, having been a graduate of the College of Physicians and Surgeons. Dr. Leduc has always enjoyed a high reputation as a physician and a skilled and careful pharmacist and his business has proved a successful one. The premises occupied are 26 x 50 feet in dimensions and are tastefully fitted up with plate glass show-cases and cabinets, etc. A fine stock is carried of fresh and pure drugs, chemicals, fancy and toilet articles, soaps, perfumes, druggists' sundries, proprietory medicines of acknowledged merit and standard reputation, as well as those articles required by physicians in their practices A specialty is made of the compounding of physicians' prescriptions and family receipe. with care and accuracy at moderate prices. Dr. Leduc is a native of the Province of Quebec, and is well-known in professional circles and to the public and gives employment to a competent assistant and two clerks in conducting his business.

J. B. Pilon, UNDERTAKER, 2517 NOTRE DAME STREET, MONTREAL.—The business of the funeral director is one requiring great delicacy of feeling and tact, and cannot be successfully conducted by everyone. From its peculiar character and the sad associations of afflicted friends and relatives, it requires considerable experience to manage all details in a satisfactory and unobtrusive manner. One of the most successful funeral directors in this city is Mr. J. B. Pilon, whose undertaking rooms are located at No. 2517 Notre Dame Street. This gentleman established his business sixteen years ago, and soon established a high reputation for the manner in which he conducted all arrangements. Mr. Pilon has a large patronage from the leading famlies in the city and surrounding districts, being considered one of the best and most considerate in his line, he has had a long experience in every detail of the business and in the quiet management of funerals has no superior in the city. He takes entire charge of the obsequies entrusted to him and furnishes everything, from the mourning badge to the casket and carriages, and the opening of graves, etc., so that mourning friends need have no extra trouble in the hour of affliction. He keeps in stock, coffins, caskets and other funeral requisites, as well as four herses which he furnishes at the lowest possible prices. Mr. Pilon is a native of St. Scholastique, and is well-known in this city by a large circle of the community, by whom he is held in the highest respect and esteem. Mr. Pilon is also Vice-President of the Funeral Director's Association of the Province of Quebec.

Ligget & Hamilton, DRY GOODS, CARPETS, ETC., 1883 AND 1885 NOTRE DAME STREET.—The commercial energy and stability of Montreal have increased in a most marked manner of late years, a result due in no small degree to the enterprise and prominence of our leading dry-goods houses.   In this line one of the best representative houses is that of Messrs Ligget & Hamilton whose large and handsome establishments are located at Nos. 1883 and 1885 and also 1884 Notre Dame street.   The premises occupied by the dry-goods house consists of a substantial 3 story structure 55 x 150 feet in dimensions.   These are fitted up in a very handsome manner and the stock is displayed to the best advantage. The stock carried is a very large and complete one and contains some of the finest lines of goods obtainable in the market,   Among the lines carried might be mentioned silks, satins, velvets and velveteens, plush, brocades, dress goods of beautiful fabrics and fashionable styles, laces, trimmings, gloves, hosery notions, underwear, blankets, woollens, cloaks, and many other lines too numerous to mention in detail.   In house furnishings the stock is very large and elegant and has been selected with much care and with that judgment that long and practical experience could suggest.   Last year they opened in the Glenora Building one of the finest carpet stores in the Dominion.   The store is 46 x 135 feet in dimension and occu-pies 3 floors with large plate glass windows admitting a flood of light so that the elegant stock of carpets carried can be shown to the best advantage.   The stock of carpets and oil cloths is one of the finest in the country and has been specially imported from some of the most celebrated of European manufacturers.   Messrs. Thomas Ligget and Henry Hamilton have a thorough knowledge of every detail of the dry goods and carpet trade and give their customers the benefit of their lengthened experience.   They are members of the BOARD OF TRADE and those forming business relations with their house may rest assured of receiving the most liberal and honorable treatment.

Ronayne Brothers BOOTS AND SHOES, CHABOILLEZ SQUARE, MONTREAL.— One of the oldest established, best known and most popular houses in the boot and shoe trade in this city is that of Messrs Ronayne Bros., which is located at Nos. 2034 and 2036 Notre Dame street, on Chaboillez Square, where it has been a landmark for years. The premises occupied consist of 3 floors, 28 x 35 feet in dimensions. This business was established here twenty-six years ago and from a small beginning has been built up to its present extensive proportions.   The store is generally well filled with customers from morning till night and in the evenings and on Saturdays the ten clerks em-ployed are kept constantly busy waiting on customers.   The stock of boots, shoes, slippers, rubbers, mocassins etc., carried is very large and complete and embraces all weights and grades from the finest of kid to the heaviest kip and made up in the latest and most fashion-able styles.   The firm have always made it a rule to sell the best quality of grades at the lowest possible prices believing—and rightly to that "nimble six pence is better than a slow shilling."   As an evidence of the popularity of the house it may be mentioned that a large number of customers who commenced to purchase goods here at the opening of the estab-lishment have ever since continued to favor the house with their patronage, a fact which bespeaks their entire satisfaction with the treatment accorded to them.

Mr. Edward P. Ronayne the Proprietor, is a native of Montreal and is a live active and enterprising business man, and a member of the Montreal Board of Trade·

Cunningham Bros., MARBLE AND GRANITE, 91 BLEURY STREET, MONTREAL, ST. LAWRENCE MARBLE WORKS—The sculptors' art has been highly eulogized by the great master of art and human feeling, Shakspeare, in the "Winter's Tale," in the following dialogue:—

> "What was he that did make it ? See, my lord,
> Would you not deem it breathed ? and that those veins
> Did verily bear blood ?
>   Masterly done !
> The very life seems warm upon her lips,
> The fixture of her eye has motion in't,
> As we are mock'd with art ;
> Still, methinks,
> There is an air comes from her ; what fine chizzel
> Could ever yet cut breath ? Let no man mock me ;
> For I will kiss her."

The art of sculpture was brought to a high state of perfection during the palmy days of Greece and Rome, and there are many worthy representatives of the art in the Dominion at the present day. Among those deserving of special mention in a work of this nature at the present day, is the well-known firm of Messrs. Cunningham Bros., proprietors of the St. Lawrence Marble Works, at No. 91 Bleury Street. This business was established in 1847 by the late Mr. William Cunningham, succeeded to by his sons, who are all dead now, except W. H. Cunningham, who carries on the business under the name of Cunningham Bros. Ever since the inception of the business it has held a high place in the trade and has proved uniformly successful. The yards are large and commodious, and here a staff of twenty-two skilled hands are given steady employment. This is the only wholesale house in this line in the Province of Quebec, Mr. Wm. H. Cunningham, the proprietor, being the wholesale representative for the Province of the Producers' Marble Company. Their specialty is cemetery work. However, they do all kinds of house finishing, marble work, etc, and his trade extends from Kingston, Ont., to Quebec. The work done here is beautiful in design and perfect in finish and has received the highest praise from competent critics. While his work is unsurpassed his prices are very reasonable, and those requiring any work of this nature would but consult their own interests by calling here and examining specimens and prices before leaving their orders elsewhere. Mr. Cunningham is a native of Vermont, but has resided in this city many years, and has thoroughly identified himself with its interests and progress and has been a leading spirit in whatever tends to Montreal's welfare, being at the present time a member of the Board of Aldermen.

Nap. Jalbert, WATCHMAKER, 2325 NOTRE DAME STREET.—Among the most ancient and honorable of trade, is that of watchmaking and jewellery. Watchmaking, of course, only dates back to the beginning of the 15th century but the manufacture of jewellery was prosecuted many centuries before the Christian era. It flourishes most in communities where people are the most prosperous, for where people have to struggle hard for the bare necessaries of life they cannot afford to indulge in the luxuries. Among those engaged in this line of business in this city, and deserving of more than a mere general notice is Mr. N. Jalbert, whose store is located at No. 2325 Notre Dame Street. This gentleman established his business three years ago and is only twenty-four years of age, during that comparatively short space of time, has succeeded remarkably well, his trade having steadily increased from time to time. A fine stock of goods is carried, consisting of English, Swiss and American watches, clocks, chains, rings and many other articles of jewellery, of beautiful design in gold and silver and rolled plate. A specialty of the business is the repairing of watches and jewellery on short notice, in the very best manner and at moderate prices. Mr. Jalbert is a native of Quebec and is a skilled, practical jeweller.

Dobson & Brodie's, PERFECTION SMOKE CONSUMER AND FUEL ECONOMIZER.—The advantage of an apparatus which will really act as a Smoke Consumer are so throughly patent to all users of steam power that it is not surprising that many efforts have been made to supply the want, but up to this time no Smoke Consumer has been produced which will effect its purpose without interfering with the draft of the furnace, or increasing the expenditure for fuel.

Besides this, most of the Smoke Consumers which have been offered to the public require a special construction of furnace, thus involving in making the necessary alterations, heavy expense and loss of time.

The proprietors of " The Perfection Smoke Consumer and Fuel Economizer," in presenting it to the public, confidently state that the defects of previous smoke consuming devices are obivated.

The principal of its construction is that a certain regulated proportion of the air admitted into the ash-pit is taken in a heated condition into an air chamber placed immediately in rear of the bridge, and thence passes out in finely divided streams to mingle with the gases holding in suspension the particles of carbon arising form the fuel, at the point at which they are most highly heated, igniting them and consuming the carbon which would otherwise be carried away into the atmosphere.

The draft in the fire-chamber proper will be increased by the more perfect combustion in rear of the bridge, and inferior fuel or even waste products can be used to fire with.

Our Smoke Consumer is in first cost and in comparison with others inexpensive and requires *no alteration in the construction of any existing furnace.* It can be placed in position ready for operation within a very few hours, say between 11 p.m. and 4 a.m., or at the end of the week's work, so that absolutely no time need be lost by its introduction.

The Canadian Pacific Railway Company were the first steam users to adopt it and after a year's use the parts are found to be perfect, and a saving of about 12 per cent. steadily maintained, The Canadian Rubber Company, The Montreal Warehou-ing Company, and the City's Water Works all have it attached to Lancashire boilers, to which it is specially adapted. In his report to the Water Committee the Chief Engineer states that never in the history of the Water-works has the consumption of coal been so low as since the use of this appliance. The saving being estimated at about one ton per day. To effect ordinary combustion of bad provincial coal, the fires have to be frequently stirred up and the firing is of the roughest and heaviest manner. The apparatus has therefore, been subjected to the severest test during these eight months at those works, and is pronounced by experts to be the best appliance for this purpose that science has produced. The precaution of smoke in flued boilers is by no means its least recommendation. The universal and ever deepening feeling against the pollution of the atmosphere with black smoke is one which with every right thinking mind must sympathise. Indeed it is difficult to see why any manufacturer should trangress in this matter when by adopting suitable appliances he may not only cease to annoy his neighbors, but also greatly benefit himself, for any economy in fuel materially lessens the cost of production.

INDEX TO BUSINESS HOUSES.

SADLIER'S
DOMINION
THOLIC TEXT BOOKS
COMPRISING
ILLUSTRATED
Spellers, Readers, Histories, Etc., Etc., Etc.
D. & J. SADLIER & CO.,

) Notre Dame Street,	115 Church Street,
MONTREAL	TORONTO.

) page 50,

The Press.

The Montreal Press has grown with, if not in advance of, the city, and has led in enterprises, especially during the later years, of a public character. Twenty-five years ago, the press was very often influenced by private opinion, and was nothing if not political. Then there were four English, and three French dailies, and a large number of French and English weekly and monthly publications. The style of the writers was pure, and their genius, perhaps, as fiery as that of to-day if not more so. There was lacking, however, the commercial spirit that now enters into the management. Montreal now boasts of five English and five French newspapers, the work on either of which is greater to-day than was that on all put together twenty years ago. It was the Montreal Daily *Witness* that marked out this advance. For many years, the late John Dougall had published a weekly newspaper, in the interest of the Protestant people. He gave to the city, the first one cent afternoon daily published on the Continent, and it has been a success. It was religious, prohibition, moral and fearless under his control. It retains all these features to-day, under the editorial management of the present proprietor, Mr. J. R. Dougall. The *Star* followed, started by Marshall, Langevin & Co., and afterwards became the sole property of Mr. Hugh Graham. Its price is one cent, and its success has been phenomenal. Its claim is to the largest circulation in the city. These newspapers are independent of political dictatorship, and are published in the afternoon. The *Post*, owned by a stock company, and edited by Mr. Carroll Ryan, an afternoon newspaper in the interests of the Irish Catholics, is managed by Mr. P. Whelan. The *Gazette*, the leading Conservative newspaper, is owned by a stock company, but the stock is principally held by Mr. Richard White, and the heirs of the late Thomas White, whose son, Mr. R. S. White, is its able editor. The *Herald*, is the organ of the Reform or Liberal party, is edited by Mr. St. John, a brilliant journalist, and is owned by the Hon. Peter Mitchell, who inspires its tone, and manages it. All these are thriving commercially and otherwise.

The strides made by the French press is even greater, by comparison, than that of the English, as they were much more backward until within the last ten years, when a spirit of emulation has produced among them, a revolution. The newspapers are *La Minerve*, Conservative, edited by Mr. J. Tassé; *La Patrie*, owned and edited by Mr. H. Beaugrand; *Le Monde*, Independent, owned by Mr. F. Vanasse; *La Presse*, Independent, owned by Messrs. Wurtele & Co., edited by Mr. G. A. Nantel; and *L'Etendard*, Ultramontane and Castor in politics, edited by F. P. A. Trudel. There is also published in Montreal, a weekly illustrated English paper, the *Dominion Illustrated*, and a French weekly, *Le Monde Illustre*. There are the *Trade Bulletin* of Mr. Henri Mason, *The Journal of Commerce* of Mr. Foley, and a number of other English weekly, and French weekly newspapers of more or less importance.

B

www.ingramcontent.com/pod-product-compliance
Lightning Source LLC
Chambersburg PA
CBHW030826020726

47499CB00006B/2088

* 9 7 8 3 7 4 2 8 4 2 4 6 6 *